DEATH BY FOOD TRUCK

4 COZY CULINARY MYSTERIES

JOI COPELAND
CYNTHIA HICKEY
LINDA BATEN JOHNSON
TERESA IVES LILLY

BARBOUR
PUBLISHING

Published by Barbour Publishing, Inc., 1810 Barbour Drive, Uhrichsville, Ohio 44683,
www.barbourbooks.com

Our mission is to inspire the world with the life-changing message of the Bible.

UN-LUCKY NOODLES

JOI COPELAND

DEDICATION

To my beautiful, amazing friend, Jaqueline Quirke-DePalatis, for not only being willing to give me insight on the Japanese culture but also for being my friend. I love you so very much, and I praise the good Lord that He had our paths cross thousands of miles from our original homes all the way in Ireland.

ACKNOWLEDGMENTS

Jesus, thank You for allowing me to write.
May You receive all the glory!
Chris, my love, my best friend, what would I do without your support and encouragement? I love you always!
Garrison, Gage, and Gavin, best sons ever!
My fantastic editor, Barbara Hand, thank you for your patience with me as I write these stories. You are amazing, and I cannot do this without you!

CHAPTER ONE

I couldn't breathe. I tried to inhale, but I couldn't catch my breath. My heart plummeted to my feet like when I rode that elevator ride at Disney World. No way was he here. I'd been living in Maine for a solid year with no word from him. I didn't even tell my own mother where I'd moved. Like she'd care anyway.

The only person who knew where I relocated went with me. Well, she and her husband, Mark McGreggor. Wei was my best friend and co-owner of our food truck, Lucky Noodles. The day Wei betrayed me would be the day Jesus stopped forgiving sinners. Never.

I leaned my body out the window, stretching my neck to get a glimpse of where I thought I saw him. I scanned the lines outside the nine other food trucks on Birch Point Lake and ran my gaze over the people standing by the Crunchy Taco. What was I thinking? Paul Davis never liked tacos. Anytime I suggested Mexican food, he'd glare at me and call me all kinds of names.

By the time I finished scanning the rest of the food trucks, I realized he wasn't there. I blew air out the side of my mouth, thankful it was just my overactive imagination. Why would Paul come all the way to Maine from Texas? He wouldn't still be hunting for me. . .would he?

"Hey, Mey." Wei nudged me with her hip. "What's the matter with you?"

I grabbed my soda cup and took a long gulp. The carbonation soothed my parched throat. Sweat trickled down my back. Summer in Maine proved to be hot and humid on most days. Not that I minded. Texas had the same weather.

"I think I'm imagining things." I shook my head, my long black ponytail swooshing against my bare shoulder.

Since I wasn't the cook of Lucky Noodles, I opted to wear comfortable clothing. Wei was the mastermind behind the meals. I kept the books, did the purchasing, greeted the guests, and took their orders. Wei made brilliant Japanese food, the best in all of Maine, maybe even the East Coast. Who was I kidding? The world.

When Wei agreed to partner with me, I hit the jackpot. I couldn't do it without her. My best friend since I was eight years old, Wei knew the good and the bad of my life. The blessings and curses. The ups and downs. Without Wei, I wouldn't have gone to church and accepted Jesus as my Lord and Savior. That simple action changed the course of my life and drew Wei and me closer together as friends.

Wei's almost-black eyes filled with concern. "What do you think you're imagining?"

I forced a laugh. "I thought I saw Paul."

Wei's face lost its color. "Paul Davis?"

"Do you know any other Paul?"

"Of course. Paul Newman. Paul McCartney. Paul Bunyan." Wei tapped her nose, a habit that appeared when she was thinking. "Paul from the Bible. Pope John Paul. Paul Revere. Paul Rudd, Paul Simon, and Mark-Paul Gosselaar. Wait. Does he count since his first name isn't Paul?" She waved aside her question. "Paul—"

"Okay, okay!" I laughed. "I get it. You know, or know of, a lot of Pauls. Yes, Paul Davis." I rolled my eyes. "But I guess I'm seeing things."

Wei chuckled along with me. "See what happens when you're snarky with me?" She tossed me a cheeky grin then sobered. "But seriously. You really think you saw Paul?"

"I hope not." Dear Lord, don't let it be so.

Paul Davis, my ex-boyfriend. I held in a shudder. The last person I expected to see on the lake would be Paul. We dated for almost four years, but after I became a Christian, I realized he wasn't the man for me. I couldn't take the belittling, the rough way he'd grab my arm in public. Add in the manipulation, the guilt, and the mind games. Yeah, he wasn't the man for me.

"How would he find you? We've been so careful." Wei crossed her arms in front of her.

"I don't know. That's why I think I imagined it."

"Mey, I'm not sure about that." My friend frowned. She leaned against the counter and poked her head out the window. Good thing we didn't have customers yet. She may have scared them away with her scowl.

"Why? What do you see?" I mimicked her actions.

"I don't see anything." Wei straightened and sighed. "But I think we need to be on the alert. I'm going to text Mark, just in case."

Wei whipped her phone out of her pocket. I grabbed it before she found her husband's name. "Don't do that until we have concrete evidence he's here."

Wei snatched her phone back. "Like what? When he corners you, guilts you into believing you shouldn't have left him, and verbally assaults you?" Wei shook her head. "No. I'm not going to stand by and do nothing like I did last time."

My frustration seeped out of me. I'd made too many excuses for Paul when we were dating. Excuses Wei never believed. Not that I wasn't a good liar. She just saw through the lies to my fear.

That was when I became a Christian. Because of Wei and Mark's unconditional love.

"You didn't do *nothing*. You tried talking to me about him for years. I didn't listen."

Wei sniffed as tears filled her eyes. "I hated seeing you with him, Mey. He turned you into something you weren't. I should've done more to get you away from him. If I'd tried harder, you wouldn't have suffered so much."

"It wasn't your fault. I didn't listen to your advice." I blinked back tears of my own. "God showed me my need for Him through all of that. He also opened my eyes to see how destructive my relationship with Paul had become." I squeezed Wei's hand.

"Please, let me text Mark. Just to let him know."

I rolled my eyes. "We both know what he's going to do. He's going to come down here and work from that table right there." I pointed to the table not far from our food truck.

"You're the sister he never had. You know how badly he wanted to pummel Paul every time the man spoke to you." Wei fiddled with her phone then typed something I couldn't see. "Please?"

I dipped my head in consent. "Fine. But I beg you, tell him there's no need to come down here. He'd get more writing done in his office at home than in today's hot, humid weather."

"I will. I can't guarantee he'll listen though." Wei finished typing and tucked her phone into her back pocket. "Promise me you'll stay in here until we can figure out if it's Paul or not."

"I will. I'm not a reckless person by nature. You, of all people, know that."

Wei's phone buzzed. She took it out and read what, I could only imagine, was a text from Mark. She shook her head, a slight smile lifting her lips. "He's on his way."

I smacked my forehead with the palm of my hand. "Oh, good grief."

"Listen, Charlie Brown, I warned you. He said he'll be here in ten minutes and that you're not to step foot out of this truck."

"Who's going to wipe the tables when the customers are done eating? You can't. You'll be cooking or cleaning up in here." I wagged my finger at her. "And I'm not Charlie Brown."

Wei giggled and tossed her apron over her short black hair and tied it around her waist. "Keep talking like Charlie Brown, and that's what I'll call you."

I glared at her and pointed to the back of the truck. "Shouldn't you be doing food prep or something?"

"Just promise you won't leave the truck until Mark gets here, or I'm going to have to tackle you and tie you up." Wei wiggled her eyebrows. "Wouldn't want to make a scene, not after the successful year we've had."

"Like you could tackle me." I rose to my full height of a whopping five foot four, fists planted firmly on my hips, and tried to look as menacing as possible. Fake bravado. Pure and simple. Because Wei not only had me by four inches, but she also had more muscular arms. She and Mark exercised every morning for over an hour, and her body proved it.

"I'm not even going to dignify that with a response." Wei turned her back on me and began preparing for the lunch rush we were sure to get.

I straightened up the counter and hollered over my shoulder, "You did respond, by the way, so your comment is null and void."

Wei snickered in return but opted not to say anything further. I chuckled and turned on the local Christian radio station. Nothing helped lift my spirit like some TobyMac or MercyMe. Okay, if I'm honest with myself, I wanted a distraction, because if I did see Paul Davis, my nice and safe life would disappear like a vapor.

I wasn't a pessimistic person by nature. On the contrary. I was overly optimistic, some said. But for the first five months after I left Texas to get away from Paul, I was always looking over my shoulder. Anytime I heard a noise, I imagined him hiding in the bushes or breaking into my house, which was situated behind Wei and Mark's. I never thought I'd date someone for so long who stripped away all of my self-worth. I guess it made sense, though, since my mom started when I was young.

The first customer of the day sauntered up to the window. "Hey, Mey. How's it going?"

"Hiya, Devon. I'm good." Not really a lie. Aside from my slight scare, I really was good. "How are you?"

"Great. Can't wait to eat some of Wei's noodles."

I wrote Devon's order on a pad of paper, connected it to a clip on a metal slider, and pushed it down to Wei. She plucked it off and started up the fryer.

"You know the drill, Dev." He handed me his card with a nod. I slid it into the machine, pulled off the paper, and handed the card and receipt to the fifty-year-old man who'd fallen in love with Wei's cooking the day we opened.

"I don't even remember what I ate for lunch before you gals came to Maine." A slow smile slid across Devon's tanned face.

"I'm sure you chose another one of these fine food trucks. I'm just glad you stick with us now." I tossed him a wink and a grin.

"If you were twenty years older, Mey, I'd scoop you up and marry you."

I giggled at our regular line of teasing. "Oh, come on. You know I'm not the chef of this truck. If Wei were single and twenty years older, you'd marry her and leave me behind." Wei handed me Devon's order.

"Nah. I come for the food, but I stay for the company." He winked back at me, tossed a five-dollar bill in our tip jar, and strolled away.

I laughed. The perfect way to start my day. Then I saw Mark setting up his laptop on the table just outside the window of Lucky Noodles. Mark must have felt the burning glare I sent his way, because his gaze rose and met mine, narrowing in the process. A slight shake of his head, meant only for me to see, told me what I already knew. He wasn't going anywhere anytime soon.

I broke eye contact and yelled over my shoulder, "Wei, my bodyguard's here. Can you put together his favorite meal?"

Wei's laugh drifted out of our truck and must have landed on Mark, based on the slight lift of his lips. "You bet. Coming right up."

While I loved Mark and Wei, they could be overbearing at times. Like when we first moved to Maine, and they wouldn't let me sleep in my house by myself. They stayed with me for over two weeks. When I couldn't handle the closeness any longer, I sent them home. Which was only twenty paces away.

Again, if I'm honest, I didn't mind them staying with me for the first week. I was like a skittish puppy, always worried someone was out to get me. Maybe I let my guard down over the last year. I got comfortable and stopped looking over my shoulder. I expected Paul to finally let me go. I hadn't heard from him in months. Of course, it helped that I changed my phone number and moved out of the state.

Mark's order came up. I grabbed his soda and took him his meal. "You didn't have to come. And you're not going to be able to see a thing with the sun glaring on your laptop."

Mark rolled his eyes. "That's why I brought my sunglasses. After I eat, I'll put them on and get some work done. I'm not leaving until the truck is closed up for the day."

"Mark, that's hours away. You can't stay here that long."

A growl escaped Mark's lips. "I can, and I will. I'm not taking any chances, and neither should you."

"I'm not. I don't know if who I saw was even Paul. Maybe it was his doppelgänger. You know we all have one somewhere in the world." I pasted on a smile I didn't feel.

"Mey." My name came out more of a sigh. "Please. Don't. I'm here to stay. It's for your own good and safety."

"Fine," I conceded. "But know I'm not happy about it."

"Really?" Mark put his sunglasses on. "I couldn't tell."

I punched Mark in the arm and then scurried back to the food truck as a few people gathered around the window.

I helped a dozen or so more customers, taking orders, making change, running credit cards, and chatting with them all, of course. Some were our regulars. Some were brand-new to our food truck. Probably tourists, since Birch Point Lake had a lot to offer in the summer.

Eight hours later, sweat dripping down the sides of my face, I locked up the cash register, the day's proceeds tucked away in my purse. The kitchen portion of the truck all cleaned and in ship-shape, Wei left the stifling heat of the truck to enjoy the breeze outside with her husband.

I studied my friends as they sat across from each other, holding hands, staring into one another's eyes. They were the cutest couple I'd ever known and the most sickening. Truthfully, I hoped to find that kind of love one day. In the meantime, I had Lucky Noodles to keep me busy. And several good books to take my mind off the loneliness that often plagued me at home.

I knelt behind the counter, making sure we were all prepared for tomorrow's lunch and dinner. Some days we were ahead of the game. Others, not so much. Today just so happened to be the former. My heart soared at how well we'd done today.

With a thankful heart, I jumped up and looked into a pair of eyes I had hoped never to see again.

CHAPTER TWO

M ey Hirano," Paul gushed, as if I were a long-lost friend and not the verbal punching bag he used me for. "You're pretty good at hiding."

I swallowed my fear, though it felt ready to erupt like Mount St. Helens. I let my gaze slide to the now-empty table.

Paul followed the direction of my eyes. "Oh, you're looking for your watchdogs?" he snarled. "They left you here all alone."

I knew he was lying. Mark and Wei probably left to put his laptop in the car. They wouldn't leave me by myself. My dearest friends in all the world had my back. They'd show up soon enough. I just had to distance myself from the man standing in front of my food truck.

"Come on out, sugar, so we can talk." Paul's ocean-blue eyes held no warmth.

I doubted his sincerity. I knew deep down he was going to try and convince me to go back to Texas with him. I tried leaving him one other time, but he was such a smooth talker. He listened to everything I said about how he made me feel, and he promised to change. For some reason, I believed him.

"I'm not leaving this truck."

Danger lurked in his eyes. "If you don't come out, I'll come in and trash everything you've worked so hard for."

"How? I have the door locked." Taunting him wasn't a great idea, but I had to keep myself away from him.

I was no match for his five-foot-eleven body-builder's physique. If he really wanted to, he could find a way to break down the door.

Paul reached through the window and grabbed my wrist. For one so large, he had amazing reflexes. I should have known what to expect from him.

I tightened my jaw against the pain shooting through my arm. "You're hurting me."

Paul's hold lessened. "That wasn't my intention." His smooth voice softened. "Please come out."

A teenage couple walked past the food truck, people I didn't recognize. They cast a curious look our way.

Paul tossed them one of his most charming smiles, the one that won me over to begin with. "Just admiring my girl's lovely hand."

They snickered and hurried away. I wanted to shout out to them. But what could they possibly do? And would they believe me anyway?

"Fine," I growled.

I pulled the rope to the metal blockade, closing the truck up, and moved toward the door. *Do I really want to go out there? He can't really force his way in here, can he?* My thoughts raced.

Mark and Wei had been gone for a while. They were sure to arrive before I even had to say another word to the maniac outside Lucky Noodles.

"Mey," Paul said in a singsong tone, but I knew what he really meant. That was what he used to do when his patience ran thin, right before he'd start telling me how weak I was and how much I needed him to protect me.

I inhaled a shaky breath and pushed open the door. Once it was locked, I turned around and found myself staring at Paul's chest.

"Finally." His hand grasped my elbow.

"Let me go or I'll scream." I was not bluffing this time.

Paul must have believed me, because he released me. I stormed away from him and into the open. Just in case he felt the need to start an argument, I wanted to have plenty of witnesses. Even though most of the food trucks were closed, a few people were milling about the area, some even occupying a table or two.

I took the closest table to Lucky Noodles and pointed to the opposite side. "You can sit there."

Paul raised an eyebrow but sat down without making a scene. "I want to talk. That's all."

"I don't have anything to say to you." I stretched my neck around his big head to see if there was any sign of my friends. No such luck.

"Why'd you leave, baby?" Paul snatched my hand before I had a chance to move it.

"I think you know the answer to that. And don't call me *baby*." I tried to yank my hand away, but his hold tightened.

"I don't mean to hurt you. You make me do it, you know." Paul's eyes pleaded for understanding.

"I don't make you do anything. You choose to demean me."

"If you only did what I said, I wouldn't have to." Paul squeezed my hand.

"You're stopping me from working. Now let me go."

He shook his head. "Not until I've had my say."

I sighed, pushing down the anger bubbling inside the pit of my stomach. I was tired. Tired of running, tired of living in fear, tired of getting beat down. "Then say it."

"I love you, Mey. I always have. I want to start up our relationship again. Come to Texas with me. We'll start over." Paul ran his fingers over the back of my hand.

"I'm not leaving Maine. This is my home now." I tried to release my hand from his vise-like grip, but he clamped down on my fingers.

"I've changed. I won't treat you that way again."

My eyes felt like they were going to pop out of my sockets. "You just threatened me and forced me to come out here and talk with you. How's that changing?"

"It was the only way I could think of to get you to sit here with me." Paul's face morphed into sadness.

"I've listened to this before, Paul. As soon as I do something you don't like, you'll tell me how dumb and ugly I am, how no man will ever want me." War raged within me. One side battling the words he used to hurl at me, the other clinging to who God says I really am.

Emotions swirled across the man's face. From guilt to anger to sorrow. I couldn't tell which one was real, and I didn't want to have to decide. I wanted this conversation to be over. *Where are Mark and Wei? What's keeping them?*

He interrupted my thoughts. "Listen, I know I'm not going to change your mind today. Why don't you go home and pray about it and see if God gives you peace about coming back with me?"

Wait. Did he just say *pray*? "What do you know about prayer, Paul?"

"I've had a religious experience, let's say. I'm like you. A Christian now."

Hairs prickled on the back of my neck. Somehow I didn't think he was sincere. I shouldn't be so judgmental, but I found it odd that my abusive ex-boyfriend suddenly became religious less than a year after I did. Not to mention his words had not matched his actions since I set eyes on him ten minutes ago.

I narrowed my eyes at him and yanked with all my might. His fingernails scratched my skin, but I finally got my hand free of his.

I pushed myself up from the table, ready to go look for Mark's car on my own. I couldn't sit here a second longer and listen to Paul's poison.

"I don't have time to talk to you tomorrow. I work."

"I know." Paul stood, towering over me. "But maybe you can meet me for coffee? I'll bring your favorite. By the lake."

"I'm not meeting you."

"You don't have to come by yourself," Paul rushed on. "You can bring your watchdogs. . . . I mean friends."

"If I say yes, will you leave me alone?"

Paul nodded. "I won't bother you anymore."

"Fine. Tomorrow morning meet me at the lake, no coffee, at eight a.m. I'll give you fifteen minutes, and that's it." I turned on my heel, ready to make a grand exit, when he clasped my wrist once again.

"You won't be sorry."

"I already am," I replied.

"Hey!"

My head snapped in the direction of the voice I'd waited to hear since Paul first appeared. "Mark," I whispered. Wei was hot on his heels.

"Let her go," he growled, fire in his eyes.

Paul dropped my arm as Mark moved between us.

Wei reached me, her chest heaving. "I'm so sorry we left you."

I blinked back the sudden tears hindering my eyesight. "It's okay. Let's go home."

"Stay away from her." Mark jabbed a finger in Paul's chest.

"She's already agreed to meet me tomorrow at the lake." Paul smirked. Then he must have realized I was still watching him and changed his expression to fake fear.

"Over my dead body." Mark backed away from Paul.

"Let's go home, you guys." The fight suddenly left my body.

All I wanted to do was go home, curl up under a blanket, put on a romantic comedy, and not think about my life. Already questions were running in my mind faster than I could answer them. How did Paul find me? Who gave away my location when only three of us knew where I was? Why did he come all this way?

It certainly couldn't be because he really loved me and missed me. And definitely not because he became a Christian and suddenly saw the error of his ways. Neither of those ideas rang true.

Lord, forgive me for doubting You can change someone, but I know Paul. There's no way he's serving You now.

Once I was safely tucked in the back of Mark's car with Wei beside me, the flood let loose. I couldn't stop the river of tears if my life depended on it. I sobbed and sobbed while my best friend's comforting arms held me close. Her own tears dropped on my head.

"I'm so sorry we weren't there," she repeated. "We went to take the laptop to the car, and a woman asked us if we could jump her car. We kept trying and trying then finally gave up."

I shook my head. "It's okay. You had no idea he was here."

"Yes, we did." Mark met my gaze in his rearview mirror. "That's why I came out today, remember? You saw him." He slapped the steering wheel, making me jump. "I shouldn't have left you. I'm so sorry, Mey."

I wiped my face with the back of my hand, the tears still flowing. "Listen, you guys," I said between hiccups, "it isn't your fault. By the end of the day, we all thought I was just seeing things."

Silence filled the car. My tears finally subsided, but the fear in my gut was active. We pulled up to our homes, and my stomach started swirling like a tornado. I started to shake, and sweat formed on my hairline. I hopped out of the car just in time to hurl my lunch all over the concrete.

"Oh, Mey," Wei whispered, holding my hair back.

I kept heaving, my stomach releasing all of its contents. Was this how intense fear affected people, or did I have the flu all of a sudden? I slowly stood, and Mark handed me a napkin he must have found in his car.

I wiped my mouth and inhaled a shaky breath. "I'm fine."

"You sure?" Mark looked skeptical. Couldn't say I blamed him.

I nodded. "Um, I know I only live twenty feet from you two, but can I sleep at your place?"

"We wouldn't have it any other way." Mark spun his keys on his finger. "Let's go grab your things, and then we'll order pizza for dinner."

"Can your stomach handle pizza?" Wei asked, walking close to my side.

"I'm not sure. After I get my stuff, I'll let you know."

To be honest, I couldn't tell what I was feeling. My emotions were all jumbled. Anger, frustration, fear, sadness, confusion. I still couldn't believe Paul found me. I didn't know how. I was so careful. I rarely used a credit card or bank card. I paid with cash because it was easier to be unnoticeable that way.

I unlocked the door to my small home. I didn't even see what was around me. All I wanted to do was collect my clothes and toiletries and escape to Wei's.

Within five minutes, we were headed to my friends' house. I took a shower to try and wash away any sign of seeing Paul, covering my ears, trying to force his voice from my head. My teeth chattered, even under the hot water. I just couldn't shake the fear surrounding me.

Once I was out of the shower and dressed, I started to feel more like myself. And since I gave up my lunch on Mark's front yard, my stomach growled. *Yep, I can definitely eat some pizza.*

With the order placed, I sat in the reclining chair, a blanket covering me because Mark liked to keep his house below sixty-five degrees in the summer. My eyelashes practically had icicles dangling from them, but I held my tongue, since they were letting me stay with them.

"What did Paul say to you, Mey?" Mark leaned forward and folded his hands between his knees.

I repeated our conversation, Paul's confession of being a Christian, and the few times he threatened me.

Wei snorted. "Doesn't sound like he's changed at all."

"I think we need to let the police know about him." Mark pulled out his cell phone, ready to call the local police station.

I shook my head. "Not yet. He's only verbally threatened me. They won't do anything with that."

"And the bruise around your wrist?" Wei pointed out.

I snorted. "You know how easily I bruise. He didn't mean to do that. I'm not concerned about that."

"And you really want to meet him tomorrow at the lake?" Wei's black eyes filled with concern.

"I just want him to go away. The sooner the better." I ran my hand through my damp hair. "If that means I talk with him for fifteen minutes, so be it."

"And he said we can be there?" Mark raised his eyebrows.

I nodded. "I wouldn't have agreed otherwise. No way do I want to meet him at a secluded spot alone."

"All right." Mark leaned back just as the doorbell rang. "I'll get it."

I moved to stand. "I'll take care of it."

Mark shook his head. "I don't want you anywhere near the door. What if it's Paul?"

"Good point." I relaxed in the chair and waited for Mark to come back with the pizza.

Sure enough, my adopted brother carried in the night's dinner with a bottle of Dr Pepper for me. It was a guilty pleasure of mine. One I tried not to dive into very often.

A movie played on the television while we ate. I couldn't seem to focus, let alone keep my eyes open. As soon as my stomach filled, I relaxed on the soft cushion and let sleep overtake me.

CHAPTER THREE

When I woke up, my nerves were shot. Why did I agree to meet with Paul? Apparently, I didn't have a brain in my head. If Wei and Mark weren't going to be with me every step of the way, I just wouldn't have shown up. But I decided to go.

So we headed off to Birch Point Lake, the lake near the food truck court. I loved spending time at the lake when I had the opportunity. It was a place my soul felt closer to God. I saw His beauty in the stillness of the water, His power when the waters were choppy, and His majesty as the sun bounced off the top, creating sparkles only the Lord Himself could make.

Not today. This morning I couldn't get my hands to stop shaking. No matter how hard I prayed or listened to the prayers of my friends as we drove to the lake, my body wouldn't relax.

Even when Mark stopped the car and I climbed out, the air suffocated me. Maine was known for its humidity in the summer months, but I felt as if I could barely take a deep breath.

Wei was silent as we waited for Paul to show up. I knew my best friend was praying. She always got a specific look on her face, like she was focused on something otherworldly. And she was.

Boy, was I grateful for her prayers. Because no matter how many times I came before the Lord that morning, my prayers seemed to bounce off the sky. Nothing took away the knots in my stomach.

I was not doubting God's existence. My vision was clouded.

"Hey." Mark interrupted my thoughts. "It's gonna be okay. We're here, and today we aren't going anywhere."

I dipped my head. "Thanks. I don't know why I can't seem to stop shaking."

"You're scared," Wei chimed in. "And rightly so. You've rebuilt your life after leaving Paul. Even your therapist said you've come a long way."

"I probably should have called her last night."

"You'll have a lot to talk about at your next appointment." Wei offered me a smile. "For now, remember God has not given you a spirit of fear, but of power, love, and a sound mind. And God's perfect love casts out fear."

I closed my eyes and breathed in the words straight from the Bible. A peace I hadn't experienced before settled over my soul. My hands stopped shaking, my heart stopped running a thousand miles a minute in my chest, and my breath came out more slowly.

I opened my eyes, the air suddenly less stifling than before. The sun seemed a little brighter than it had been a few minutes before. Maybe, just maybe, everything was going to be okay.

I leaned against Mark's car and checked my watch. "He's late."

Mark frowned. "Isn't he normally punctual?"

"If I was even a second late, he'd go off the deep end." Hope started to build in my chest. "Do you think he decided he doesn't want to talk? That maybe after seeing me yesterday, he realized he can't have me back?"

Wei bit her bottom lip. "I don't know, Mey. That doesn't sound like him, does it?"

"But he said yesterday he's a Christian now. Maybe he went to his hotel last night and prayed about it, and God told him to go back to Texas." I couldn't stop the hope building within me. "That has to be it!"

Mark shook his head slowly. "Don't get your hopes up. I really doubt that's the case. He's probably running late is all."

And just like that, my friends let the wind out of my sails. I sighed and leaned against the car, shutting my eyes once again. The sun kissed my face. A slight breeze ruffled my hair, tickling my sleeveless shoulder. The day promised to be warm and beautiful, like most days in Maine.

"How long do we wait?" I checked my watch once more.

"I say let's give him another fifteen minutes. You gals have to get Lucky Noodles set up." Mark set a timer on his watch.

"You think a timer's necessary?" Wei giggled.

Mark gave her a wink. "Anytime I can use my tech watch, you know I will."

"So, Mark, how's the writing coming along?" I liked hearing about Mark's newest novels. He had a way with words I envied.

"It's good. I'm ahead of schedule, so my editor and publisher are pleased. If this book sells well, I'll be going on tour."

Mark's latest novel had sold over five hundred thousand copies. Wei didn't have to work if she chose not to, but she loved cooking.

I wanted his books to sell, I really did. But if he left for a tour of the United States, where would I find someone who could protect me from my abusive ex-boyfriend?

"When you become even more famous, will you remember little old me?" I grinned at him.

"How could I forget you?" Mark's eyes twinkled with mischief. "You're my wife's best friend. You'll always be a part of my life, whether I want it or not."

I smacked his rock-hard abs as his laughter shook his stomach. "I don't know why I put up with him."

"Because you love him. He's the brother you always wanted." Wei wrapped her arm around his waist and kissed his cheek.

"Or the brother I never wanted," I teased. "All right, how much time is left?"

"One minute and thirty seconds." Mark crossed his arms over his chest. "Do you know how hard it was for me to sleep last night after that movie?"

"What?" I pretended I was shocked. "You didn't like *The Proposal?*"

Mark shrugged. "I don't know. Ryan Reynolds seemed too young for Sandra Bullock. Don't you think?"

"No!" Wei and I both said at the same time.

Mark chuckled. "All right. I guess it wasn't that bad."

"Whew!" I wiped the very real sweat off my forehead. "I thought I was gonna have to disown you for a second."

"We don't want that. Now do we?"

"Sarcasm does not become you, Mark." I smirked.

Mark's timer went off. Finally, we could leave the lake without having to confront Paul Davis.

"Time to go." Wei practically pranced to the passenger side of the car, like she'd been waiting with as much anticipation as I had.

It made sense. She walked with me through my relationship with Paul. She saw me go from a woman already knocked down by her mother's verbal abuse to a shell of a human being in four years. Wei fought the lies Paul told me on a daily basis, even when I didn't believe the truth she spoke into my life. My best friend prayed with me and for me, and offered me her quiet strength and not-so-quiet advice.

When I finally came to my senses, she and Mark left everything they had in Texas to help me start fresh. I didn't even have to beg, though I was prepared to do so. But my best friend suggested it before I had the chance. I was so very glad.

Mark walked us to the door of the food truck and waited until we were safely inside. "I'll be back in an hour. Do not open this truck or come out of it until I return. Got it?" He gave me a pointed look.

"I don't plan on going anywhere until you knock on this door and tell me I can put out the umbrellas over the tables." I raised my hand. "Scout's honor."

"That doesn't count." Mark rolled his eyes. "You were never a Girl Scout."

I turned a frustrated glare to Wei. "Must you tell him everything?"

Wei giggled. "I must."

"And do not open the metal barrier either." Mark wagged his finger at me. "Only when I get back. I'm setting up shop where I did yesterday."

"I may have argued about that before, but I won't be doing that today." My cheeks puffed out with my long sigh. "I sort of wish Paul had been at the lake this morning, just so I can move on and stop wondering where he is or if he's going to show up today."

"Me too." Mark shrugged. "I'll be back in an hour."

I locked the door after Mark closed it, and turned to my best friend. "I know I give you both a hard time, but I really am glad you're in my life."

"We're glad we are too. You mean a lot to us, in case you couldn't tell." Wei tied her apron around her waist and clapped her hands together. "Now, let's get going on prepping."

I groaned. I didn't like prepping. It was my least favorite part of my job. But since Wei was the chef of our food truck, I wanted to help her out as much as possible.

I pulled out the recipe card for yakisoba. Japanese stir-fried noodles always went over well with the customers. I didn't enjoy cutting onions, but I powered through. The carrots, shiitake mushrooms, and green scallions took less time to prepare than I thought.

I glanced over at Wei. She was putting together the sauce for the yakisoba without even looking at the recipe card I held in front of me. She was such a brilliant cook. I couldn't believe I got to be her partner. She could be making so much more money in a five-star Japanese restaurant. But no. She said she was more than content working side by side with me.

The food truck court wouldn't be open for a few more hours. We were definitely early. I was sort of glad. I would much rather be early and not talk to Paul than be late and have a discussion I knew would send me over the emotional edge.

"Want me to get the ingredients together for the Soba Noodle Salad?"

Wei tapped her finger to her nose. "Sure. It never takes long to prepare if everything is ready."

I put on a Christian radio station as I prepared the ingredients and dressing for the salad. Wei and I both sang along with MercyMe and danced around to "Grace Got You." We laughed as we sang the wrong lyrics but quickly caught up to the right ones.

"I love that song." I glided across the floor. Maybe glide was too strong a word, but I did my best anyway.

A pounding on our door stopped our joyful noise. I opened it, expecting Mark to be grinning back at me. Instead, a police officer with a frown greeted me.

"Excuse me. I'm looking for a Mey Hirano."

"I'm Mey. How can I help you?" I wiped my hands on the towel on the counter.

"Ma'am, can you step outside, please?"

Mark's warning came flying at me. Don't leave the truck for any reason. But the man before me was a police officer.

Or was he?

"Do you have a badge I can see?"

Wei came up behind me. "What's going on?"

"This man says he's a police officer. I'm just asking for credentials before I step outside."

Wei squeezed my arm. "Good idea," she whispered. "You can never be too careful."

The dark-haired man squinted at me like I was some sort of criminal. He yanked his badge out of his pocket and shoved it in my face. "Satisfied?"

"Sir, after what I've been through, you wouldn't fault me for asking for a badge." I didn't mean to be snarky, but come on.

"Now please step outside." His comment left no room for argument.

"Can my friend come with me?"

The officer inclined his head. "It may be a good idea."

I stepped outside, Wei close behind me. "What's this about?"

I followed him around the corner of the food truck, and he pointed to the center where all the tables were set up. I had not put out our blue-and-white umbrellas yet, but one of our tables was occupied.

I gasped. "What's he doing here?"

"I can't believe he'd show up here and not at the lake where you said you'd meet him." Wei planted her hands on her hips. "The nerve of some people."

"Ms. Hirano, do you know that man?"

"Yes, I do. He's my ex-boyfriend. What's wrong with him? Did he drink too much this morning?" I squinted against the sun.

Paul was slumped over our table.

"No, ma'am." The officer glared at me. "He hasn't been drinking."

I sighed. I was tired of the games Paul had been playing. Clearly, he had no intention of meeting me. Why, I didn't understand.

"Sir, I was supposed to meet him at the lake this morning. My friend and her husband went with me because he was abusive during our relationship in Texas."

"Mey, don't say anything else." Wei's warning struck me as odd.

"I have nothing to hide, Wei."

The officer crossed his arms and smirked. "Then by all means, keep talking."

"Mey. . ." Wei whispered again.

"I was closing the food truck yesterday when he showed up. I've been hiding from him for a year, but he tracked me down somehow. He threatened me until I promised to come out and talk to him, begging me to go back to Texas with him. We argued, he grabbed me, and then Mark and Wei came to my rescue."

"Is that so?" Officer Smirky turned to Wei. "Is what she says true?"

Wei fiddled with her phone then held it up to her ear. "I think I'd better get my husband down here."

"Wei, just confirm what I told him, please." My best friend was being really weird, and I was confused. "Why isn't someone waking Paul up? He'll tell you the exact same story I just did."

"Ma'am, don't you see the yellow tape around your table?" Officer Smirky pointed.

For the first time, I took in the scene around me, not just Paul's slumped body. There was, in fact, yellow crime scene tape around the few tables we had set up. People milled about, whispering behind their hands and casting curious glances my way.

I gulped. Paul hadn't moved a muscle since I came outside. That right there should have sent up red flags. The second I came into view, Paul was usually all over me, up in my face.

"Officer Sm—, I mean, sir, what's wrong with my ex-boyfriend?" I held my breath, waiting for the words I didn't want to hear but somehow deep in my soul knew would come.

"Miss Hirano, I am afraid your *ex-boyfriend*"—he stressed the word—"is dead."

"Dead?" I whispered, the world turning into a Tilt-A-Whirl carnival ride.

"Dead," he repeated. "And ma'am, you're under arrest for the murder of Paul Davis."

Black spots appeared before my eyes. The last thing I remember was Wei screaming my name.

CHAPTER FOUR

I groaned and forced my eyes open. "What happened?"

The kindest green eyes I'd ever seen held my gaze. "You fainted, miss."

"Well, at least I didn't have far to fall." I pushed myself off the hard ground.

Mr. Green Eyes chuckled. "Take it slow now."

He reached out a hand. With his other one under my elbow, he helped me stand. I tried to remember what caused me to be in a horizontal position in the first place.

"Wait." I spun around, instantly regretting that decision. My gaze landed on Paul, still slumped over the table. "Is he really dead?"

"Afraid so, miss." Mr. Green Eyes sighed.

"And am I really under arrest for his murder?" I darted my eyes back to the man next to me.

He scowled at Officer Smirky. "No. You're not under arrest."

My knees gave out, and I found myself trying to kiss the pavement once more.

Mr. Green Eyes switched his arm to around my waist and caught me just in time. "Why don't you sit down for a few minutes? You've had a lot of information thrown at you."

He guided me to a bench—not close to Paul, thank the good Lord. I shivered despite the sun warming me from head to toe. I couldn't believe he was dead. Less than twenty-four hours ago, we sat at that very table and argued.

Oh no. We argued. Who saw us? The teenage couple, but that was when I was inside the food truck. I couldn't remember if anyone walked by us. I was so focused on trying to get away from my abuser.

Wei was by my side in a matter of seconds. "You all right?"

Mr. Green Eyes turned on his heel and had a low conversation with Officer Smirky. I couldn't hear what they were saying, but I wanted to.

"I'm fine. I can't believe this is happening."

Wei's shoulders slumped. "Mark should be here any second. He said not to say anything else until he gets here. He also called his friend who's a lawyer. He'll be here soon too."

I dropped my head into my hands. "I am such a nuisance to the both of you."

Wei snorted. "Because you were abused by your ex-boyfriend, and now he's dead? None of this is your fault."

I lifted my head, ignoring the pounding behind my eyes. "I'm still shocked. How did he die?"

Wei shrugged. "When you were taking a nap on the ground, I was trying to hear what was going on. Someone said he doesn't have any wounds, so they think it may be poison."

"Taking a nap?" I nudged her with my shoulder. "You have a funny way of looking at things, my friend."

"Unfortunately, I doubt my humor is going to get you out of this." Wei's eyes filled with worry. "I know you didn't kill him. Mark and I can attest to your innocence."

"They must have some inkling I'm guilty, or else why would Officer Smirky say I was under arrest?"

"Officer Smirky?" Mr. Green Eyes interrupted, a smile lifting his tanned cheeks.

Heat traveled to my face. When did his discussion come to an end? I needed to pay more attention to everyone around me.

"I, uh, didn't catch his name, so I started calling him that in my head." I forced a chuckle, but it came out sounding like a duck.

Wei coughed behind her hand, but by the shaking of her shoulders, I knew she was really laughing. Great. The last thing I needed was my best friend laughing while I made a fool of myself in front of Mr. Green Eyes.

"I'd say the name fits." He crossed his arms, the material of his shirt accentuating his muscular chest and arms. He spread his legs, his slacks barely reaching his shoes. "What name have you chosen for me, since I haven't introduced myself yet?"

"Don't do it," Wei mumbled.

I shrugged. "Mr. Green Eyes."

His smile stretched from ear to ear then. "Well, I guess it could be worse. Not that I want you to stop calling me that, but I'm Detective Grayson Lang."

"Detective." I held out my hand. "Mey Hirano."

Detective Lang's hand engulfed mine, and a feeling of safety washed over me. I'd never felt that way with a man, aside from Mark, before. Especially since my relationship with Paul.

"Just Grayson, or Gray, is fine. Miss Hirano, I do have some questions for you." He squatted in front of me. "But I think you should have representation here before I ask them."

"She does."

I tore my gaze away from Gray's furrowed brow. "Mark."

Wei stood and moved into Mark's embrace. "Thanks for coming, hon."

Mark nodded and waved his hand behind him. "This is my lawyer, Mr. White."

"Ladies, Detective."

"How'd you know he's a detective?" My eyes swung between the two men.

"It's written all over him," Mr. White explained. "The badge on his belt, the way he's dressed."

Detective Grayson stood. I'd missed all the signs indicating who he was. I really needed to pay closer attention.

"Glad you're here, Mr. White." Detective Grayson gave him a nod then turned to me. "Can you tell me how you knew Paul Davis?"

I glanced at Mr. White. He dipped his head. "I used to date Paul in Texas. He was abusive, so with the help of Wei and Mark, I left him and moved here."

"So, he hurt you?" The handsome detective took out a notepad and started writing.

"Yes."

"What did he do, exactly?"

That sick feeling I got every time I had to talk about Paul's abuse filled my stomach. My therapist was still working with me on that, but it was taking a lot more time than I thought it would.

"Detective," Wei interjected, "this isn't something that should be spoken about in front of a group of people. It's rather private."

"Agreed," Mr. White warned. "If you want to go down this line of questioning, take her to the station."

The detective pursed his lips into a line. "I'd rather not make it that formal. Is there someplace quiet we can go?"

Mark sighed. "We can go back to our place. Wei and I live close by."

"What about Lucky Noodles?" I asked. It was our livelihood. I didn't want to close it right now. We made a lot of money in the summer. It sustained us throughout most of the year, in fact. Closing for even a day wasn't high on the list of things I wanted to do.

"Miss Hirano, I suggest closing for the day." Detective Grayson spread his hands. "I don't think you'll get a lot of business with a dead body in front of your truck."

I palmed my forehead. "That isn't good for business."

A chuckle surrounded me, settling my erratic nerves. "I'm sure it'll pick up once again, Miss Hirano. I've heard of your food truck, even in York." Detective Grayson sent me a smile. "If you wouldn't mind giving me some time, I'd like to ask you a few questions."

I stood, Wei on one side, Mark on the other, and nodded. "Follow us, then."

Mark and Wei would not let me walk my normal brisk pace, not after fainting. I still felt woozy, but I wanted to get to the car, hide from all the people looking at me, and collect myself before answering questions about Paul.

Unbidden tears filled my eyes. *I can't believe he's dead.* Did he really become a Christian, or was that just a lie? It was too late for me to know now, but I couldn't help but wonder if I should have spent more time with him yesterday, asking him questions.

I closed my eyes after getting into the car, begging my mind to take me back to sitting across from him. Was there sincerity in his eyes when he spoke about his faith? I couldn't even remember what he said exactly.

"You don't have to tell the detective anything you don't want to." Mark interrupted my thoughts.

"I think I do." I laughed, even though there was nothing funny. "He's a cop, Mark. I can't say no to a cop."

"You can tame down what you say." Mark held my gaze in the rearview mirror. "Like instead of saying you fought yesterday, you say you had a discussion."

"We did have a discussion. I wouldn't say we fought. Not like we used to."

"That's what you should avoid saying." Mark's eyebrows furrowed. "Don't give away too much."

"Mark." I stopped short and inhaled, hoping my chin wouldn't quiver. "Do you think I'm a prime suspect or something?"

"I don't know, Mey. I really don't. But you're the only one who really knows Paul. . . .Sorry. . . knew Paul. They might just need to get information and wait for the autopsy." Mark pulled up to the house.

I got out of the car, slammed the door, and took a deep breath.

"We'll be right here with you, Mey. And we'll be praying the entire time." Wei's arms wrapped around my shoulders. I leaned into her strength, taking as much of it for myself as possible. "And if they decide to send you to jail, Mark knows a guy who can break you out." She wagged her eyebrows at me, forcing me to laugh.

"You're the best, you know that?" I returned her hug.

"I don't really know a guy, by the way, unless you count Mr. White." Mark smiled. "But we'll help you no matter what."

We waited for Mr. White, the detective, and Officer Smirky. I still didn't know his name, but I was fine with his nickname. Within seconds, their separate cars came to a stop. Both law enforcement officers climbed out, as different from each other as night and day.

Officer Smirky, while taller than me, barely came up to Detective Grayson's shoulder. The cop's beady eyes made me doubt I could trust him. His closely shaved head didn't do him any favors. Neither did his beer belly.

Now, Detective Grayson, on the other hand. Green eyes, hence his nickname. Tall, probably about six feet or more, hair as dark as night, longer on the top than the sides, and a chiseled chin that I swear Michelangelo himself carved.

Mr. White finally pulled up then joined us.

"Gentlemen." Mark motioned with his head. "This way."

We all followed Mark in single file down the walkway and into their house. Wei immediately went into hospitality mode, offering tea, coffee, and baked treats. Both lawmen accepted coffee. The lawyer took tea and a muffin. I needed something in my hands, so I agreed to peppermint tea, decaf because I didn't want anything to make my hands shake.

We were all seated, making small talk, until Wei appeared with a tray full of drinks and goodies. I couldn't take much more. My nerves were strung tighter than guitar strings. I was about ready to snap.

"Okay, Miss Hirano, tell me about your relationship with Mr. Davis." The detective didn't waste any time.

"We met in Texas, dated for four years, broke up, and then I moved here a year ago." *Keep it simple*, Mark had said. How much simpler could I make it?

"You said he abused you." Doubt lingered in Officer Smirky's eyes.

"He did," Wei cut in. "She has the bruise from yesterday to prove it and the emotional scars from those four years." My best friend raised one eyebrow, a look she gave when she was about to make a challenge.

Officer Smirky opened then closed his mouth. He looked like a guppy. *Hmm. Maybe I need to change his nickname.*

"Officer Sm—" Detective Grayson's eyes widened, and he forced a cough. "Officer Sheldon, I'll ask the questions."

I held in a massive laugh that wanted to escape more than a caged puppy. I didn't even know how I was doing it. If I were to break out in giggles, I'd look guilty for sure. So I swallowed any amusement bubbling inside me and reminded myself why everyone was here in the first place.

"He did abuse me. Quite regularly. He showered me with guilt and emotional abuse, jerking me around and ripping my mental health to shreds."

"Why didn't you just close up the truck yesterday and stay inside?" The detective tilted his head.

"Because he'd find a way in." My insides quaked as memories of his last verbal tirade seared my mind.

"What would he have done?" he pushed, his tone gentle, his eyes kind.

I rolled my shoulders and closed my eyes. "I can't say for sure, but from my past experiences, he would have manipulated me and run me down until I admitted I needed him."

"Did he ever abuse you in any other way?"

Wei reached for my free hand and squeezed.

I huffed. "No. He said only a monster would hit or force himself on a woman."

The detective mumbled something, but I couldn't make out the words. He wrote something down and tapped the pencil on the paper.

Officer Smirky spoke up. "Detective, this could be all one-sided. We don't know if what she says is true."

"I can get my therapist to speak with you, if that'd help."

"Did you talk with your therapist while the emotional abuse was occurring?" The officer lifted one side of his mouth.

"No."

"So there's no record of any verbal or mental abuse."

I pinched the bridge of my nose, doing my best to hold it together. "Officer, have you ever worked with abused women before?"

"That's not my area of expertise," he admitted, albeit reluctantly.

"A lot of women don't report the abuse because they, we, are afraid of our abusers. That's why I left him in the first place. I changed my number, sold my car, closed my bank account. I pay for things only with cash, so I leave no record behind. I broke free of his cruelty, but not a lot of women do."

"Do you have any idea how he died?" Detective Grayson asked me.

I shook my head. "After our talk yesterday, I came home with these two, slept here all night, and then went to meet Paul this morning."

"Why?"

"Because he asked me to talk to him one more time, to pray about getting back together with him. Said he's changed and turned to Jesus." *Dear Lord, let it be true.*

"And you believed him?" Detective Grayson's eyebrows met his hairline.

"I don't know. I prayed about it and didn't feel any peace." I raised one shoulder and let it fall.

"Did you want to believe him?"

"No. And yes. Yes, because I wanted him to be a Christian. No, because he hurt me within five minutes of seeing me." I cocked my head to the side. "Do you know how he died?"

"Not yet. But an autopsy will tell us." Officer Smirky leaned forward. "And I ask that you not leave the city."

"Why?"

"Because if it's murder, you're our number one suspect."

Detective Grayson leaned back and shot Officer Smirky a glare. Then he turned those beautiful green eyes on me, sadness replacing his glare.

CHAPTER FIVE

I pulled down the barrier, signaling that Lucky Noodles was closed for the day. Over the previous week, business had picked up. The day after Paul's body was discovered at one of our tables, we barely sold anything. The worry in Wei's eyes tugged at my heart. If it weren't for me, she would have had lines all around the lake.

But as the week went on, people came back to Lucky Noodles. No one asked anything about the dead man. They probably wondered who he was and what he meant to me. Even if they had asked, what could I tell them? *Oh, he was my ex-boyfriend, Paul. I suffered his abuse for four years because I wasn't strong enough to leave an unhealthy relationship. When I finally came to my senses and ended things, I ran away as far as I could. But he found me.*

And then the next question would inevitably come. *Did you kill him?*

To which I would answer, *Of course not.*

Doubt and perhaps fear mingling in their eyes, they'd nod and scurry away.

Okay, okay. My imagination got away from me. But I could just see all that happening. And yet it didn't, so I was glad. I smiled for the first time in a week. A real smile.

"What has that weird smile on your face?" Wei balled up the apron she'd worn all day and tossed it in the basket.

"I just feel like everything's going to be okay. I mean, we haven't heard anything, so that might mean he died of natural causes, right?"

Something about Wei's expression told me she felt otherwise. "It's good to hope."

I leaned my hip against the small counter, the air around me thick. "Yes," I drew out the word.

"Then that's what we'll do." Wei's grin was anything but authentic. "We will continue to hope."

I wasn't upset with my friend's lack of faith. Not after all she'd done for me. She was more pessimistic than I. Unfortunately, most of the time she was right about things. I didn't want her to be right this time.

"Well, we best get outside, or we'll suffocate in here." I pushed the door open, inhaling the lighter air.

I waited for Wei to exit, then I turned around to lock the door. We moved to one of our tables. The other food trucks were closed as well, their umbrellas taken down. The donut, taco, and spuds trucks all did well during the day. When they were closed, the food truck court felt eerie.

I shivered as a bead of sweat traveled down my spine. The little hairs on the back of my neck raised, like I was being watched. *But that's ridiculous, right? Paul's gone, and he'd be the only one stalking me.* I rubbed my neck and shook off the feeling.

"You two about ready?" Mark sauntered over, a smoothie in each of his hands.

"You come bearing gifts," I said, reaching for my strawberry drink.

"Don't I always?" Mark dropped a kiss on the tip of Wei's nose.

"You know you don't have to. I'm fine, and I don't need gifts to make me feel better."

Mark snatched the drink out of my hand before my lips even touched the straw. "Fine. You don't want my gift. I'll take it back."

I tried to grab it again, but he held it high above his head. *Doggone these short legs of mine!* "Fine. I do like your presents."

"Say you're sorry." Mark lowered the drink.

"I'm sorry. It's just you've brought something every single day, and I want you to know gifts aren't necessary." I finally got my smoothie back where it belonged and took a long sip.

"I know you don't need them. But it's one of my love languages. I can't fix what's going on, but maybe a special treat here and there will help you a little bit." Mark's little boy look did me in.

"I appreciate all you've done." I gave him a sideways hug. "Can we go home now? I'm ready for a light dinner and bed."

Mark and Wei strolled ahead of me, hand in hand. Those two were the cutest couple, and I hoped someday I could find love like theirs. They had their problems. They were human, after all. But they really were two of the best people I knew.

I listened from the back seat as they discussed their day. I didn't have a lot to say, so I stayed silent. By the time we got home, my smoothie had filled me up. I wasn't hungry for dinner. I said my goodbyes and headed the twenty feet to my home.

I spent a long time in the shower, washing away the sweat from working inside a food truck all day. After drying off, I slipped on my lightest pair of sleep shorts and a tank top. I plopped down onto my comfortable sofa and turned on the television.

Just what I need. To watch a mindless show to get my thoughts off of Paul Davis. I picked up my cell phone. A text message from Wei two minutes before appeared: DETECTIVE GRAYSON'S ON HIS WAY TO YOUR FRONT DOOR.

Before I even had a chance to reply, my doorbell rang. I didn't have time to change, so I moved to the door and pulled it open.

"Detective." I tried to make my voice sound normal, but the man was far too good-looking. I know my voice kicked up a notch.

His eyes perused me from head to toe then landed on my eyes. His cheeks turned a dark shade of red. "Uh, Miss Hirano."

"What can I do for you?" I moved aside and motioned him in. "Would you like something to drink? Lemonade, tea, Coke, Dr Pepper?"

The detective cleared his throat. "I'll, uh, have a Coke. Thanks."

Moving as fast as my little legs could carry me, I grabbed a Dr Pepper, a Coke, and two cups filled with ice, and hurried into the living room.

I handed him the Coke. He popped the top and poured it over ice. "Is there a reason for your wall of birds?"

"My *wall of birds*, as you call it, is actually a group of one thousand origami paper cranes held together by strings. An ancient Japanese legend promises that anyone who folds a thousand origami cranes will be granted a wish. The crane in Japan is one of the mystical or holy creatures. It's said to live for a thousand years." I glanced over to my wall of paper cranes. I loved the beauty of all the colors. "They are also given to a person who is seriously ill." I lifted my soda to my lips and took a sip, a grin playing at the corners of my mouth. "They are commonly used for sport teams or athletes. Wishing them victory, of course. Not to mention, cranes represent a symbol of peace."

"You know a lot about cranes."

"I'm half Japanese." I shrugged my shoulders. "I doubt that's why you came over. To talk about my cranes."

"No. You're right." His eyes grazed the rest of my living room. He stood and moved to my kokeshi doll. "This may sound weird, but this doll reminds me of Nintendo's Miis. Have you seen those? You can customize them to look like yourself."

I wandered to where he stood, and nodded. "That's exactly what the Miis were modeled after."

Detective Grayson's eyes softened as he looked at me. I wondered what he was seeing, but I didn't dare ask. He was here for an investigation, I presumed, not to ask me out on a date. Even though I wouldn't mind if he did.

He cleared his throat and moved back to the couch, then pulled a pad of paper from his shirt pocket. "I'm sorry to drop by so late."

"It's not late." Then I followed his gaze to my shorts and shirt. "I was really hot at work and just wanted to get into something comfortable after showering."

He rubbed his lips together. "Well, I wanted to ask you a few more questions about Paul. I received the autopsy report today."

Please, Lord, let it be natural causes. "Oh?"

Detective Grayson flipped to a page. "Have you ever heard of Fentanyl?"

Fentanyl. Fentanyl. "Hmm. It sounds vaguely familiar. Why?"

"It was found in Mr. Davis's system. Quite a high dose, actually."

"What's it used for?" I tried really hard to remember why I knew that name.

Detective Grayson—I was sort of sad to call him that instead of Mr. Green Eyes—zeroed in on my face. "It's prescribed for severe pain."

Realization dawned on me. "Like a spinal injury?"

"So, you have heard of it."

"Yes. My doctor prescribed it. I fell and hurt my spine. Like, I almost couldn't walk." My hand automatically moved to my lower back. Once again, I felt a wave of pain go through my body.

"You all right, Miss Hirano?"

"You might as well call me Mey. And, yes, I'm fine. I get these phantom pains when I remember what I've gone through."

"So, you have those pills." A statement, not a question.

"No. I went to take them one day, but they must have fallen out of my purse while I was at Paul's, ending our relationship. My doctor warned me about taking them for too long because they are highly addictive. So as soon as I could, I stopped." I clenched my hands together. "You said they found large amounts of Fentanyl in his system? Like how much? I've never known Paul to use painkillers."

"A lethal amount, I'm afraid, Mey." Tucking the pad of paper into his shirt pocket, he leaned forward and clasped his hands between his knees. "What I'm saying is, your ex-boyfriend was murdered."

"Murdered?" I repeated. I was glad to be sitting down, because the room started to spin. So much for hoping for the best. This was certainly not the best.

"Yes. Murdered. Would you have any reason to kill him, Mey?"

The blood drained from my face. "You can't be serious."

"As a life sentence."

His words sent fear galloping into my heart. "I had no reason to kill him."

"Not to get even for all the times he belittled you?" The detective's gaze bored into mine.

"I'm a Christian, sir. I don't do the whole vengeance thing when God says it belongs to Him."

"I'm a Christian too, and I've been known to want to see justice done, even by my own hand." He raised an eyebrow.

I mimicked him. "And do you?"

"Do I what?"

"Do you take justice into your own hands, or do you leave it to God?" Oh, I hoped he left it to the Lord.

"I don't take revenge, but I seek justice at all costs."

"Even if that means breaking the law?" I pushed.

"No. I don't break the law," he finally said.

"Then we have something in common, Detective. Because I did not kill Paul Davis. I may've wished he would disappear, but I would never, never seek to do that on my own." I held my breath. Did he believe me?

Detective Grayson lowered his head in slow motion. *Hopefully, he's praying, asking for God to show him who the real killer is, because as sure as I know my own name, it isn't me.*

"I'm going to be honest. You are our main suspect."

"But I didn't do it," I insisted.

"You say that, but can you prove it? Can you tell me how he got those pills in his system? If it wasn't you, then who was it?"

"I can't tell you that because I hadn't seen him for a year until the other day."

"So, let's talk about the day you met with him again." The detective stood and started pacing. "And call me Gray."

I folded my knees under my chin and wrapped my arms around my legs. I took a deep breath and let it out through my nose. "Okay. Mark stayed all day at one of our tables because I thought I saw Paul that morning. The day flew by, and I told Wei to go sit with Mark while I locked up our earnings. I stood up, and there was Paul."

"Where were Mark and Wei?"

"I looked at the table, but it was empty."

Gray pulled out his notebook again. "All right. Keep going."

"I figured they went to put his laptop in the car. Paul said something about missing me, wanting me back."

"Typical of an abuser."

I snorted. "Tell me about it. I told him no." I finished telling him about Paul's threat, how I closed the barrier and thought about staying inside the truck.

"You probably should have." He stopped in front of me and dropped to one knee. "I know this is painful to walk through. But right now, I have to treat you like you're a suspect unless I can find evidence proving you're not guilty."

I dipped my head. "I understand." I gulped and continued. "I told him to sit across from me instead of next to me."

"Did he have anything to drink with him?" Gray rose and sat across from me on the chair.

I closed my eyes. The table was in front of me. But nothing was on the table. "No."

"There weren't any bottles, soda cups, alcoholic beverages?" Gray wrote more.

"No. Just an empty table."

"Hmm. Okay. Continue."

"We talked a few more minutes. He told me he'd turned religious. I stood up, and he grabbed my wrist and started to squeeze." Chills ran down my spine. "Then Mark yelled something, and he came between me and Paul."

"So, they might be angry with him too?"

"Not enough to kill him. They love me, yes, but they follow Jesus too and aren't about to take matters into their own hands. Besides, we were with each other all night."

"Why?"

"Because once we got home, I threw up, and I didn't want to be alone. Mark wasn't going to let me anyway. So I grabbed my stuff and slept at their house."

"Did you all sleep in the same room?"

I shook my head. "I slept in the living room."

"Did they see you fall asleep and wake up?"

"I don't know. I didn't leave until they left the next morning, to go meet Paul."

Gray wrote some more. "And he didn't show up."

"No, he didn't. And now I know why." My teeth started to chatter. "Gray, I didn't kill him. Neither did Wei or Mark."

A deep sigh left his lips. "I want to believe you. And you're innocent until proven guilty. But right now everything points to your guilt."

CHAPTER SIX

I stopped in my tracks, my heart plummeting to the ground. Wei gasped next to me and reached for my hand.

"Who did this?" Mark yelled across the food truck court.

MURDERER, written in bright red, ran across not only Lucky Noodles' tables but the truck too.

Some people stopped and shook their heads. No one confessed. And why would they? I had a sneaky suspicion Mark would pummel them if they did.

My sigh left my mouth nice and slow. I wanted to find the culprit who graffitied our property, but this wasn't the time. "Mark, call the police," I instructed, taking control of the situation. I yanked my phone out of my pocket and started snapping pictures for evidence.

"We can't clean it up until the police come and file a report." Wei's voice shook. "I'm so sorry, Mey."

"You have nothing to apologize for." I turned to her and pulled her into my embrace. "I'm the one who should apologize. I've caused you both nothing but trouble the last few years."

"Neither one of you needs to apologize." Mark shoved his phone into his pocket. "Whoever did this is a coward. They couldn't tell you to their face how they feel, so they chose childish tactics." He shook his head, a storm brewing in his eyes. "If I find out who did this, they'll be the ones who are sorry."

"I told Detective Grayson last night that we don't take matters into our own hands, remember?" I crossed my arms and raised an eyebrow. "I may be the prime suspect, but unfortunately, you two aren't off the hook yet."

"This entire thing is ridiculous." Wei moved to the door of the truck and unlocked it. "What did the police say, Mark?"

"They're on their way. I asked them to bring the detective too."

Butterflies flapped their wings in my stomach. The attractive detective had that effect on me, and I didn't really like it. Paul was my last boyfriend. To be honest, I wasn't looking for love. Obviously, I wasn't a good judge of character, or I wouldn't have been with Paul for four years.

I pressed my hand to my stomach, pushing down the flutters, to focus on the task at hand. "Let's get ready for the day. No matter what, we're going to open and not let this affect us, right?"

Wei's decisive nod sent me into action. I found the recipe card and started dicing the onions she needed for the yaki udon. The thick noodle dish with beef or chicken sounded good today. I grabbed the cabbage, carrots, and green onions and chopped them up as well. Wei worked on the seasoning for the dish, since it was her specialty.

We had everything ready for the day when Mark flung open the door. "Cops are here."

We wiped our hands, dropped the towels on the counter, and left our truck.

"Good morning, Mey, Wei." Grayson greeted us with a grim expression. "I'm sorry about this." He waved his hand in the direction of the tables and the front of our truck.

"Thanks." I moved around him. "I forgot to ask you, but did you find out where Paul was staying?"

"There was a room key in his pocket. It was the local motel." Grayson pulled out his pad of paper. "We searched his room, but we didn't find anything."

"He stayed by himself?" For some reason, that surprised me. Paul hated being by himself.

"Yes. Why?" Grayson tilted his head.

"He hated living alone or even being alone, for that matter. I never stayed overnight with him, and he guilted me something awful about that too. But when his roommate was away, he'd always call someone to stay in the apartment with him." The snapping of cameras drew my attention. My gaze followed the photographers as they moved around the truck and tables.

"Why didn't you say something before?" Officer Smirky growled.

"I wasn't told you searched his room already," I snapped back. "No one asked me anything about Paul, only my relationship with him. If you want to know more, ask better questions."

Wei put a steadying hand on my shoulder. "If you want to discuss this more, we can go down to the station."

Grayson shook his head. "I'll talk with my colleague here after we're done with this." He thumbed in the direction of the photographer. "Can you tell me what happened?"

"We arrived here and found it like this. We didn't move anything, but I took pictures, just so you know it all looks the same." I handed Grayson my phone. He thumbed through the photos, then sent them to his cell phone.

"I want to make sure they match." His eyes held an apology. "Just to cover all our bases."

I waved my hand and took my phone back. "That's fine. I don't have anything to hide." I glared at Officer Smirky.

The officer grunted. "We'll see about that." He stormed away.

"What's his problem?" I turned to Grayson.

He shrugged. "Maybe he doesn't like a murder in his town, or maybe that's just his personality. Either way, it doesn't matter what he thinks. What matters is the truth."

"She's telling you the truth." Mark narrowed his eyes at the detective. "And we'll prove it too."

"You saying you want to work together to clear Mey's name?" Grayson raised his eyebrows.

"Yes. If we can do anything to prove her innocence, we will." Wei nodded with finality.

"What motel did Paul stay at? Did anyone check in with him or at the same time?" I pursed my lips.

"He checked in by himself." Grayson skimmed the pad of paper in his hands. "We didn't find anything in his room either. Pretty clean, even though housekeeping hadn't gotten to his room yet."

I ran my sweaty palms over my shirt. "He's always been messy, never clean."

"You're thinking he was with someone?" Grayson wrote something I couldn't see.

"Yes. I just don't know who."

"Do you know any of his friends who would come with him?" Grayson tucked his pencil into his shirt pocket.

I shook my head. "I didn't spend a lot of time with his friends, not even his roommate. He sort of kept me tucked away."

"Mey, why don't you and the detective go over to the motel and talk with the manager? Mark and I can clean this place up." Wei sent Mark an unspoken message.

"That's a good idea. I don't think you need to be around this anyway." Mark took out his phone. "I'll call a cleanup crew and see if they can help us out."

"I like that idea. Now that I know a little more about Mr. Davis, I can ask different questions." Grayson nodded at me. "Are you all right with that? Maybe you can tell me more on the way to the motel."

My mouth dried up like the Sahara Desert. "We're going to ride together?"

"Mey, you rode with me and Mark, remember? He'll need his car at some point today." Wei held up her finger to the detective and pulled me away. "What's the matter with you?"

"Nothing."

"I know you better than that. Now spill it." Wei tapped her foot against the pavement.

"I've spent enough time alone with Grayson, don't you think? Last night, and now today? That's too much."

"Why? Don't you want to clear your name?" My friend scratched her cheek.

"Of course I do." I nibbled my lower lip between my teeth. "It's just—"

"You like him." Wei's eyes widened.

"No, I don't." I denied it, but she was smart enough to see through my protest.

Wei clapped her hands and jumped up and down. "Yes, you do!"

"You're twenty-five years old, Wei McGreggor. Stop acting like a teenager!"

"Then spill the beans, Mey Hirano." Her grin slipped. "I know you've been through a rough time, especially with men. You need someone who's going to treasure you the way you deserve. The way God intended."

I swallowed the boulder in my throat. The problem with Wei's statement was something I'd been working through. I'd always felt I deserved to be treated just as Paul treated me. My therapist and I had been having a lot of conversations about that.

"Since he told me last night that he's a Christian too, I'm even more attracted to him." I avoided eye contact with Wei. "And that scares me."

"Of course it does, Mey. And you shouldn't act on it if you aren't ready for a relationship." Wei squeezed my hand. "But don't run from something that could be very beautiful."

"I'll hold off on making a decision until after my name is cleared. Because heaven knows how hard it would be to have a relationship with a detective while I'm in prison."

Wei threw her head back and laughed. "So I've been told."

"If you're fine with me leaving, I'll return as soon as I can."

"Take your time. You've already prepped. I can ask Mark to take orders. It'll be fun working side by side with my husband for a change." Wei wiggled her eyebrows. "I can finally boss him around."

We walked to where Mark and Grayson stood. "Okay. I'll go. Can you bring me back here when we're done?"

Grayson tipped his head to the side. "Let's see what time we get finished. I may need to ask you more questions. Will that be all right, Wei?"

My best friend nodded, but her eyes held mischief. "Just take her home. All I ask is that you feed her a meal."

"That was my plan all along." Grayson grinned.

"Great minds think alike." Wei chuckled.

"Oh brother. Thanks, Mom." I turned to Wei and made my words as sarcastic as I could.

Wei rolled her eyes. "Sometimes it feels like I'm dealing with a teenager. Good luck with Mey today, Grayson. And if she gives you any problems, let me know."

I grabbed Grayson's sleeve to drag him away. "We'd better get out of here before she sets rules." I dropped my hand and strolled as casually as I was able next to this handsome man.

Grayson opened the passenger door and waited for me to get situated before he closed it. I took steadying breaths. I needed to get through this day without making a fool of myself. *It's about clearing my name. It's not like we're on a date.*

Grayson climbed in, clicked his seat belt, and started the ignition. "So, tell me more about Paul's personality."

"That's a broad statement." I licked my lips. "When we first met, Paul was kind, polite, and gentle. We went on a few dates. He was quite romantic."

"When did he change?"

"After about six months, I started noticing he'd speak down to me, tell me things like no wonder my mom didn't pay attention to me, because I was so stupid. I should've left him after the arguments we had, but I started to believe him." Shame wrapped around me. "I still can't believe I did that."

"That happened before you became a Christian, right?" Grayson glanced at me, then turned back to the street.

"Yeah."

"Then there's no condemnation. You're in Christ Jesus now." He leaned over an inch and whispered, "That's straight from Romans chapter eight verse one. You just needed to see how God sees and feels about you, not Paul or your mom."

My lips turned up a little. "Thanks. That's what my therapist says."

"I'm glad you're seeing a therapist. After what you've been through, I'd highly recommend it." Grayson suddenly became quiet, as if realizing our discussion was turning more personal. He cleared his throat. "Anything else you can tell me?"

"Well, like I said before, Paul's a sloppy guy. Not clean at all." I fiddled with the hem of my T-shirt. "One day I was cleaning up my living room. Whenever he came over, he'd eat and leave his dishes around. I was annoyed. He stopped by on his way home from work, and I snapped at him."

My eyes shut, reliving the nightmare soon to follow. "Paul turned from Bruce Banner to the Incredible Hulk in seconds. He started by smashing everything in the room. I got scared. I'd never seen him so angry. I tripped over the vacuum and fell into the coffee table. I still have the scars on my back."

"Mey?"

I opened my eyes and forced my eyes in his direction.

Grayson stopped at a light, his expression worried. "What did he do?"

I cleared my throat and blinked, wiping away the images of the shattered living room. "Did you ever see the *Avengers*?" At his nod, I continued. "When Hulk starts smashing, everything he touches comes to ruin. That was my life for four years. Except I ended up being ruined. No, it wasn't his fault I tripped, but I have the scars to remind me of my awful decision to stay with him."

Grayson reached for my hand, compassion flowing from his eyes. He gave it a gentle squeeze. "You weren't at fault for asking him to clean up after himself."

I shook my head. "I don't know. That night he sat in the hospital with me and cried. He felt horrible for scaring me that badly. I probably overreacted."

Grayson released my hand and stepped on the gas pedal, his nostrils flaring. "Don't do that to yourself. It isn't about you. It was his fault. A true man controls his anger, and the ones who don't, need to get help. And that goes the opposite way as well. No woman has the right to put a man through that situation either. Period."

"I agree. On both accounts." I shrugged. "But at the time, his was the only voice I listened to. After all, he loved me. He said he loved me." I blinked back the tears begging to fall. "Anyway, that's how I know there's no way the motel room was cleaned by Paul."

"Hmm. What else can you tell me about him? Did he have any enemies, jilted lovers, frustrated family members?"

"I never met his family. He said he stayed away from them because they were toxic." I snorted then covered my mouth. "Sorry. That wasn't very ladylike."

"No problem. I just about did the same thing." Grayson's grin lit his face.

"We did argue about a few female friends he kept in touch with. Ex-girlfriends who wanted him back. That was about three years ago."

"Do you know their names?"

"Um, I'll have to think about it. It's been a long time, and I try to forget a lot about our arguments. Generally, they ended only one way—him screaming and me in tears."

"Mey, I'll be honest with you, and this is off the record." Grayson pulled into the parking lot of the motel and shifted in his seat. "I've never wanted to harm a man more than I do at this moment."

CHAPTER SEVEN

I followed Grayson to the manager's office. He motioned for me to join him in the back office. Papers piled high filled the desk. The manager's hair stood on end, giving him a wild look.

"Cal, sorry to drop by unexpected." Grayson patted the chair next to him. I sat down and waited.

"No problem, no problem. What can I do for you, Detective?" Mr. Hair straightened a stack of papers.

"You've kept Mr. Davis' room free, right?" At the manager's nod, Grayson continued. "Thank you. I'd like another look around but wanted to ask you a few more questions. Did anyone check in the same day as Mr. Davis?"

"Detective Grayson." The manager folded his hands on the desk, condescension oozing from his lips. "It's summer in Maine. Many people checked in the day Mr. Davis did, as well as the next day."

"I do understand that, sir." Grayson's thin smile betrayed his calm voice. "I may need to ask some of your guests a question or two. Did you happen to notice if Mr. Davis was friendly with anyone?"

Cal leaned back in his chair and looked to the ceiling. "Mr. Davis was friendly with everyone. He'd smile and wave at whoever crossed his path. Shame what happened to him." His eyes flicked to me.

"I agree." I nodded. "No one deserves to have their life taken from them."

Uncertainty clouded the manager's eyes. "Well, yes."

"So, you're saying he got along with all your guests?" Grayson pushed. "Did he get along with any one guest more than others?"

Cal rubbed his clean-shaven jaw. "There was a gal he got to know."

My heart hammered in my chest. "Oh?"

"She had the room next to him. Hasn't checked out yet. Don't know how long she'll be here." Cal swirled his chair and faced his computer. "Name's Jamie Bolten."

I tried to keep my face impassive, but I knew that name. Grayson must have sensed something, because two minutes later, with Paul's room key in his hand, he led me out of Cal's office and up the stairs. He stopped, unlocked the door, and let me go first.

A fresh scent of lavender and mandarin orange hit me. I knew Paul's scent all too well. At the heart of his cologne, spicy coriander tangled with lily for a rich sandalwood base. I grimaced. I hated the smell when we were dating, and I hated it even more now. I sneezed.

"Bless you." Grayson eyed me. "I take it Mr. Davis' cologne does not please you."

"I'm allergic to it." I wiped my eyes with the back of my hand. "But I can tell you what's in it."

"Do I want to know this story?"

"Probably not." I turned to the window. "If I'm going to be in here, I need to open this. That okay?"

"Yes." Grayson took over my spot and forced the clunky window open. "Tell me what happened."

My gaze swept the motel room. The queen bed, no surprise there, two nightstands, a television sitting on top of the dresser. The vanity area still held his toiletries.

"One day Paul bought a new cologne. I pretty much discovered I was allergic to it right away." My legs fought to keep me up. No way was I going to sit on the bed Paul slept in. "I asked Paul what was in it. When he figured out I didn't like it and it made me ill—"

"Let me guess. He was offended and thought you were faking it."

"Yep. He screamed at me, telling me I was jealous because other women would want to date him because of the cologne." I shook my head. "He sprayed it on my wrist and made me sniff it. I kept sneezing and finally had an anxiety attack because I felt like I couldn't breathe. He stopped, but not before informing me I was weak."

Grayson groaned. My eyes grazed his face. I flinched. Not because I was scared. Grayson didn't frighten me, oddly enough, even though he had my future in his hands. His look of disgust and righteous anger soothed my weary soul.

"When did you start to plan to leave Texas?"

"After that. It took me another year. Paul must've known I was working on something. Every time I tried to break up, he came up with one excuse after another why we were so good together and treated me like a queen." I turned my back on the horrific bottle and glanced around the room once again.

"I'm going to change the subject now." Grayson moved next to me and let his hand rest on my shoulder. "I felt in Cal's office that you recognized the name Jamie Bolten."

I slammed the door on emotions and focused on Grayson. "Yes. Jamie was Paul's ex-girlfriend. The one before me."

"You think they came here together?" Grayson lifted one eyebrow.

"I don't know. I find it odd that the two of them ended up in the same place at the same time. I don't know why else she'd be here."

"Were they communicating while you two were together?" Grayson pulled out his handy-dandy pad of paper.

"Not at first. But definitely toward the end. I checked his phone once when he left it unattended and saw a few texts from her." I'd secretly hoped he found himself interested in her if it would help to end our relationship.

Grayson slid two pairs of gloves out of his pocket. "Put these on. I'm sorry to have you do this, but we need to go through his belongings. If something doesn't seem like it belongs to Mr. Davis, you'll be able to tell me, right?"

"Without a doubt. People can change in a year, but he was a stickler for routine." I waited for Grayson to grab Paul's suitcase.

Grayson tossed the case onto the bed and unzipped it. Paul's normal clothing filled one side. On the other were pictures of me and gifts with my name on them. I shuddered. He really wanted to buy me back. Not like I'd accept anything he offered. Not after the pain I went through being with him.

"He seemed quite taken with you." Grayson held up a framed photograph of me.

"Paul wasn't taken with me. He wanted to control me. I was nothing more than a puppet to him, someone he could use and abuse at his will." I grabbed the frame from him and tossed it back into the suitcase. It broke, and my picture fell out.

"What's this?" Grayson held up the photo and flipped it over. "'She'll never have you,'" he read. "Did you write this?"

"I'd never write that." I huffed. "Even when we were first together, I never claimed Paul for myself."

"Don't hate me, but you'll need to write this same thing for me to be sure."

I wasn't surprised when he handed me his pencil and pad of paper. I wrote the words and handed it back to him.

Grayson glanced between the two, a grin spreading across his face. "Your writing's awful."

"You're not the first person to tell me that." I laughed. "My teachers spent many hours trying to drill perfect penmanship into my brain. It never stuck."

"So, who does this belong to?" Grayson tapped the photo with his finger.

"My guess is Jamie. Paul was obsessed with me. She was just as crazy for him."

"We'll have to check her signature from when she signed in at the front desk." Grayson rummaged through more of the suitcase. "Anything look out of place to you?"

I muddled through his things, not seeing anything odd. "Nothing stands out to me."

"Would you really accept this?" Grayson held up a string bikini.

"Not if my life depended on it. I'd never put that on." I yanked it out of his hand and tossed it back into the suitcase.

Grayson's low chuckle filled me with warmth. "Good."

"What do we do now?"

"I think we need to get some lunch and then return and wait for Miss Bolten. I'd like to ask her a few questions." Grayson zipped the suitcase up and put it away. He closed the closet doors. "You about ready?"

"We should shut the window."

"You go on out, and I'll do that." Grayson opened the door and waited for me to leave. Once the window was closed, he came out of the motel room. "I did promise Wei I'd feed you."

"You don't have to. I'm fine waiting until I get home to eat." The rumble in my stomach contradicted my words.

Grayson arched an eyebrow. "Really?" He got me situated in the passenger seat and then closed the door.

Minutes later, we were headed to a fast-food restaurant. "I'm going to go through the drive-through because I don't want to miss Jamie. That all right with you?"

"That's fine. Makes sense."

I wished I could eat some of Wei's cooking. I never realized I'd want Japanese food if I owned a truck, but I craved it more than I thought I would. Instead of ramen, I settled for a burger, fries, and a soda. Not my favorite food, but it would fill my stomach and get the job done.

With our order on my lap, Grayson headed back to the motel. We unbuckled, said a quick prayer over our food, and dug in. The burger tasted better than I expected. And when it was so hot outside, Dr Pepper quenched my thirst. If I wasn't careful, I'd become addicted to the sugary drink again. I loved the soda from Texas. It was definitely my kryptonite.

"Do you normally eat at the food truck court?" Grayson wiped his mouth with a napkin.

I nodded. "If it's not ramen or noodles, I get a taco, or something from the Spudmobile. I'm partial, though, to our truck."

"Because you enjoy your own cooking?"

I snickered. "Oh, I don't do the cooking. That's all Wei. I help prep, take the orders and payments, and chat with the customers. But Wei's the mastermind behind our food truck."

"She comes up with the recipes?"

"Yes and no. We work together on that, but she's the one who puts it all together. She's really quite brilliant." I couldn't keep the admiration from my voice even if I tried.

"How long have you two been friends?" Grayson bit into a fry.

"Forever. Wei's been with me through my good and bad times. She's held me when I cried, prayed with me even when I didn't want to hear it. It's because of her love and faithful friendship I follow Jesus today." I sipped my drink, collecting my emotions before they spilled onto my cheeks.

"And Mark?"

"Like the brother I never had and always wanted." A grin slid across my face. "He tortures me like an older brother but protects me like a brother would too. I'm glad he and Wei have each other. They're the best things in my life."

"Family?" Grayson continued munching on his burger.

"American mom who doesn't want anything to do with me. Japanese dad who died when I was a teenager. No siblings." My turn. "You?"

"Oldest of three boys, parents live in Portland."

"Oregon or Maine?"

Grayson made a funny face. "Uh, Maine. Come on, now. Must you ask?"

I laughed. "Sorry. Remember, I've only lived here for a year."

"That's true. You're forgiven then, solely based on your ignorance." Grayson sent me a wink, which set those once-tamed butterflies fluttering around my stomach again.

"What do your brothers do?"

"One's a journalist for *The New York Times*, and the other's a high school teacher." Pride flowed from him.

"You guys close?"

"Yep. Can't imagine my life without them." He tossed his trash into the empty bag. "My parents taught us about Jesus and the value of keeping our relationship strong with each other. They would remind us while we were growing up that friends can come and go, but we'll always have each other."

"You consider them your best friends, then?"

"Absolutely. We talk at least once a week, sometimes all together, other times not." Grayson glanced at his watch. "Do you think Jamie will come back?"

"At least to sleep, right?" I finished my burger and threw away the trash. "Did you always want to be a detective?"

"As long as I can remember." Grayson leaned back in his seat and thumped the steering wheel with his fingers. "I've had a desire for justice my entire life."

Silence settled between us. Not an uncomfortable silence, where I felt like I had to say something. It was a foreign feeling, being relaxed with a man I'd just met less than two weeks before. Which unsettled me at the same time as it relaxed me. *Is it really wise, being attracted to someone who might send me to jail?*

Besides, he probably didn't even view me as anything but a suspect. I pushed down my feelings of attraction and focused on the task. *Jamie.* I'd only seen pictures of her, mostly on Paul's phone.

"I wonder what she's doing." Grayson half mumbled, half spoke. "Let's say, for the sake of argument, that she actually killed Mr. Davis."

"I like your train of thought." I grinned.

Grayson grinned back then turned to the front window. "Why would she still be here? What purpose would she accomplish by remaining where she committed a crime?"

"Maybe to make sure I get arrested."

"But what's the motive? If she loved him or had some unhealthy fascination with him, why kill him?" Grayson rubbed his stubbly chin.

"Paul begged me to go back to Texas with him, said he wanted to start over. What if she thought he had come here for some other reason?"

"And if she found out, she'd be angry because she thought she finally had him to herself." Grayson nodded, as if it all came together in his head.

"Could be. I don't know why anyone would want him. You'd have to be crazy to stay in a relationship with him." I held up a hand. "I know, and I'm not denying my insanity."

Grayson barked a laugh. "Good to know. On the serious side, Jamie just might be crazy. And if she is, then she's dangerous."

"Which means she might kill again if she thinks I'm not going to prison for Paul's murder." I finished Grayson's thought.

"We might want to get back to the food truck and talk with Wei and Mark." Grayson turned the key in the ignition. I clicked my seat belt into place seconds before he peeled out of the parking lot.

CHAPTER EIGHT

I held on to the door as Grayson turned the corner. "Do you think Jamie's with Wei and Mark?"

Face somber, he righted the car and nodded. "Call it a gut instinct. It's been over a week since Mr. Davis's death, and no arrests have been made. If Jamie feels like you're not going to be prosecuted, she may try something drastic."

I bit my lip. I always felt like I was a burden on people I loved. At that moment, it seemed I may very well have put my friends' lives in danger. My grip tightened on the door handle, my knuckles as white as a sheet. *Lord, keep them safe.*

"I'm going to try calling them." I pulled out my phone and hit Wei's name first. After several rings, her sweet voice came on the phone, requesting that I leave a message. "Ugh. No answer. I'll try Mark." Same result.

Grayson's lips turned down. He squealed into the parking lot of the food truck court. "You stay here. I'm going to make sure everything's okay."

I grasped his long-sleeved shirt. "I want to go with you."

His eyes held compassion as he patted my hand while shaking his head. "It may not be safe. I'll be back as soon as possible if they are safe."

Grayson ran toward the court, leaving me alone with my thoughts. Not a good place to be. Too warm to stay in a hot car, I climbed out and leaned against it, crossing my ankles. The breeze rustled my hair. I closed my eyes and inhaled.

"Well, well, well, if it isn't the perfect Mey."

I snapped my head in the direction of a woman's voice. "Jamie?"

"You know who I am." Delight lit her hazel eyes. She flicked her long golden ponytail over her shoulder, a gun in her other hand. "Let's go."

"Go?" I tried to stall, knowing Grayson would be back any second.

"He's not coming for you." An evil smile spread across her face. "I hit him over the head. He'll be out for a while." She waved her gun at me. "Get moving."

"Where?"

"Just to that car right there." Jamie pointed to an SUV.

I slowly moved toward the car. "You can't drive and hold a gun, you know." I glanced over my shoulder at the tall woman. Much taller than I expected her to be.

"I know."

When she didn't say anymore, my heart sped up a notch. She was planning on hurting me before we even left the parking lot.

"You killed him, didn't you?" I opened the door and climbed in.

"Shut up," Jamie growled. "I don't have to justify my actions to you."

"When you try to pin a murder on me, you do. Why'd you do it?"

Jamie pulled something out of her purse. A syringe. "Just relax. This'll all be over before you know it."

"That's what I'm afraid of," I murmured.

With catlike reflexes, she jabbed the needle into my arm. Within seconds, my body felt heavy, my eyelids closing against my will.

My head rolled back. I grimaced and tried to force my eyes open. They felt like they'd been glued shut. That was impossible, of course, but I've never had such a hard time opening my eyes, even when they were swollen from weeping.

I moved my hands to rub my eyes, but they were tied together behind my back. I was sitting in a wooden chair, as far as I could tell, with my legs tied to the legs of the chair. Whatever she had planned for me wasn't good.

A maniacal laugh floated my way. "Doesn't feel good, does it?"

"What did you give me?" I managed to croak.

"It won't kill you, so don't worry." A chair scraping sent shards of pain to my head. "Open your eyes, Mey. I want to get a good look at you."

I didn't want to do as Jamie said, but if I didn't obey, I was afraid she'd do something even more dangerous. Scrunching my face, I pried my eyes open to slits. The dark room had little in it. Two chairs, a wooden floor, a bed.

"Are we at the motel?"

"That would be stupid, don't you think?" Jamie snarled. "Why go back to where I stayed? That'll be the first place the detective looks."

"He may not even care. He doesn't believe I'm innocent."

Jamie snorted. "If only that were true." She gave an indulgent sigh. "If he thought for a second you were guilty, you'd be behind bars, awaiting bail. But no. Something you told him made him believe in your innocence." She towered over me. "What did you tell him?"

"The truth. I didn't kill Paul."

Jamie's hand landed on my face. My head lobbed to the side. "Don't you dare say his name. You're not worthy to even speak his name."

My cheek stung from the contact. I tasted blood in my mouth. I must have bit my lip or cheek. "I didn't deserve that," I dared to say.

"You deserve so much more. But I'll refrain for now."

She was crazy. Though she wasn't saying anything I didn't tell myself. Or that I hadn't heard from Paul. He used to play the guilt card too. If I cared about him, I wouldn't make him so angry. If I just listened to him, he wouldn't have to scream at me.

On and on the excuses went as to why I was abused. None of it was ever Paul's fault. It wasn't like he had an anger issue or wanted control. No, it landed squarely on my shoulders. According to him anyway.

"Did he ever scream at you, Jamie?" I swung my gaze to her.

The woman turned her back on me. I really wanted to see her expression. Instead, she moved to the wall and leaned her head against it.

"Only once." Jamie straightened and spun toward me. "But then, I did everything he asked. I was the perfect girlfriend. He never had a reason to scream at me again." She glared at me. "Until you came along."

"What do you mean?"

"The day he met you, he changed. He no longer wanted me. He told me we could be friends but nothing more." A tear slid down Jamie's face. "I was going to marry him."

"You wouldn't want to." I shook my head. "He wouldn't ever stop abusing you, no matter how perfect you were."

"You lie!" Jamie screamed. "Even after you left, when we got back together, he didn't raise his voice to me. He loved me."

"Then why'd you kill him?" I taunted. I shouldn't have, but I had to keep her talking until Grayson found me.

"Paul asked me to go away with him." A dreamy smile lifted her lips as she sank onto the chair across from me. "I knew we were going to get married. Why else would he want to go away with me? He wouldn't tell me where we were going, just that it was a surprise."

"Did you get married?" The answer was as plain as the nose on my face, but I waited for her to answer anyway.

"No. He found out where you escaped to. I didn't know that until we pulled up to a car rental place. He told me to get out and rent a car. I did as he asked. We met at a diner outside of town, and he told me he wanted to talk with you one more time before the two of us drove to New York to spend the week there."

"You believed him?"

Jamie narrowed her eyes at me. "Why wouldn't I? He's never lied to me before."

I snickered then pursed my lips together to keep from getting slapped again. "So, what happened?"

"Paul knew you wouldn't talk to him without your friends, so we had a plan. I'd ask them for a battery jump in the parking lot and keep them detained for as long as possible."

"You were the woman who needed help?" I should have known Paul was behind all of that.

"Of course." Jamie's face filled with pride. "He said he'd only need half an hour. That's it. To show you what you were missing out on and that he was finally happy."

"That's not what he said at all, Jamie." Pity filled my heart.

"Don't you think I know that?" she yelled. "He accidentally called me while talking with you. I heard everything. Said he loved you, wanted you back, that he became religious." Her laugh sent waves of fear down my spine. I'd never heard anything so wicked.

"He didn't become a Christian?" My shoulders sagged. Though I'd never have gone back to Paul even if he did decide to follow

Jesus, I still hoped that what he'd said was true so he'd be in heaven with the Lord.

"Paul only said that to get you back. He mocked religion every chance he got. He thought he'd win you over with that lie."

"I didn't love him, Jamie. I had no intention of starting our relationship over again. He wasn't the man for me. He hurt me too much."

"I thought so too, and then you said you'd meet with him the next day." Despair covered her face. "He met me in the parking lot, happy, excited that you considered giving him another chance." Deep lines ran across Jamie's forehead. She stood and started pacing in front of me, her agitation growing with each word. "I asked him what about us, and he laughed. Laughed!" Her wild look sent chills running through my veins.

"That wasn't very nice of him."

"No, it wasn't. Thank you for saying that." Jamie's shoulders sagged. "But he put on his charm and asked me to go get the pills from his car. The ones you used to take. So I did. I grabbed his soda and dumped them all in there."

"How'd you get him to my table?" Paul wasn't a small man. But then again, Jamie wasn't tiny either.

"I asked him if he'd go with me to get a drink at the food truck court. He said we couldn't be seen walking together, but he'd take his drink and we could sit at different tables." Jamie chuckled. "I couldn't have planned it better myself."

"What do you mean?"

"I watched him sit down and drink his entire soda. I just sat there, knowing that the medication would take effect quickly." Jamie's eyes turned hard. "He shouldn't have laughed at me, Mey. He shouldn't have pretended he loved me when he wanted you back all along."

I shook my head, hoping against all hope she saw my sincerity. "No, you're right. He was wrong. I told him I didn't want to be with him anymore. He could've been with you."

"But then you said you'd talk to him one more time. If you hadn't told him that, we would be in New York, married and happy." Jamie's voice hardened.

"I only said I'd talk to him because I was going to tell him I didn't love him. But I needed my friends there to protect me."

"To protect you? From my loving and caring Paul?" She giggled like a little girl. "He wouldn't have hurt you, because he knew I was waiting for him. Don't you see? He needed you to turn him down that first day and not agree to meet with him. You ruined everything."

"I gave him no hope that I'd return to Texas with him. Think about it, Jamie." I softened my tone, as if talking to a child. "I have a life here, one where I'm happy. I own a food truck and love Maine. I'd never leave here with P—him."

"But because of you, I had to kill him."

"Why? I didn't do anything wrong," I insisted.

"He was infatuated with you. He still had your pictures up in his apartment when we started dating again. He said it was because he wanted you to see how happy he was with me." Jamie sniffed. "But I think he lied. He always lied when it came to you."

"Not because I wanted him." I wiggled my hands behind me. The ropes were too secure to escape. "I ran away from him because he tried to control me. He didn't love me."

"You made him that way. He wasn't ever that way until you came along." Jamie grabbed the gun off the table. "And now you'll die for making me kill him."

"You said he screamed at you before me." I tried to make her see reason, though it may have been pointless.

"Until I became the perfect girlfriend." Jamie waved the gun around. "Don't you see? He had everything with me. Then you flaunted yourself in front of him and stole him from me. Now I can't have him."

I licked my lips. "But if you kill me, you're going to make us be together forever. Is that what you want?"

"Make you be together?" Jamie blinked, as if it was a new thought.

It wasn't an accurate thought, that was for sure, but one I'd let her believe if it would stop her from putting a bullet in me. "Yes. We'll both be dead. Which means we'll be together forever. . .without you."

"No. He'll never be with you forever. When you die, you die. There's nothing else."

"That's not true. There's heaven and hell," I pushed.

Jamie aimed the gun at me. "Paul didn't believe in heaven and hell. Only you crazy Christians believe in that sort of stuff. No, when you die, if there is a heaven, you'll go there, and Paul will be far away from you."

"Jamie, please, think about this. You don't want to do this. What if the detective finds out where you are? You'll go to prison for killing me and Paul," I pleaded.

"The detective doesn't know I killed Paul. Only you. And I'll be long gone before he finds me."

The door to the room was kicked in. Jamie jumped, pulling the trigger. The bullet slammed into me, and searing pain coursed around my head. I fell back, chair and all, onto the hardwood floor.

Another gunshot rang through the room. I tried to lift my head, but everything swirled around me.

"Paul!" Jamie screamed before silence surrounded me.

I forced my eyes to stay open, not sure where I was hit. Grayson leaned over me. "Stay with me, Mey."

I tried to talk, but nothing came out. I stared into his beautiful green eyes before my eyelids closed without permission and blackness surrounded me.

CHAPTER NINE

The beep of a machine grated against my nerves. *What is that racket, and would someone please make it stop?* I peeled my eyes open. Dim lights greeted me. That beeping? I glanced to my left. A monitor of some sort stood next to my bed. I was in a hospital.

"You're awake!"

I turned my head to where my best friend occupied a chair. "So it seems."

Wei reached out and squeezed my hand. "I'm so glad. I was worried."

"Are you and Mark all right? What happened?"

Wei's face clouded. "That woman was crazy. She snuck up on us while we were cleaning the tables outside and forced us into the truck at gunpoint. She had Mark tie me up, and then she tied up Mark."

"Did she tell you why?"

My friend shook her head. "But we knew she was after you." Tears filled Wei's eyes. "I don't know what I would've done if she'd killed you."

I tightened my hold on Wei's hand and forced a smile. "You would've had a more peaceful life."

Wei sniffed and shook her head. "Don't joke. I'm serious."

"So am I. I've caused you nothing but grief." I fought my own tears. "Thank you for always sticking by me."

"You'd do the same for me."

"Where's Mark?" I shifted my gaze away from her face and, with slow movements, glanced around the sterile room.

"He's in the hall. The nursing staff didn't want more than one person in here at a time after visiting hours. Oh! I almost forgot." Wei gave me a sly grin. "Someone wants to talk to you." She jumped up and yanked open the door. She motioned to someone outside. "He's been waiting for you to wake up for a while." She wiggled her eyebrows and closed the door behind her, leaving me alone with the handsome detective.

"Why am I in a hospital? I sort of hoped to avoid them for a while." I tried to rub my eye, but my right arm was in a sling.

"You don't remember what happened?" Grayson stood at the door of my hospital room, looking far too good for any man. Except for the dark circles under his eyes.

"I remember parking at the food truck court. Jamie made me get into her car, then drugged me with something."

"That's what happened?" Grayson eased onto the chair next to me. "I couldn't figure out where you went at first."

I nodded then instantly regretted it as pain shot around my head like a ping-pong ball. "Ouch."

"Don't move too fast. You hit your head when you fell." Grayson brushed a strand of hair away from my face.

Warm flurries flowed over me. I hadn't been touched like that in my entire life. Not even from my own mother. Maybe my father, but it had been so long, I could barely remember. I leaned into his touch.

"You had us all worried for a while." Grayson slid his finger down my cheek.

"How'd you find me? Jamie said she knocked you out."

"She did." Grayson flinched. "When I came to, I found your friends tied up in Lucky Noodles."

"You mean Un-Lucky Noodles. That food truck is starting to feel like it's cursed." I frowned.

"It's not cursed." Grayson smiled. "That's how I was able to meet you." He cleared his throat. "As for your question, Wei said you put a tracking device on your phone after you escaped Paul."

"Yeah. I didn't know what he'd do to me, and I wanted her to always know where I was."

One side of Grayson's lips lifted. "Good thinking. If it weren't for that, I fear you may have met our Maker."

"I remember Jamie shooting her gun. I don't recall anything after that." I scrunched my nose.

"I think I scared her when I burst through the door. She pulled the trigger when she saw me." A muscle in Grayson's jaw ticked. "After her gun fired, she turned it on me."

"And you shot her." I finished for him.

His head dipped. "I did. I had no choice."

"Of course not. It was either that, or she'd get you first."

"It wasn't fatal though. I made sure of that. Just skimmed her hand to make her drop the gun. She'll be in prison for a long time." A weighty sigh left Grayson's lips. "But thank God she's not a very good shot. She only hit your shoulder."

I scowled. "That's why there's this tremendous pain." I pointed to my shoulder then smiled. "Good thing for me she can't aim very well." I sobered instantly. "She was very sick in the head. That much I can tell you." I sighed, grateful she might have another chance to repent of her sins. "She told me she killed Paul."

"I found the prescription bottle in her purse."

"So I'm not a suspect anymore?" Hope rose in my chest.

"Nope. You're free and clear." A grin covered Grayson's face, relief filling his eyes.

A nurse bounced into the room. "Well, well, our patient has survived." She turned to Grayson. "Detective, you're going to need to go out in the hall. I want to check Miss Hirano."

"Yes, ma'am." Grayson stood then leaned over me. "You better do everything she says. She's quite the taskmaster, from what I've heard." He whispered loud enough for the nurse to hear.

She giggled and wagged her finger at him. "Oh, you. Out with you now." She checked my machine once he'd left. "Your young man's been pacing the halls out there. At one point, I thought I'd have to tackle him to get him to stop."

"Oh, he's not my young man." I shook my head, pain sending black spots before my eyes.

The nurse tilted her head to one side. "You could've fooled me. I've seen a lot of smitten men before with that same look."

"I think you're mistaken." Deep inside, I hoped she wasn't. What would it be like to be loved by such a man? Heat traveled up my body and landed on my face.

"Ah, your heart rate just spiked." She eyed me. "I can see the feeling's mutual." Nurse Cupid gave me a decisive nod. "Good. He's been spending a lot of time praying for you."

Those butterflies appeared in my stomach once more. I wasn't used to anyone other than Mark and Wei praying for me. Even in our new church here in Maine, I hadn't made a lot of friends. When I was younger, I didn't have my guard up when it came to meeting people. After being with Paul, however, I often doubted the sincerity of those I met.

As a believer, I knew I shouldn't. My therapist said it was natural and, in time, I'd stop doing that as long as I was aware and wanted to change. I didn't want to continue down the path of distrusting others.

Oddly enough, Grayson didn't make me feel that way. I wanted to trust him. I knew he was a kind man who was passionate about his work yet not tainted by it.

"How do I look?" I desperately wanted to change the subject. I wasn't comfortable talking about my nonexistent love life with Nurse Cupid, since we just met.

"You look good." She fiddled with a few more things, checked my chart, and smiled. "I'll send the doctor in soon. He'll be able to tell you when you can go home."

I breathed a sigh of relief. "Thank you. Nothing against hospitals, but I've had my fill of them."

Sympathy filled her eyes. "I saw the scars on your back. I don't know what happened to you, but I'm really sorry it did."

Emotion clogged my throat. "Thank you," I answered around the lump. "I appreciate that."

Nurse Cupid blinked, the sympathy replaced by professionalism. "There's one more man outside waiting to see you."

Mark. She didn't have to tell me. He'd let Grayson in first, so he wasn't worried I'd die, but the fact he hadn't gone home showed me he wasn't comfortable leaving unless he heard from me that I was okay. I loved this man I called brother.

Nurse Cupid left, and in walked Mark. His brows met in the middle of his forehead as he rushed to my side. "You all right?" He slid into the chair up against my bed.

I gave him a very slow nod, having learned my lesson a few moments before. "The nurse said I'm doing well, and the doctor will let me know when I can go home. How are you?"

Mark chuckled and leaned back in his seat. "Better than you." His eyes roamed over my face and shoulder. "I'm sorry I wasn't there for you."

"Mark, you were with Wei, which is exactly where you needed to be. I'm sorry Jamie got to you before we did." I raised my good shoulder and let it fall. "She had it all planned out."

"Grayson said she had distracted me and Wei with her car. The thought crossed my mind when she was tying me up, but it was nice to have it verified." He ran a hand through his hair. "You sure you're okay?"

"I'm positive. In a little pain due to a bullet wound and bump on the head."

Mark scowled. "Because of that jerk's crazy girlfriend."

"It breaks my heart that Paul didn't make peace with God before he died." I fiddled with the edge of the blanket with my good hand. "I wonder if I'd asked Paul more questions that day, maybe he would have actually become a Christian."

"Don't do that, Mey. He had the opportunity in his life. Besides, who knows what God did in Paul's last moments?" Mark tapped his fingers on the chair. "I've heard stories about people who call out to Jesus right before they die. Maybe Paul did the same thing."

"I hope so." I held up my hand. "Not because I have feelings for him. I just don't want anyone to suffer needlessly." I sighed. "And I hope that Jamie can find salvation also."

"Despite everything those two crazy people have done to you, you still want what's best for them." Mark shook his head. "You astound me."

"I'm an optimist, remember? It's who I am."

"You believe the best and want the best for others no matter what." Mark rubbed his chin. "I seem to remember a Bible verse about that. That's real love, little sister."

"Must you always put the word *little* in front of *sister*?" I feigned annoyance. "We both know you're taller than I am. Shoot, that fake tree in the corner is probably taller than I am."

Mark threw his head back, his laughter bouncing off the white walls. "I will forever call you 'little sister,' even though you're a few months older than I am."

"Well, at least you finally admit I'm older."

Mark snorted. "No one heard it but you, I'm afraid. So it's now your word against mine." He tossed me a wink and stood. "You look done in. I'm going to take my wife to get something to eat, and then we'll be back."

"Go home, Mark. I'm fine. I'm safe. You both deserve a good night's rest."

Mark pursed his lips. "You sure? I don't think Wei's going to like that."

"If you need me to tell her myself, send her in. But honestly, I'm okay. I'll sleep anyway." As if on cue, my shoulder began to throb. "Actually, would you ask the nurse for some pain medication?"

"I'm surprised it took you this long."

"I don't want to overuse medicine." I pasted on a smile. "But seriously, go home."

"I'll make Wei come home with me. Do you have enough energy to talk with Grayson some more? I know he wants to come back in here." Mark glanced toward the door and then at me.

"Probably to take my statement. He hasn't done that yet." I stifled a yawn. "Sure. Send him in."

An unrecognizable look passed in Mark's eyes before he pivoted and moved to the door. "I don't think that's what he has on his mind." He winked at me again. "Get some rest, little sis. We love you and are praying for a pain-free night for you."

What was with my roller coaster of emotions? A tear slid down my face. No one but Mark made me cry at the drop of a hat. "Thanks, bro. I appreciate it."

His Adam's apple bobbed before he opened the door and left. I expected Grayson to come in, but instead Nurse Cupid glided in, medicine in hand.

"This should help your pain." She held the little cup up to my mouth, then grabbed a large cup with a straw. I swallowed the pills with the water.

"What is it?"

"Just Extra-Strength Tylenol with codeine. Mark said you didn't want anything too strong."

I exhaled. "Perfect. Thank you."

"It'll hit pretty quick, so I'll send in the detective. And don't push yourself. When you start to feel tired, tell him no more questions and send him on his merry way." She plopped one hand on her hip and looked at me over the top of her glasses. "Got it?"

"Yes, ma'am. I won't let him stay too long."

She smiled and spun around.

"And thank you," I mumbled before she left the room.

Nurse Cupid's eyes softened. "You're welcome, dear."

Silence filled the room. I closed my eyes as peace settled over me. For the first time in over five years, I didn't have to worry about Paul. I didn't have to fear him finding me or lashing out at me. I didn't have to always be looking over my shoulder, wondering if and when he'd show up.

Fear no longer resided in my heart. What a weird feeling! For years fear and I had been constant companions. Just when I thought I had it under control, it would rear its ugly head, stealing peace from my life.

While I didn't want Paul to die, I was finally able to live a life of freedom. What did that even look like? I didn't have all the answers, but I knew the one who did. And so I determined to put my complete trust in Him. *No matter what may come, He will always be with me.* After all, He was always with me, never letting me go, despite my fears, worries, and kidnapping.

Peace continued to wash over me. My eyes remained closed. I didn't think I could open them even if I wanted to.

I probably should so that I can answer all of Grayson's questions when he comes in. But for now, I just want to sit and rest in God's embrace, allowing His arms to wrap around me and remove the pain and heartache of the last five years.

CHAPTER TEN

The first thing I saw when I opened my eyes was poor Grayson, slouched in the chair next to my bed. Grayson! Oh no. We were supposed to talk last night. I racked my brain, trying to remember if I even saw him enter my room. I recalled my eyes closing after Nurse Cupid came in and gave me pills. I was only relishing the peace finally surrounding me, not meaning to fall asleep. Apparently, I did just that.

I studied the man sleeping next to me. His long lashes rested against his cheeks. His tan face appeared to be relaxed. He certainly deserved it after the two weeks he'd had trying to find Paul's murderer. Strong arms crossed over a muscle-rippled chest while his legs were spread apart.

Grayson didn't stir. The rise and fall of his chest were the only things confirming he was still alive. Otherwise, I'd wonder if he'd met the good Lord. How could one move so little in sleep? *Unless I'm forced to remain in one place, like I am now, I always toss and turn. What's his secret?*

"You done ogling me?" One side of Grayson's mouth quirked up.

I gasped. "I'm not ogling you."

His lips turned into a full-fledged grin as he scooted up. "Sure you were. But that's okay. I was doing the same thing to you last night before I fell asleep."

"You watched me sleep?"

"Yep. Even saw the cute little puddle of drool on your pillowcase." Grayson's green eyes crinkled at the sides.

I wrinkled my nose. "Ew! I do not drool."

A low rumble flowed from Grayson's throat. "Maybe when you aren't on pain medication. That stuff can knock anyone out and make the driest of sleepers drool."

I felt my pillowcase. Not an ounce of moisture on it. I shook my head and laughed. "I'm surprised they let you sleep in here."

Grayson blew on his fingernails and rubbed them across his chest. "I do have some sway, being a detective, you know."

Disappointment bounced in my stomach. So he only wanted to take my statement. I squared my shoulders as much as I could and pushed the button that would bring the bed to a reclining position. I couldn't sit up straight yet, but reclining was better than lying down.

"Whoa. Should you be doing that right now?" Grayson stilled my hand. A spark passed between us.

I raised my gaze to his. By the slight rounding of his eyes, I knew he felt it too. I tugged my gaze away. "If I keep lying down, I'm going to get a bad headache. I already have a slight one because of the lump on my head."

"Just don't overdo it. That way you can leave sooner rather than later." He slid his hand off mine.

"I'm sorry I was asleep when you came in. I didn't mean to be."

"I think you've earned your rest. You had a challenging day yesterday." Grayson's gaze searched my face. "How are you feeling today?"

"Better, actually." A real smile filled my face. "I feel at peace for the first time in years."

"That's good. No one should ever have to go through what you did. I'm sorry you experienced that."

"Thank you. I don't wish it on anyone, that's for sure." A pain shot around my shoulder, and I sucked in a sharp breath.

"Pain?" Grayson's eyes clouded with concern.

I grunted. "Little bit."

"Want me to get the nurse to give you more medicine?"

I shook my head and tightened my jaw. "It'll go away in a second. Besides, I need to be awake in order to give you my statement."

"Your statement?" he repeated.

"Yeah. That's why you wanted to talk to me, right?" I tilted my head.

Grayson shifted in his chair and rubbed a hand on the back of his neck. "Well, uh, not exactly. I do need to take your statement, and I should've done that last night. But I wanted to make sure you were okay first."

"So, what'd you want to talk about?" Drat those butterflies! Would they ever stop flapping their wings in my stomach?

"Once the case closes, we won't be seeing much of each other." Grayson licked his lips. "I mean, that's pretty obvious. Not that we saw a lot of each other the last couple of weeks."

"True."

"But ever since I met you, I can't stop thinking about you."

It was my turn to lick my lips, which drew his attention to them. Heat swarmed my face. "Me?"

Grayson nodded. "Yes. I find it odd for me that I was so drawn to you right from the start. That's new for me."

"You're drawn to me? What does that mean?" I was pretty sure I was muddling this, but his word choices confused me.

"I'd like to ask you out on a date, is what I'm trying to say."

A date! I laughed then covered my mouth with my good hand. "I'm sorry. I don't find that funny. Really, I don't."

"That's why you laughed, then?" One of his eyebrows turned into an upside-down *V*.

"Yes. I wasn't expecting you to say that so matter-of-fact." I bit my lower lip. "If you live in York, how would we go on a date? It doesn't seem quite logical for us to start something if we live so far apart."

"The thing is, I don't want to rush a relationship with you. You've been through quite an ordeal, and I don't want to force you into something you may not be comfortable with. So, no matter how far apart we live, we can talk on the phone, and I can come here on the weekends. We can meet halfway if you get a day off, and spend the day together."

"You've really thought about this, haven't you?" I reached out my hand. He entwined our fingers together.

"I had a few hours on my hands while you were napping." Grayson's eyes sparkled.

I tried to pull my hand away, giving him a taste of his own teasing, but he tightened his hold then brushed his lips against the back of my hand. Pleasure sent tingles up and down my spine.

"I'm not in a hurry to start a serious relationship." I gulped, hoping beyond all hope I didn't scare him off. "I jumped right into mine and Paul's without really getting to know him."

"That's why I'm okay with talking on the phone, texting each other. Even video calls when we can't see each other in person." Grayson's gaze drew me in. "You can control the tempo. I'm not going to make you do something you don't want to."

"You sure?" I couldn't help the doubt mingling with my words. I'd never had someone treat me with such care.

"We've only just met. This will give us time to get to know each other. What I do know, I admire."

"Like you said, we've just met. You can't admire me that much." I rolled my eyes.

"Wanna bet?" he challenged. "I know you're a survivor, determined, courageous, and strong. You're funny and witty. You've shown me how you strive to seek the Lord in your daily life, which is not an easy characteristic to find in a woman. Believe me, I've tried."

A grin tugged at my mouth. "Any woman who didn't follow the Lord after meeting you is crazy."

"What do you mean?"

"One look at you, and she has to know there's a God. Because only He could create something so perfect." I squirmed under his intense gaze.

Grayson sported a giant grin. "Well, I've never been told that before. See what I mean? Witty."

Laughter bubbled inside of me and spilled out. "My wittiness may be your undoing. Just ask Wei and Mark."

"Oh, I've already talked at length with them both about this." His confession shook me.

"Really?"

"Sure. We had a lot of time to talk while you were in surgery. I wanted to make sure they were okay with me courting you." Grayson traced a line on my hand. "Mark was a little more difficult to get to agree. He's very protective of you."

"He is at that. He's the brother I've always wanted. . . sometimes. Other times, he's downright annoying."

Grayson threw his head back and laughed. "He said the same thing about you."

"See what I mean? We're not even related, but my adopted brother has to get the first and last word in."

"That is true. He did say if I hurt you, he'd find a way to destroy my life." Grayson lifted one eyebrow. "I thought you said he wasn't a violent man."

"No. I said he wouldn't take the law into his own hands." I giggled. "He'd pummel you if need be."

Grayson laughed.

I could get used to that laugh. For the first time in years, my future with a man looked promising. I didn't know where we would be two weeks from now, let alone two months. But I knew I could trust Grayson.

I held in a yawn, but Grayson saw right through it. "I should let you sleep, and also go back to my hotel room and shower. I do need to get your statement before we can make our dating official. Otherwise, it'll be a conflict of interest."

"I understand." A yawn escaped this time. "Will I see you soon?"

Grayson dipped his head and stood. "I'll be back in a few hours. Hopefully, by then you'll know when you can be discharged."

"Okay."

Grayson moved to the door.

"Grayson?"

He turned his gorgeous green eyes my way. "Yeah?"

"Thank you."

A smile lit his face. "I don't know what for."

"For saving my life, for believing I didn't kill Paul, for not rushing a relationship with me." I swallowed down the emotions threatening to overwhelm me. "I really appreciate everything you've done for me."

"Some of that's part of my job." He sent me a slow wink. "The other is simply because I find you amazing."

Grayson exited before I could respond. Probably a good thing, since I didn't even know what to say to that. I'd never been told by a man that I was amazing. Stupid, dumb, unlovable, imperfect, sure. But amazing? What else did Grayson say about me? *He finds me courageous, determined, and strong.* Comfort like a warm blanket surrounded me. *If this is what it's going to be like being courted by him, sign me up! Oh, wait. I think I just did sign up for that.*

A knock sounded on the door. Wei poked her head in. "We saw Grayson. He said you were getting tired. Care for a few minutes of company and a yummy donut?" She held a bag in front of her.

"You know I'd never say no to either of those two things," I chided.

"How about some good old-fashioned ribbing?" Mark asked from behind my best friend.

I glowered his way. "That I may be able to do without. I am wounded, you know."

Mark snickered and entered the room, a coffee cup in his hand. "Then you can't have the mocha I brought for you."

"Good old-fashioned ribbing it is, then." I reached out my hand, my mouth salivating in anticipation.

Mark chuckled and gave me my drink. "I knew that'd getcha."

"So. . ." Wei sat, pulled out a donut, and handed it to me on a napkin. "Grayson take your statement?"

I rolled my eyes. "Oh brother."

"What?" My friend's eyes turned as round as a plate.

"Don't 'what' me. You know very well he had no intention of taking my statement last night." I shot her a frown of fake frustration.

"He said you were asleep before he even sat down. Did he stay here the entire night?"

"Yes. But as you can see, nothing inappropriate happened. I stayed in bed, not even knowing he was here."

Mark choked on the bite he swallowed. Wei pounded him on the back and his coughing subsided. "I never said that or even implied that."

"I just wanted you to know." I gave him a snooty smile.

"Sisters." Mark shook his head. "I don't know why I put up with you."

"You love me. Grayson confirmed it, so you can't deny it now." I couldn't stop the smug feeling running over me.

"Great. Now I have to be careful what I say around that man. He may be in our lives for a long time, and I don't want to add to your big head," Mark grumbled, his voice still raspy from his choking.

"Enough, you two," Wei groaned. "Tell us what happened with you and Grayson."

"It's still all so new. I don't really know how to explain it." I filled her in on our conversation anyway, trying not to appear too excited. "I don't want the same thing to happen with Grayson as it did Paul."

"He and Paul are two very different men, Mey." Wei wiped her lips with a napkin. "Grayson isn't going to hurt you like Paul did. He may say things that will hurt your feelings, by mistake, but that's human nature. Even Mark and I don't get along all the time."

"I know. I just don't want to rush into anything."

"And that's a good idea." Mark nodded his agreement. "Take things slow. As you both said, he doesn't live close anyway, so it's a good time to get to know one another."

We chatted for a few more minutes before they left with the promise of coming back as soon as I let them know my time of discharge. I hoped it would be soon. I would rather sleep in my nice, comfortable bed than in a hospital bed. I liked being in my own home, and I was ready to go.

Of course, my body told me otherwise. As sleepiness started to overtake me, I closed my eyes and let my body relax. *I'm so thankful for the friends God has given me. I'm thankful for God's protection over Wei, Mark, Grayson, and me while uncovering the truth of Paul's death.*

And Grayson was right. My food truck wasn't *Un-Lucky Noodles*. Because without it, I wouldn't have met Grayson and started a new chapter in my life.

AUTHOR'S NOTE

Dearest Reader,

Thank you so much for reading *Un-Lucky Noodles*. When I first sat down to write this novella, I didn't expect it to take the turn of abuse. I knew Mey would be running from her abuser, but as I was writing it, I discovered just how much abuse can stay with a person. And Mey was no exception.

I'm glad she had friends who were willing to be with her, to help her walk through the difficult parts of life. I'm even more grateful she gave her life to the Lord, because He can help heal her scars. And therapy. I, myself, have a wonderful therapist who's helped me walk through anxiety and the lies anxiety tells. It's very different from any form of abuse, but I'm a firm believer that finding the right therapist, a Christian one in my case, can help people deal with wounds that desperately need healing.

If you've been physically, mentally, emotionally, or sexually abused, please seek help. You don't have to walk through it alone.

And please, if you ever feel like reaching out, you certainly can by emailing me at booksbyjoi@copelandclan.com.

Blessings to you as you navigate this journey we call life!

In His grip,
Joi Copeland
Philippians 4:6–8

Joi Copeland is an award-winning author. She has written more than twenty books and desires to share her love of hope and redemption through each story she pens. Joi and her incredible husband of more than twenty years have three fabulous boys and currently lives in Ireland. She is passionate about Jesus, Bible study, and the people of Ireland.

DEAD AS DONUT

CYNTHIA HICKEY

CHAPTER ONE

The fulfillment of a dream. I, Angel Stirling, proud new business owner, stepped back from the pink-and-white food truck sporting a sprinkle-covered donut on the roof and the words DREAM DONUTS swirled across the side. As it was the first truck in line, everyone who entered the food court would have to pass me.

Tears pricked my eyes. Even seeing it right there in the food truck court seemed almost unreal.

"It's beautiful." My grandmother, Ida, as everyone called her, even me, since she abhorred the word *grandmother*—she said it made her old—clapped her hands. "I'd like to be your first customer."

"It's on the house for you. If not for you, I wouldn't have had enough money to get started."

Ida grinned. "We're partners, remember? I'd still like the first donut. Make that a dozen. I'm going to drum up business with samples."

"What a great idea." I quickly put together a box and opened the slide-up window to signify the truck was now open.

With Ida strolling the early morning crowd carrying a tray of delicious treats, it didn't take long for a line to form. I'd have to get up extra early tomorrow to increase my daily quota. At this rate, I'd be out of donuts before noon.

"Good morning." A deep voice greeted me.

I turned and lost my breath. The man removed his hard hat, revealing tousled hair almost as dark as a raven's wing and eyes the same color. "Good. . .good morning. What can I get for you?"

"Chocolate éclair, please." A dimple winked in his right cheek. "I'm Jack Lowery. New to town. I work for Johnson Construction. We're doing some work around the food court."

"Angel Stirling. Not so new to town." I'd grown up in Birch Tree and had no desire to live anywhere else. I handed him an éclair wrapped in a piece of parchment paper. "Enjoy."

He nodded and placed the correct amount of money on the counter. "I'll be seeing you."

I certainly hoped so. I couldn't remember ever seeing anyone that handsome before.

"If you're finished gawking at one of my workers, I'd like to purchase some donuts, not to mention so would the rest of the men."

I tore my gaze away from Jack to the disgruntled man next in line. "I'm so sorry. Caught me in a daydream."

"Not very professional, the way you ogled Jack."

I widened my eyes. "I was not ogling. Who made you the local law enforcement?" I bit my tongue to stop more bitter words from escaping.

"Hmm. I'd like six chocolate-glazed."

I packed them quickly and handed the pink box to the man. "Enjoy."

"Humph." He stepped aside to allow another man in a hard hat to step up.

After he left, I muttered under my breath, "What a rude man."

"Two chocolate-glazed." The middle-aged man grinned and patted his stomach. "Should only get one, but I need the strength for an unpleasant task. Don't worry about Larry. He's our boss and always on the gruff side. You did nothing wrong."

"I hope your task isn't too horrible." I gave him his order, grateful for his kind words.

"Kind of like ripping off a Band-Aid, I reckon. Best to just get it done."

I supposed so. At one p.m. I closed shop for half an hour and purchased a fully-loaded baked potato from a nearby truck, the Spudmobile. I carried my lunch to one of the tables in front of Dream Donuts and settled down to enjoy the break with a good book.

"This seat taken?" Jack stood across from me with a plate of barbecue beef and a bun.

"No, please sit." I closed the newest mystery book I'd purchased. While I'd been looking forward to reading the book, getting to know Jack would be nice too. "How do you like our fair city?"

"It's great." He filled the bun with beef. "Beautiful scenery, nice people... Haven't found anything not to like. I didn't expect anything like this food court. Sure makes it easy for us working guys to get food. Your donuts are delicious." He awarded me with his dimpled smile.

"Thank you." I ducked my heating face. *Say something brilliant, you dope.* "What are y'all building?"

"Just repairs to the concrete fixtures. With a crowd like this coming every day, there are things to fix." He grinned. "My first job is to dig up that patch of hemlock over there."

I grinned back. "You're doing the food trucks a service. Wouldn't want anyone to mix that in someone's food."

He laughed. "Remind me to check my donut next time." He wiped his mouth with a napkin and got to his feet. "Lunchtime is over." He held out his hand. "I can throw your empty container away, if you'd like."

"Thank you."

"See you tomorrow." With a long-legged stride, he headed for the trash cans.

Loud voices came from behind the brick building that housed the public restrooms. Being a nosy person by nature, I wanted to investigate, but a glance at my watch sent me rushing to reopen my truck.

The afternoon passed far less busy than the first part of the day. I'd expected it to. Donuts were more of a breakfast food for a lot of people. I leaned my elbows on the counter and watched as lines came and went at the other vendors. They weren't as busy past lunchtime either.

Now the crowd seemed more interested in the sparkling lake than in food. I couldn't blame them. The view next to the food truck court would never grow old to me. My gaze fell on Jack ripping up the hemlock.

He caught me watching and raised the wildflowers in a toast.

Smiling, I took an inventory of what product I needed to replenish. With the success of the first day, I'd have to get up at four a.m. to be ready to open at six.

Ida waited at home with a plate of spaghetti and a salad. "Figured you'd be hungry."

"Thanks." I sat back, a smile of satisfaction on my face. "I have to get up at four."

"Profitable day." Ida raised a goblet of ice water. "Here's to more of those."

I agreed. Getting up before the sun was part of being a baker. Maybe I should hire help. No, it was far too early for my business to be that ambitious. "While you were mingling this morning, did you hear anyone requesting a donut flavor we don't have?"

"Birthday cake."

I frowned. "Isn't that similar to our sprinkled one?"

"Made from cake batter." Ida shrugged. "The chocolate and the chocolate-glazed seemed to be the most popular."

"Yes, they did." One of my favorite ways to relax was to come up with new donut ideas. "I'll think on the birthday cake. For now, we'll focus on what we know sells."

The next morning, Ida beat me to the oven. "I couldn't sleep, so I got started early. This way we don't have to rush."

"Thank you." I kissed her cheek. "What a grandmotherly thing to do."

"Shut your mouth." She grinned, wagging her finger from me to her. "Partners."

"I hope you still say that if things hit a rough patch." I donned a canvas apron and measured the ingredients for a batch of plain glazed twists. "Will you help me get these to the food truck? Other than that, I don't think I need you the rest of the day."

"I'll try to drum up some new business before leaving." She placed a pan in the oven. "Then I'll most likely take a nap."

Her regular routine, it seemed. I teased her about getting up early, but Ida had done that for as long as I could remember. A few hours' sleep here and there seemed to do okay for her. It worked for both of us, and Ida felt important by readying the morning's baking.

Donuts baked or fried, cooled, and decorated, I closed the back of her SUV, ready to start the day's business. "I'll see you there."

Ida flashed me a thumbs-up and got into her sedan.

The sun had just made its appearance as I got the last tray in the truck. The other food truck owners had yet to make their appearance, not selling breakfast as I was.

Jack tossed me a wave as he joined the rest of the construction crew across the way. The men stood, glancing around them as if waiting for someone. When Jack joined them, they continued to watch.

Seemed like strange behavior. I shrugged and climbed into my truck and pressed the button for the lights to come on. When they didn't, I clicked again. With a sigh, I climbed down to check the connection behind the truck.

The cord had definitely come unplugged. And it was easy to see why.

A man with a half-eaten chocolate-glazed donut in one hand lay faceup across it.

CHAPTER TWO

I staggered back, a hand clasped over my mouth to hold in a scream.

"What is it?" Ida peered around the corner of the truck. "No lights."

"That's because there's a dead man lying on the cord. A man who bought donuts from me yesterday. He must have pulled it out when he fell across it."

"Are you sure he's dead?" Ida joined me.

"I'm pretty sure the wide-eyed, nonblinking stare signifies that he is, Ida." I checked for a pulse anyway.

Nothing.

Footsteps sounded behind us. I whirled and stared into Jack's stunned face. "Call the police," I said to him.

"Already done," Ida said, showing me her phone. "I called 911 while you checked for a pulse."

A crowd had gathered. Gasps and murmurs filled the air.

Jack's boss, Larry, scowled. "Looks like that chocolate donut did him in."

I narrowed my eyes. "That, sir, is not funny."

"Didn't intend for it to be. Way I see it, he died eating your donut. Seems clear to me."

"Don't speculate without the facts." Ida turned on him like a crazed raccoon. "Let the authorities come to their own conclusions."

By now, the harm had been done. Folks shrank back from my food truck as if whatever had killed this man would rub off on them. "He told me yesterday he had some unpleasant business to tend to," I said as an officer in uniform approached. "He was a nice guy."

"What kind of business?" the officer asked me, while another pushed the people back from the scene.

"He didn't say."

"Who owns this truck?" He showed me his identification.

"I do. Angel Stirling." I sagged against Dream Donuts. "I found him when I came out to see why I didn't have any electricity."

"Napkin." Officer Murphy held out his hand.

I grabbed a napkin from inside the truck and dropped it into his palm.

He removed the donut from the dead man and dropped it into a bag. "The lab will process this. The medical examiner will determine the cause of death. Don't go anywhere, Miss Stirling."

My mouth dropped open. "I'm a suspect?"

"You're a person of interest until we determine whether or not the donut killed him."

I turned away from the suspicious glances sent my way. How could yesterday have been so wonderful and today so awful?

Ida put her arm around me. "No one in their right mind will believe you killed this man."

"Look at their faces. They all think I did it." Rather than stand around being looked at as if I had just landed on the planet, I decided to do some searching of my own.

Averting my gaze from the poor dead guy, I looked under my truck, under a nearby bush, and under the dumpster, using a napkin to gather anything that looked like evidence. Then I carried my loot to the nearest table.

I'd found a plastic knife with chocolate frosting on it—*frosting*, not glaze. When I looked closer, I could see tiny little green flecks against the dark brown. I really needed to see that donut again.

"What's this?" Officer Murphy frowned at my stash.

"Can I see the donut in evidence?"

"Why?" He narrowed his eyes.

"Because I don't think it's mine."

"It was found behind your truck, ma'am. Your *donut* truck."

"Please?" I put on my most imploring look.

He sighed and showed me the donut. Just as I suspected, it had been frosted, not glazed. "Not mine."

"Why do you say that?"

"Because I don't frost my chocolate donuts. I glaze them. This isn't nearly as shiny as mine." Why would someone try to frame me? "The things on this table are evidence." I gave an authoritative nod. "You may proceed."

High spots of color appeared on his cheeks. "Are you trying to tell me how to do my job, Miss Stirling?"

"Not at all. I simply read a lot of mystery—"

"God spare me from meddlesome wannabe crime solvers." He bagged the rest of the evidence though. "Don't interfere."

I crossed my arms and glared at his back as he marched away. "I ought to know whether it's my donut or not."

"You're saying someone else gave him that donut?" Jack tilted his head.

"Yes. Are you saying that you think I killed him?" That sent a knife right through my gut.

"Of course not. I ate here yesterday, and I'm still walking around. Maybe he died of something else, like a heart attack."

That made me feel better. "That's right. We don't know for sure that he was poisoned." Why get myself all worked up without the proper evidence to say how he died?

Several hours later, after being questioned within an inch of my life, I was allowed to remove only my personal items from the truck, which meant my purse. Everything else had to stay until the truck was cleared. Which meant no business and no income.

How was I going to occupy myself? I couldn't stay home with my grandmother, watching soap operas and game shows. If the news came that it was the donut that killed the guy, then I'd spend my days clearing my name. Please, God, let the man have died from something else.

———

The next day, I roamed the food truck court, ears strained for any news about the police investigation. So far, all I'd gathered was that the police in York had been called in to head the investigation since Birch Tree had such a small force.

Stern stares and avoiding glances were mostly what I found. I plopped down at one of the tables in front of my truck and placed my face in my hands. I struggled not to break into tears.

I opened my eyes as someone sat across from me. A calloused hand removed mine from my face.

"It'll be okay," Jack said. "I'll help you find out the truth."

"You've heard something."

He nodded. "Poisoned. They suspect hemlock."

I froze. Jack had removed hemlock the afternoon before I discovered the body. I swallowed against the fist-sized rock in my throat. "Are they sure?"

"Yes."

"Mr. Lowery?" A stern-faced police officer stopped by the table. "I'm taking you to the station to answer a few questions."

Jack paled. "Regarding?"

"The death of Mr. Bruce Whitton."

While I'd prayed for eyes to be cast elsewhere, this wasn't the answer I'd expected or looked for. I watched as crime scene tape was removed from around Dream Donuts. I jumped to my feet.

"Can I reopen?"

The officer shook his head. "Most likely tomorrow. They have to prove you and Mr. Lowery didn't work together."

"So, Jack is a suspect."

"I cannot divulge that information. Have a good day." He shoved the tape into the dumpster and marched to a waiting squad car.

So I wasn't completely in the clear. I really needed to stop jumping to conclusions.

Ida sped into the parking lot, narrowly missing the tailgate of one of the construction trucks. Seconds later, she moved quickly toward me, arms pumping as if she were running a marathon, and wearing a hot-pink sweat suit. "Come." She continued past me, heading for the hiking trail.

With a shrug, and curiosity consuming me, I followed. "Why are you acting so weird?"

"They don't think you killed anyone." She stopped and gasped for breath. "As for my ruse, I didn't want to act suspicious."

I bit my lip to keep from grinning. She'd attracted the attention of everyone within sight. "I already know. They suspect Jack Lowery. I wonder how they knew he pulled up the hemlock."

"Well. . .that might be my fault." She gave a sheepish grin. "The ladies in my gardening club and I video chatted last night, and I gave them the rundown on everything going on with the food court. Trying to drum up business, you know? Anyhoo, I might have mentioned that the area was now clear of the hemlock, and it was safe for them to bring their fur babies."

"I don't think dogs eat hemlock, Ida."

"Just trying to get them to come spend their money." She gave a heavy shrug. "One of them must have called the police after the news last night about a man being poisoned. They're very bright, dear. One of them must have put two and two together."

Someone else who read mysteries or watched crime shows like I did, most likely. A person would have to be inclined to think and rationalize in a certain way to put the pieces together.

I hung around the food truck court for the rest of the day, ignoring the stern glances but eavesdropping every chance I got. Even the construction workers thought I was involved.

"Why are you framing Jack?" one of them yelled. "What did he ever do to you?"

"I'm not framing anyone." I wrapped my arms around my waist and kept walking.

He fell into step next to me. "Folks say different. You talked to him about the poison flowers, you made the donut, now Bruce is dead. And since Jack pulled up the flowers, seems to me you're too involved not to be involved. Know what I mean?"

Unfortunately, I did. "If law enforcement focuses on me, they won't find the real killer." I shot him a look, clearly telling him to leave me alone.

He must have received the message, because he looked startled and stopped in his tracks. Good. I could give a look even Ida would be proud of. She'd always told me not to let anyone stomp on me. I gave the same look to the other construction workers, then went to the Lucky Noodle to get something for lunch.

"I can't believe you have the nerve to show your face around here after what you've done." The woman in line before me glared over her shoulder.

"Soon enough you'll see that I'm not responsible." I kept my head high and my gaze straight. *Hurry up and order so I can get out of here.*

After a long, uncomfortable time of fidgeting under her stern gaze, I breathed a sigh of relief when she finally turned back around.

"Don't think on it for a second," the woman behind me said. "You're a local. Locals don't kill people."

"That's right," someone else said. "People from Birch Tree stick together."

Tears sprang to my eyes. This town really was filled with wonderful people. Knowing they supported me filled me with hope. God might not have answered my prayer in the way I thought He would, but He had answered in a good way nonetheless.

Bowl of noodles in hand, I smiled at the woman who had spoken badly to me and sat down with my book to have lunch. I'd no sooner read the first paragraph when Jack dropped onto the seat next to me.

"They think I killed Bruce." He shook his head. "With the hemlock. Did you say something to them?"

I'd expected him to deny the accusation right away. "No, but my grandmother thinks one of her friends did. They were talking about the food court and all the changes."

He rubbed both hands down his face. "This is all so unbelievable."

"Why?" I tilted my head. "People were thinking I did the deed. Why not you?"

"Do you think I killed Bruce?" He got to his feet. "Because I thought we were friends, and I was hoping you'd help me."

"Help you in what way?"

"Clear my name."

CHAPTER THREE

I da felt bad about putting the suspicion on Jack, even in a roundabout way, so the next day she told me we had to help him. "If he's guilty, the police will thank us for helping. If he's innocent, then Jack will be the happy one."

I doubted the police would like our interfering, regardless of the outcome. "I don't know the first thing about sleuthing."

"Hogwash." She crossed her arms. "That's what you were doing with all that stuff on the table yesterday. What good is all that reading if you aren't going to put the knowledge to use?"

"Entertainment." Oh, I had every intention of snooping. I just didn't want to sound too eager, which meant a certain amount of reluctance was required. "Besides, I'll be too busy. I can reopen business today."

"I doubt you'll have any customers." She slid a pan of éclairs into the oven. "You'll have those wanting to poke their nose into what doesn't concern them, but don't expect the rush of the first day."

"Okay, Debbie Downer. There are plenty of people in town who know I'm not a murderer." I sprinkled multicolored flecks of sugar over a just-frosted donut.

"I'm going to enlist the garden club to help us. Those ladies know everything about everyone in this town." She wiped her hands on her apron, something my grandmother never did. Her aprons, unlike mine, rarely looked as if she used them.

"What's got you so nervous?"

Ida lowered to a kitchen chair. "In every movie I've ever seen, when someone gets involved in trying to solve a murder, the killer comes after them."

"You don't have to do this." I put a hand on her shoulder. "I can do this alone. With Jack's help, of course."

She grinned and leaped to her feet. "I knew you'd come around with a bit of coaxing."

"You're a trickster." I laughed. "And quite the actress."

My nerves were strung tight as I opened shop. Was my grandmother right? Would no one come?

Jack did. He entered the food court and made a beeline for my truck. "Two chocolate-glazed, please." He lowered his voice. "Are you going to help me?"

"Are you sure you want these? Bruce died from one."

"People need to see that you don't sell poison donuts."

"Unless I wanted to off someone."

He took a deep breath through his nose. "Are you going to help me or not?"

"Yes, Ida and I will help you." I handed him his purchase. "Did the police grill you very bad?"

"Brutal. They gave up when my story never changed. Everything they've got on me is circumstantial, and they know it." He bit into one of the donuts, closing his eyes as he savored the treat. "Just because I excelled at chemistry and botany in high school doesn't mean I could do something like this."

My heart skipped a beat. I really hoped this gorgeous man wasn't a killer. But someone who knew plants could easily poison a donut.

"Thanks." He opened his eyes. "Catch you at lunch. I better get to work."

The other construction workers scowled as he approached them. I sighed. People were often so quick to condemn.

A young man slapped a flyer on the counter before rushing to the next truck.

I glanced down to see the announcement of a fishing tournament tomorrow. That might be a good chance to mingle and ask questions. Don't men get all chatty while fishing? Or are they afraid of scaring away the fish?

Larry Johnson approached the truck. "Too bad I like donuts even if they might kill me. I'll take two of what got rid of Bruce."

"The only way my donuts might kill a person is if they eat too many, get fat, and die of a heart attack." I put two donuts in a little white bag and handed them to him. "Want me to take a bite to show they aren't poisonous?" I smiled, hoping to take some of the sting from my words. No need to take my stress out on someone else.

His face darkened. "You've got a smart mouth, you know that?" He snatched the bag and marched to his workers. With a snide glance over his shoulder in my direction, he handed a donut to one of his men.

I rolled my eyes and wiped the counter for something to do. I didn't have to wait long. A line quickly formed in front of my truck. Most likely because of Larry. By buying donuts himself, people had seen they were safe.

I tossed him a reluctant smile and started filling orders.

"If you didn't kill that poor man, who did?" Mrs. Olson, my third-grade teacher, stood at the front of the line. People leaned forward to hear my answer. "Because I cannot believe that a man as good-looking as Jack Lowery would kill anyone."

"There have been handsome killers before." I shook my head. "As for who the culprit is, I have no idea."

"Aren't you going to try and find out?" She arched a brow. "You may not be the top suspect anymore, but you aren't fully cleared. Mark my words, the authorities are watching you."

With those comforting words, she left with half a dozen strawberry-filled donuts for the ladies of the garden club. It was no secret what the topic of conversation would be, and it wouldn't be who had the best rosebush in town.

By lunchtime, my stomach growled. I always had a donut for breakfast, but that didn't hold down my hunger until one. Today I wanted Mexican. I got in line at the Crunchy Taco.

"At least no one died eating tacos," one of the construction workers behind me said.

I turned to glare. "You saw Larry eating his donut. He didn't drop dead."

"You must not have a beef with him."

I growled and turned back around. The best way to deal with jerks was to ignore them.

As soon as I had my tacos, I headed for the table I usually sat at, not surprised to see Jack already there with his favorite food, barbecue. "Before you ask, I don't know anything." I took a seat across from him. "What I would like to know is why that man over there"—I pointed to the jerk—"thinks harassing me about Bruce is fun."

"Scott Turner's been bothering you?" Jack stared in the direction of the other man. "I'll talk to him."

"Why is he?"

"He's got nothing better to do." He returned his attention to his food. "The man is like a gnat. If he figures a way to bug you, he'll keep it up until you find out how to stop him."

Like finding out who killed Bruce. "Are you entering the fishing tournament tomorrow? It's Saturday. You don't work on Saturday, do you?" I asked.

"Yes, I'm entered. Why?"

I shrugged. "It's the best way I can think of to ask questions."

His eyes widened. "People don't talk much while trying to catch the biggest fish. Your best bet is to keep snooping around the food court. Folks will have their guards down. I'll do what I can on the water, which won't be much."

"What can possibly be more important than finding out who killed Bruce?"

He smiled. "A thousand dollars for first place. If I catch the biggest and the most, that's two first-place prizes."

"What will you do with the money?" I wiped my mouth and collected my trash.

"Buy a better boat. Wanna meet up with me this evening to make a game plan? We can't just hope we stumble across the information we want." He took the trash from me.

"Sure. Come for dessert and coffee." I'd text Ida to whip up something.

I spent the rest of the day trying to think up an idea about sleuthing that wouldn't make me look like an idiot. All I needed to do was think about all the mysteries I'd read and put them into action.

I shoved aside the point about a killer coming after me. Ida might have been fooling around that morning, but I was afraid there was a lot of truth to her words.

CHAPTER FOUR

H ere's the scoop." Ida set a coffee cake on the table along with three plates. "The ladies at the garden club have managed to dig up some information the police don't even know yet. Or so they say."

"Are you going to share what they found?" I filled three cups with coffee.

"Thought I'd keep it to myself." She frowned then shook her head at Jack. "Angel isn't always the sweetest thing."

"Oh, I think she is." Jack tossed a wink my way.

My heart did the somersault thing. Again, I prayed he wasn't the killer. I really wanted the chance to get to know him better.

I cleared my throat. "Can we focus, please. Tell us what they found out."

Ida sat, a satisfied smile on her face. "Seems Bruce, Larry Johnson, and some cute guy with an attitude were in an altercation around three o'clock the day before you found the body. Some harsh words and a bit of shoving were involved."

"That gives us two main suspects." Jack poured a liberal serving of vanilla creamer into his coffee.

"How did they find out?"

"Greta was at the food court buying a special order of tacos for a party and saw the whole thing. You know she'd have been glued to the fight."

I should have paid more attention to the argument I overheard that afternoon.

I hope she'd stayed out of sight. If one of those men did kill Bruce and saw Greta. . . "How do we find out what they were fighting about? Did it have something to do with Bruce saying he had something unpleasant to do?" I reminded them of my conversation when the man purchased donuts. "He bought two from me, so either the one that killed him was his third, or someone got ahold of one of the first two. Do the construction workers leave their food lying around?"

"We keep our lunch boxes in our vehicles until time to eat," Jack said. "I've found it easier to buy something from one of the food trucks, but Bruce did sometimes bring his lunch."

"Where would he have put a donut he wanted to eat later?"

"His truck."

"Did he usually lock the doors?"

Jack shrugged. "I don't know. I'm thinking the poisoned donut being his third sounds like it makes the most sense. Bruce isn't the type to have saved one for later."

The man had had quite the paunch. "Okay. So there was a fight, and then someone gave him a poisoned donut. Doesn't make sense that he would've taken one from the guys he just fought with."

"Unless they were 'apologizing.'" Ida made finger quotes.

That made sense. "Where do we go from here?"

Jack squared his shoulders. "As much as I dislike the idea, I'm going to have to buddy up to Larry and Scott."

"At the fishing tournament."

"As long as doing so doesn't cause me to lose." Jack narrowed his eyes. "You aren't asking me to lose on purpose, are you?"

"Would you?" I raised my brows. That would really help him make friends if one of the other men won and Jack acted happy for them.

"No." He dug into a thick slice of cake as if finishing it quickly would take back my question.

"Make sure you win." Ida patted his hand. "Really get them riled up. Angry people make mistakes. That's when they get caught."

At least that's how it worked in books.

Saturday morning dawned bright and beautiful. High seventies, blue skies, and a slight breeze put a pep in my step as I waited on the last customer in line.

I craned my neck for a glimpse of Jack. There. He slid a V-hull boat from his boat trailer and into the water.

One by one boats entered the lake. I glanced at my watch. They couldn't start fishing for another fifteen minutes.

When the signal to go sounded, engines roared to life and boats sped off in all directions. My heart leaped into my throat. Someone was going to have an accident.

"They do this every year," a woman said. "We're left here wondering who will come back unscathed."

"People get hurt?" Goose bumps prickled my skin.

"Yep. Fishhooks in body parts, sometimes a drowning, snake bites from them falling into the boats from trees."

Absolutely nothing she said held any appeal for me. "This is insane."

"It used to be a man thing, but now there's women." She cut me a sideways glance. "I've been meaning to ask you something."

"Okay?" What could a woman I'd just met need to ask me?

"It's about the. . .murder." Her voice dropped to a whisper. "I was in the food court the night before the body was found."

My blood chilled. "And?"

"I heard arguing, something about it being wrong."

"What was wrong?" My heart rate increased. I was about to get some juicy tidbit to solve this case.

"One man said it was wrong what the other man was doing. I couldn't hear exactly what he meant." She turned her gaze to the water. "I should tell the police." Her eyes glistened. "What if I could have prevented that man's death?"

"Why didn't you tell the authorities?"

She took a deep, shuddering breath. "Because I have an unpaid speeding ticket. Two, actually. I'm a horrible person."

I rushed from the truck and put a hand on her shoulder. "It's not too late to tell them. You'll have to pay your fines, but it's never too late. You can always ask for forgiveness."

A slight smile teased at her lips. "You sound like a preacher."

"Heavens no, but I do know about forgiveness." Being a forthright, sarcastic person kept me apologizing more times than I cared to count. I felt pretty certain God often shook His head at me while looking down from His throne. "Would you like me to make the call for you?"

"Yes." She turned her eyes back to the water.

Of course, it had to be Officer Murphy who responded to the call. He listened with a grave expression as I told him what the woman had said before he went to hear her repeat the news and before he led her to his car. Her sad face impaled me as she stared out the back window. I hadn't even asked her name.

The morning bled into the afternoon like a tiny cut. Just enough business to keep me from closing the truck. Mostly from the families milling about waiting for their fierce fishermen to return.

I found myself searching the lake many times for Jack's faded red, white, and blue boat. My neck and shoulders ached from the tension of wondering how he did out there. Had he caught anything? Heard anything? Been harmed?

Jack and I weren't even a couple. Barely friends. Someone needed to tell my heart. Or maybe I had been without a boyfriend for too long.

Slowly, the boats started returning to shore as the sun lowered in the sky. I closed up the truck and joined the others to see who had won and who managed to return unscathed.

Jack stood at the front of the crowd with a string of bass, one hand held awkwardly to his side. One fish was so big, I was sure Jack had to be the winner. Sure enough, his name was soon announced for having the biggest fish. A grin spread across his face, and his gaze searched the crowd, finally settling on me.

Once he received his prize money, he strolled toward me, still carrying his fish. "Mind giving me a ride to the ER, and do you have a fridge in your truck?"

CHAPTER FIVE

I do. Is that a fish hook in your thumb?" My stomach rolled.
"Yeah, hurts like the dickens too. Someone in the ER can remove it." He ducked into my truck, returning a minute later minus the fish. "I'm ready."

I wasn't sure I was. I grabbed a water bottle from inside Dream Donuts and guzzled half of it for courage. "Let's go."

Luckily, the closest ER was only twenty minutes away and wasn't crowded. A nurse took Jack's vitals and ushered us into a room with promises that the doctor would be in soon.

"How did you do this?" I peered closer. The large hook was buried all the way up to the little eyelet thingy. The barbed end was poking out again through the pad of his thumb. Nausea grew again in my stomach, causing me to turn to my bottle of water.

"Squeamish?" Jack grinned.

"A bit. How can you be so calm?"

"Beats crying."

The door opened, and a heavyset man in a wheelchair entered. He held up a pair of pliers. "Need a fishhook out?"

Spots appeared before my eyes. My legs weakened.

"Just kidding. I'm Doctor Norris. Be right back." He laughed. "I'm messing with you." He set the pliers on the counter and left.

What kind of place was this? My startled gaze met Jack's amused one.

"I like him. I bet he knows what he's doing." He hopped onto the bed.

I sure hoped so.

A nurse entered and gave Jack a shot to numb his thumb. She patted him on the shoulder. "Don't worry. This isn't the first hook the doctor has removed this season. He'll be in once the shot has taken effect."

It helped knowing Jack wouldn't be in pain while the doctor worked. "Guess what I found out today?" Talking about Bruce's death would take my mind off Jack's thumb. I told him about the woman who had overheard an argument and been taken to jail.

"I wonder what the guy meant about "it" being wrong." Jack frowned. "That's a lot better than my news." His eyes widened. "Hold on. Maybe it's tied into what I heard."

"What?"

The door opened, and the doctor joined us. "Feel anything in your thumb?"

"No sir."

"Good. Mind telling me how this happened?" He snipped the eyelet off.

"I tried slingshotting my line to get it under some low-hanging branches. Embedded it into my thumb instead." Jack shrugged. "Tried something new, and it didn't work."

"I have to agree." The doctor's shoulders shook with suppressed laughter.

No matter how old I get, I don't think I'll ever understand men. I watched as the doctor pushed the hook the rest of the way through. Without the part the line was tied to, it took little effort.

"Had your tetanus shot?"

"When I was a kid."

"I'll have the nurse give you one." The doctor wrapped the thumb in a clean bandage. "I'll also prescribe an antibiotic. Just in case." He patted Jack's arm. "Better luck next time."

"I won." Jack's grin widened.

Back in the car, I brought up what Jack had started to say before the doctor returned. "What did you hear?"

"It's why I got hooked. I was eavesdropping instead of being careful." He clicked his seat belt into place. "Sound carries on the water, so I'm not sure which boat the voices came from, but they were just around the bend. Someone said there were rumors that the job on the new strip mall had been done with shoddy workmanship. That corners were cut." His face grew serious. "Johnson Construction did that job. I wasn't working for them yet."

I gasped. "You think Larry killed Bruce?"

"If the rumor I heard was true. . .maybe."

"How can we be sure? We need a plan. Something to help us."

"Slow down. What we need to do is contact the authorities with the information."

I wrinkled my nose. "It's only a rumor. We need something more before going to the police. Do you have any clue who you heard talking?"

"No, but I can get a list of participants and the area they fished. We were assigned zones through a drawing. That'll at least narrow things down. This could be dangerous, Angel."

"We're just going to ask a few questions." I turned the key in the ignition. "You get that diagram, and we'll be good to go."

He dug his cell phone from his pocket and made a call while I drove us back to the now-empty food court. The sun had started its descent, casting most of the place in shadow. Spooky with all the empty trucks and tables.

A leaf skittered across the concrete. A few feet away sat Jack's truck. A piece of paper flapped from under the windshield wiper.

"I should have the list by Monday morning. Want to ask questions after work?" Jack slid from my car.

"Sounds great." I smiled and watched as he snatched the paper from his window.

He stiffened, his features grave.

I turned off the car and hurried to his side. "What is it?"

He handed me the paper.

Typed in a large font were the words DO NOT REPEAT WHAT YOU THINK YOU HEARD OR ELSE.

"The lake wasn't so large after all." I returned the page. "Someone knows you were there and what you heard."

"Which makes getting that list all the more important." He glanced around the area. "I'll follow you home to make sure you get there safely."

My blood chilled, and I nodded, grateful for his presence. Whoever knew Jack had overheard something might also know he'd tell me.

———

Jack was my first customer Monday morning. "I've got the list. Pays to have a friend in the fish and game commission."

"It does." I glanced to where his coworkers mingled. One of them, possibly Larry himself, was a murderer. I'd bet my last donut. "Be careful today. Accidents can happen on a jobsite."

"Since we're still repairing things around here, not so much. When we're done, though, our next job is an apartment building. Let's hope we can close this case before I'm on the third floor with nothing but a rope keeping me from falling."

The picture he painted filled me with dread. "We'll work fast."

"Get to work, Lowery. I'm not paying you to talk to the ladies." Larry stepped in line behind Jack. "Get your donut and go."

"Yes, sir." Jack mouthed, *See you later*, before heading to where the others stood.

"He's injured, Mr. Johnson." I frowned.

"If he showed up to work, he isn't that bad off. I'll take my regular, please."

I bagged two chocolate-glazed donuts. "Did you participate in the competition yesterday?"

"Yep." He took a bite.

"Any luck?"

"Jack won."

"Yes, but did you catch anything?"

His eyes narrowed. "Why all the questions? If you were that interested, you should've participated yourself." He marched away.

I wanted him to be guilty simply because I didn't like him. After a quick prayer of repentance for having bad thoughts toward him, I greeted the next customer with a smile.

"You're back," I said to the woman Officer Murphy had taken away the day before. "I never got your name."

"Susan Bower." She smiled. "I was released after paying my fines. Officer Murphy said my guilt over not saying anything had been punishment enough."

"That's good news. Did he say anything about the murder?"

She shook her head. "He wouldn't though, would he? Not to me, at least. I'm a civilian."

I supposed not. Still, I had to try. "Jack Lowery won the competition."

"That's good. He's a nice guy." She purchased a donut with sprinkles. "Thank you for your help yesterday."

"Anytime." I leaned on the counter as she left. Finding out anything about Bruce's death was like picking fleas off a squirmy dog. Hopefully, Jack and I would have better luck later.

By lunchtime, my feet ached from a busy morning, and I was more than happy to sit down with a bowl of Japanese food from the Lucky Noodle.

Jack joined me, a pained look on his face. "I think Johnson is purposely giving me work that hurts my thumb."

I cringed. "That might be my fault. I told him you were injured. You know, so he'd maybe take it easy on you."

He chuckled. "Don't help, okay? My boss isn't exactly my friend. Neither is Scott, for that matter. Now he and Johnson are close." He entwined his fingers. "They go out for a drink after work most days."

"We're together most days. Doesn't mean anything strange is up." I glanced at him from lowered lashes as I twirled noodles onto my spork. What would it be like to be more than friends with him? I sure wanted to find out.

"What is strange, though, is that Johnson has me and Scott working closely together for the first time since hiring me."

"Keeping an eye on you?" Suspicion leaped to my mind.

"That's what I'm thinking."

"That would make the two of them involved."

"Not necessarily." He straightened in his seat. "Don't jump to conclusions. It could simply be Scott keeping tabs on the new guy during my probation period."

"Well, since Johnson is the only suspect we have, I'm sticking to my idea." I finished my food and got to my feet. "I'll close the truck at four today so I'm ready by five."

"Sounds good." He smiled up at me. "I'm not disputing your idea, Angel, just saying for you to keep an open mind. Don't fixate on something without concrete evidence."

Good point. I returned his smile. "See you at five. Did you keep the warning?"

"Yep. Put it away for safekeeping until we decide when to hand it over to Murphy." He threw away his trash and strolled back to work.

The stoniness of Scott's stare as he watched Jack sent a chill through me. When he turned that same stare on me, the chill became frigid. The man definitely didn't like either Jack or me. Since we were no longer suspects, at least not seriously, why did he still treat us as if we'd killed Bruce Whitton?

I shuddered and headed for Dream Donuts. My skin prickled, feeling the weight of the man's glare. I almost expected to feel a knife plunge into my back.

CHAPTER SIX

J ack came to my food truck at precisely 5:00 p.m. with a smile on his face and his phone in his hand. "Let's get this show on the road," he said.

"How was your day?" I asked as we headed for his king cab pickup. "Your thumb doing okay?"

"It throbs a bit." He opened the door for me. "But I'll live." He closed the door and rushed to the driver's side. Once in the seat, he turned to me. "Scott was a real pain though. Surly, complained about everything I did. I'm not sure how much longer I can work with him."

I arched a brow. "You're thinking of quitting?"

"Maybe." He started the engine. "But I won't make any decisions until we find out who killed Bruce. I've also thought about it, and I think we should let Officer Murphy know about the warning note. Mind if we go there first?"

"He'll try to stop us." The last thing I wanted to do was let the police know what we were up to.

"I don't plan on telling him we're sleuthing." Jack grinned and turned the truck in the direction of the police department. "Besides, anything like this takes more of the suspicion off us."

True. "Okay, but don't say anything more than you have to."

He parked in front of the building. As we walked toward the door, he took my hand in his, giving it a gentle squeeze.

My heart skipped a beat. If I was going to track down a killer with anyone, I was glad I was doing so with Jack.

Officer Murphy stood at the front desk. He turned from his conversation with the receptionist as we entered, and a scowl replaced the smile. "What now?"

"I got this on my car." Jack handed him the paper.

His frown lines deepened. "How do I know you didn't print this out yourself?"

A muscle ticked in Jack's jaw. "Why would I?"

"To throw—"

"For crying out loud." I snatched the paper from his hands. "Believe us or not, but Jack thought you should know. I tried talking him out of it." I marched for the door.

"Miss Stirling." Officer Murphy's voice boomed behind me. "My office, please. Both of you."

Jack shot me a look that seemed to say, "You've done it now."

I shrugged both shoulders, then squared them, prepared to do battle if necessary. There were no grounds for us being detained. So why take us to his office?

"Sit." Officer Murphy pointed to two chairs opposite his seat.

I sat and crossed my arms. "Why are we here?"

"So you don't throw a scene in the reception area." He mimicked my posture. "Why do I get the sneaking suspicion the two of you are sticking your noses where they don't belong?"

Since I couldn't lie to the police, I didn't say anything.

Jack spilled everything he'd heard at the lake as if his words were a raging waterfall. When he stopped for breath, I butted in. "So we weren't actually snooping."

"Humph." Officer Murphy narrowed his eyes. "The shoddy construction was a complaint after the mall was built, but no one could really prove anything. Doesn't mean that Johnson killed Whitton though. Don't be making any accusations."

Good. He didn't tell us not to do anything else. I stood. "Absolutely not." I pasted on a smile. "May we go?" Did he see how nice I was being? Didn't make a scene or get upset at all.

He didn't look convinced but waved his hand in a dismissive gesture. "Don't do anything stupid."

I felt pretty certain that questioning potential murder suspects would fall into the category of stupid. Again, I didn't say anything and increased my pace to get out of the building as soon as possible.

"Where to first?" I asked as soon as we were in the truck.

Jack pulled up the list of names on his phone. "Hopefully, you know some of these people. I'm new to town, remember?"

I recognized the first name, Walter Reed. Avid fisherman. Widower. Ran me and my friends off his lawn when we were kids. "I know where he lives. Cranky, but I can't imagine him killing anyone." Actually, I couldn't imagine anyone I knew committing murder.

"We should still pay him a visit. He might have heard something around town."

"True. He always did seem to know everyone. He lives across the street from me and my grandmother. I'd like to let her know what you heard about the building of that strip mall. If the rumors circulated very long, she or her garden club ladies would know about them."

"Great. We'll take supper to her."

I sent Ida a text. She replied immediately. "She's already cooked something and says there's plenty for you."

"Great." He grinned and headed for my house.

Over a delicious meal of oven chicken and rice, we filled my grandmother in on what had been happening. "Did you ever hear the rumors about the mall?" I asked.

"Sure I did." She buttered a hot roll. "After the mall, everyone knows Larry Johnson isn't someone you want to hire unless you can't afford better. Guess that's why they hired him to fix up the things that need fixin' around the lake. No budget."

"If they couldn't prove shoddy construction, why stay away from Johnson?" It didn't make sense to me. Obviously, there was more to the story. That was what Jack and I needed to find out. Bruce had discovered something that got him poisoned. Jack and I would have to be more careful. I wouldn't take anything from anyone if I didn't see them make it with my own eyes.

"People believe the rumors. Cheap roofing tiles, cheap flooring. . .things that look good at first glance, but upon closer inspection are inferior. I'm not sure whether any of it is dangerous. No question about it being unethical." Ida bit into her roll. "But if Mr. Whitton was killed because of knowing something about corners being cut, that might suggest there was, indeed, something not done correctly. Something that could get someone hurt."

"The only way to find out is to ask enough questions and hope to get an answer to some of them." I slumped in my seat.

"You could talk to the owner of the mall. It's owned by the Shirley family."

"Really?" I went to school with one of the Shirley kids. "We definitely will."

My mind whirled, trying to figure out how to visit everyone we needed to and get home in time to go to bed. Donuts still needed to be made in the early morning hours. Solving this would take days, if not weeks.

Of course, the police would probably solve the case before we did, but they were understaffed. So far, they hadn't called in detectives from York, a nearby, larger city. Why? Was Murphy that confident in apprehending the killer?

After we finished eating and cleaned up, Jack and I headed across the street. Mr. Reed sat on his front porch in a rocking chair, an unlit pipe in his mouth. He'd quit years ago but didn't want to give up how he relaxed at the end of the day. Rocking with his pipe.

"How's the donut business?" he asked, not getting up. "Heard you poisoned someone?"

"That has been proven false." I frowned. "Can we ask you something about the new mall?"

"Why?" He leaned forward. "Haven't you seen it? Shopped there?"

"Well, yes, but. . ." I cleared my throat.

"Sir, Angel thinks you have a wealth of knowledge about the folks here in Birch Tree. What we're wondering is whether you heard the rumors about the construction, whether you believe them, and do you know who might have wanted Bruce Whitton dead? What did he know?" Jack smiled.

Mr. Reed drummed his fingers on the arm of his rocking chair. "Of course I heard them. Haven't cared for Larry Johnson since. As for who killed Bruce, well. . ."

I held my breath, waiting for an answer.

"I have no idea. Don't know what he could have dug up either, but if I were investigating, I'd find a way into the construction office and look at some blueprints. Maybe get into Whitton's place of residence too. See if he left something behind." He chuckled. "I thought you'd have figured this out, Angel, seeing as how you said you read all them crime books."

"Both of those things are against the law." I lifted my chin.

"So? You want to find out who tried to frame you or not?"

I glanced at Jack. "I do, but—" Did I really want to risk Murphy slapping handcuffs on my wrists? Of course, if we actually found the killer, the police would be happy, right? "We'll think about it. Thank you." I jerked my head toward Jack's truck. If we went now, we could visit Lindsey Shirley, and I could still be in bed by eight and get my six hours of sleep before baking.

While I didn't spend time with Lindsey, Birch Tree is a relatively small town, and I knew where she lived. I gave Jack directions to an upscale apartment complex.

I read the names on the mailboxes until I found hers, then pressed the intercom button.

"Hello?"

"Lindsey? It's Angel Stirling."

"Wow. Hey. I'll buzz you up."

The gate next to us buzzed, and Jack pushed it open. "Nice."

"Birch Tree is trying to keep some of the younger folks from leaving town by supplying these types of amenities." I preferred living in the small house with my grandmother on our quiet residential street.

Lindsey lived on the second floor and waited with her door open. "This is quite the surprise." Her gaze flicked to Jack. "I've been meaning to come by your donut truck but haven't made it yet. I'm not really a food truck/outside/hang-by-the-lake kind of person. Come in."

I perched on the edge of a white leather sofa, running my hand over the buttery surface. An orchid in a square vase provided a bit of color to an apartment decorated in glass and leather.

"What brings you here, and who is this?" She tilted her head and smiled at Jack.

"This is Jack Lowery. He works for Larry Johnson."

Her smile faded. "And?"

Jack's gaze fixed on her face. "We're checking out the allegations that he cut some corners when he built the mall."

"You're the second person to ask that question."

"Was the first Bruce Whitton?" My heart rate increased.

"Yes."

"We suspect he was killed because he found out something about the work on the mall."

Lindsey jumped to her feet, her face paling. "I was afraid of that. I shouldn't say anything. Not if a man died because of what I told him."

"Please? Someone tried to convince the authorities that I killed Bruce. Jack and I need to find out what Bruce knew so we can help catch the killer." I got to my feet and took her cold hands in mine. "Then they turned their attention to Jack."

She took a shuddering breath. "It's best that I show you." She pulled free and led us to a room she obviously used as an office.

After fishing a key from a hook behind an oil painting, she opened a safe behind another painting. She unlocked the safe and pulled out a few pages. "I spent days locating the materials quoted and the ones actually used. The ones used were of a much inferior quality than what was promised. I gave a copy of this to my father. Bruce was one of my father's friends. Dad must have confided in him."

I frowned and scratched my head. "No one has come after you or your father?"

"Whoever killed Bruce obviously doesn't know where he got his information. I'd prefer to keep it that way." Her hands shook as she handed me the pages. "Take photos of these so I can lock them back up."

I nodded and spread the pages on the floor. Jack and I both took pictures of each page. When we'd finished, I glanced up. "If these pages were to become public, it would destroy Johnson Construction."

Jack swallowed hard. "That's why someone is willing to kill to keep it hidden."

The biggest question I had was why hadn't Lindsey shown this to the police?

"I was going to," she said when I asked, "but then Bruce was killed. I didn't want anyone, not even the authorities, to know I had this information."

"They need to be told." Jack shook his head, sliding his phone into his pocket.

"I agree." I glanced from her to him. "But are we willing to have a target on our back?" The news might leak about who turned in the pages. Was I willing to take that risk?

CHAPTER SEVEN

The week passed uneventfully. Nothing happened, and we found out no new information. Ida and I spent the week doing our usual baking and selling of donuts. Jack was busy with work. By the time Saturday came around again, I itched to get back into the mystery.

Unless there was a special event, like the fishing tournament, I closed my truck on weekends. Jack and I had decided to risk passing the papers on to Murphy. Not only that, but we planned on sneaking into the construction office of our number one suspect. One more thing to add to the "don't do anything stupid" list.

Ida's brows rose as I came downstairs. "That isn't suspicious at all." Her gaze roamed from my black sneakers up to the black yoga pants and T-shirt to the black beanie on my head. "You go into the police station looking like you plan on robbing something, and you'll end up behind bars lickety-split."

"I don't want to be easily seen." I removed the beanie. I could put it on after the visit to the police department.

"What are you doing that warrants that remark?" She crossed her arms. "Something illegal and dangerous, I'm guessing."

"Yes to both." I kissed her cheek. "The less you know, the better. If I'm not home by midnight, call the police. I'll leave my phone on so you can track me."

"I'm liking this less and less." She opened the front door and let Jack in. "You'd better not let anything happen to Angel."

"I'll do my best." He grinned my way. "Very burglar-like attire."

I smirked. "Better than that white shirt you're wearing."

"I thought it best not to look suspicious if we're seen," said the voice of reason. "Too late to change now. Murphy said we had to get there in ten minutes or see him tomorrow."

With that warning, we hurried to his truck and to the police department where Murphy waited outside. "Almost missed me. What's so important you have to see me tonight?" He frowned at my clothes and shook his head.

"It's best we go inside." Jack glanced around the parking lot.

"Okay, I'm intrigued." Officer Murphy opened the door and led us to his office. His eyes widened as Jack explained about the pages we'd photographed.

Jack handed the officer his phone. "Do you want me to email them to you?"

"Absolutely. This is proof that Johnson cut corners with the mall, but it doesn't prove he killed Whitton." He tilted his head. "You aren't fabricating these clues to remove suspicion from yourself, are you?"

"No, these are legit, but I am trying to prove to you that I did not kill Bruce Whitton."

Officer Murphy handed the phone back with a business card. "My email is on there. Now, I really do have to go. I suggest once you've emailed those, you delete them from your phone."

"Why doesn't he see what's plain as day?" I got into Jack's truck.

"No concrete evidence." Jack tapped his head. "Open mind, remember?"

I groaned. "You know as well as I do that Johnson has to be the person who killed Bruce. All we need to do is find the right evidence."

"Do you expect to find hemlock lying around his office?" Jack started the truck. "If he's the one who offed Bruce, he's not going to leave the evidence lying around."

If, if, if! I'd have to prove Johnson was the killer, since everyone else seemed a bit skeptical.

Jack sent the photos to Murphy then deleted them. Did he always do the right thing?

I didn't, no matter how much I tried. All my life I'd made wrong choices and had to ask God to forgive me. Maybe I needed to change my ways. "I don't think we should investigate any further. It's wrong."

Jack's eyes widened. "I thought you wanted proof."

"I do, but we're breaking the law, and I've decided to always do the right thing." I crossed my arms to show I was serious.

"Clearing our names beyond a shadow of a doubt is the right thing."

"You're confusing." I shook my head. "One minute you're following instructions from Murphy without question; the next you want to break into a business."

His brow furrowed. "It is contradicting, isn't it?" He shrugged. "Let's finish what we started. I've never been a quitter."

I studied his serious face for a few seconds then nodded. "You're right." Murphy hadn't come right out and said my name was cleared, although I felt pretty sure it was. Jack was still a suspect in Murphy's mind. I'd do almost anything for a friend. I nodded again then turned to face the windshield.

We made the rest of the drive in silence. Guilt still tickled my mind regarding breaking the law. If we were caught and arrested. . . Why, I could lose my business. The urge to quit swarmed me.

Jack reached over and put his hand over mine. "It'll be fine. We'll be in and out, hopefully with a major clue. That way, if we do get caught, we at least have something to give Murphy, which might prevent him from hauling us to jail."

"Blackmail?" Maybe Jack wasn't so perfect after all.

"No, leverage." He pulled into a large vacant parking lot.

At the far end sat a metal building. Behind the building were construction trucks and other equipment. We were going through with the insane idea. I squared my shoulders as Jack drove behind the building, cut the headlights, and parked in the shadows.

"How are we getting in?"

"There's a guard here." He motioned to a building not much bigger than a closet. The line from its window illuminated the ground a few feet. "Hopefully, he left a door open."

The guard had not seen us arrive, or he would have yelled out. I pulled the beanie over my head, put my hand on Jack's back, and let him lead the way.

Two doors were in the rear, one of which opened easily under Jack's hand. We should have worn gloves! Taking a deep breath, I followed him inside, where he softly closed the door before clicking on a flashlight.

"Larry's office is this way." Jack headed down a long hallway with four glass-walled offices, which would leave us exposed if the guard came looking.

Fancy for a construction company. I'd expected something more rustic.

Johnson's office was locked.

Jack pulled a key from his pocket.

"You stole his key?"

"Of course not. He dropped it the other day."

"And you didn't return it."

"Be my conscience another time. I plan on giving it back. He's already made himself a new one anyway." Jack unlocked the door and ushered me in.

A desk, two filing cabinets, a chair, and a sofa filled the room. Sparse and plain. The fancy windows down the hall allowed him to watch his employees. "I'll take one filing cabinet, you take the other," Jack said.

I didn't expect it to be as simple as a file marked *Whitton*, so I perused the labels for something out of the ordinary. Spotting *Birch Tree Mall*, I lifted out the folder and flipped through a few pages. Nothing more than the estimate and the bill marked PAID IN FULL. I returned the folder and kept looking.

A flicker of light caught my eye. "Jack," I hissed, ducking.

He glanced over his shoulder then dropped to the floor. We both scurried behind the desk and huddled together. A waft of cologne drifted to my nose. The man smelled good. Real good.

Focus, Angel.

Footsteps tapped the wood laminate floor of the hallway. The flashlight beam swung from left to right. The guard passed the room we hid in, and my heart rate slowed. When he turned back and opened the door, my heart lodged in my throat.

Jack put a hand over my mouth and shook his head.

Eyes wide, I nodded.

The guard swept his beam across the desk. Seconds later, the door closed, and the light moved away.

"That was close." I pushed to my feet.

"Too close. Let's hurry." Jack returned to his search.

I flipped through all the other folders and found nothing. Somewhere Johnson had to have something telling him that people, at least Bruce, knew how he did business. Otherwise there was no need to kill to keep someone from talking. The filing cabinet wouldn't be safe enough.

I crouched and searched the desk drawers, searching for a hidden panel. When that didn't pan out, I got under the desk and searched for. . .something. There. A slightly protruding button that looked like the top of a wooden screw.

I pressed the button. A drawer slid from the side of the desk and hit me in the head. I put a hand to the bump, stifling a cry. That would leave a bruise.

I reached over and felt the inside of the drawer. My fingers came in contact with an envelope. I grabbed it and crawled from under the desk, remaining on the floor so I wouldn't be seen. "Found something."

Risking light, I brightened the screen of my phone. The envelope contained two typewritten letters, both accusing Larry Johnson of cutting corners and one with the promise of coming clean to the police. None of them were signed, which didn't prove they were sent by Bruce. The saving grace was the fact that very few people used a typewriter anymore.

"We're getting nowhere." I groaned. "We get the same proof every time. The whole town knows Johnson is dirty. This doesn't tell us what we want to know."

"We're definitely missing something." Jack perused the pages again. "If I wrote these letters, I'd have a backup somewhere in case they were lost."

"That means we need to get into Bruce's house."

"Yep." Jack snapped photos of the pages and handed them to me. "Best put them back. We don't want Johnson to know anyone saw them."

I returned the envelope to the hidden drawer.

Jack stood near the door, peering through the glass at the hallway. "We can't leave yet."

"Why not?"

"The guard is blocking our way, talking on his cell phone."

My heart stopped. "Do you think he suspects we're here and is calling for help?"

"He didn't act like it when he entered the office, but anything is possible." He turned back to me. "We wait and see."

"What do we do if someone does join him?" I leaned against the desk.

"Worry about that if it hap—" Jack waved me forward. "He stepped outside. Let's exit through the other door."

"He'll know it's unlocked."

"Hopefully, he'll think he didn't lock it."

"Mr. Optimistic, you are." I put my hand on his back and followed as he set off at a quick pace to the second rear door.

He took a deep breath and opened the door just enough to peer out. Then he took my hand and kept a tight hold, entwining his fingers with mine. "We'll skirt around the opposite side, staying in the shadows."

I nodded, although the dark was too thick for him to see it. My heart beat so loudly, I thought people in the next county might hear.

The rough concrete of the outside wall pulled at my shirt. I stepped an inch away to stop the rasping sound.

Jack stopped so abruptly, I smashed my nose against his back. "Shhh."

I clapped my hand over my mouth to silence any sound my breathing might make.

Footsteps sounded around the corner. The guard was coming! We'd be discovered. I yanked free of Jack's hand and sprinted for the car.

Jack thundered behind me.

"Stop!" The guard's order did nothing to deter us from our goal.

I jerked open the truck door and dove inside as Jack did the same. Seconds later, the truck squealed its tires as we sped from the parking lot.

"Do you think he could tell what we look like?" I glanced at Jack.

"Guess we'll find out when I go to work on Monday. If the guard describes me well enough, Johnson will fire me."

CHAPTER EIGHT

My mind whirled as we drove to Bruce's house. I didn't know anything about the man. Had he lived alone? What if we surprised someone there? Someone with a gun.

I reached over and clutched Jack's hand. "Tell me Bruce lived alone."

"As far as I know. He never mentioned anyone." He gave my hand a squeeze.

"What if the guard calls the police?"

"I doubt he knows who we are."

"He might have seen our faces. He can give a description. He'll know he saw a man and a woman."

"He saw us from the back, Angel. Relax. It'll be all right." One more squeeze of my hand, and he let go. "If we see any sign of someone at the house, we'll drive on by."

"Okay." I felt marginally better. Jack was right. The guard had only seen our backs.

Bruce had lived in a small redbrick house in what had once been a nice neighborhood. Now lawns held weeds, roofs needed repair, and cracked sidewalks stretched on one side of the road.

His house showed a bit of pride with flowers in pots on the postage-stamp front porch.

Thankfully, no crime scene tape fluttered from the railing. No car sat in the carport.

Jack parked a few houses down the street. "Take off the beanie. We're a couple taking a nighttime stroll."

On the sidewalk, he tucked my hand in the crook of his arm. I'd be lying if I said I didn't enjoy the feel of his muscles.

When we reached Bruce's yard, Jack quickly tugged me behind a juniper bush. Then, when no one cried an alarm, we made a dash for the backyard. The gate squeaked as we pushed it open, freezing us in our tracks. After a tense second or two, we continued.

"What if everything is all locked up?" I whispered.

"Then we made the trip for nothing." He stood a few feet from the house and studied the windows. "These don't look locked. Bruce must have been a trusting man." He opened a window to a small dining room. "I'll boost you up."

"I'm having second thoughts." I glanced at the neighboring houses. Lights shone in their windows. "It isn't late enough for breaking and entering."

"The longer we stand out here, the greater the chance of someone seeing us."

Good point. I moved to the window. With one lift, I found myself sitting on the sill then standing on a floor covered with worn linoleum.

A cat meowed and rubbed against my legs. "Jack, there's a cat." Oh, please let someone have been feeding the poor thing. I made my way to the kitchen as Jack climbed through the window. My heart settled to see self-feeding food and water dishes. Why hadn't someone come for the poor thing? Did the neighbors know Bruce owned a cat? I'd have to find a way of letting Murphy know without him knowing we were inside the house.

I roamed through the house, the light of the moon guiding me. Three bedrooms, one bath, maybe a thousand square feet. Bruce hadn't been gone long, but already the house seemed sad to not have its owner.

I paused in the doorway of the room he used as a home office. On a small table sat a vintage typewriter. A laptop lay closed on the desk. A printer sat off to the side. I pulled a sheet of paper from it, rolled it into the typewriter, and typed my name. Same font as the letters we'd found in Johnson's office.

"Bruce found out about Johnson's dirty deeds," I told Jack when he joined me. "The odds of someone else having an old typewriter aren't great."

"No, they aren't." He pulled the paper from the typewriter and shoved it into his pocket. "We need to find a way of telling Murphy without ending up behind bars."

"That task seems more impossible with each minute. Can we go now?"

"Absolutely." Jack took the time to fill the cat's food and water to the very top before helping me out the window.

I really wanted to bring the fluffy pet with me. Leaving it behind seemed wrong somehow, but taking it would be theft, and I had enough on my head. "Want to go to church with me and Ida on Sunday?" I really needed church right then.

He shot me a look over his shoulder. "Sure. What time?"

I told him the time and the place, cringing at the squeak of the gate. My heart leaped into my throat at the sight of an elderly woman walking up the driveway, a baseball bat in her hand.

"Who are you, and why are you sneaking around Bruce's place?" She raised the bat. "I was quite good at softball in my day, so don't make me use this."

"We, uh, fed his cat." Not a lie.

"How did you get in? Bruce hasn't been home in days."

"Oh." She didn't know. "He always leaves his windows unlocked."

"Ma'am"—Jack sighed—"Bruce Whitton is dead. Has been for over a week."

Her face fell. "Oh. That explains his absence. Well, climb back in that window and fetch me Fergus. I'll care for the cat. Bruce didn't have any family."

Jack rushed to do her bidding, leaving me standing there fidgeting.

"I'm Addie."

"Angel." I smiled. "Thank you for caring for Fergus. I live with my grandmother, and she's allergic."

"I've got five already. What's one more?" Sirens wailed in the distance. "Oh. Since I didn't know you were friends of Bruce, I called the police."

My heart dropped to my toes. Murphy would never buy our story like Addie did.

Jack handed over the cat as Murphy's squad car stopped in front of the house. Another police car stopped behind him.

"It's all right, officers," Addie said. "They're friends of Bruce's. I didn't know they were here to feed the cat."

Murphy narrowed his eyes at us. "We'll take it from here. Thank you, ma'am."

She shot me a questioning look, her brows rising as Murphy ordered us to turn around and put our hands behind our backs. "Officer, really. . ." She shrugged and marched home with Fergus and her baseball bat.

"We can explain," I said. "Did you know Bruce had a cat? Someone had to take care of it."

"Right. That's why you're here." He snapped the cold, hard steel around my wrists.

I started to tell him what we'd found but didn't know how to without getting into more trouble. "We're only trying to help," I mumbled.

"On the contrary." He took me to his car while another officer led Jack.

I met Jack's gaze before Murphy opened the door to the back seat. Without speaking to Jack first, I didn't know what to say in answer to the questions I knew were coming. "I need to talk to Jack."

"Not going to happen." He slammed the door shut and got into the driver's seat.

Ida was going to kill me. When we arrived at the station, I demanded my one phone call.

"After I ask you some questions." He led me to a room with a table and two chairs. "Sit."

I obeyed.

"You cannot deny that you were in Johnson's office this evening. You were caught on camera. The questions I want answered are what did you find and why go to Whitton's house?" He crossed his arms.

"Are you arresting me?"

"Maybe." A muscle ticked in his jaw. "You were trespassing, and Mr. Johnson is livid. It didn't take a genius to decipher that it was you and Lowery at Whitton's when the call came through. Spill it, Miss Stirling."

"We gave you the papers from the mall. Jack and I knew we needed more proof to get you to listen to us and realize neither of us killed Bruce. So we entered Johnson's company. The door wasn't locked, so we didn't break in." I lifted my chin.

"You went after hours. Go on."

"Under Johnson's desk, I found some letters threatening to expose him. If you uncuff me, I can show them to you. I have photos on my phone."

He pulled a key ring from his belt and uncuffed me before returning to his seat across the table. He wiggled his fingers for my phone.

I pulled it from my back pocket, swiped to the pictures, and handed it to him. "Then, at Bruce's house, we found the typewriter that typed them. He sent the letters to Johnson. Johnson killed him."

"Still no proof Johnson killed anyone."

How dense could one man be? "Are you serious? Johnson is the only one with a motive."

"There are factors you know nothing about, Miss Stirling."

"Then tell me."

"I cannot give you the details of an investigation."

"An investigation Jack and I are solving for you!" I slapped the table.

He glowered. "Would a night in a cell calm you down? Get you to keep your nose out of where it doesn't belong? Because, Miss Stirling, the things you and Mr. Lowery are doing can get you killed."

"Can I go home?"

Without answering, he left me alone in the stark room. I folded my arms and laid my head down on the table. Why did someone have to kill Bruce behind my truck and try to frame me? All I wanted to do was run my little business and make people happy with fabulous donuts. I really didn't think that was too much to ask.

I must have fallen asleep, because the next thing I knew, Murphy was shaking me awake. "Go make your phone call. Hopefully, it's to someone who can give you and Lowery a ride back to his vehicle."

"You're letting us go?"

"This time. Look, Miss Stirling, I cannot have the two of you interfering. Do so again, and I will arrest you. That is a promise. Do you understand me?"

I nodded, getting to my feet. "Completely." Besides, we'd already proven who killed Bruce. Murphy would see that in time. Our work was done.

I called Ida and explained multiple times that I did not need bail money. Only a ride.

"Seems to me like you'd be arrested after that little adventure," she said as I climbed into the car. Jack slid into the back seat.

"We got lucky." I glanced at Jack. "Did he ask you about why we were at Johnson's and what we found?"

"Yes. Guess our stories matched enough to satisfy him." He grinned. "He did tell me that I was no longer a person of interest in Bruce's murder. Thanks to you, my name is cleared."

"We did it together." A flush of pride washed over me. "Life can now return to normal."

"Normal is boring," Ida said. "The two of you did such a good job with this case, you really ought to find another one."

"No way." I laughed. "Jack?"

"I'm good."

We dropped him off at his truck with promises to see him tomorrow at church.

As Ida and I drove home, I filled her in on everything we'd discovered. "We really did do a good job, didn't we?"

"Yes, you did. At finding evidence. But there is still one little problem."

"Like what?"

"I found out Johnson wasn't in town the night Bruce died. He'd gone to visit his sister. She swears by his alibi. The killer is still unknown."

CHAPTER NINE

I got little sleep that night wondering who, if not Johnson, killed Bruce. I'd stayed up far too late talking to Jack, but neither of us had any ideas. What we did decide was that Murphy knew of Johnson's alibi, and that was why he kept telling us we had no proof.

Now I sat at church fidgeting like a bored child until Ida elbowed me. Jack glanced over. His mouth twitched.

I snorted, holding back a laugh, and strained to keep my gaze forward. The pastor's teaching on patience definitely did not hold my attention.

"This is something you should listen to," Ida whispered, her voice carrying a bit of a growl.

I clapped a hand over my mouth to hide a grin.

Jack's eyes twinkled, and it was evident from the pressing together of his lips that he was trying desperately not to laugh. He shook his head and, hunched over, apologized to people as he squeezed past.

It didn't take but a breath before I copied. Getting outside before bursting into laughter was a necessity.

We raced around the corner. I sagged against the building, giggles escaping me. "I do believe I got scolded."

"Big-time." He laughed. "Why were you so twitchy?"

"Thinking about last night, all that happened, and Johnson. If not him, who? All I could think about was the who."

"Don't look now, but we're being watched." Jack stepped closer, as if to shield me.

I peered around him to see Johnson, Scott, and a few of the other construction workers, all decked out in their Sunday best, watching us with stern faces.

"Looks to me like you're the one in trouble." Johnson wouldn't fire Jack at church, would he?

"Yeah." He exhaled heavily. "Let's sit on the bench over there until the service is over." He led me to a concrete bench under a maple tree.

"How'd you like our church?" I took another look at the group of men who had dispersed except for Scott and Johnson. Why were the men outside and not in the sanctuary?

"I think I like it," Scott said. "Hard to tell when I didn't stay very long."

"What about your coworkers? Why are they outside? Church seems a strange place for a work meeting."

"Yeah. Uh-oh." He jerked his head to where Murphy pulled into the parking lot. A couple of minutes later, he was talking to Johnson.

Johnson's face turned dark. He shot a stony look toward Jack and me, then marched into the building. Scott scurried after him like a crab.

Without glancing our way, Murphy returned to his car and drove away.

"I must admit, Angel, that your church is definitely entertaining." Jack smiled. "I'll be back."

"It isn't always like this." I laughed and stood as Ida headed our way.

"You two are embarrassingly childish." Head high, she headed for Jack's truck and into the front passenger seat. "You can sit in back, Angel."

Chuckling, I got into the back seat and clicked my seat belt into place. "How was the sermon?"

"As if you care," Ida snorted. "What had you in such a state?"

"My mind was everywhere but on church, and when you elbowed me and Jack tried not to laugh, I lost control." I smiled at Jack's eyes in the rearview mirror. I really hoped he would want to remain friends once we'd solved this murder. The days wouldn't be nearly as much fun without him.

"How about lunch?" Jack asked, pulling out of the parking lot. "We could go to the diner."

Ida and I agreed. A few minutes later, we were seated in a booth perusing menus.

"I should have a salad, but the bacon mushroom burger is calling my name." I shrugged and closed my menu.

"You only live once," Ida said. "So I'm getting the salad." She slapped her menu on the table. "What's next on your plan to find out who killed Bruce Whitton?"

"No idea." Jack set all three menus at the end of the table. "Since neither of us is considered a suspect or person of interest, we might as well quit trying to figure it out. We accomplished what we set out to do. We cleared our names."

I sat still, trying to figure out how I felt about being done. It felt like relief on one hand and disappointment on the other. Playing detective had given me a thrill I'd never experienced before. But, yes, Jack was right. I could 100 percent focus on my career now.

I thrust out my hand. "Finished."

He returned the shake, lingering a bit. "Finished."

Ida scowled. "The two of you look as if you'll never see each other again. Can't you stay friends without danger following?"

Our gazes met. In unison we said, "Friends."

But I wanted more than friends.

The waitress came by and took our orders and filled our drinks. But conversation at our table had ground to a halt.

We'd said the word *friend*, and now it seemed as if neither of us knew how to be one. I cleared my throat. Someone had to break the ice. "Guess I'll have time to experiment with new donuts now."

"I'm sure I'll be looking for a new job."

"I know someone who's hiring," Ida said. "One of the women in my garden club's husband owns a much better construction business than Johnson's. He needs a new foreman. I'll put in a good word for you." She pulled her cell phone from her purse and sent a text. "There." She smiled. "I'm sure you'll be hired."

"Won't I need to meet with him?"

"I sent him your picture."

His brow lowered. "When did you take my picture?"

"The first time you showed up at the house. I also know someone who can run photos to see whether you're a criminal." Seeming completely unashamed for stepping over boundaries, she smiled. "If you know the right people, you can get anything done."

"Amazing." Jack sighed.

I'd watched the exchange in amusement. There was absolutely nothing my grandmother couldn't do or get done. At least I'd never found her weakness.

The rest of our mealtime was sprinkled with chitchat, the previous uncomfortable atmosphere gone. When we finished, Jack paid the bill and we headed back to his truck.

"It's been a good Sunday, ladies. Thank you."

Ida glanced at her phone. "Richardson wants to speak with you, Jack, when you're able. This afternoon is fine. I've forwarded you his number. He's the owner of Richardson Roofing and More."

"You do move fast." He opened the passenger-side door for her.

"At my age, you have to." She patted his cheek and climbed in, leaving me in the back again. "Time to go home. I like to rest as much as possible on Sunday before the rush of the week and baking."

Me too. A leisurely day, with an early night to bed and hope that Jack would show up for a donut in the morning.

After Jack glanced in the rearview mirror for the fifth time, I looked behind me. A truck jacked up so high that all I could see were the headlights followed far too close. "Are they following us?"

"I think so," he said, "and they keep getting closer."

Goose bumps prickled my skin. "Do you think they'll hit us?"

"Maybe they only want to intimidate us," Ida suggested.

"I hope so. Do you recognize the truck?"

"Not from what I can see." She gripped the handle near her head. "I hope this truck has airbags."

"It does. Hold on." Jack increased his speed. "Let's pray we don't have to test them."

From the rumble of the engine behind us, I knew we could never outrun the truck. "You can outmaneuver them. They won't be able to turn very fast on those oversize tires." Maybe they'd flip.

"Hard to do on the interstate." Jack whipped the wheel to take us down an off-ramp.

My head snapped to the side and hit the window. "Ow!" I put my hand to the injured spot.

"Sorry." He made a fast left, crossed a bridge, went down another ramp, and got back on the interstate.

It'd be a miracle if I didn't end up with whiplash. Even my grandmother let out a gasp or two instead of her usual steely resolve.

Horns blared as we weaved in and out of Sunday traffic. People leaving church and headed home. So much for us enjoying a restful afternoon. I wouldn't have to worry about getting up to make donuts if we died in a fiery car crash.

"I don't think it matters if the two of you stop snooping," Ida said. "Someone wants you out of the picture permanently."

"Which means we know something." Jack's knuckles whitened on the steering wheel.

"If only we knew what that something was." I tightened my seat belt and continued watching the vehicle behind us. Did we know who the killer was but didn't realize we did?

The truck slammed into us.

Jack's truck fishtailed.

Ida and I screamed.

When Jack regained control, he ground a question through clenched teeth. "Would someone please call 911 so the cops can come stop this maniac from killing us?"

Ida nodded. She placed the call then told us reports had already been called in by several other drivers. "Police should be here in less than five minutes."

"We could be dead in five minutes!" Another ram jerked me hard against my seat belt and sent us spinning.

My eyes widened as we headed for a minivan. My mouth opened in a silent scream.

We went over the median, past other cars, and into the ditch on the opposite side. The truck we were in mowed down saplings and tall grass before coming to an abrupt stop against a fence post.

Airbags deployed, slamming against us and releasing a fine white powder.

"Everyone okay?" Jack asked, fumbling with his airbag.

"Yes," Ida said.

"I'm okay too." I freed myself from the seat belt, turned around, and got on my knees to search for the truck that had hit us. It sped down the interstate away from us. The cops would never catch them. I didn't get the license plate number, but I did notice the truck was a black newer-model Ford on tires three sizes too big. Hopefully, someone driving by got the plate number.

Jack got out of the truck and rushed to the passenger side. He yanked on the door. "You'll have to come out the window, Ida."

"In a dress? I think not. I'll sit right here and wait until they use the jaws of death and cut me free so I can slide out like a lady."

"I'm not as fussy." I kicked at the shattered glass in the window and climbed out.

"Your door wasn't stuck." Jack opened and closed it.

"Oh." I smoothed my skirt, my face heating. "I guess car accidents knock a person off-kilter."

A police car screamed to a stop on the interstate. Close behind it came an ambulance and a fire truck. Within minutes men worked on cutting my grandmother free while she sat primly on the seat doing her best to fix her hair.

"You're bleeding. Right here." Jack lightly touched my forehead.

I touched the spot, and my fingers came away bloody. "Didn't feel anything until now." The area burned. I stared up at him. "Why do this? What do we know?"

"We need to go back over everything we've discovered and find out." He reached into the truck and retrieved his phone. "I need to call Richardson, tell him I'd like to talk about the job but that I can't start for a day or two because I have to get a new truck. And we need to tell Murphy." His eyes flashed. "I will find out who did this. I loved this truck."

I turned my gaze back to the interstate. It should be pretty easy to find out who owned a truck like the one that had hit us. But that was the problem. Easy could be dangerous.

CHAPTER TEN

J ack wasn't the first in line the next morning to purchase a donut, but he was there. He'd pulled up in a battered old Chevy.

"Nice ride." I jerked my chin toward the truck. Every movement made my body ache. I had bad bruises from the seat belt and the airbag.

"Borrowed from a neighbor. She may shake, rattle, and roll, but she gets me where I need to go." He glanced to where Johnson and the others stood next to their own vehicles. "They should be done today or tomorrow. I'll take two chocolate-glazed, please. I'll need them in order to face the consequences of trespassing in Johnson's office."

I bagged them up and handed them to him with a sad smile. "On the house. We were both in the office. Good luck."

"Thanks. I'll need it." He moved away from the food truck and stood stoic as Johnson marched toward him, Scott on his heels.

Scott stopped a few feet behind Johnson and crossed his arms. An arrogant expression twisted his features. The man seemed eager for what was coming. Why did he dislike Jack so much?

Johnson waved a finger in Jack's face. While his tone was loud, I still couldn't make out his words. Jack didn't move, taking the shouting with squared shoulders and a straight back.

Seeing me watching, Scott approached the donut truck, stepping to the front of the line. When one man complained, Scott glared then turned back to me. "This is your fault, you know. Him getting fired."

"How so?" I narrowed my eyes.

"If you'd have let things be, the police would've figured out you didn't kill Bruce on their own. Instead, you and Jack had to meddle."

"Are you purchasing anything?" I almost wished for a bit of poison to slip into a donut for him.

"Sure. It's a day of celebration. Give me a baker's dozen for the guys."

"Why do you dislike Jack so much?"

"Because he was in line to get the position I will now get. Foreman." Rather than look ashamed of his actions, he seemed full of pride.

"Doesn't matter. He's going to be foreman at Richardson Roofing." A laugh escaped me at the startled look that crossed his face. I hoped Jack wouldn't be angry that I let his news slip. "Found out yesterday," I said as I packed his donuts. "That means your meanness was for nothing, unless this is your normal personality. If it is, I almost pity you."

When I turned around, the hatred in his eyes froze me in my tracks. I set the box on the counter and slid it toward him. "Have a nice day."

He snorted, tapped his card, and carried his purchase to the other workers. I sure hoped Jack was right and their time near the food trucks was about over. Since there weren't a lot of them, business wouldn't be hurt by their absence.

After what seemed like a very long lecture, Jack sat at one of the tables in front of my truck and ate his donuts. I waited on the rest of my customers before joining him. I sat across the table and folded my hands.

"You okay?"

"Absolutely. I have a better job starting tomorrow."

"The food court won't be the same without you."

"Oh, I plan on still coming every morning."

His words warmed my heart. "That's great."

"We're friends. I plan on introducing your donuts to my new work crew."

Friends. Ugh. Be careful what you wish for, right? I'd wanted to be friends, and now that I was, I wanted more than just friends. "That's nice of you. What did Johnson say about us being in his office?"

"Said, 'How dare you,' a few times, said we should both be locked up for a very long time, said to stay away from him and his or we'd be sorry. . .the usual stuff." He shoved the last bite of his donut into his mouth. "Not sure when I'll be able to join you for lunch after today, but I will as often as possible. I've got to settle into my job to know for sure." He stood and balled up the empty pink-and-white-striped donut bag.

"I understand. I'll make sure to always bring a book. What now in regard to who killed Bruce?"

He rubbed his jaw. "I'll be here at lunch today. Let's talk about it then. I've got to head to my new job and fill out paperwork."

"Okay." I nodded. "We can try to figure out what this bad guy thinks we know." I headed back to my food truck where two customers waited, one being Mr. Johnson. "I'm so sorry."

The other, a woman with her toddler, said, "We've only been waiting a minute." She smiled at the child. "Sprinkles?"

The child jumped up and down in glee.

Mr. Johnson cleared his throat, clearly growing impatient.

I finished with the mother and child before greeting him. "The usual?"

"No. You have lost me as a customer forever." He took a deep breath.

Very dramatic. "Then what can I do for you?"

"Stay back. You have no idea what kind of an anthill you've disturbed, Miss Stirling."

"Are you threatening me?" I glanced around for anyone close enough to hear our conversation. My blood boiled. "Do you happen to drive a jacked-up Ford, Mr. Johnson?"

"My truck is over there."

"Perhaps you have more than one truck."

"For your sake, please stop playing detective." He spun and marched away.

Our conversation left me feeling as if there was more to Mr. Johnson than I'd found. He definitely knew about the big truck. I'd seen the flicker in his eyes. Did he also know who killed Bruce?

The next two hours crawled by. When Jack arrived, I raced to meet him, feeling a bit like a puppy whose human had been gone too long.

"I had my own little talk with Johnson," I said as we headed to the taco truck.

"Glad you didn't miss out." Jack chuckled and ordered three street tacos for me and five for him.

"He said, verbatim, 'For your sake, please stop playing detective.' That's after he told me I've stirred up an anthill." Tacos in hand, we moved to a table as far away from the crowd as possible. "Doesn't that sound like a threat?"

"Yes." He unwrapped a taco and squeezed hot sauce from a little packet onto it. "I think that answers the question about whether we continue or not. I say we back off, let some of the heat dissipate."

"What if we're threatened again anyway?"

"Then we'll face it head-on."

Ida slapped a sheet of paper onto the table.

I flinched. "Don't sneak up on a person like that, Grandma."

"Ida." She tapped the page. "Read that."

Jack and I peered at the paper. "'You and that gardening group need to back off before someone ends up six feet under,'" I read. I glanced at her. "You got this? What have you and your friends been doing?"

"Asking questions." She sat next to me. "Mostly about Johnson and his business dealings. I think he's the killer."

I exchanged a shocked look with Jack. "But you said he had an alibi."

"Maybe he snuck out long enough to do the deed." She crossed her arms. "I have no idea whether he owns the truck that hit us, or borrowed or stole it, and I don't care. He definitely had a motive to kill Bruce, and we haven't been able to find anyone else who did."

I didn't like the fact my grandmother had been threatened. "I think you should go visit Aunt Lilly for a while. Just until this is all over."

She frowned. "I won't let anyone drive me from my home." She got to her feet and snatched the paper. "I'm heading to the police department to demand an officer follow me around."

I didn't think it worked that way but hugged her goodbye. "I want a text from you every hour on the hour."

"Don't be silly." She bustled away.

"You made me do it as a kid," I yelled at her retreating back. I turned to Jack. "We need a plan. I couldn't bear it if anything happened to her."

"I'm drawing a blank. Everything pointed to Johnson, then it didn't, and now we're back to him. I have no idea how to get more information when what we've found hasn't gotten him arrested."

I sat back down, glancing to where the construction workers laid paving for a new walkway. Scott leaned against a tree while the other men worked. Johnson had left the food court/lake area right after our altercation.

Scott caught me looking and saluted. "Scott told me he didn't like you because before Bruce died, you were in line to be foreman," I said to Jack.

"I was?" Jack's brows rose. "I didn't know that."

"I also let it slip to him that it didn't matter anyway, because you were going to be the new foreman at Richardson Roofing." I gave a sheepish grin. "I'm sorry, but he got under my skin."

"That's fine. It's not a secret. Johnson already knew. Said Richardson called him for a reference. I guess, despite his anger, he gave me a good one." He laughed. "My new job is better, with a higher salary. Let him chew on that. I've never had patience with jealousy in the workplace. See you tomorrow." He clapped me on the shoulder and left.

Yep. Friends.

The afternoon dragged by. I spent it brainstorming new donut ideas until the time came to clean up and put everything away.

The construction crew filed by, willing to purchase anything left over for half price. Said they wanted to celebrate finishing the job. I was more than happy to oblige. Whether I sold them today or tomorrow, either way, the day-old donuts would be discounted.

Scott hung back, a smirk on his face as if he were too good to ask for anything but fresh. I rolled my eyes and kept boxing up what little I had. Then I wet a rag and wiped down the counters I'd finished cleaning before the men came by.

I hung the wet rag over the faucet to dry.

The light in the truck flickered off. *Not now.* The light bulb shouldn't be bad. It wasn't that old.

I stopped midreach for the bulb. The last time I'd lost power, someone had been murdered and fell across the cord. Did I really want to check today? What if I didn't and someone needed me?

Every B movie I'd seen with a heroine too stupid to live flashed through my mind.

With a groan, I decided I had to be that person. I pushed open the door and peered out. Not seeing anyone, I climbed down and moved to the rear of the truck. The power cord had come unplugged.

I bent to plug it in.

Something bashed me in the back of the head.

The world went dark.

CHAPTER ELEVEN

M iss Stirling?" Officer Murphy peered down at me. "Do you know where you are?"

"I'm on the ground." I held out a hand for him to help me up.

"Let the paramedic check you out before you get up." He stepped aside so another man could shine a light in my eyes and check out the back of my head.

"Who called you?"

"One of the other food truck owners," Murphy said. "They thought it was strange that your car was still here and came to check on you. Unfortunately, they didn't see who hit you."

I winced as the paramedic pressed the spot where I'd been hit. "At least I wasn't killed."

"I don't think you should be anywhere alone until this is over. You could have easily met the same fate as Whitton." He crossed his arms.

"She's got a nasty bump," the paramedic said. "Best she go to the ER to get checked further. We can take her or she can get a ride."

"Her grandmother is on her way. Thank you." Murphy helped me to my feet and to the closest table. "I asked you to stop snooping."

"I haven't since then. Jack and I decided to stop. Now I can't."

"Yes, you can." His brow furrowed.

"No, because this person will keep coming at me until we put them behind bars."

"There is no 'we.'" He glanced to where Ida rushed toward us. "Straight to the hospital, ladies. I'll follow you."

His worry was contagious. Ida nodded, eyes wide, and helped me to her car.

She drove as if she had a crate of eggs in the front seat.

"We'll both be old by the time we get there." I closed my eyes and leaned my head back.

"I don't want to jostle you." She sniffed.

"Are you crying?" My eyes popped open.

"I could have lost you tonight, Angel. That would have been very bad for me."

I put my hand on her arm. "You didn't though. Remember why I'm named Angel?"

"Of course. It was my idea. We named you Angel so there would always be angels around you."

Angels would be around me anyway, but I loved the sentiment. "One watched over me tonight." I peered out the window as we pulled in front of the hospital emergency room doors. "Jack's here."

"I called him to meet us so he can help you inside while I park."

"You wait right here until I'm inside. Then he can go with you to park the car and walk you in. No being alone, Murphy said. That goes for both of us. Do you think Jack should move into the guest room for a while?"

"Doesn't hurt to ask."

I got out of the car.

"You okay?" Jack put his hands on my shoulders and stared into my eyes.

"A bit of a headache, but I'm sure it's nothing more than a concussion. Once I'm inside, please go with Ida to park. Murphy doesn't want us to be alone until the killer is caught. I think that means you too. We've got a guest room you can use."

He nodded, his expression grave, and handed me into the capable hands of the admitting nurse. With a glance over his shoulder, he stepped outside and into my grandmother's car. By the time they joined me, I was already in a hospital gown in a cubicle, waiting for a doctor.

"Tell us what happened," Jack said after fetching a second chair from another room.

"There isn't much to tell. Someone unplugged the power to my truck. When I went out to plug it back in, that person—I'm assuming it was the same person—hit me. I woke up to the sight of Officer Murphy looking down at me."

"Not a bad sight to open your eyes to." Ida wiggled her brows. "He's a handsome man."

"Is he?" I shrugged. I'd never looked at the man that way. I turned the conversation back to what had happened. "We need to dig deep to find out what we know." I drummed my fingers on the bed, doing my best to ignore the dull throbbing in my head.

"We know that Johnson had a motive." Jack pressed his lips together. "We know that Scott doesn't like me—"

"That's it!" How could we have missed it? "Scott killed Bruce. Think about it." I sat up suddenly, sending a sharp pain through my head. "He wanted the foreman job. I bet he was acting foreman during the building of the strip mall. He might have cut corners to save money for Johnson in hopes of securing the position. Bruce found out, and Scott had to kill him."

"That means Johnson has to know, or at least strongly suspect, that Scott did the deed."

"It's kind of a stretch," Ida said. "But it's worth digging into Scott's background. I'll get the garden club right on it." She took her phone from her purse and started pressing buttons.

"Scott knew we'd put the pieces together when he let it slip about his dislike of you. That's why he hit me. I think he really meant to kill me."

"Good thing you have a hard head." Jack's smile trembled.

"Yeah," I said hoarsely. Of course, there were always the angels.

The doctor came in and took a look in my eyes and at my head. "Pain level?"

"About an eight."

"You've got a concussion. I'll prescribe you some pain meds, but if you promise to take it easy for the next couple of days, I'll let you go home."

"I own my own food truck. There is no taking it easy."

"I'll run the truck for the next few days," Ida said. "No excuses. I'm perfectly capable of making and selling donuts."

"Okay." I'd agree to anything in order to go home, but Ida couldn't run the truck alone, and Jack had his own new job to do.

They stepped from the cubicle to allow me to put my clothes back on. Why did hospitals automatically make you put on a hospital gown? Were they hoping to admit everyone who came through their door?

A few minutes later, a nurse arrived with a wheelchair. "Policy," she said when I argued.

With a sigh, I took a seat and let her wheel me to the door while Ida and Jack went to fetch the car. Jack would have to drive alone to his place, grab some things, then come to our house. I sent up a prayer for God to send down angels to watch over him.

"We need to speak with Johnson," I muttered.

"Larry Johnson?" the nurse asked. "Only family is permitted to visit at this time."

I jerked to face her. "Will he live?"

"That's all I can tell you."

"He's my friend's boss." Or was. Spotting Officer Murphy in the waiting room, I asked the nurse to wheel me to him, then leave us alone for a few minutes. "I'm guessing you're here about Johnson."

He gave a few rapid blinks. "How did you hear about him?"

"Little bird." I wouldn't rat out the nurse. "Have you seen him?"

A horn honked outside. Ida would have to wait.

"No, they haven't let me speak with him yet. Go home, Miss Stirling. Take care of your head, and make sure you always have someone with you."

"I will." Although the three who would be together were the three Scott wanted out of the picture. "Scott Turner is the man you're looking for." I told him my theory. "And now it seems as if someone is trying to clean up all the loose ends."

"You should be a detective, the way you ferret out information."

That was the best compliment he could have given me. "Thank you." I waved to Jack, who was searching the room for me.

He rushed over and grabbed the handgrips of the wheelchair, smiling at the nurse who had just returned. "I'll take her out. Ida is having a fit in the car."

Jack wheeled me outside and helped me into the car, where I quickly filled him and Ida in on what I'd found out. Feathers smoothed, she drove us to a twenty-four-hour pharmacy. She pulled up to the drive-through to get my prescription and then drove home, ordered me to bed, and handed me a pain pill.

"Not yet. I'm going to wait for Jack." I lowered myself to the sofa and eyed the pill in my hand. It would make my brain fuzzy. I'd hold off until I went to bed.

"I'll fix up the guest bed." She headed down the hall.

I closed my eyes, my mind whirling. As the realization that I was most likely meant to die that day hit me, nausea rose, and my body started to tremble. I didn't stop until Jack arrived and put his arm around me.

"Everything will be okay. Have faith."

"Why did Bruce have to be murdered behind my truck?" I buried my face in his shoulder. "Why did Scott try to frame me? That very first day he acted as if he thought I killed Bruce."

"To throw suspicion off himself, I guess."

He didn't answer the rest of my questions, but I supposed they really didn't need an answer. I most likely just got unlucky, and where Bruce died was where the argument took place.

"Go to bed," Ida ordered from the doorway. "Sleep in. Jack can help me make the donuts."

"I can?" He stiffened. "I don't know anything about making donuts."

"Just follow my instructions." She clapped her hands. "Come on."

I got slowly to my feet and took the pain pill. "You can do the work tomorrow, but I'll be going with you. No one left alone, remember? I'll sit on a chair and stay out of your way."

Neither of them looked convinced. Sitting up all day would not be resting. They must have realized they wouldn't change my mind, because they didn't argue.

I woke the next morning to the aromas of frying donuts and sizzling bacon. The two best smells, in my opinion. Since we had a houseguest, I showered and dressed before heading to the kitchen.

Ida and a glaze-splattered Jack moved around each other like a choreographed dance team.

"Good morning." Jack smiled. "I got fired from decorating and assigned to cooking breakfast. Something I do know how to do. How are you feeling?"

"Like someone hit me in the head, but I did get a good night's sleep." I sat at the kitchen table. Anger that I didn't have the luxury of actually relaxing after the attempt on my life rushed through me. If I ever saw Scott again, I'd bash *him* over the head.

Ida's phone dinged. "That's a text. Go ahead and read it for me."

I grabbed her phone. "Johnson's brake lines were cut."

Jack turned, a slice of bacon in the tongs he held. Grease dripped to the floor. "Scott, if it was Scott, didn't even try to make it look like an accident. It's easy to tell when brake lines are cut."

"Why make it so obvious?" Ida asked.

"I don't know, but you have other texts here. Ones that came in last night." I skimmed through the texts from her garden club members. "'Scott did not go home last night,' Trudy says. 'Scott was the foreman on the mall build,' Mabel says. 'A jacked-up truck was stolen the other day and discovered last night in a wheat field.' That's from Alice. Wow. Your friends could probably dig up dirt on anyone."

"They sure could." Ida beamed. "Our group is a force to be reckoned with. We have friends or family in every job that counts in this city. The local police department should always use our services."

I laughed. "They aren't using your services now." But they were benefiting from Ida and her friends.

"Oh." Jack put the bacon on a paper towel then bent down to clean up his mess. "I'm not liking the two of you going to work today."

"The same goes for you." I tilted my head. "You'll be completely alone."

"I'll be surrounded by construction workers."

"We'll have a food court full of people."

"The two of you need to stop bickering." Ida took her phone from me and slipped it into the pocket of her apron. "The real thing to consider here is that Scott is no longer trying to hide the fact that he will commit murder. He'll be braver, thinking he has nothing to lose."

"Except his freedom," I said.

"He's already lost that by being forced to hide. What he'll want now is revenge."

CHAPTER TWELVE

The next morning I sat in a rolling office chair and filled orders while Ida took payment. "Sorry," I said after running into her for what had to be the tenth time.

"Stop doing that." She glared.

"There isn't much room in here." I sighed and reached for another chocolate-glazed.

"Did you hear about what happened to Larry Johnson?" a woman in line said. "Brakes cut. His foreman is missing. Do you think someone killed him?"

"No, I do not." Ida handed her a bag. "His foreman cut those brake lines."

"How do you know?"

"I just do. Have a nice day."

"Good job not spilling crucial information." I patted her arm. "The garden ladies still asking around?"

"Absolutely. Good morning, Jack. Thought you might not be able to make it."

I rolled to the window. "Hey."

"Wouldn't miss seeing my two best girls. Besides, I promised my crew the tastiest donuts in the state." He grinned.

My heart swelled. "An assortment?"

"Sounds perfect." He stepped closer and lowered his voice. "Lots of speculation about where Scott might be hiding out."

"Such as?" I grabbed a box but kept my attention on him.

"Some say a fishing shack on the other side of the lake, someone else says a hunting cabin on the mountain, others a hotel. . . ." He shook his head. "The police have been run ragged with all the alleged sightings."

I couldn't get Ida's warning about Scott wanting revenge out of my mind. All I could do was hope and pray the pressure on him would make him flee too far away to be of any harm to us.

"Where are you getting this information?" Ida took his money.

"The men I work with mostly. Any word from your friends?"

"Not yet, but it's early. Mark my words, it'll be the garden club that finds Mr. Turner."

"Somehow, I don't doubt it." Jack laughed and took the donuts I quickly packed.

"Well," the man behind him said, "I know for a fact that the Turner family owns an auto repair shop. I bet they know where he is."

I was sure the police would have already questioned any immediate family or acquaintances. Regardless, I had no intention of asking anything. All I wanted to do was get through all this alive. I couldn't relax until Scott was behind bars.

I watched as Jack got into his truck alone. No matter how much I wanted him to heed Murphy's advice, I supposed it would be difficult for him to always have someone with him.

"Don't worry. He'll keep an eye out for trouble." Ida smiled. "Jack's no dummy." She leaned close to my ear. "I'm packing."

"Packing what?" I tilted my head. "Are you going somewhere?"

"A Taser, Angel. I have a Taser in my purse. I borrowed it from Mabel."

Oh, Lord, help us. "Do you know how to use it?"

"Of course." She looked at me as if I'd lost all my sense. "I'm from the South, dear."

"Oh." As if that explained anything. I prayed she'd have no need of the Taser.

I took over at lunchtime while Ida went to get some lunch. I already missed lunch with Jack. A grin split my face when he approached with boxed lunches from the Lucky Noodle. "This is a surprise."

"A man's got to eat. I'll set these on the table and help you out of the truck. Ida is still at the Spudmobile."

I fidgeted as I waited for him to come get me and flipped the sign to say I'd be back in half an hour. By the time we arrived at the table, me moving slower than usual, Ida was already seated.

The excited look on her face alerted me to the fact she'd heard something interesting. "Guess what?" She wiggled her eyebrows.

"Just tell us, please." I sat and opened my box of chow mein.

"Fine. You're no fun. As with our line this morning, everyone is talking about Johnson and Scott. Johnson had surgery this morning for a broken back. Whether he'll live is still up in the air. If he does, it's doubtful he'll ever walk again. If he doesn't make it, that would make Scott a double murderer." She stuck her fork into her baked potato. "I also heard that Scott was sighted in Monroe. Of course, this is all hearsay, but if he is in Monroe, he isn't far enough away for my taste."

Not with Monroe only fourteen miles away. "Do you think that if he's that close he intends to come after me again?" I glanced at Jack.

Worry creased his face. "I think it's highly likely." He scanned the surrounding area. "And I don't like it one bit."

Neither did I. The back of my neck prickled as if someone watched us, and I turned to do my own study of the area. No one seemed to be paying us any attention. Still, I'd lost my appetite, and the delicious noodles lost their taste.

I knew that during the slower afternoon hours, my mind would fill with every worst-case scenario my imagination could come up with. If not for the fact I usually sold out by discounting the donuts left, I'd close up shop early.

Jack cleaned up after us and rushed away. I waved off my grandmother's offer of leaning on her. "I'm perfectly fine other than a mild headache." And fatigue. I'd never been so exhausted. "I think I'll take a nap in the car."

"Make sure to keep a window cracked. Even though it's nice weather, it'll get hot."

I shook my head. Ida still treated me like a child a lot of times.

I lowered all four windows and stretched out in the back seat, something I hadn't done since I was a child. A smile crossed my face. I'd forgotten the luxury of a nap. My eyes drifted closed.

When I woke, the food court had grown silent. I sat up and looked around. At least half the vendors had already left. The other half were closing up.

A sheet of paper flapped from the windshield wipers. I groaned and climbed from the car. All sleepiness left as I read the words SEE HOW CLOSE I CAME TO YOU WITHOUT YOU SEEING ME?

I swallowed past the lump in my throat. A breeze tore the page from my fingers. Oh no. I scrambled after it. Without the threatening paper, I had nothing to show Murphy. I clutched the page as it stilled next to the tire of a car.

Keeping a tight grip, I approached the donut truck and slapped the paper onto the counter. "Another warning."

Ida's eyes widened as she read. "I would have noticed if Scott was in the food court."

"Did you see who put this on the window?"

"Well, no."

Still, as much interest as people had in Scott's whereabouts, there would have been a shout of alarm if he'd been anywhere near. I sat on the steps of the truck and dialed Murphy, who promised to be here in ten minutes.

When Ida finished wiping everything down and closing the awning, she joined me. She stopped halfway to a sitting position. "Angel, look." She pointed toward the lake.

I gasped at the sight of a man who looked like Scott. "He's too far away to be sure."

Ida entered the truck and emerged with her Taser.

I widened my eyes. "What do you plan on doing with that?"

"Chasing him down and demanding answers." She headed off at a fast pace, considering her age.

I couldn't let her go alone. Weaponless, I followed, calling 911 while I went.

Ida got close before the man looked over his shoulder and saw her. It wasn't Scott, but the fact the man started to run led me to believe he had something to hide.

"Stop or I'll shoot." Ida stopped and gasped for breath. "Please."

The man stopped.

"Hands. Over. Your. Head."

He complied.

I approached him with caution. "Why are you running from us?"

"Because you have that." His gaze landed on the Taser. "I think there might be some kind of law against chasing a stranger with a gun."

Ida looked shocked. "It's not a gun. It only looks like one, but let me tell you it will do the job it needs to. Tell us right now, young man, who you are and why you were watching us."

"Danny Matthews. I was paid to put a note on a car then watch to see what happened. Man, lady, you sleep a long time." He glared at me.

"Concussion." I frowned. "Was the man who paid you Scott Turner? The one the police are looking for?"

He shrugged. "I don't know who it was. He came up to me while I was fishing."

So, Scott had been close. I'd bet a box of glazed donuts that he'd been watching everything. But from where? Where could he hide that no one would see him? "Come with us."

He exhaled heavily. "Can I put my hands down?"

"As long as you walk real slow in front of me while I keep this thing on you. If you run, we'll find out whether it works or not."

"Grandma!" I shot her a shocked look.

"It's Ida, dear." She jerked her head toward Danny.

For Pete's sake. I shook my head and headed to where Murphy waited.

His eyes narrowed at the sight of the Taser. "What in the world are the two of you doing?"

"Not my idea." I resumed my seat on the truck step.

"With Scott trying to kill Angel, I'm not taking any more chances," Ida said.

"Put that thing away. Let me see the note. Stay right there, Danny. I'm sure you're involved in whatever this is." The young man had tried scooting away.

I retrieved the note from the truck and handed it to Murphy. "This guy put it there. Someone paid him to. I think Scott was close enough to watch the whole thing. He's trying to scare me."

"Better than kill you." Murphy turned in a slow circle, his sharp gaze roaming over every building. He headed toward one used for providing electricity to the food court. Leaving Ida to guard Danny, I followed the officer.

The lock on the door had been cut. Murphy drew his weapon and opened the door. "Stay here, Miss Stirling."

I obeyed but craned my neck to see inside.

Empty water bottles, fast-food bags, and a sleeping bag attested to the fact someone had been sleeping there. "Scott?" I asked Murphy.

"Could be a homeless person."

"Why do you always discount anything I say?"

"Because we can't jump to conclusions without absolute facts. Please stand back. This is a site of potential evidence." He headed for his car.

I jogged to stay on his heels, ignoring the pounding in my head. "What about Danny?"

"I'll take him in for questioning. I seriously doubt anyone else cares about terrorizing you besides Turner." He pulled a roll of crime scene tape from his trunk.

Minutes later, he had it strung across the door. "Go home, Miss Stirling. Lock your doors. I'll send a patrol car around to keep an eye on the place."

"Thank you." Instead of making me feel better, the fear grew. Murphy wouldn't think an officer outside our door was needed unless he suspected Scott would make another attempt on my life.

Ida must have thought the same thing, because her hand trembled as she dropped the Taser back into her purse. "Let's get home and pray Jack is there and safe."

Amen to that.

When we got home, Jack's truck was parked in the driveway. With four slashed tires.

Ida pulled up alongside it. "I'll call Murphy again. Don't go in the house without me, Angel. I mean it."

I shoved my car door open. "Then make the call quick, because Jack could be lying injured inside." Or worse.

CHAPTER THIRTEEN

Jack had been idly flipping through channels, waiting for us to return, oblivious to the fact that someone had ruined the tires on his borrowed truck. He was still complaining about it the next day.

"I'm not having much luck in the way of vehicles." He groaned.

"Tires are an easy fix." Ida patted his back on her way to the door. "I've got a garden club meeting. The two of you stay safe inside."

"You can't go alone." I started to get to my feet.

"Mabel is outside waiting for me. I'll be perfectly fine." She clutched her purse. "I'm armed, remember?"

"Don't remind me." I'd been shocked, terrified, and amazed yesterday at her bravery while carrying a weapon. Thankfully, no one had been harmed. "I'll be working on paperwork. Jack?"

"I'm going to do absolutely nothing." He grinned. "Except for getting new tires anyway. It's been a rough week."

I had to agree. After Ida left, I headed to my room and my laptop. I had monthly expenses and income to log. What I'd rather be doing was sitting on the couch with Jack and watching a movie. Maybe later.

"Angel, you might want to see this," Jack called from the other room. "It's important."

With a sigh, I got up from my desk. I froze in the doorway to the living room. Squad cars and news reporters were on the television. They all stood in front of a house. The ticker at the bottom read: HOSTAGES HELD AT GARDEN CLUB MEETING. My cell phone rang.

"Ida?"

"Yes, it's me. I'm, uh, well—"

"This is Scott Turner. If you don't want me to shoot every one of these lovely ladies, starting with your grandmother, then I suggest you and Lowery get over here. Now." He hung up.

Tears sprang to my eyes. "He's got Ida and wants us to come."

"I'll get my shoes." Jack sprang to his feet and thundered down the hall.

That's what I liked about him. Even though we might not live through the day, most likely wouldn't, he hadn't hesitated. The world could use more men like Jack Lowery.

I prayed for protection as we hurried to my car. I stared at the house for a second before backing out of the drive, wondering whether I'd see it again. Live there with my grandmother another day.

"It's going to be okay." Jack put his hand on my arm. "We've come this far since Bruce was murdered. Whatever happens, it'll be okay. Have faith."

I nodded. He was right. Whatever happened, whether I was here or in heaven, it would be okay.

I stopped the car outside the crime scene tape. An officer stopped us when we tried to cross.

"Please bring Officer Murphy over here." I didn't have time to follow the rules.

"Let them in." Murphy marched our way. "I've received a call. Probably the same one you got. I'll say this though. We'll do everything possible to keep you from entering that house."

Head high, I made my way to the sidewalk in front of Mabel's house. "My grandmother is in there. You'll have to shoot me to keep me out."

"I could put you in the back of my car."

"Please, don't." Jack's sad gaze pleaded with Murphy. "Let's try to make sure everyone walks out of there."

"You and Miss Stirling most likely won't." A muscle ticked in Murphy's jaw.

"That's a risk we have to take." Jack reached over and took my hand. When Murphy didn't protest further, we made our way slowly up the sidewalk.

The door opened before I could raise my hand to knock. With a glance over my shoulder at the reserved face of Murphy, I stepped inside, still clutching Jack's hand.

Scott sat in a large armchair. The garden club ladies filled the sofa. Mabel, who had opened the door, perched on the arm of the sofa.

"Glad you made it. Stand over there." He waved his gun toward the women. "In front of the window. The two of you make a good shield."

"You shouldn't have come." Tears slid down my grandmother's cheeks.

I reached for her.

"Do not touch her," Scott barked. "Get back by Lowery. I'm finalizing plans in my head and don't need any distractions."

We did as instructed. The curtains were open just enough that I could peer out the inch or so opening. Hopefully, the sniper, if there was one, would be able to see I wasn't Scott. A SWAT team pulled up. Things were about to get serious.

"Look," I whispered.

Jack nodded and exhaled long and slow.

The tick of a clock sounded loud in the silence. One of the women cleared her throat. A bird came from the clock and cuckooed the hour.

I shrieked.

Scott leaped to his feet and whirled toward the clock. "Shut that thing off. I could've fired my gun. I start shooting in here, and those goons outside will storm the place. I plan on being long gone before that happens." He glared in my direction. "You two will be going with me." He resumed his seat.

Eyeing all the unfinished glasses of tea on the coffee table, I asked, "Is it all right if they finish their drinks? Older women need a lot of hydration."

"Sure. Whatever."

Ida shot me a questioning look but reached for her glass.

Throw it, I mouthed.

She raised her arm.

Scott glared at me. "Not funny. Glasses down, ladies." He came and stood so close to me I could feel his breath on my face. "Stop playing games or I'll shoot your boyfriend and risk the cops storming in. Got it?" He tapped the gun on the top of my head.

"She's recovering from the concussion you gave her," Jack growled.

"A headache is the least of her worries." He shoved the gun into Jack's stomach. "Don't be a hero, buddy."

Scott resumed his seat, crossing one ankle over his knee and drumming the fingers of his left hand on the arm. "I could send the other women out and kill you here."

"Not in my house." Mabel hitched her chin. "Don't leave that memory here."

He shrugged. "Or I could force the cops to let us pass by, making a human shield. I'd need two more people though. You volunteering, Miss Mabel?"

She wrinkled her nose.

"No? Then we need to consider my first option. Unless I come up with something better." He sat back down.

The man had clearly come unhinged. Otherwise, he'd be making a quick getaway. Sitting here didn't accomplish anything. The cops would get antsy. Who knew what would happen then?

"Let's just go." I motioned to the back door. "There'll be fewer officers out there." Jack or I could maybe grab a garden tool as a weapon or one of those crystal vases I knew Mabel had. Something, anything, to defend ourselves. I might know my eternal destination, but it didn't mean I wanted to go today.

"Hush, Angel. The man is trying to think." Ida frowned and mouthed, *What are you doing?*

I gave a one-shoulder shrug. I really didn't know. I'd never been a hostage before. In addition to maybe finding a weapon of some kind, being outside would give the authorities a better chance of rescuing us.

"It's a plan," Scott said. "Let me ruminate over what could go wrong." He picked up one of the women's tea glasses and downed the remains.

Where was my grandmother's Taser? I didn't see her purse anywhere close. So far, none of my ideas had done any good, and Jack remained strangely calm and quiet.

I glanced up at him. He looked almost bored. Trying not to look like a threat? Because he was taller than Scott by a couple of inches and was in better physical condition from what I could see. Smart.

I, on the other hand, needed to do something. If I could distract Scott, then maybe Jack could act on whatever was running through his mind.

"I'm thirsty."

"Don't care." Scott glared.

"I need to use the restroom."

"Shut up."

I slouched. My head started to ache. "I need to sit down."

"I won't tell you again. Now, act like the angel you're supposed to be and behave."

I gritted my teeth so hard I thought I might break one. "You don't get to say those words to me. Only my father could say them." And had on several occasions.

"Since I'm the one in control here, I can pretty much say and do whatever I want." He tilted his head. "I'm starting to reconsider leaving this house. I doubt I'll make it out alive, so why should any of you?"

"These women did nothing," Jack said quietly. "Let them go."

Well, Jack and I hadn't done anything worth dying over either, but I agreed. "They didn't mess up your plans for the future. I agree with Jack." I nodded toward the door. "It would be a good show of faith to the officers." I glanced through the curtains and spotted some men wearing FBI vests. "SWAT and the FBI have arrived."

"Good. The FBI might be more willing to negotiate. Call Murphy on your phone. Give the phone to me when he answers."

I pressed the numbers to reach Murphy.

"What's going on in there?"

"Scott is thinking. He wants to speak with you." I handed the phone over.

"How can I leave without incident, taking Angel and Jack with me? The others I'd leave here." His face darkened. "So you'd rather they all died instead of two? Tsk-tsk, Officer. Think it over. I'll call back in fifteen minutes." He set my phone on the end table next to him and resumed drumming his fingers.

"We have to do something," I whispered.

"I'm thinking on it." Jack nudged me with his shoulder. "Move to the other side of the slit in the curtains."

"Stop talking!" Scott shot us a sharp look.

I scooted over as soon as he turned his attention back to his thoughts. Now a sniper would have a clear shot if Scott moved where they could see him. Somehow, I needed to get him up again.

After the longest fifteen minutes of my life, Scott called Murphy back. He listened for a few minutes. "Try again in another fifteen." He hung up.

Jack slowly slipped his hand in his pocket. "Get him talking," he whispered.

"Why'd you kill Bruce?" I asked, then smiled as Jack's pocket flickered. Hopefully, he'd called Murphy, and whoever was on the other end would figure out what was happening and not make a sound.

"Because he knew too much. Couldn't keep his nose out of things. Same as you two, and these nosy ladies. Always asking questions. I lost my job because of all of you."

"You lost your job because you cheated."

"What part of 'no talking' do you not understand?"

"Are you on medication?" I arched a brow. "For your mental state?"

His face turned a frightening shade of red, but he remained in his seat. "You aren't too bright, are you? I see what you're doing." He waved the gun around. "Trying to distract me so all of you can overpower me. Well, it isn't working."

Scott started to get to his feet but grabbed another glass of tea instead. "I might have to risk one of you running off. There's a plate of sandwiches on the kitchen table I could really use right now."

The dining room curtains were fully open, and he'd have to go through there to get to the kitchen. "You have the gun," I said. "You can see us from in there. Get them yourself."

"Nah, you get them." He laughed. "Go on. I'll even share."

With a cautious glance at Jack, I shuffled to the kitchen. At the table, I lifted the tray of sandwiches and stared out the window at Murphy, who nodded.

Good. I prayed the sniper's aim was true.

CHAPTER FOURTEEN

I spotted Ida's purse on the counter and set the tray beside it. Could I injure a person? I knew nothing about weapons. I retrieved the Taser and slipped it in the back of my waistband as I'd seen in the movies and pulled my shirt down to hide it.

Determined to get Scott in the line of fire, I picked up the tray of sandwiches and set it on the coffee table instead of offering it to him.

He scowled. "Ida, get me a sandwich."

As Ida kept his attention with food, I whispered to Jack that I had the Taser.

Shock crossed his features, but he gave me a long, slow nod before a smile teased at his lips.

"Go ahead, ladies, get one for yourselves. Someone give Jack and Angel something. Wouldn't want them to faint before I take them out." Scott bit into the cucumbe-and-cream-cheese sandwich. "Women's food."

"It's a women's gardening club." Ida shook her head and brought Jack and me each a sandwich.

Not my favorite, but I was starting to get hungry, and I had no idea how long before I'd get Scott in position. "Are you okay?" I asked Ida.

"I'm fine. Tell me you used your head in the kitchen."

I nodded and smiled. "Maybe Scott will let you bring us something to drink." Then she could slip out the back door.

"Not a chance," he said. "Go sit down."

Why hadn't a smart mouth like me gotten him angry enough to get up and threaten me yet? I had seriously lost my touch. "Why did you try to kill Johnson?"

"You mean he's still alive?" He sighed. "Because the idiot's conscience was bothering him. I really had hoped that you were stupid and wouldn't figure all this out."

"How did Johnson figure it out?"

Jack's hand inched toward my waist. Good. The Taser seemed to burn my skin.

"He saw the whole thing. Saw me putting ground hemlock in the frosting. Then, when Bruce ate the thing, he saw that too. I'd told him to stay in the car and that I'd deal with Bruce. The fool. How else could we make him not say anything?"

"You were the idiot," I said. "You shouldn't have done it with Johnson around."

"I had the opportunity!"

There was the anger. "Sometimes a person should think before he acts."

Jack's hand rested on the Taser. The only problem was, he now blocked the sniper's view.

Sweat trickled down my back. *Look away, Scott.* Jack was in the line of sight for too long. What if the sniper's finger twitched? Accidents happened, didn't they?

Ida must have seen the panic on my face. She suddenly knocked over a glass of tea.

Jack took the chance, pulled the weapon from my waistband, and stuck it in his.

I breathed a huge sigh of relief and almost sagged to the floor.

"Somebody get her a chair before she falls down." Scorn twisted Scott's features.

Mabel jumped to her feet and grabbed a kitchen chair. "Here, dear." After placing the chair for me, she rushed back to her friends, tossing Scott such a look of disdain it surprised me that he didn't burst into flames.

"Why try to frame me?"

"Again, opportunity." The man's expression screamed arrogance and condescension. "I'll use small words so you'll understand. I bought a donut from a bakery. Added a little something special to it. When we were at the bar, I told Bruce to come with me to check something behind your truck. Offered him the donut. The rest is history."

One of the women on the sofa collapsed and sagged against Ida. "Alice?" Ida shook her.

The woman didn't respond.

I made a move forward.

"Stop right there," Scott said. "There are plenty of women to tend to her."

"You've got to let a paramedic in here. Please." Worry choked me. "Don't let another innocent death be on your hands."

He thought for a moment. "Fine, but get over here by me."

I stepped in front of him. He pressed against my back, the gun pointed at my head. "Get a paramedic, Jack," he said. "Just one. Don't do anything stupid."

My legs started to tremble.

At the door, Jack spared me a glance then squared his shoulders. His hand gripped the doorknob. The door gave a slight creak as he pulled it open and stepped outside.

"We need a paramedic," he yelled. "Just one, or he'll shoot Angel."

Minutes later, two men with a gurney burst inside, Jack on their heels.

"I said one."

"What if she has to be taken out? Surely, you'll allow her medical help."

His grip on me tightened as one of the paramedics glanced at us. "Everyone else is fine. Get on with it. You can take her, but no one else."

The two medics lifted Alice to the stretcher and rushed her outside. One less life to worry about, I hoped. One of them said she was still breathing.

I yanked away from Scott. My skin crawled from his touch. The sandwich threatened to come back up as I returned to the window with Jack, being careful not to stand in front of the gap in the curtains.

The room grew silent again. What was Scott waiting for now? The fifteen minutes for Murphy to have made up his mind had passed.

Scott took a deep breath and reached for my phone.

The dining room window shattered as two armored SWAT team members crashed through. Before Scott could raise his weapon, a shot rang out, and he fell to the rug.

"My Persian carpet," Mabel wailed as blood started to pool.

Scott groaned, dropping his weapon and clutching his arm.

The SWAT team darted forward, each grasping an arm.

"Hey, that's where you shot me!" Scott squirmed.

Stoic-faced, they marched him outside. I threw myself into Ida's arms. "Are you sure you're okay?"

"One hundred percent. Jack, you may return Mabel's Taser. We no longer need it." She caressed my cheek. "What an adventure that was."

Murphy entered the house. "Good job on turning on your phone, Jack. We heard everything going on in here."

"Now you have the irrefutable evidence to convict Scott of killing Bruce and trying to kill Johnson," Jack said.

"Unfortunately, he succeeded. He's got two murders on his head. Johnson passed this morning." Murphy shook his head. "Senseless. We'll need your statements. You can either stay inside or come out."

"Outside." I didn't think I'd enter Mabel's house again for a good long while. "Is Alice okay?"

"She just fainted." He smiled. "We had a lucky day."

Jack and I followed him out but stopped on the porch. Jack's expression grew serious. "All this has made me think."

"Oh?"

He put his hands on my shoulders. "I don't want to be friends anymore, Angel."

My heart fell. "Why not?"

"Because I think I want to give more than friends a try." The twinkle returned to his eyes. "What do you say?"

"I most definitely say yes." Just like that, all the tension from the last few days slipped from my shoulders. A future getting to know Jack without a murder looming over us sounded fantastic. A handsome boyfriend, a growing business—the future seemed bright indeed.

Cynthia Hickey is a multipublished and bestselling author of cozy mysteries and romantic suspense. She has taught writing at many conferences and small writing retreats. She and her husband run the publishing press Winged Publications, which includes some of the CBA's most well-known authors. They live in Arizona and Arkansas, snowbirds with two dogs and one cat. They have ten grandchildren who keep them busy and tell everyone they know that "Nana is a writer."
www.cynthiahickey.com

LETHAL SPUDS

LINDA BATEN JOHNSON

CHAPTER ONE

S hanice, look what someone did to Mr. Spuds."

My grandpa waved the Spudmobile's four-foot metal mascot, a cross between Mr. Potato Head and Mr. Peanut, which served as the symbol for his business. The metal sculpture held a board with the day's special. He pointed to the large block letters that proclaimed LETHAL SPUDS as the Wednesday offering.

"Bring Mr. Spuds inside. I have hot dishwater. Maybe they used a washable marker." I opened the door of the retired school bus that Tater, my grandpa, had converted into a food truck. The outside was green with several pictures of baked potatoes, a list of prices, and a drawing of Mr. Spuds saying, "We Cater Taters," in a speech balloon. The inside was organized for efficient and effective food preparation in a small space.

"Lethal spuds! How dare he! Lyman Ernst did this. I'm going to give him a piece of my mind."

"Oh no." I grabbed Tater's arm and pointed to the cluttered counters. "You're not going to escape work. Your rule is that no one leaves until this stainless steel interior gleams to mirror quality."

"Why would he do this? Lyman and I have been friends since we were kids. I don't get it." Tater grabbed a cloth from the dishwater and attacked the counter. "He's been telling church folks that the health and safety department needs to investigate me. His gossip campaign is killing our business."

I scrubbed the skulls and crossbones off the body of Mr. Spuds. "Might have been kids instead of Lyman. Anyway, you should calm down before you talk to him."

"Is that your prescription?" he asked.

"Nurses don't prescribe medicines, and besides, I gave up that career four months ago."

Retreating to Birch Tree had been my way of dealing with burnout from treating ICU patients. I felt guilty for leaving when the hospital remained short-staffed, but watching my mom die while on a ventilator robbed me of my will to continue my profession in critical care. I'd thought working with patients in the severe trauma section was my calling, but when my mother was admitted to the unit, things changed. I began to associate more closely with accident victims and their families, those paralyzed by falls, and stroke victims. Seeing other patients and their families in situations similar to mine, where life was so fragile, overwhelmed me. I left Augusta for the small town in rural Maine where Grandpa Tater lived, to reconsider my career choice.

For me, Tater's town seemed as idyllic as a Norman Rockwell painting in the middle of the last century, with sensible values and a place where everyone had loving and open hearts. But today my grandfather was saying negative things about his lifetime friend who had been a part of my life since the day I was born.

"Could your disagreement have anything to do with Helen?" I asked.

Tater rubbed the stainless steel fridge until it gleamed. "Don't think so."

"I thought Helen and Lyman were keeping company last year. Did you win the fair Helen's affection?"

"She's a nice lady." Tater's smile revealed a big gap between his upper front teeth.

I had a similar gap. My parents wanted me to get braces to push the teeth together, but I refused. That gap represented a bond of affection between Tater and me.

"Helen is very nice," I teased. "I see her every day, if you ever want me to pass a message to her."

"I can do my own talking, thank you," he said.

The subject of his lady friend had taken his mind off the defaced Mr. Spuds. I did see Helen every day, as she was my landlady. Helen Randall owned the quilting business on Main Street, which included two apartments above the shop. I rented one, and Helen's lone employee leased the other.

Over Tater's protests, I insisted on my private space instead of moving in with him. My decision hurt his feelings, but I needed peace and quiet after I left my career and hometown. I'd found even talking to loved ones required energy I didn't have after losing my mother and tending day after day to patients teetering between life and death. Here I alternated between solitude and hard work in the Spudmobile, and both restored my body and mind. Another restorative cure for me was singing. I'd always found music to be an excellent release and a way to rejuvenate my spirit, especially in a choir format, when I am "inside" the music, but recently my absolute joy came when singing in a trio at church.

"Looks like Mr. Spuds has a broken foot." I held up the metal man who had long rods on the bottom of his flat feet to push into the dirt so he could stand.

"That will be my excuse to go see Lyman. Manuel, who runs Lyman's garage, made Mr. Spuds for me. You know, Lyman's been stirring up trouble with Manuel too. Lyman promised to sell Manuel the business earlier this year then backed out. Lyman told Manuel that he could continue managing the shop and living in the house next door, but no sale. That was the big news here five months ago. Now, Lyman's picking on me."

"Grandpa, you're talking about Lyman. You can't be serious." I deliberately called him Grandpa instead of Tater to let him know how concerned I was about the rift in the friendship.

Birch Tree was one of those places where everyone knew everyone, and everyone knew everyone else's business. Lyman and Tater joined the army right after high school, served in the same unit, and returned home to start their lives. My grandpa married and had two children, but Lyman remained a lifelong bachelor. Growing up, I spent summers in Birch Tree with my grandparents and belonged there as much as in my Augusta home.

I eyed the inside of the Spudmobile. "Shipshape. Looks ready for another busy day tomorrow."

"You can handle it," he said.

"We can handle it," I corrected. "Tater, let me talk to Lyman about Mr. Spuds. You two have been friends forever. I don't want you saying something you'll regret."

"He started the trouble." Tater looked around the inside of the gleaming food truck. "Shanice, I'm going to take a vacation."

"Vacation? You take time off when the food court park closes for the winter. This is June." To prove my point, I pointed at the blue-lettered calendar hanging above the interior menu board.

"Changing things up. I'm taking time in June this year." His smile and easygoing nature won most people to his side, but he wasn't smiling, and his determined tone told me he wasn't joking.

"I'll buy you an ice cream cone, and you can tell me why you're planning to leave during the food court's peak business season." I tossed my brown-and-green apron into the laundry bin and grabbed my wallet. "Should we ask Helen if she wants to join us?"

"Sure. Helen likes strawberry." He tucked Mr. Spuds under his arm. "I'll put this guy in the trunk, pick up Helen, and meet you at the Creamery."

"Shouldn't you call her?"

He chuckled. "Helen's expecting me."

The short walks to and from work provided the high points of my days. The mix of freshly turned dirt, mown grass, and outdoor grills sending forth mouthwatering aromas of burgers, brats, and hot dogs would make even the grouchiest person smile. I loved seeing showy stands of purple iris and orange oriental poppies, birds circling over the town's lake, and youngsters heading for the fishing pier with nothing more than a pole and a container of worms. In June, I believed the sign that greeted people entering my home state—WELCOME TO MAINE, THE WAY LIFE SHOULD BE.

My merry attitude melted when I spied Lyman sitting on the bench outside the Creamery, eating a chocolate sundae. Best to face the man before Tater arrived.

"Mr. Ernst, may I join you?"

Lyman, who wore his signature bow tie and jacket even on the most oppressive summer days, shifted to the end of the bench to give me a place to sit. "Pretty formal today. You always call me Uncle Lyman. Where's Tater?"

"He'll be along soon. He's. . ." I hesitated, not wanting to mention Helen. "Well, Mr. Spuds suffered damage today. Someone covered his body with skulls and crossbones, painted a patch over one eye, and put the words *Lethal Spuds* on the daily special board."

"Is that so?" Lyman hadn't slowed his ice cream eating, and his sundae was nearly gone.

"Who would do such a thing?" I asked.

"I hear some people got sick after eating at the Spudmobile. Some people think the health inspector should shut down the business," Lyman said.

"Then 'some people' should identify themselves. Uncle Lyman, what's going on between you and Tater?"

"There's your grandfather," Lyman said.

I waved as Tater pulled up in his Toyota Camry and postponed my peacemaking endeavor for another day. I'd allowed Lyman's comments to get under my skin, and I was a tiny bit gratified to see disappointment register on his face when he saw Tater open the passenger-side door and offer his hand to Helen Randall.

Over the years visiting Birch Tree, I had watched Helen's hair go from brown to brown with silver streaks, and now it was silver with brown streaks. But it was always impeccably arranged. She stood almost five nine, which I thought was a perfect height for Tater, who was a couple of inches over six feet. Tater's physique was rounded, Helen's was spare. Tonight she wore navy slacks, a navy-and-green top, and sneakers. She wore comfortable shoes because she stood most of her days. Helen helped regular and returning clients in her shop, which drew customers from as far as Boston. A master quilter, she kept samples of her personal work on the walls, which needed constant replenishing. Buyers snatched up her offerings because they admired the workmanship and the colorful designs.

Helen grabbed my hand and smiled broadly, showing off even, white teeth. "Shanice, thanks for inviting me to join you. What's your favorite flavor? I think about switching from strawberry, but when I get to the head of the line, that's what I order."

Lyman tossed his empty sundae container in the garbage. "Tater, Helen."

Tater started for Lyman, but I blocked my grandpa's way, and Lyman slid behind the wheel of his Cadillac without looking back.

I returned to Helen's ice cream question. "I order something different every time, but Tater's stuck on mint chocolate chip. Lucky for me, Iris works here and gives me samples."

When Tater opened the Creamery door, we saw a long line. Iris, the high soprano in our trio, bent over the tubs, scooping out servings for little sluggers, both boys and girls, in uniforms with ERNST GARAGE on the back.

"I'll be right with you," Iris said without lifting her head.

Helen patted my arm. "Too bad Winnie isn't here. You could treat the customers to a song. You three girls sing like angels. Your hymns are the high point of Sunday service for me. What do you have planned for this week?"

Tater rocked back and forth from heel to toe, looking a bit uncomfortable and staring at the empty spot where Lyman had parked.

"William has a wonderful voice too." Helen patted Tater's arm.

I cocked my head. "You call him William?"

Helen laughed. "Your grandfather has a distinctive name. William Henry Williams. He also has a good voice. When he was younger, he used to sing in church. We called him Hank Williams. Do you remember people calling you that, William?"

Tater stuffed his hands into his pockets. "I do. I think Iris is finishing up the orders for the kids."

"Hank Williams? Tater, I never knew you were called Hank Williams. Hank makes more sense than William Williams. I always thought it was strange that your parents named you William Williams."

Helen waved a dismissive hand. "That wasn't so uncommon back then, was it, William? We knew Jack Jacksons, John Johnsons, and other William Williamses. I think it was a fad for a time."

"I like the nickname I have now," Tater said. "You know how I got it?"

I did. Everyone in Birch Tree did, but my grandfather loved telling the story, and he rolled out the familiar tale again.

"I was a fussy baby, and one day when my auntie was holding me at the dinner table, she managed to get some mashed potatoes past my lips. Auntie said I looked shocked, said 'Mmm,' and opened my mouth wide. She kept shoveling potatoes into me and announced she planned to nickname me Tater. People called me that before I could even sit up by myself. I've loved taters ever since, in any form or fashion."

Helen nudged him. "I think Iris is ready for us to order."

"Evening, Iris. We'll have three cones. A double scoop of mint chocolate chip, a single strawberry, and whatever Shanice wants."

I eyed the containers. "I'll have a single cherry jubilee, please."

Iris pushed up her oversize glasses and waited.

"No, butter pecan," I said.

Iris, a seventeen-year-old with short curly hair dyed sunlight yellow, wore more makeup than her mother approved of. She completed the orders for Tater and Helen before peering at me. "Do you need to taste test?"

"No. I'll take the cookies and cream. Final decision." I stepped back.

Despite her youth, Iris possessed an abundance of confidence. God had given her a beautiful voice, pure, clear, and clean. Singing with her was a true pleasure. I provided the melody, Winnie Green, the alto or lower harmony, and Iris, the high soprano. Singing with the other two for church each week soothed and invigorated me and contributed to the healing I'd experienced here in Birch Tree. Rehearsals and praising God with church songs reopened a channel of communication with my Creator that I couldn't explain.

I accepted the cookies and cream. "'It is well with my soul,'" I sang after tasting my first bite.

Iris sang back, "'Praise God from whom all blessings flow.'"

My heart felt light until I remembered promising Tater that I'd pay a visit to Lyman to find out what was going on with him and why he was trying to sabotage his good friend's Spudmobile business.

CHAPTER TWO

As a nurse, I'd worked the second shift, and my body battled the transition to the early hours as Tater's food truck helper. I yawned as I riffled through my bag, checking for phone, keys, tissues, and lip balm. Before I closed my door, Nila Tran emerged from her unit across the landing. The two of us occupied identical apartments above the quilt shop on Main Street and shared the joint landing and staircase to the street level, but I'd never been in her place, and she hadn't visited mine.

"Morning, Nila."

"Shanice." Her smile didn't reach her eyes as she nodded to me, but they opened wide when she touched her neck. "My *ngoai*'s necklace." She flung open her apartment door and hurried back inside.

Waiting for her to return, I peeked into the room. Her place looked as sterile as an operating theater. I'm neat but not a neat freak. Nila wasn't the talkative type, but I felt uncomfortable with only name acknowledgments when we met. I hoped to see something within her apartment that might help me start a conversation. Fresh flowers graced the small dining table, and a framed map appeared to be the lone wall decoration.

Nila returned to the landing and fingered the carved wooden beads around her neck before shutting the door and inserting the key.

"I don't bother with keys here in Birch Tree," I said as we started down the stairs together.

"You should," she said.

"I noticed you have a map on the wall." I waited for her to respond.

"My country."

"Vietnam, right? My grandpa and Lyman Ernst served there."

"You call destroying my family's village a service?" She punctuated her bitter remark with a derisive snort. "My grandparents lived in Quang Nam province along the coast. When they applied for asylum after losing everything, officials told them you sometimes must destroy a village to save it in war. Can you believe that?"

Determined to be pleasant, I persevered with a different topic. "I've noticed you always wear that necklace."

Her fingers touched the individual beads as if saying a rosary. "It belonged to my ngoai. That's our word for grandmother. She was wearing this necklace when she fled. She gave it to my mother, who passed it on to me. I can't chat. I'm opening the quilt shop today." Nila turned to the quilt store's front door on Main Street.

So much for becoming better acquainted with my neighbor. The Tran family history with Birch Tree went back fifty years. Helen Randall's mother, Sarah, became a peace advocate when her husband died in the early days of the twenty-year Vietnam War, leaving her a widow to raise baby Helen alone. Community members either lauded or loathed Sarah's strong opinion about the war but admired the actions backing her stance. She offered to share her home with Vietnamese refugees in the resettlement program, and Nila's grandparents lived with Sarah until they got on their feet and moved. When Nila returned to Birch Tree several years ago, Helen offered her a job and rented her the apartment over the quilt shop.

The walk to the Spudmobile took ten minutes from my apartment in town. I stopped at Dream Donuts, the donut truck in the food park, for chocolate-glazed donuts, a dietary habit Tater and I should break. My clothes fit a little snugger since my move to Birch Tree. As a nurse, I'd done well over my ten thousand steps a day. As a food truck worker, my step count was minimal.

Tater flung open the door. "Got your coffee ready, Shanice."

Potatoes waited for scrubbing in the sink. A single oven rack already held rows of potatoes, but we always started with two.

"What's the special today?" I accepted the green mug with the Mr. Spuds logo and held out the donut box.

"Super Mashed Mixture." Tater snagged a donut but continued to stand, shifting his weight from foot to foot. "Been thinking about Lyman all morning. I don't get it. Since first grade, we've been inseparable—went to church summer camps, played football, and got into trouble together. Then we joined up, went overseas, and served in the same unit side by side. He was best man at my wedding when I married your grandmother."

I refilled my mug and held the pot toward Tater. "Could it be Helen? A love triangle?"

He shook his head. "With all we've been through, I don't think so. Lyman did ask Helen to marry him. I didn't start courting Helen until long after she turned Lyman down. I wouldn't do that to my best friend. Helen wouldn't bad-mouth anyone, but she said Lyman showed a different side of his personality after she refused him."

The lone donut in the box called my name, and I grabbed it. "I can't imagine Uncle Lyman doing anything mean to you, Helen, or anyone. It's not in his nature."

"Helen said he continued to offer her unrequested advice after she refused him. She knows Lyman and I are like brothers. Helen thinks he was jealous."

"Jealousy is called the green-eyed monster," I said. "Want me to clean potatoes, or make the mixture?"

"I'd better do the special. I know the secret of how much cream cheese, sour cream, butter, and—"

"Stop. Write down the recipe. There might be a time when you're not here and I'll need to make the Super Mashed Mixture by myself."

"Maybe so, but I'll do it today. You clean those potatoes for baking," Tater said. "Lyman left a phone message for me to meet him tonight at nine at the lake gazebo."

"Good. You two can settle your differences." I slipped the apron opening over my neck, tied the strings at the waist, and picked up the scrubber.

"I can't be there at nine. Got something to do. You go in my place. Ask Lyman to tell you everything."

I shrugged and nodded but wondered what could be more critical to Tater than mending a damaged relationship with his lifelong friend. I kept my mouth closed and my hands busy.

"We have another problem. The young upstart who runs the food court, Donald Price, is paying us a visit today. He called this morning. He needs to talk to me about permits and complaints. The guy told me the charges are serious. Donald wouldn't even have this job if his parents hadn't given it to him."

My grandfather's fidgety behavior was out of character. I'd always known him to be jovial, upbeat, and optimistic.

"And then there's Mr. Spuds." Tater continued his downbeat litany. "It's silly, but I'd like to have him back in his usual spot outside the Spudmobile. I took him over to Manuel Ortiz at the garage last night. He promised to make our little metal friend look like new." Tater glanced at the clock. "We have almost an hour before we open. Let's put the potatoes in the oven and then go see if Manuel has finished the Spudmobile's mascot."

The idea seemed foolish to me, but Tater removed his apron, shoved two loaded racks of potatoes into the oven, and jingled his keys.

"Shouldn't I stay here, since the oven's on?"

"They should be okay. We won't be gone long."

Tater parked his car across the street from the Ernst Garage. "You know Lyman tinkered with cars his whole life. After returning from Nam, he went to an auto mechanic school while I earned my teaching certification. Now his arthritis keeps him from the shop floor. Manuel does the shop work, and Lyman does the books."

"All the bays are full, with cars waiting."

"This is a good business. Manuel's a wizard with anything that runs on gasoline. People come here from all over the state. A good mechanic is as hard to find as a good woman." Tater grinned at his joke.

Manuel, who wore Ernst Garage overalls, pulled a rag from his back pocket, wiped his hands, and waved for us to follow him. His salt-and-pepper hair was full and thick and the same color as his toothbrush-style mustache, while his thick eyebrows retained their dark brown color. He was a stocky man with a full face and laugh lines around his eyes, but he wore a serious look today.

Manuel pointed to Mr. Spuds. "What do you think?"

"I'd say he looks as good as the day you made him. Thanks, Manuel. Do I pay you or Lyman?"

Manuel shrugged. "I wouldn't have charged you a cent, but I'm not the boss. Lyman said twenty bucks."

Tater grinned and pulled out his wallet.

Manuel put the bill in an envelope and wrote my grandfather a receipt. "Tater, you know Lyman better than anyone in this town.

Can you explain why he's been acting so mean lately? We had a handshake deal that I'd take over the garage this past January. Then he changed his mind. I'm doing all the work, and he's putting all the profit in his pockets. We'll have two kids in college next year, and I don't want them to have to start life with buckets of debt."

Tater shook his head. "Lyman's telling folks the Spudmobile's food is no good. I think he's the one who marked up Mr. Spuds and then asked me to pay to repair him."

Manuel thumbed toward the house next to the garage. "My wife's more upset than I am. When Lyman reneged on our agreement, he pulled the rug out from under our plans. We're not big spenders, but we want to provide a good education for our boys. The garage would let us do that."

"So John's off to college next year? Time flies. I taught him in middle school. He's a good boy, Manuel. You and your wife can be proud of your kids."

Manuel basked in my grandfather's compliments. "Both aim to become pharmacists. When they start talking about drugs with names as long as my arm and their side effects, I'm lost."

I spoke up. "Some patients go to several doctors and receive prescriptions that can cause adverse reactions when taken together. Fortunately, most use the same pharmacy, and a conscientious pharmacist who watches for drug interactions is invaluable."

"Shanice is a nurse. After she battled severe health conditions in the ICU, she came to Birch Tree for some R and R and to make delicious spuds." Tater squeezed my shoulder.

"We did leave potatoes in the oven." I tapped my watch.

"Right," Tater said. "Manuel, thanks for repairing Mr. Spuds, and when I figure out what's up with Lyman, I'll let you know."

Tater didn't speak on the ride back but groaned when he saw a black Jeep parked in the Spudmobile's assigned parking slot.

A young man in black jeans and a gray lightweight sweater paced in front of the food truck. His thick, black-rimmed glasses matched his black goatee and the soul patch under his lower lip. I estimated him to be in his late twenties, but his plump face showed no character lines.

"I've been waiting." He punctuated his nasal remark with a sneeze into his handkerchief. "I don't like waiting."

"You didn't set an appointment time. If you had, I'd have been here. Donald Price, my granddaughter, Shanice Williams." Tater pushed the tines of Mr. Spuds into the soft dirt near the door. "Had to pick up my mascot. Someone tried to ruin him, just like someone's trying to ruin my business."

"That someone might be you, Mr. Williams. As the food truck court manager, I'm getting complaints about your Spudmobile."

"Who's complaining?" Tater demanded.

"I've received calls and notes. People don't have to give their names or sign the letters. I hear this place is known as Lethal Spuds now."

"Should I check on the potatoes?" I asked.

"We'll get back to work when Donald leaves," Tater said.

Donald pulled out his phone and used his thumbs to enter notes. "I have a file on you. As a courtesy, I'm letting you know that your city permits are not in order. Address them before the end of the week. Now I'd like to inspect the interior."

"Be my guest. You won't find anything amiss." Tater unlocked the door.

Donald entered first and looked over his shoulder. "Found something—an open donut box. Leaving trash on the counter attracts bugs." He touched the oven door. "And the oven is on! You left the premises with the oven on?"

The question seemed rhetorical, so neither of us answered. Tater and I watched Donald make more notes and open cabinets and drawers.

Before leaving, Donald pulled a folded paper with Tater's name on it from his back pocket. "I found this taped to your door.

It says, 'Tater, I ate your loaded spud yesterday and threw up all night. Are you trying to poison your neighbors?'"

"You read something that was addressed to me?" Tater reached for the note.

"Isn't mail, wasn't sealed, and the Spudmobile occupies a rented spot. Anyone could read it." Donald folded the block-printed message and offered it to Tater.

Seeing Tater's tight neck muscles and fisted hands, I reached for the scathing letter. "Donald, thank you for the information about the permits. We'll take care of that this week. Tater, I'm sure our guest has other food trucks to visit."

"I do. I don't know why my parents invested in this property. I have to protect their financial interests. This place is a lawsuit waiting to happen. I've received bad reports about the Pretzel Place too." Before leaving, he turned to Tater. "I've warned you."

The phone rang with take-out orders for our Super Mashed Mixture. I took orders from Manuel at the Ernst Garage and Nila at the quilt shop, a request from Lyman at his house by the lake, and an order for the mayor's office at city hall.

Instead of helping, Tater sank onto the stool and sat, head down. He looked deflated and defeated. "My life savings are in the Spudmobile."

I took orders at the window, put together take-out orders, and replenished supplies while Tater sat. Comforting my grandfather felt like a role reversal. "Tater, my friend Winnie works at city hall in the permit section. I'll ask her to help me file the documents. We'll figure this out. I can handle the business today if you want to go rest or take a walk."

"And you'll meet with Lyman tonight?"

"I can, but I think you should," I said.

"You do it. I'm going to Helen's, and then I have a trip to make." He walked out without another word.

When the lunch rush shifted into high gear, I called Helen to see if she could spare Nila for an hour to deliver orders. Tater decided to pull his disappearing act on a particularly busy day. When Donald Price returned, I plastered on a smile. "Do you want to try our special of the day?"

"Is Tater here?" he asked.

"Gone, and I have delivery orders piling up." I waved to the bags on the counter behind me. "Helen said the quilt shop could spare Nila for an occasional hour if I got in a pinch. Would you mind taking them there? They're all the Super Mashed special. The boxes are numbered, and I have a list here of who gets them."

Donald hesitated then held out his hand. "I'll take them."

His kindness seemed out of character, but reminding myself of the adage about not looking a gift horse in the mouth, I handed the take-out parcels to Donald Price and prayed I wouldn't regret it.

CHAPTER THREE

After turning the sign from open to closed and bringing Mr. Spuds inside, I stared at the sink full of dishes. Lyman would be waiting for Tater at the gazebo at nine, and I craved a soak in a hot tub and some time for meditation. Snapping my fingers to have today's cleaning and tomorrow's prep work done magically would be nice, but I didn't have superpowers. I grabbed a soda with caffeine and attacked the chores.

The meeting with Lyman intrigued me. He'd asked my brother and me to call him Uncle Lyman because he said Tater was like his brother, which made Tater's children and grandchildren kin.

Even when I was little, I sensed a sadness about Lyman. Tater said his friend never got over the treatment soldiers received here in the States when they returned from Vietnam.

Although Lyman worked as a mechanic and grew a successful business by having grease under his nails, he always wore a jacket and bow tie when he went out. Tater teased his friend about his soldier's ramrod-straight posture and meticulous attire, and Lyman asserted that a man had to look respectable to gain respect. Their banter was a habitual thing and a symbol of affection. I did not understand how any conflict had escalated into a major row and vowed to do my best as their intermediary.

Maine's late spring evenings reluctantly ceded to a dusky light at nine, leaving enough brightness for me to glimpse the hillside gazebo that overlooked the lake. I was surprised not to see Lyman's silhouette, because punctuality meant five minutes early to him.

Breathing out a sigh of relief, I slowed my steps, noted a hawk soaring, and listened to children's giggles coming from the playground. Birch Tree's slower pace and friendly ambience proved curative to my body and soul. I softly sang the hymn "There Is a Balm in Gilead," substituting Birch Tree for Gilead. Taking a leave of absence had been the right decision. I missed the healing part of nursing, but my permanent critical care assignment presented an intense and unabated bombardment on my emotions. After facing the daily issues in the ICU, repairing the split between Tater and Lyman seemed a simple task.

I was still singing when I reached the gazebo and saw Lyman. He lay unmoving on the concrete floor.

I screamed his name then yelled, "Call 911!"

"Uncle Lyman, open your eyes!" I did a quick assessment. He had a bump on his head, which I chalked up to his fall. An aneurysm? A heart attack? I checked the carotid artery, then the wrist, and detected no pulse, but he was still warm, so I checked his airway, tilted his head back, and began CPR. I talked to him as I performed chest compressions. I reminded him how much our family loved him. I encouraged him to fight. I told him how much I'd loved it when he dressed up as the Tin Man and took me trick-or-treating. Why hadn't I ever told him that?

Large hands pulled at me. "We've got him, miss."

The local police officers, the volunteer fire crew, and the town's doctor filled the gazebo.

I staggered to the pavilion's wraparound bench and sat. The awfulness of finding Lyman washed over me. He was a beloved uncle figure, a part of my life since childhood. I bit my lip, and tears filled my eyes. Tater would be devastated.

"Shanice." Someone shook my shoulder, and another person clasped my hands.

"Winnie? Iris?"

My fellow trio singers helped me to my feet. Iris put a blanket over my shoulders while Winnie led me by the hand to her car. In a small town, people follow the sound of sirens, willing to offer comfort, prayers, and help to the person in need. I shouldn't have been surprised to see my friends, but I was.

"He's gone, Shanice."

"No. He was warm when I found him." I struggled with them and finally broke free to go back to where the firemen were putting Lyman's body on a stretcher.

The doctor shook his head. "I'm sorry."

"He wanted to meet here to talk about something. Now I'll never know what he had on his mind. He wasn't my uncle, not my real uncle, but as real as any uncle could have been. What do you think happened?"

"I'll let you and Tater know when I know. You should get some rest."

"I don't think I'll be able to," I said.

Winnie pulled me aside and said to the doctor, "We'll take Shanice to her apartment."

"I should go to Tater's," I said.

"Pastor Brandon is on his way to your grandfather's," Winnie said. "We're taking you to your apartment. You're shaking. Since you're a nurse, you know you're in shock." She secured my seat belt before getting into the driver's seat.

The staircase to the landing was only wide enough for two, so Winnie went ahead and opened the door. Iris held on to me as we took the steps one at a time. My friends tried to put me into bed, but I balked.

"I'm okay," I said.

"I'm making hot tea with lots of sugar for you." Winnie filled a cup with water and punched numbers on the microwave panel.

"Lyman and Tater quarreled. They didn't have a chance to patch up their differences." I pulled the blanket I wore as a shawl closer. I thought about my mom's prolonged health battle. She'd been able to see her family and hear them offer loving expressions. Lyman didn't have any grace period. He was alive in the morning and dead by evening.

Winnie handed me a mug. "Sip some first. Your microwave settings may be different than mine."

Iris placed a kitchen chair in front of me and lifted my legs to rest on the seat. She pressed the bridge on her oversize glasses, moving them back into place, and peered around the apartment, searching for another task.

"Why don't you make tea for yourselves? I'd like it if you stayed for a bit." My cell phone trilled its signature ring.

My friends fussed with tea making while I talked.

"Thanks. He said he was going on a trip." I pushed the end button. "That was Pastor Brandon. Tater's not at home."

"Try his cell. He'll want to know about Lyman," Iris said.

I hit the speed-dial number for Tater, but his phone went straight to voice mail. I turned to Winnie and Iris. "Tater's gone and not answering his phone."

"Where did he go?" Iris asked.

"I don't know. He was secretive about his destination." I pictured Tater sitting slump-shouldered on the stool in the Spudmobile. "He was pretty despondent this morning—worried about the Spudmobile's profits and glitches with permits. Lyman's death will hit Tater hard."

"And the Spudmobile's problems will become your problems. I can help with permit paperwork," Winnie said.

"We're the terrible trio—one for all and all for one." Iris held out a hand, but neither of us placed a hand on top of hers. She shrugged when her attempt at lifting the mood fell flat.

"I should call my dad. We all considered Lyman family," I said.

"Why don't you wait until tomorrow? It's nearly midnight. More tea?" Winnie took my empty mug.

"No thanks. You two don't have to babysit me. You should go home."

"I can work at the Spudmobile tomorrow until I have to report to the Creamery—if you plan to open," Iris said.

"I will. I can't sit around here all day."

Winnie nodded. "Let Iris help you with the food, and let me sort out the permit problems Tater has."

"The problems with the Spudmobile seem inconsequential now. Donald Price gave us several bits of good news today." I held up fingers to number Donald's list. "Our permits are not in order. Tater's business garnered negative reports filed with the Board of Health. The food truck court management has received complaints about Spudmobile food. And he's raising the rents for the plots."

"Permits are issued through the office where I work. I'll check to see which ones weren't filed and which need an update." Winnie kissed my forehead. "Try to sleep."

I hugged my friends goodbye and went to bed, but I didn't sleep.

When I stopped at Dream Donuts the next morning, the co-owner, Ida, quizzed me about Lyman's death. I choked up and hurried to the sanctuary of the Spudmobile, tears threatening to spill down my cheeks. I lifted my head and blinked to keep them from escaping. I'd seen extreme pain, grief, and death in the hospital, but seeing Lyman's lifeless body was unexpected and personal. I wondered who would oversee his affairs. Tater was the logical choice, and he was gone. Where was he, and why hadn't he told me his plans?

True to her word, Iris arrived as I positioned our mascot, Mr. Spuds, with the sign for today's unique baked potato—chicken à la king. I tossed her an apron and pointed to the donut box and coffeepot.

"I don't drink coffee, and I just had breakfast. What should I do?" Iris asked.

Thankful to focus on food prep, I set Iris to cleaning the large baking potatoes while I worked on the chicken à la king and peeled smaller potatoes for our mashed specialties. I finished both jobs before Iris filled one tray for the oven. The interior of the food truck, a converted school bus, meant tight quarters, and somehow small-framed Iris took up a lot of real estate. When I needed to move from one spot to another, she would stand up and stretch or choose that precise moment to turn and check the menu board or the clock. She'd offered to help, but I think her willingness had waned.

Peppering my morning conversation with "Excuse me," "I need to get to the fridge," "Behind you," and "Squeeze in," I was ready to fire my volunteer before noon. Tater and I managed to navigate the space without bumping into each other, and Iris was half Tater's size. I suggested that she open the table umbrellas and check the garbage bins to get her outside.

By my third coffee, the food was ready, and I flipped the sign to indicate we were open for business. Many townsfolk stopped to pay Tater condolence calls concerning the death of his best friend. This mandated I explain Tater's absence, leading to additional exchanges clogging up the line of paying customers. My helper's skill in taking orders, plating food, and serving was as abysmal as her food prep, but we managed to fill the customer requests.

Winnie arrived after the lunchtime peak with a fistful of papers. "Donald Price told you the truth. To operate a food truck in this county, you need eleven permits. Overwhelming, right? Tater only filed for seven, so he's been operating illegally. Price is digging through all the food truck files, not just the Spudmobile's. I don't know whether he's trying to avoid problems or create them."

"What should I do?" I asked.

"First, you need a food handler's permit, Shanice. Technically, you shouldn't be here. Tater didn't file for a special event permit, the fire certificate, or the parking permit. Even though all the vendors pay Donald's food truck fees, each must file a separate parking permit with Birch Tree. I have all the paperwork. The ugly truth is the Spudmobile business has overdue fines for noncompliance."

Iris tugged at my sleeve. "Want me to do the paperwork? I might be better at that than preparing and serving food."

"Thanks, but that's a job I'll need to tackle," I told my reluctant potato preparer. "I appreciate your work today. You should probably rest since you're working at the Creamery tonight."

Iris sang the first line of "My Soul Finds Rest in God Alone."

Her hymn choice made me smile. "Mine too, Iris. I appreciate your help."

After she left, Winnie leaned forward. "I added up all filing fees and back penalties. You're looking at over five thousand dollars."

"What?"

"And Donald Price is pushing for compliance before the summer promotion he has planned," Winnie said. "Don't be surprised if he makes you close the Spudmobile until you get your food handler's certificate."

"He didn't mention it yesterday, and he actually agreed to help me out by taking lunch orders to Nila to deliver."

Winnie grinned. "That doesn't sound like Donald Price to me. Are you sure he got them to Nila and didn't mess them up?"

"All the deliveries he took were for the same thing—the Super Mashed Mixture. I asked him to take them to Helen's shop. She'd offered to let Nila help out when needed. Didn't get any complaints, so I assume the deliveries went smoothly. One was earmarked for city hall."

"I didn't notice a delivery from the Spudmobile, but that doesn't mean it didn't arrive. I need to get back, Shanice. Once you complete the paperwork and have the payments, I'll expedite the filing." Winnie hurried toward city hall, her brown curls bouncing as she walked.

Other food trucks had continual lines while the Spudmobile's sputtered. Had the Lethal Spuds posting and negative comments killed Tater's business?

———————

A banging on the Spudmobile interrupted my quiet afternoon of filling forms instead of orders. I leaned out the window, and the man wearing a white dress shirt and cargo pants held up a badge.

"Jerry Rilke, York Police detective. Are you Shanice Williams?"

"I am."

"Our station received a call from the coroner about the suspicious death of Lyman Ernst. Since you discovered the body, I'm starting my inquiry with you. Close up, and we'll go to the gazebo where you found Mr. Ernst's body."

"I'll miss the dinner crowd. Can this wait?"

"Murder doesn't wait," the detective said.

His line sounded quite dramatic, which made me wonder if he'd used it before. Surely he didn't have a plethora of murders to investigate in York, Maine. I took my time, moved Mr. Spuds inside, and locked the door, mentally calculating how far in the red the Spudmobile would be when I balanced today's till.

A "Rock-a-Bye, Baby" ringtone sounded, and Detective Rilke fished a phone from the side pocket of his cargo pants. I watched him from inside the Spudmobile to give him some privacy. The detective was a solidly built man who appeared to work out in his spare time. He had hazel eyes, and his shaved head was more prominent because of his sandy-colored beard and mustache.

"Hey, little man, can you help your mama with the baby until I get home? We can kick the soccer ball around. . . . We don't have to play soccer. We can play with your cars or put together a puzzle. Why don't you think about what you'd like to do? Let me talk to Mommy, please."

The detective's bargaining with his young adversary didn't appear to be going smoothly. I worked until the detective banged on the door again.

"Let's go." His voice was firm and strident, devoid of the honeyed softness he'd used on the phone.

We walked to the gazebo, and he bombarded me with questions along the way. At first, inquiries concerned my specific timing about the walk to the gazebo and anyone I saw along the way. Some details popped to the surface, but not enough to satisfy the detective. He had me stop at several spots to check my visual perspective of the park structure. Since the enclosed bottom of the circular building accommodated interior seating, I couldn't see Lyman's body until I was within five feet of the structure.

He stopped. "This is where you were when you saw him?" he asked.

"Yes. I saw Lyman, screamed his name, rushed inside, and checked for a pulse. When I didn't find one, I started CPR."

He moved ahead of me into the pavilion, settled on the wooden bench, and opened his tablet. "Why?" he asked.

"His body was warm to the touch. I yelled for someone to call 911 while I worked on Lyman."

"Could you have been mistaken?" Detective Rilke entered my answers.

"About?"

"The sequence of events. The local police mentioned a raised lump on Ernst's head." Detective Rilke waited.

"I saw the bump. I assumed it happened when he fell. What makes you think the death was suspicious?"

"He'd ingested sleeping pills, enough to put him to sleep permanently. Not many people planning to commit suicide set an appointment and then go to the meeting. They tend to stay at home, or at least somewhere comfortable."

"Sleeping pills? I never remember Lyman taking sleeping pills."

"The autopsy results showed the pills were mixed into the mashed potatoes. Did he order mashed potatoes from the Spudmobile yesterday?"

His insinuations were insulting, but the information he'd disclosed was unnerving. "I think you know the answer. But other people ate the special, and they didn't die. There were four delivery orders, and Lyman's was one of them."

"Did you drop them off?"

"No. Donald Price was supposed to take them to Nila Tran at the quilt shop, and she was going to deliver them for me."

"Was there a feud between your grandfather and Lyman Ernst?" The detective switched subjects.

"Maybe a misunderstanding. The two were lifelong friends. They would have worked things out."

"I heard Lyman complained about the Spudmobile's food quality."

"Are we talking hearsay or facts? It's hard to chase down gossip, isn't it?"

"I'm not in the business of gossip. The facts as I see them are your grandfather, William Williams, believed Lyman was spreading damaging information about his food. He agreed to meet Lyman last night. Instead of honoring his promise, he skipped town without telling anyone where he planned to go. Do those actions seem suspicious to you?"

"I know it was a misunderstanding," I protested.

"Then there's a scenario that implicates you, not your grandfather. You prepared the potatoes laced with sedatives and then went to meet Lyman on your grandfather's behalf. You suggested his death was a heart attack or an aneurysm. As you are a nurse, people believed you. Fortunately, the authorities ordered an autopsy."

"Lyman was like family. He's always been in my life. I wouldn't want to kill him any more than Tater would," I said.

"Would your grandfather benefit from his friend's death?" the detective probed.

"I have no idea. As far as I know, Lyman had no kin, but he was close with Manuel Ortiz, who manages the garage, and he liked everyone in town. He'd lived here all his life," I said. "Lyman and Tater were best friends. He showed up for all our family celebrations because he was one of us."

"Since Mr. Ernst was like family, I guess you were devastated when you learned the man had been diagnosed with B-cell acute leukemia from Agent Orange and had only a month to live."

"What?" I stumbled back and sank to a bench, and the harshness of Lyman's death washed over me again.

If Detective Rilke meant to shock me, he'd succeeded. The loons on Birch Tree Lake chose that moment to sound their haunting call, and I shivered.

"You didn't know?"

"No. Lyman had a heart scare around Christmas, and he'd developed a paunch. Tater blamed the meds Lyman's VA doctor prescribed."

The detective moved next to me and spoke softly. "Wanting to spare a good friend a painful, prolonged death would be understandable. Lyman went to the VA hospital in Augusta. That's where you worked, isn't it?"

"I worked in an Augusta hospital, but not the VA." My mind reeled. Had the prognosis caused the alteration in Lyman's behavior?

"You're a professional person. Why are you in Birch Tree working at a food truck?"

"Because my mom died in the ICU wing where I worked. I needed a break. The hospital administrator told me they would take me back as soon as I was ready."

"Did you ever think it was a good thing when one of your patients died?"

"Sometimes the end of suffering seems a blessing for the patient and their family."

Detective Rilke entered notes on his tablet. "I have more questions about your grandfather. Did you report him missing?"

"No. Tater told me he had to go somewhere. I didn't question him. He loved surprising people. I just thought he was cooking something up."

"And he left last night, before the discovery of Lyman's body." The detective checked his screen. "Pastor Brandon Caulder couldn't find Tater to tell him the news of Lyman Ernst's death."

I stood. "Tater would not be involved."

The "Rock-a-Bye, Baby" ring demanded Detective Rilke's attention again.

I paced while he engaged in baby talk with his little one. He had a sheepish expression on his face when he put his phone away.

"I don't mean to be disrespectful, but I need to finish cleaning up the Spudmobile and get ready for tomorrow," I told him.

"Fine, I need to get back home too. Don't make any out-of-town trips like your grandfather did."

I resented the insinuation, but I held my tongue.

CHAPTER FOUR

Solid and welcoming, the Birch Tree stone church with the cross on the metal roof pulled me like a magnet. The central section looked like a face with two elongated eyes, a round stained-glass window for a nose, and a wide wooden door painted bright red for the mouth. The wings on each side swept out like a long, trailing veil. Before the Civil War, local believers hauled stones to the construction site in horse-drawn carts and wagons, and this building was a testament to their faithfulness. The continuity of worshippers who sat in the pews we now occupied inspired and awed me.

Winnie and Iris waited for me in the choir room to rehearse for Sunday's service. We didn't need a pianist, because Iris has perfect pitch, which is good and bad, as she cringes when Winnie or I miss a note.

"We might want to go over some music for Lyman's service," Winnie said. She was engaged to Pastor Brandon, so she had the inside scoop. She informed us Lyman's burial would be at the Maine Veterans Memorial Cemetery in Augusta Wednesday afternoon after celebrating his life in this church that morning.

"You knew him, Shanice. Do you have any suggestions?" Iris thumbed through the hymnal listing of ideas for funeral services.

"He loved 'Blessed Assurance.' Lyman always requested that hymn when we sang as a group." I pictured past Thanksgivings and Christmases when our family gathered around the piano with my mother playing and Lyman adding his rich baritone to the melodies. This coming holiday season, those two precious faces would be absent.

"Good choice. Our whole community is reeling from the news. We could all use some blessed assurance," Winnie said.

Iris sang the notes for "Bless-ed" to give me the pitch, and I began the melody.

"'Blessed assurance, Jesus is mine! O what a foretaste of glory divine! Heir of salvation, purchase of God, born of His Spirit, washed in His blood.'" The words soothed me as we sang.

After an hour's practice, I asked if they wanted to go with me to Tater's house.

"Why?" Iris pushed her glasses up on her nose.

"A detective from York came to Birch Tree today. He said Lyman's death is questionable. He seems to suspect Tater or me. I denied Tater's involvement and defended him to the detective. . . ."

Winnie finished the thought I didn't want to verbalize. "But Tater's sudden departure, without explanation, has you worried."

I nodded.

"Let's go." Iris rubbed her hands together.

Even though the talented soprano was ten years younger, the age difference between us seemed exaggerated. She had just received her high school diploma this month, and I felt as if I'd lived two lifetimes during the past year. Still, I appreciated her unabashed eagerness to help.

Tater's house was within walking distance of the Main Street storefront shops. A sharp-angled roof and dormer windows relieved the home's boxy appearance. The steps from the sidewalk led to a porch deep enough for a swing on one side and two wicker chairs on the other.

"I'll go through the back and unlock the front for you." I hurried off before they could offer to join me.

Tater had been gone less than a week, and yet the place smelled abandoned. Turning lights on didn't dispel the gloom. I flipped the porch light switch and held the door for Winnie and Iris.

"If we're being detectives, what are we trying to detect?" Iris asked.

"Anything to tell us where he's gone and why. Tater never learned to use his phone for note-taking. He jotted things down on sticky pad sheets or scraps of paper. You two look in the kitchen and the den, and I'll check his bedroom."

His sleeping quarters were as tidy as the Spudmobile's interior at closing time, but a surprise awaited me in his closet. His good blue suit was gone. Tater had only one and called it his wedding and funeral outfit as he'd adopted more casual clothes for church or dining out. He might wear a button-down shirt and a sports coat and tie for services or a nice restaurant, but he reserved the suit for special occasions. Why would Tater take a suit with him? I hurried to see if my pals had discovered anything.

"Found something of yours." Winnie held up an envelope. "Isn't this where you worked?"

I took the letter that showed my hospital's return address in the upper left corner and ripped it open. The postmark showed a date in May.

"Is it important?" asked Winnie.

"A reminder that my leave is up at the end of June, and that they're still shorthanded. They're asking me to contact them about a restart date."

Iris whined, "Oh Shanice, you can't go."

"I don't think I can leave right now." I tucked the letter in my pocket and wondered why Tater hadn't mentioned it. "Did you find anything else?"

Winnie and Iris glanced at each other.

"Spill!" I ordered.

Iris pointed to a drawer filled with overdue notices and unpaid bills and handed me some papers. "Your grandfather is having financial problems."

The papers were Tater's bank statements. Both the savings and checking account totals showed declining balances over the past two years, and handwritten notes next to the amounts showed monies going out to cover shortfalls in the Spudmobile business. The records made a case for giving up the Spudmobile, but I knew the food truck was an extension of Tater's identity, and he'd be unwilling to let it go.

"Find anything else?"

"Not really," Iris said. "Your grandfather has a big pad of paper on his desk with scribbles all over it."

"I should look at that." After pulling out my phone, I took a picture. On the lower right corner, I spied an Augusta telephone number. Tater would have told me if he had planned a trip to Augusta, so I doubted that was his destination. And a trip to Augusta wouldn't require a suit. Where would he need his best attire?

I encouraged Iris and Winnie to head home, telling them I planned to stay a little longer, and they reluctantly said their goodbyes. They obviously relished participating in clandestine activities. After they left, I called my dad. I'd told my family about Lyman's death but not about Tater's unexplained absence. "Dad, sorry to call you so late."

"That's fine, honey. How are you holding up? Do you have information about the funeral?" The tone of his voice told me how much he worried about me, even though he still grieved for his wife of forty years.

"The funeral is Wednesday. I'll email the information."

"How's Tater? He must be taking it hard. He and Lyman were inseparable."

"Tater's not here. He went on a trip and didn't tell anyone where he was going. Did he say anything to you?"

"Not a word," Dad said. "I'm the son-in-law. He'd confide in you before me."

"He was secretive about the trip. I'm at his house now. He took his blue funeral and wedding suit."

"Did he?" Dad was quiet. I could picture him rubbing his chin and thinking. "Maybe he confided in someone else. Lyman is the only one who comes to mind."

"Dad, Tater has a girlfriend. She doesn't know where he went either."

"So Tater has a girlfriend? He's sure kept that quiet." Dad sighed. "But tell me about Lyman's service. Your brothers and I want to attend. In fact, I have Lyman's eulogy. He and Tater wrote their eulogies and gave them to your mother to hold. Strange thing to do, if you ask me. I ran across them when I was going through her papers. Never dreamed either Lyman or Tater would need them this soon."

"Tater leaving town right before Lyman died doesn't look good."

"The two events are unrelated, I'm sure," Dad said. "Tater would never leave if he'd known Lyman's heart was about to give out."

"The detective is treating the death as suspicious. He's hinting that Lyman's life might have ended sooner than it should have."

"That's nonsense. Who would want to hurt Lyman?"

Instead of telling my dad that the detective considered both Tater and me as possible suspects, I echoed his statement. "My thoughts exactly, Dad. Who would want to hurt Lyman?"

"Well, I'll email that eulogy to you. I'm sure Tater will want to speak at the funeral. He won't miss Lyman's service. You doing okay, sweetie?"

"Still reeling from Lyman's death, and the hospital sent a letter saying they want me back the first of July. I think I need more time. Can't see my future in Birch Tree loading baked potatoes with toppings, but I'm not ready for the patient floors yet."

"You could work in a doctor's office, as a school nurse, or maybe for some big company," he suggested.

"That may be where I end up. Critical care is not for me. I'll keep my options open. Love you," I said as a farewell.

"To the moon and back," Dad responded.

As I ended the call, I reflected on my rich life. Because of my blessings, I would return to nursing, which I considered a calling and a career, but I couldn't leave here until I cleared my grand-father—and myself—of suspicion in the death of Lyman Ernst.

———◆———

Sitting in the choir, I gazed at the faces of my friends in Birch Tree. They'd welcomed me as Tater's granddaughter and into their community of believers. Tater told the choir director that his granddaughter's voice was as beautiful as his daughter's had been and encouraged me to join the choir where my mom sang during her teen years. I hadn't wanted to sing when I retreated to my grandfather's town as a refuge. Chorus and small group singing always filled me with joy, but after Mom's death, I saw the lyrics more as a chant than a tune. Weekly rehearsals slowly edged the darkness from my heart, and when Winnie and Iris asked me to sing melody in a trio, I agreed. The harmony recreated a sense of wholeness and accord for me.

Singing with the two calmed my soul when I needed it most. But the trio's life would end in August. Iris would be off to college,

Winnie and the pastor, Brandon Caulder, would marry, and I'd be back in Augusta.

We'd decided to use "Blessed Assurance" for today's service as well as for Lyman's service. I allowed the lyrics and harmonies of the hymn to wash over me and savored the chords and the potency of the words.

Pastor Brandon announced that Lyman Ernst's memorial service would be in the church next Wednesday at ten, followed by his burial in the Maine Veterans Memorial Cemetery that afternoon at three. Carpool sign-up sheets for the journey from Birch Tree to Augusta would be in the vestibule. The minister invited congregational members to send anecdotes about Lyman for sharing either in written form or for reading at the memorial. He suggested the individual remembrances would be more appropriate than a sermon to celebrate Lyman's life.

This morning Pastor Brandon's message stressed serving others, and he spoke of how Lyman served his country and then his community by keeping all their machines, not just their cars, in working order. He mentioned Lyman's dress code and proposed the men wear bow ties to the Wednesday service in honor of Lyman.

Our trio closed the service by singing "God Be with You Till We Meet Again," and I wondered if Tater, wherever he might be, sensed that his best friend had passed from this world to the next.

Helen Randall stood by the carpool sign-up sheets in the foyer. "Shanice, most of the cars are full. If you want to go with me, I'll drive."

"Thank you. I'm closing the Spudmobile so I can attend both services."

Helen fiddled with her earring, something I'd seen her do countless times. "The friendship between Tater and Lyman suffered because of me. I've not told anyone the reason."

I didn't comment, and she drew in a deep breath as if ready to explain. But at that moment, Iris exited the sanctuary and looped her arm through mine.

"Ready for lunch? My folks are waiting." Iris nodded to her parents sitting in their sedan.

Helen stepped back and waved me off. "Shanice, I'll see you Wednesday at the church service. You gals sang beautifully today, as you do for every service. I think half the congregation comes to listen to your trio."

The opportune moment for Helen to tell me about the other trio of Helen, Lyman, and Tater vanished. Maybe she'd find the courage to tell me the story on the drive to Augusta.

Some sweet congregational family usually invited me to their home for dinner after Sunday morning services. My absence allowed Helen and Tater to share a meal without me. Today I thought of Helen eating alone, and my mind raced with scenarios of what she almost, but didn't, confess.

CHAPTER FIVE

On Monday morning, I scurried downstairs, hoping to catch Helen in her quilt shop before Nila arrived. Helen's greeting seemed subdued.

"Helen, do you really not know where Tater went? Detective Rilke quizzed me on his sudden trip, but I have no clue where he went or why."

"I don't know, Shanice. But your grandfather assured me I'd be very happy when he returned. He'd been on his phone a lot recently, always ending the call when I came within earshot."

I pressed Helen for more information. "Did he tell you how long he'd be away?"

"You know your grandpa. Tater said he'd stay until the job was done but didn't tell me what the job was."

"I talked to my dad last night, and I've decided my place is in Augusta—when Tater returns. I know he needs an extra set of hands at the Spudmobile, but he's managed to take care of the business by himself this long, and I'm sure he'll find someone else. I've enjoyed being with him, but I was called to nursing. I just went into the wrong specialty."

Helen seemed distracted, so I didn't mention the eulogies Tater and Lyman wrote, in case the words turned out to be some silliness the two friends cooked up. If Tater didn't show up to do the honors for his friend and the eulogies were genuine, I'd read Lyman's words at his memorial service.

Helen squinted at the front window. "Do you know that man?"

Detective Jerry Rilke marched back and forth in front of Helen's quilt shop, checking his watch at the end of each pattern.

"That's the York detective here to investigate Lyman's death," I said.

"We should open the door for him, but if he wants to talk to me, I'd prefer our conversation be in the back. I'll make a pot of coffee. Nila is punctual. She can unlock for business." Helen perused the shop a final time and tapped her manicured nails on the counter before retreating to the break area in the rear of the store.

I unlocked the door and greeted the detective.

"Came to see Helen Randall," Detective Rilke said. "You have any luck locating your grandfather?"

"No." I chose to be as curt as the detective, who hadn't bothered to say hello or good morning.

"His hasty disappearance doesn't look good for him. In our investigation, we learned that your grandfather threatened Lyman on more than one occasion and in front of multiple witnesses. I should tell you we did search his house, and there's a warrant for his arrest."

"What? Why? My grandfather didn't harm Lyman. He wouldn't. Wait. You searched his house? Is that legal?'"

"We had a search warrant. He and Lyman were no longer best friends as you portrayed them. Your grandfather is a murder suspect. You'll tell him to turn himself in when he calls, won't you?"

"I will if he calls. Now I need to get to the Spudmobile." I turned toward the back and raised my voice. "See you Wednesday for our trip, Helen. Detective Rilke is here to talk to you."

"Hold up," the detective said. "You're not planning on leaving town, are you?"

"Helen and I will be attending Lyman's graveside service at the Maine Veterans Memorial Cemetery in Augusta on Wednesday."

"I'll see you there. Killers often attend their victim's service. Maybe your grandfather will show up."

"If he does, it would be out of respect." I spoke a bit sharper than I should have to a law officer.

Helen emerged, doing that fidgety thing with her earring again, and invited the detective to the back of the store. Why should Helen be nervous about talking with the detective?

I substituted an egg taco for my morning donut. The food trucks offering breakfast items opened earlier than the Spudmobile. Being a bit selfish, I was delighted Tater didn't have an early morning menu. The days were long enough with the lunch crowd appearing when Mr. Spuds was stuck in the ground at ten with his board proclaiming the featured item. Today's special would be meatless. I'd returned to the Spudmobile last night and chopped vegetables. Today, as I lined up the boats for the baked potatoes, reality hit me. Since Jerry Rilke believed Tater was guilty, saving my grandfather would be up to me. I'd have to become an amateur sleuth and follow the clues to save my beloved grandpa.

———————

Iris arrived at the Spudmobile brimming with enthusiasm but not much work efficiency. We continued to bump into each other, even with fewer customers than we'd served when Iris helped me a couple of days ago. The loaded vegetarian potato didn't sell well. I'd have to come up with something more interesting tomorrow so I wouldn't lose the ingredients I'd chopped.

Iris pulled handles on the drink machine to dispense sodas for both of us. "Shanice, if your grandpa doesn't return, he may not have a business to come back to."

Her comment resonated with truth. I needed to do two things. Save Tater's business and preserve his reputation. But I wasn't sure how to do either.

"Since we're not barraged with visitors, I'd like to go to the bank."

Iris assured me she could manage the Spudmobile and reminded me that her second job at the Creamery began at six.

I removed my apron and combed my hair—not that a tidy presence would sway a banker who dealt with black-and-red ledger entries.

———

Inside the bank, a vice president invited me into her office. She waited until I sat before offering me something to drink, which I refused.

"Can you tell me if my grandfather has mortgaged his home?" I asked.

"That's no secret. It's a matter of public record. He did, but he's not making the monthly payments. We kept his loan in the Birch Tree branch because our bank officers have known Tater all his life, but he has yet to make a payment. We may have to foreclose. I gave your grandfather the name of a Realtor, hoping she might talk him into sprucing up the house in case he has to put it on the market."

The name of the Realtor went into the notes app on my phone, and I mentally debated about asking for financial information on the Spudmobile. My curiosity won, and I blurted out the question. "How is the Spudmobile business doing?"

"Tater owned his house free and clear. Then he took out a mortgage and poured most of the money into a charitable foundation and the rest into the Spudmobile. News travels fast in small towns. I've heard Lyman said some nasty things about your grandpa's food. A good friend bad-mouthing the Spudmobile hurt its reputation and profitability." The banker paused. "Your grandfather has also been delinquent in the Spudmobile's financial obligations."

"I don't understand. Tater believed the negative comments came from Lyman, but Lyman placed a take-out order with us on the day he died. Why would he do that if he thought the food was tainted? If I can't sort out these crazy allegations, Tater will be ruined financially."

The banker straightened her blouse then leaned forward. "I hope you can talk some sense into him. He loves you, brags about you every time he's in the bank."

I opened my bulging bag and removed the sheets Winnie provided and riffled through them. I asked for cashier's checks for license and permit fees with the additional penalty amounts, using my personal funds since I used the same bank in Augusta.

"It's generous of you to cover these fees for your grandfather." She added up the amounts and handed me the receipt. "I'm sure your grandfather will repay you." She stood and shook my hand.

I didn't know how Tater could repay me, since both his checking and savings bank book accounts showed less than a thousand dollars. I didn't ask the amount of Tater's delinquent mortgage payments.

I mumbled my thanks and left the building. I could see the Spudmobile's bright green form from my view outside the bank's front door, and the food truck parking area was practically empty. I hurried to city hall with the forms and checks. Winnie worked her magic as promised and gave me paid receipts. If Donald Price showed up, at least one of his grievances would be satisfied. I also inquired about the complaints to the Better Business Bureau and the health board, and Winnie suggested names and offices of where I should go. Those trails died quickly, as most grievances or criticisms were anonymous.

My phone showed a few minutes past three, so I headed to the gazebo. Perhaps a visit might jog my memory. After the shock of seeing Lyman on the ground, I'd focused on him. Maybe if I sat and let my mind go blank, I'd remember people or things I'd seen or heard but not recalled at the time.

———

I approached the gazebo from the same direction, remembering the hawk, the children's giggles, and the barking of dogs. Edging forward until I could see the floor of the gazebo, I stopped in the spot where I'd seen Lyman's body and searched for anything that might spur a recollection. The path circling the lake started to the right of the gazebo. A bag dispenser for doggie leavings and a garbage can marked the beginning of the trail. I squeezed my eyes shut. In my mind, I saw a broad-shouldered man starting down the path, a leash stretched taut in front of him. My mind couldn't recall the dog, but the man's outline favored Donald Price's. Donald didn't seem the dog type. I visualized Nila Tran, who seemed to hate both Lyman and Tater because they'd served in Vietnam, stopping to speak to the man with the dog. Perhaps my vision was skewed. I didn't want Tater to be guilty, so I conjured up two others who might want Lyman dead.

I closed my eyes again and imagined Manuel's pickup and Helen's sedan. My fancy worked overtime coming up with ideas about why anyone might want Lyman dead. However, picturing someone I knew actually killing any individual was incomprehensible.

Sitting on the bench inside the gazebo, I let my mind wander. Suddenly I bolted upright. What if Lyman hadn't been murdered? What if he'd died by his own hand? Lyman ordered the mashed takeout that day. He could have mixed the pills into his potato special. But why would he do that?

Some amateur sleuth I was. Instead of narrowing the list of suspects, I'd added one to my list—the dead man.

CHAPTER SIX

The next morning, Donald Price's Jeep occupied a space next to the Spudmobile's designated picnic table, and the broad-shouldered man alternated between sipping from a silver tumbler and eating a donut. When he saw me approach, he quickly closed the top of the box, even though I saw four more circular treats he could have shared.

"You're early." I placed the key in the lock and swung open the Spudmobile's door.

"You're late with taking care of business," Donald countered. "I checked yesterday morning, and you didn't have the permits and fines resolved."

"Did it yesterday afternoon. The Spudmobile is legal for operations. All permits filed and all fines paid." I left the door open—in case he wanted to do another inspection.

Donald followed me inside. "I reminded you and Tater about the increase for the lot rental. Do you have my check?"

"Since you told us last week, I assumed it would start next month." I pulled out a box of potatoes and dumped them into the sink.

"I made the increase effective as of the first, and I sent official notices. Your grandfather probably missed it. He receives a lot of food complaints and overdue notices."

"What's the difference in the amount? I might have the cash." I needed to begin my prep work, or any loyal customers who showed up would have no spud dishes.

As Donald consulted his phone, I watched his face, which seemed a study in contrasts. Was I imagining kindness and concern there? When he stated the amount, he actually sounded apologetic.

"On second thought, why don't you send an invoice? When I receive it, I'll send a check. I like a paper trail for taxes, don't you? Cash payments might be forgotten."

He nodded his agreement. "Fine. By the way, I've started a 'Welcome to Summer' promotion. Set it up for this weekend, with food trucks open from eight in the morning until ten at night, both Saturday and Sunday. I could overlook the Spudmobile not opening until one on Sunday."

Donald knew Tater and I were churchgoers and never opened until after services on Sunday.

"I'll bring some flyers about the promotion," he said. "I'd appreciate it if you'd post them around town and on the Spudmobile."

Donald walked past a napkin with chocolate icing on it then backpedaled and tossed it in the garbage bin. He went to his car and returned to the Spudmobile with the flyers. "I'll bring more after you post these."

"My hands are wet. Please put them on the shelf above my head."

Donald did so, waved, and walked to the next food truck.

I used the back of one of Donald's flyers for my hand-printed announcement about the Spudmobile's Wednesday closing out of respect for Lyman Ernst. Then I added the times and locations of Ernst's memorial service in Birch Tree and graveside service that afternoon in Augusta. After posting the announcement and the rest of the flyers, I worked on the day's special.

The banker I'd spoken to yesterday called midafternoon to say that Tater's house payment would be overdue on the fifth. She explained that Tater had left my name as the emergency contact, and since my grandfather seemed to have disappeared, the banker thought I should know. I had savings, but not enough to pay Tater's bills and my obligations and to keep the Spudmobile afloat. As soon as we ended the conversation, I regretted not asking her about the charitable foundation where Tater had siphoned his life savings. I jotted a reminder on my phone to ask her, and I'd do that. . .if I remembered to check the notes section on my phone.

The Southwest Spud filled with chili garnered compliments from our faithful customers, and when I tallied the contents of the cashbox that evening, it showed a profit for the day. Tater would need that revenue to help pay the mortgage on his house.

After overseeing the food truck all by myself for the day, I walked to my apartment on Main Street, exhausted and looking forward to a long soak in a hot bath. Instead, I found Nila Tran waiting outside my apartment door.

"I wondered if you've heard from your grandfather. Unusual that he'd leave."

"Haven't heard anything yet. Would you like to come in?" My mother brought me up to be polite, and I honored that teaching, even though I yearned for quiet time alone.

"Yes."

"I can offer you water or orange juice," I said, placing my heavy bag on the kitchen counter.

"Nothing to drink. I've been thinking about your grand-father and wanted to know if he ever talked to you about his time in my country." Nila's fingers touched each bead on her grandmother's necklace.

I poured a glass of juice for myself and drank some before answering. "No. He and Lyman were both pretty closemouthed about their experiences overseas."

"I know they were in my village," Nila said.

"I thought America was your home. You were born here, right?" I asked.

"I was born here, but Tater and Lyman said they'd been to the village where my grandmother lived. These are her beads." She took them off and handed them to me.

The individual wooden beads had carved symbols, and the necklace emitted a sweet cinnamon aroma. I returned the necklace, not sure where this awkward conversation was headed.

"The separations remind me of the rosaries some of my friends use when saying their prayers," I told her.

Nila refastened the necklace. "I use them for meditation. American soldiers destroyed my grandmother's home. I've often wondered if Lyman and Tater could have been with that group."

Nila's allegation required a giant leap with no logical basis. The two young soldiers could have been in the village at any time, if at all, and to be there on the singular night of the destruction seemed preposterous. I hoped my face didn't reveal my annoyance. I took another long drink of orange juice to stifle an unkind retort I'd later regret.

"As I said before, neither my grandfather nor Lyman talked about the war. Some people didn't respect their military service and treated them unkindly when they returned home. I do know that disturbed them."

"The Americans were wrong to be in my country. I could have grown up in that beautiful place, surrounded by family."

People smarter than me have debated the Vietnam engagement for years, and I didn't want to argue with my neighbor. "Your family moved to Florida, didn't they?"

"Yes," Nila said.

"But you chose to stay in Maine, didn't you?" I hinted the distance from her family members was her preference. Through

Helen, I knew Nila's parents were still alive and that she had two brothers and a sister and was an aunt to several youngsters.

"Soldiers killed people in our village. Your grandfather and Lyman Ernst might not be the kind and helpful people you think they are."

I rinsed my glass and placed it in the dishwasher. "People surprise us, don't they? Thanks for coming to visit."

Nila pursed her lips as if she'd tasted something unpleasant. "People do surprise us, and not always in the way we'd like."

I followed her to the door and locked it behind her. I hadn't bothered with locks in Birch Tree, but Nila's visit changed my mind. Had I seen her in the park on the day of Lyman's death?

My comforting bath slipped to the end of my to-do list. I made tuna salad and flipped through my letters, mostly junk mail, while I ate. I messaged my dad, reminding him about sending Tater's and Lyman's eulogies to my email account. If the two men created them to be read at their funeral, then Lyman's words deserved to be heard by his friends. This morning, Detective Rilke said they'd searched Tater's house. He didn't say why, but I decided to return to my grandfather's home to see how the search crew had left the house.

After washing dishes and selecting clothes to wear for Lyman's services, I changed into comfy sweatpants and sneakers, planning to run to Tater's house. The exercise routine I'd maintained while working in the ICU suffered a decline after the move to Birch Tree. I stuffed a flashlight in my pocket to compliment my phone's app on the off chance Tater had stopped paying his electric bills as well as his mortgage.

A streetlight illuminated the exterior of Tater's boxy house. The potted plants on the porch bowed their heads, begging for water, and the wicker chairs were missing their cushions.

The lights blazed when I flipped the inside switch. Whoever searched Tater's home had left the outdoor chair cushions leaning against the front wall, and I replaced them in their spots before I watered the plants. Someone had ransacked my grandfather's place. No, *ransacked* was the wrong word; perhaps *rearranged* better described the changes. The detective said he'd searched the house, but had others? Knowing Tater, half the people in town had a key to his front door. I searched for items missing or not in their usual places.

Tater's computer was gone, probably taken by the police, but he was more of a paper-and-pen guy. The big calendar pad remained on the desk. Maybe the police photographed it, as I'd done, instead of confiscating it. I examined each day of the current month. Most were food order lists, chore reminders, or appointments. When I lifted the corner to see whether the next month had noteworthy entries, I saw Lyman's name surrounded by black-colored hearts, my name, and four numbers. Were they the last digits of a phone number, or of a bank account, or of that charitable organization? Why had Tater written my name and Lyman's together? I photographed the calendar's exposed edges and headed to Tater's bedroom.

I rechecked his closet, hoping to see his wedding and funeral suit in its dry cleaner's bag. The police wouldn't notice missing items of clothing, but Tater's suit and dress shoes being gone was as unfathomable as Lyman's death. Where was my grandfather?

CHAPTER SEVEN

O n the day of Lyman's services, the morning dew glistened on the grass, birds trilled, and puffy white clouds patterned the brilliant blue sky. I dressed not in black but in green, the color of regeneration, growth, and healing. Winnie, Iris, and I would wear choir robes for the church service, but wearing green underneath my choir attire cheered me.

The bright red doors of the stone church opened to welcome those coming to celebrate Lyman's life. A flag-draped casket stood in front of the altar with two framed pictures on a nearby table bedecked with a red, white, and blue floral arrangement. The first picture was of Lyman as a young soldier, the second as an elderly gentleman wearing a suit and his trademark bow tie.

I clutched Lyman's eulogy. The words were powerful and poignant. Pastor Brandon had suggested I read Lyman's comments, so I'd rehearsed and hoped to get through the words without breaking down. Lyman's friends should hear his personal thoughts about his life from a reader with a clear, firm voice.

After the pastor shared the scriptures and offered words of comfort, he asked me to read Lyman's farewell thoughts.

LETHAL SPUDS

As I unfolded the sheet of paper, I noticed Detective Jerry Rilke sitting in the back row. The pews were packed. I wondered if Lyman would have been surprised by the large turnout.

I studied the faces in the congregation. "My grandfather and Lyman were lifelong friends. I only found out this week that the two of them had decided to write their own funeral speeches. Here is Lyman's eulogy in his words:

"'Friends, when you think of me, I hope it will be with a smile and not a tear. I know some people pity me because I never married and had a family. I don't have a family. I have *many* families. I have my church family, friends who sustain and encourage me in difficult times and who try to fatten me up at potluck suppers. I also consider my fellow garage workers and customers as kin. My fellow soldiers are family. We were young when we enlisted, but we bonded in foxholes and on patrols. Those terrifying moments spent together not knowing if we would live or die created unbreakable bonds, and we kept in touch over the years with letters, phone calls, emails, and sadly, obituaries.

"'This community of Birch Tree is also a family unit. We may not think alike, but because we're family, we put up with one another's opinions—even when they're wrong. Finally, Tater Williams, who is as close as any brother I can imagine, invited me to share his family. They include me in all their gatherings, and I've watched the kids in the family grow up.

"'I love working with my hands and giving tired old machines renewed life. My body is now a tired old machine, but when you hear this, I'll be in God's hands with a renewed body. Hallelujah!

"'To the group listening today, I don't know whether you'll hear my words or Tater's first, but I hope you'll sing "Blest Be the Tie That Binds" as you leave this service. Ties have bound Tater and me since elementary school, through fighting on another continent, and through old age, and those connections will bind us in heaven. A mighty God has blessed my life.

"'How many people who have walked this earth can say they've been blessed with so many families and lived their life with a true friend by their side?'"

After I finished, the pastor said a final prayer and the congregation sang "Blest Be the Tie That Binds" as they passed by the casket on their way out of the church.

Helen's new silver SUV was practical for carrying bolts of fabric for her quilt shop and comfortable for passengers. At the last minute, Winnie and Iris opted out of the trip to Augusta for the military graveside service, so Helen and I were the only ones in her car.

"I wonder when Lyman wrote his farewell remarks. Do you know?" Helen nosed her SUV into the caravan heading to Augusta for the second part of Lyman's services.

"My dad said the eulogies were dated three years ago. He found them in my mom's papers."

"The words reminded me of the Lyman I'd known in the past but not this year. He changed, but I'm sure you know that." Helen's voice sounded sad.

"I knew he was giving Tater a hard time—lodging complaints and not coming over for Sunday football games. His eulogy reminded me of how much Lyman was a part of our family, so I want to understand what happened, if I can. How did Lyman's behavior change for you?" I hoped my question would encourage her to offer her insight.

Helen maneuvered the car into traffic before speaking. "Tater married soon after the two returned from Vietnam, and Lyman and I dated for a short time. The relationship was doomed. My mother was a strong peace advocate because my dad died over there before it was even a war. She took me with her to peaceful protests from the time I could walk. Lyman was proud of his service and devastated by the treatment of Vietnam veterans. Our basic prejudices precluded any romantic notion at that time."

"That was then, but Tater said you and Lyman had dated recently," I said.

"Lyman began asking me out around the holiday season last year. I always liked him, but then he became pushy and insistent. He believed I should give up my business and fire Nila because he thought she was taking advantage of me."

"That was about the time Lyman found out about his heart problems," I prompted.

"He didn't tell me about the diagnosis. Instead, he pushed to get married and travel the world. I never make hasty decisions—which might explain why I've remained single all these years. He even asked the pastor for available dates for our wedding ceremony. I felt like I was being steamrolled, so I told him I had no intention of marrying him at any time."

"Was that the end of it?"

Helen switched lanes to stay with the other Birch Tree cars in the funeral procession heading to Augusta. "I wish I could say it was, but Lyman persisted. He wanted to give me advice on running my business, which I've done successfully on my own, thank you very much."

"Did his treatment of Nila change at the same time?" I recalled Nila's bitterness toward Tater and Lyman.

"Yes." Helen added nothing more.

"I never saw that side of Lyman. His feud with Tater was a shock to me."

Helen nodded. "I felt the same. When Tater told me about Lyman's heart problems, I chalked up Lyman's behavior to the medicine or anxiety about his future."

"Did you confront him?" I asked.

Helen shook her head. "No. What could I say? In the quilt shop, he talked with Nila as much as me, and their conversations seemed contentious too. When I quizzed Nila, she said it had to do with Vietnam. Couldn't coax much more out of her."

"As a nurse, I've seen a patient's personality change when facing a serious diagnosis."

Helen glanced from the road to me. "Tater told me Lyman's heart problem was under control, and everyone our age has medical problems."

Helen's statement told me she didn't know about the terminal leukemia, which made me wonder if Tater knew.

Helen continued. "When Tater and I started dating, Lyman's actions intensified. He went after Tater and his business, then tossed over their lifelong friendship and became buddies with Donald Price."

I saw the sign for Maine Veterans Memorial Cemetery. "Here's our exit," I said.

"Shanice, I'm ashamed that I let Lyman's recent actions change my opinion of the overall life of the man, but his recent behavior infuriated me." Helen glanced my way. "You must think I'm a terrible person."

I didn't know what to think. Was Helen angry enough to want Lyman dead?

As we exited the highway, I decided the time was right for me to tell Helen my decision about my living arrangements. I wouldn't tell her about Tater's failing to pay his bills. "Helen, I've decided to move out of the apartment. You shouldn't have any difficulty finding a new tenant for the summer."

"I won't, but where will you go?" She followed the cars into the cemetery and toward the pavilion.

"I'll move into Tater's house for a while. Then I'll return to Augusta. It's time to go back to nursing. I've missed it. I think I was in the wrong place. I'm not right for the ICU, but nursing is my calling. My place is caring for people instead of serving baked potatoes."

"Your grandfather enjoyed having you here, but he'll understand."

———————

My father and my brothers waited in the gathering area, and I waved to them. "Helen, if you'll excuse me, I'm going to talk to my family. Be right back."

"Join them. I'll sit with the Birch Tree group." Helen shooed me off.

My family's encompassing hugs made me feel like a kid again.

"Did you read Lyman's eulogy?" my dad asked.

"Yes. Thanks for sending it."

The cemetery representative joined our circle. "Shanice Williams, right? I understand you read words from the deceased at the church service. Do you want to repeat them here?"

I shook my head. "Most of the people here have already heard them." I didn't include my immediate family because I knew we'd read Lyman's words again at our future gatherings.

"Please follow me. You'll be in the family section." He escorted our group to the front then invited everyone else to fill in the remaining chairs.

A military chaplain read the Twenty-Third Psalm followed by the details of Lyman's life as listed in the official obituary, and then offered words of comfort before a prayer. The playing of taps by a lone trumpet followed, and the poignancy of the slow majestic notes gave me goose bumps. A rifle detail offered a salute, and then uniformed service members lifted the flag from the casket, folded it, and presented it to me.

For a brief moment, I pushed the triangular flag back toward the gloved hands. The sacred emblem representing Lyman Ernst and his service should not be mine. Who should hold it? All Lyman's blood family was gone. Ours was the closest to a real family that Lyman had, but I shouldn't be the recipient. Tater should be here to accept the flag. Where was he?

My father placed his arm around my shoulders, and when I turned to face him, out of the corner of my eye I saw Detective Jerry Rilke in the back, wearing sunglasses and moving his head slowly from left to right as if identifying every person in attendance.

CHAPTER EIGHT

A disheveled Detective Rilke with bloodshot eyes showed up at the Spudmobile the next morning, clenching his coffee cup as if it were a lifeline.

"How old is your baby?" I'd seen that look on both my brothers' faces during their children's infancy.

"Six weeks, and we have a toddler who's only eighteen months." He gulped the coffee. "My wife and I thought it would be a good idea to have kids close together since we're older. I'm forty, but I feel twice my age today."

Without his stern working face, the detective appealed to my sympathetic nature. "I saw you at both of the services for Lyman."

The unkempt father morphed into the efficient detective. "Your grandfather didn't show, but we just had a lead pay off. Officers in North Carolina spotted his car. We expedited the paperwork. If he doesn't slip through our fingers, we should have him back here in our custody in the next couple of days."

"North Carolina?" I racked my brain to come up with a connection with the Tar Heel State and came up with nothing except good college basketball teams.

"You don't know anyone he would have been visiting there?"

"No." I placed my hands on my hips. "My grandfather would never harm Lyman Ernst."

Rilke rubbed his eyes. "Sometimes when you hear a person deny something over and over, you begin to wonder about them. How's the business? Any more poison notes or complaints since Mr. Ernst's death?"

"No, but business hasn't picked up. According to Tater's books, June is one of our best months, but not this year."

His phone sounded the lullaby tone, and he cringed. "My sweet wife is with the two little insomniacs all the time, while I escape to my work. Don't misunderstand. They're both adorable."

When he turned his back to the Spudmobile, I smelled trouble and spun around to see an oven belching black smoke. Trashing a whole tray of bacon wouldn't increase this month's profit.

I'd invited Helen to dinner at my apartment as a thank-you for driving to Augusta and to talk about my moving date. I suspected she charged me lower than the typical rate, so my departure would earn her more income. A quick move would also save me the money I needed to cover Tater's bills until he came back and took a hard look at his finances.

Helen rapped on the door just as I removed a chicken-and-rice casserole from the oven. I'd promised her our dinner would be potato-free since I cooked plenty each day at the Spudmobile.

Still clutching a pot holder in my left hand, I opened the door where Helen stood with a vase of spring flowers. To my surprise, Nila Tran waited behind her with an inquisitive look. Helen and I performed an inaudible dialogue. I tilted my head toward Nila, and Helen responded by lifting her shoulders slightly.

"Nila," I said, "would you like to join us for dinner?"

She didn't answer but returned her apartment key to her pocket and followed Helen inside.

I quickly set another place at the table, divided two salads into three, and placed bread fresh from the oven in a basket. Helen and I made small talk about my impending move to Tater's house while a mute Nila studied my apartment's furnishings.

Once seated, I held my hands out to them to form a prayer circle. "Father, we are thankful for the many blessings we enjoy, and we thank You for the life of Lyman Ernst and the joy he brought into our lives over the years—"

A chair scraped on the wood floor. Nila released my hand, and the apartment door opened and closed.

Mumbling a hasty "Amen," I looked at Helen. "That was weird."

"Nila disliked Lyman. She's quiet but can be dramatic when she's angry or wants to make a point. Walking out during your prayer was rude." Helen flicked open her napkin, obviously annoyed with her employee, and smiled. "Your casserole smells delicious."

Helen and I continued our conversation about the apartment transfer, and I promised her I'd move my things early Saturday morning, clean after work that day, and return the key.

"I didn't need to advertise. Just mentioned to friends that the unit might be available, and two people are interested," Helen said.

"I hope you're charging them more than you did me." I offered her the bread.

"These two units came with the storefront. My quilt shop provides my living. I use the rental money for causes I support."

Our evening passed amiably. Could I remove Helen from my suspect list? She'd been open with how she felt about Lyman and his actions over the past years. She said she'd refused Lyman's offer of marriage. I hoped she wouldn't refuse Tater if he asked. My grandfather's face lit up when he talked about Helen. Even though Tater and Helen were in their seventies, I could envision them starting a life together.

If Helen agreed.

If Tater got his finances in order.

If my grandfather explained why he'd left so suddenly.

If Detective Rilke believed Tater had not been involved in the death of his best friend.

After Helen left, I remembered the slip of paper I'd seen on Tater's desk. I hadn't been able to place those four digits. My mind associated them with a phone number, one I'd called before. I stacked the dishes for washing, retrieved my phone, and scrolled through the phone numbers, hoping to see duplicate ending digits.

Suddenly a creaking of floorboards and soft footsteps sounded outside. I flung open the door.

Nila jumped back.

"Yes?"

"Your prayer said Lyman was a good man. He wasn't."

"You have your opinion. I have mine." I didn't want to hear her litany of Lyman's supposed misdeeds in a country on the other side of the globe when he was an eighteen-year-old private. Especially when the man was not even cold in his grave.

"I'm telling the detective the facts I know about Lyman and Tater." Her words sounded like a warning.

I said goodbye and willed myself not to slam the door. Clearly the threat came from a misguided person, but did it have any merit?

———◆———

The encounter with Nila made me want to vacate this place immediately, so I packed the boxes I had, threw a sheaf of clothes hangers over the top, and took the stairs. I hip-bounced off the railing as a precaution, since my arms held the cartons and clothing. Stuffing everything into the trunk of my car, I kept an eye out for Nila to make another appearance. I'd be exhausted tomorrow, but right now adrenaline coursed through my veins.

Entering the back of Tater's house via the garage, I plopped an armload of hangers with clothes over a kitchen chair and reached for the light switch. A large hand over my mouth muffled my scream.

"Guess I surprised you." Tater's amused voice didn't slow my heart's rapid beating. "Don't turn on the lights."

"Tater! Where have you been?" I breathed in and out to calm my jitters. "And why shouldn't I turn on the lights?"

"Because I don't want anyone watching to know I'm in here."

"But if they're watching, they know I'm in here. Wouldn't they think it's strange if I don't turn on a light?"

"You're right. Turn on the lights, maybe the TV too. I'll hide in the pantry and talk to you from in there."

"What are you doing here?" I asked after I flipped on the lights and turned the TV volume to the level suited for a watcher who needed hearing aids. "Where have you been? I'm happy you're back, but you had me worried sick."

"Told you. I had to go away."

"So why are you hiding?"

"Police came to the place where I was staying and told the owner I was a person of interest in a homicide. What's going on, Shanice? What homicide?"

"Lyman Ernst is dead."

"Lyman? No, no, no!" Tater's breaths sounded like panting. "Didn't think it was his time. Oh no. And I wasn't here. Was someone with him when he passed? How did it happen? When?"

"The detective from York says he died from an overdose of sleeping pills in mashed potatoes. He's treating Lyman's death as a homicide. Lyman ordered our take-out special the day you left town, the Super Mashed Mixture. Detective Jerry Rilke thinks you killed Lyman because of the feud you were having over the 'lethal spuds' thing and Lyman telling people not to eat at the Spudmobile."

"That's ridiculous. I'd never kill my best friend. He's like a brother. . .well, *was* like my brother."

I shrugged. "Rilke's pegged you as the prime suspect."

"You believe me, don't you?" Even with his voice muffled by the pantry door, I could sense Tater's sorrow and his need for affirmation.

"Of course I do."

"When's Lyman's funeral?"

"Yesterday. You missed it. I read the eulogy Lyman wrote for himself. There were two services. The church was packed for the memorial here, and for the burial, which was in the military cemetery in Maine."

Tater made no comment, and I allowed him time to reflect on the unexpected news.

"Who would want Lyman dead?" Tater's voice trembled.

"You're the one the police are considering. Folks know about your recent arguments with Lyman about the Spudmobile and about the two of you both liking Helen."

"Who else is a suspect? You know I didn't do it!"

"Detective Rilke doesn't confide in me. But my guess is that his other persons of interest include me, Manuel, Helen, Nila, and Donald Price."

"Lyman's death had to be an accident," Tater said.

"That's what I told the police, but the detective said the dose was too large to be accidental. I don't believe Lyman would try to kill himself, do you?"

"No. He wouldn't. Some buddies from our army unit chose that route. Lyman took their deaths even harder than I did. He always said you never know the plans God has for your future. He wouldn't take his own life."

"I found a drawing on your calendar with Lyman's name, my name, hearts colored black, and four numbers. You know I can't make heads or tails of your doodles, and those may have been from different days."

"You know Lyman had heart problems," Tater said.

"He took his heart pills, didn't he?"

"His heart problems were under control, but Lyman had a death sentence hanging over his head. He had B-cell acute leukemia from Agent Orange. It had moved into the bone marrow, causing him repeated infections. Doctors said he didn't have long to live."

"I learned that from Detective Rilke. Why didn't you tell us? Lyman was family."

"Lyman and I had some important things to do before he passed. Oh, I can't believe I wasn't with him. The doctor says the particular strain Lyman had affects the lungs. Lyman wanted me to get tested."

"Did you?" My concern was now for Tater.

"Yep. Don't have it now, but that leukemia can stick its ugly head up whenever it feels like it."

"When did Lyman find out?"

Tater rubbed his chin. "Guess it was back in January. Had to be January, the month he was born, and the month he always had his annual physical at the VA hospital in Augusta."

"Tater, you should turn yourself in."

"I might tomorrow night, but I have something important to do during the day."

"What's more important?" I asked.

"Helen's birthday," Tater said.

His attitude annoyed me. "Well, I'll be busy too. I'm moving out of Helen's apartment and in with you because of what your banker said."

"Why were you talking to my banker?"

"I had to get checks for the permits, so I went to the bank." I paused, then blurted out the rest. "I looked through your house, trying to find out where you might have gone. I found your unpaid bills."

"The Spudmobile will pay the bills." Tater sounded confident, but he obviously hadn't taken a hard look at the business accounts.

"Your house and the Spudmobile are both in jeopardy. The banker might help arrange payments, but first we have to convince Detective Rilke of your innocence and mine. You need to turn yourself in."

"After tomorrow," Tater repeated.

"I'll be violating the law if I don't report you. I'm going back to the apartment. You know what you need to do."

"I'll sleep on it." Tater didn't speak for a moment. "Shanice, Lyman recorded major events of his life on cassette tapes. They're important. You have to save them. They're in the back of his guest room closet. Will you do that for me? For Lyman?"

"Okay, but tonight I need sleep. I have spuds to sell tomorrow."

"Wish I could be there. What's the feature?"

"Haven't decided. Do you have any ideas?"

"How about a Hot on Top special? Give them a standard loaded potato with a few shakes of hot sauce on top."

"Sounds easy. Good night. I'll turn off the TV and the lights. Tater, do you have anything to eat?"

"Crackers and peanut butter. You'll come back tomorrow, won't you?"

"I will if you tell me where you went and why."

"You'll know everything soon," Tater promised.

Right then, I felt like I could sleep for a week, but I feared I'd repeat what I'd done during the grueling days of working in the ICU. When my head hit the pillow, my eyes would fly open, and I'd worry about the patients and their families whose lives had changed in a single moment.

CHAPTER NINE

B etween serving the Hot on Top baked potato special and worrying about Tater's sudden and secretive return, I heard the wail of Birch Tree's police car blaring progressively louder.

"Do you think our local law enforcement officer decided to make an example of a speeder today?" I asked a customer as I lined up his order of four Hot on Top taters.

He shook his head. "Siren's coming from the residential area, not the highway."

My stomach sank. I had the horrible feeling Tater was the person in the back of the patrol car. With two customers waiting, I concentrated on orders and ignored my premonition. Today's business was better than the day before, which gave me hope. For Tater to avoid foreclosure on his house, he needed his business to be profitable.

"Shanice?" Helen Randall ran toward the food truck.

I blinked twice. Running was out of character for the dignified, imperturbable Helen.

"Is everything all right?" I threw open the Spudmobile door and hurried to meet her.

Helen bent over and blew out a big breath. "The police arrested Tater. He called to see if I could get him a lawyer, and he wanted you to know before you heard it from someone else."

"Sit down. Catch your breath." I guided her to a picnic bench.

Helen glanced around to see if anyone might be listening. "Before Tater left town, he went to Lyman's house. He says he saw Donald Price's Jeep leaving Lyman's just as he pulled into the driveway. Do you think the detective knows?"

"Detective Rilke is trying to link the delivered order to Lyman's death, but Donald delivered four Spudmobile orders that day. No, wait, Donald didn't deliver them. I asked him to take the orders to your quilt shop and ask if Nila could take them to the customers."

Helen looked puzzled. "That's right. I'd forgotten that. He did drop them off. But then why did Tater see him at Lyman's? This is too confusing. The lawyer is the important thing. Shanice, the one lawyer in Birch Tree would be overwhelmed with a possible murder defense. Do you know anyone in Augusta? Would they be willing to come to Birch Tree?"

"Be right there," I said to a customer who stepped up to the window. I turned back to Helen. "I'll call my dad and have him check with my brothers. I'll give them your number. I'm sure they'll call by tomorrow." I hugged Helen, which surprised both of us. "Don't worry. We know he's not guilty."

Helen headed back toward Main Street's row of shops. She'd run toward the Spudmobile, but now she trudged away as if weighted by a huge burden. As she left, I remembered that today was her birthday and that Tater had wanted to do something special for her. I doubt going to jail was the surprise he'd had in mind.

———◆———

Winnie and Iris, my eager accomplices in another clandestine activity, chattered nonstop as I drove the worn path behind Lyman's house. As concerned as I was about Tater's being in jail, my grandfather's anxiety about retrieving Lyman's cassette recorder and tapes moved up to number one on my to-do list. I unlocked the door with the key hidden under the back mat, and we used our phones' flashlight apps to explore. Somehow, not turning on lights made this adventure more exhilarating.

The computer no longer sat on Lyman's desk, and my guess was the police had taken it. Winnie and Iris checked the office drawers and cabinets and whispered they'd found nothing. Iris headed to the bathroom to check for prescriptions. I wanted to know exactly what Lyman had been taking. Winnie went to the kitchen, and I went to the guest room. I entered the closet Tater described and turned the flashlight's brightness to its highest setting.

Dust coated the old-style cassette player which rested on top of a box. After opening the box and seeing it was full of cassette tapes, I placed both it and the player in the bag I'd brought and began searching the room. I was almost through when headlights lit up the bedroom window. A car moved slowly down Lyman's long driveway.

"Douse your flashlights and head to the back door. Someone's coming," I hissed. I reached the porch last, locked the door, and indicated they should hurry to the boat tied to the pier.

"Who is it?" whispered Iris as she lifted the tarp of the small fishing dinghy.

"Don't know, but I'd like to," I said.

I motioned Winnie to climb inside. I followed, and Iris came last. The little boat rocked as I stepped off the pier. Once hidden, we held the tarp up slightly so we could see the house. I glanced at the spot where I'd parked. My car was close to a clump of trees and in shadows. A person wouldn't notice it unless they were looking.

"It's a Jeep. Doesn't Donald Price drive a Jeep?" Winnie asked.

"He does. What's he doing here?" I spoke my thoughts aloud.

"It's definitely Donald. The moon's bright enough for me to make out his face, and he's messing with a key ring." Iris was on the end, with the best vantage point for viewing.

Lights blazed in the house. While Donald looked through the rooms, we huddled in the boat, listening to the tune of lapping water, buzzing mosquitoes, and hooting owls. We waited for Donald to complete his search so we could leave.

"I wish we could see what he's doing," I said.

Iris crooned softly, "Be Thou my vision," and we all giggled. We enjoyed the challenge of coming up with a song lyric to express our feelings for all situations.

I slapped my arm. "Mosquitoes love my blood. I wish he'd hurry."

As if he'd heard me, Donald exited the front door, slid into the Jeep, and turned on the ignition.

"Finally," I said.

"Not so fast," Iris warned. "There's a second person."

"With Donald?"

"I'm not sure." Iris pushed up her glasses and leaned forward. "Looks like a female silhouette, and she came from behind the Jeep. I don't know if she was with him or hiding—like we are."

"Do you think we could risk going over there? After all, Donald and his friend would have to explain why they're here too," Winnie said.

"You're right. Remind me, why are we skulking around in the dark and hiding in Lyman's fishing boat?" I asked.

The Jeep roared to life, and Donald made a U-turn, exiting the same one-lane road.

"Did she go with him?" Winnie asked.

"Don't think so. We should stay here a bit longer." Iris relished being the boss, an entitlement her superb viewing spot gave her.

We all sniffed the acrid smell simultaneously.

"The place is on fire!" Iris beat at the tarp covering and struggled to climb out of our tight quarters. "She's running away, going through the trees. I wonder if Donald is waiting for her."

I threw back the tarp. "Let's go. If the fire reaches my car. . ." I raced ahead, Iris and Winnie right behind me. The person who started the fire must have used an accelerant liberally. In minutes the flames licked at the windows, and breaking glass and hissing sounds forecast devastation.

"I'm calling the fire department," Winnie said as we piled into the car.

"Not sure they can do any good." I started the engine, pushed the accelerator, sped up the driveway, and turned left onto the road toward the subdivision where Iris lived.

Sirens screamed, cars filled the road, and houses lit up. I drove cautiously, not wanting to draw attention to us. In front of Iris' house, I finally breathed a sigh of relief, unbuckled my seat belt, and turned to my fellow sleuths.

"Did you get a list of his prescriptions?" I asked.

Iris held up her phone. "Photographed them. I'll email them to you."

"I struck out. Didn't see anything unusual. Mr. Ernst was well organized," Winnie said.

I pointed to the bag. "I snagged the tape recorder and a box of tapes Tater wanted me to get. I'll listen to them and see if there's anything Detective Rilke should know."

Iris reached for my hand. "We're lucky we escaped tonight. This was fun, but our undercover work is becoming a little scary."

"I agree," echoed Winnie. She sang, "'Sweet hour of prayer.'"

Laughing, I reached for their hands to form a prayer circle. I thanked God for my friends and for our safety and asked for wisdom and patience. Clearly, I needed patience, because I couldn't wait to listen to Lyman's words on the cassette tapes.

———

Back in my apartment, I ignored my partially packed boxes and plugged in the tape machine. There wasn't a cassette in the recorder, so I looked through the shoebox holding the tapes. Lyman had labeled them by date and event. Their titles tugged at my heart because they involved milestones, and many included our family, such as "Joining up to serve my country," "Starting Ernst's Garage," "Buying my first house," "Tater's wedding day," and "Birth of Tater's daughter." My eyes filled with tears as I read the titles.

This box held the oral history of two lives woven together for over sixty years. I wanted to listen to every one of them, but I didn't know if Tater wanted me to find a specific tape or just save these precious memories. About midway through the box, I spied one named "My Death Sentence," dated January of this year. I set it aside and thumbed through the rest. The January recording appeared to be the last one Lyman made.

I checked the time on my phone. It was after two thirty. I would be exhausted at the Spudmobile in a few hours, but I inserted the tape and pushed play. Nothing. When I hit rewind, the swishing sound of the plastic tape whirling through the spindles reassured me. This time, when I pressed the button, Lyman's voice boomed out.

"This is Lyman Ernst, and I have something to say—"

A scream came from across the hall. I hit the stop button and rushed to the other apartment door. "Nila, are you okay?" I pounded until the lock turned.

Nila, face ashen, stood peeking from behind her apartment door. "I had a horrible nightmare. I'm sorry." She frowned at me. "What are you doing?"

"Nothing. Why do you ask?"

"You're still in your clothes, and it's the middle of the night." Nila's eyes traveled up and down my black attire.

"I'm moving this weekend. Will you be able to go back to sleep?"

"Yes. It was just a bad dream. I go to sleep quickly." Nila closed the door and turned the dead bolt.

I retreated to my own apartment and sniffed. Had Nila smelled of smoke, or was the scent coming from my clothes and hair? Could Nila have been racing about the county with Donald Price or out by herself tonight?

I lowered the volume of the recorder and hit play again. This time the words emerged in a low singsong, telling me the batteries were shot. I emptied the batteries from the back of the machine. They were not a size I kept on hand.

As I got ready for a quick shower to rid myself of the smoky smell, I thought about Nila's nightmare. The wall between our apartments was thin. I often heard her radio. Had the sound of Lyman's voice caused her bad dream? Did her reaction mean she was guilty of arson? Of murder? Just what was on that tape?

CHAPTER TEN

M y morning donut stop for a sugar high coupled with generous amounts of caffeine didn't stop my yawning as I prepared for another day serving tasty taters from the Spudmobile.

Helen, followed by Nila, met me as I opened the umbrella over the picnic bench.

"Shanice, I've asked Nila to give you a hand today instead of working in the quilt shop. She said you were up late packing. I feel guilty about mentioning the new apartment tenant when you've got so much going on." Helen placed a hand on Nila's shoulder.

"I'll feel better after I move. Did my dad or brothers have any suggestions for a lawyer?"

"They gave me three names. I spoke with all of them yesterday. A Mr. Higgins seemed the best to me, and he promised to be with Tater in court on Monday for the arraignment. This is happening so fast." Helen tugged at her earring.

Nila, silent while Helen and I talked, sat on the picnic bench and toyed with her phone. I turned to her. "Nila, I'd love your assistance. Could you stay until about one? That would take me through the noon rush."

"Miss Helen said to help as long as you wanted, but I'm more comfortable with quilts than food." Nila remained seated.

Helen pulled out a twenty and handed it to Nila. "Why don't you buy us lunch when you finish? We can relax and let the customers browse while we eat."

"Do I have to buy from the Spudmobile?" Nila pocketed the bill.

"Well, I like the potatoes, don't you?" Helen seemed flustered by Nila's comment.

"Don't want to die," Nila said. "The potatoes killed Lyman, didn't they?"

Helen glared at Nila. "Other people had contact with Lyman Ernst's food before he received it, including you. Buy the spud special for me. You can eat what you want."

Helen's sharp retort startled me. Maybe the woman needed a break from her quilt shop helper.

"Come on, Nila. Let's get to work."

Nila rose, face expressionless, and followed me inside the Spudmobile. Her mannerisms could be abrasive, but perhaps I could learn something about Nila working with her in these close quarters.

Nila's demeanor told me she wasn't looking forward to our joint workday. Hopefully, she wouldn't attempt to sabotage the morning's routine. Other food court vendors managed business by themselves, but despite Tater's numerical task list, I kept falling behind in the daily activities. And today I wanted time to sneak away to buy batteries so I could listen to the tape recording.

"Come on, Nila." I spoke with a cheery tone to the somber-faced young woman.

"I'm here because of Miss Helen's kindness. Your grandfather and Lyman destroyed my village."

I handed her an apron. "Nila, you and I are the same age. You were born in the United States, as was your mother. You never lived in that village."

"But my grandmother came here because she had nowhere to go. I could have been born and grown up in Vietnam, and I should have." Nila wrapped the apron strings around her small waist and tied a bow in the front.

This crazy assertion made no sense, and we'd already had this no-win argument. I pointed to the potatoes in the box. "Thanks for helping. I'll work on the barbecue for today's special. Would you scrub those potatoes, please?"

She scrubbed the spuds vigorously, and I appreciated her industry.

"Heard at the donut shop that Lyman's house burned down last night." I kept my tone light.

Nila dropped the potato she was scrubbing. "He won't be using it anyway."

"But the house belonged to someone. We'll have to wait until the will is read to know, but someone lost a lovely property."

"I heard he had things from Vietnam in his house. Did he?" Nila asked.

"Some," I said.

"Probably things he stole from villages like mine. Potatoes are done. Now what?"

"Refill the salt, the pepper, and the silverware bins, and then please peel some potatoes for the mashed recipes." I checked around the tiny kitchen as I read Tater's daily to-do list.

Every person who appeared at the food court talked about nothing else but Lyman's house burning down. Customers with friends or relatives affiliated with the fire department or those who followed the sirens to the scene all declared arson caused the destruction.

Tater needed to know about the lawyer coming on Monday and about the burning of Lyman's house. The fire would be another blow for my grandfather. The two men were in and out of each other's homes with the regularity of sunrises and sunsets. Tater would feel the loss of Lyman's property keenly. I slipped out and rang Helen during a lull and asked if she'd talked to Tater.

"Called him this morning, and I'm going to the jail—how I hate to say that word—this afternoon when Nila is back to mind the shop. Oh, Tater said you should concentrate on the Spudmobile and moving. He wants you to wait until next week to visit him."

"Sounds like my grandfather. Always calling the shots. Well, give him my love, and tell him I found the package." I punched the end button so I didn't have to explain. Then I returned to the Spudmobile and filled orders, pleased that today's lunch traffic proved steady.

When I went to the order window and saw the bloodshot eyes of Manuel Ortiz, I gasped. "Are you okay? Take a seat, and I'll bring you some water."

Manuel nodded and stumbled toward a bench. I asked Nila to take over for a few minutes and grabbed two bottles. Before sitting, I twisted the cap on one and handed it to Manuel.

He took a big swallow. "Tater back?"

I opened my own bottle. "Back to Birch Tree and in jail. He's in custody as a suspect for Lyman's death."

"Jail?" He raked his fingers through his salt-and-pepper hair. "That's crazy. He'd never hurt Lyman."

"I know." I paused, then asked why he'd come.

"Oh, I hoped Tater might be back. I wanted to talk to him about Juanita. Your grandpa knew that my wife and I expected the garage business to be ours in January, but then it didn't happen. I still believe things will work out, but Juanita is the worrying type." He shrugged. "She frets about little things, like what to have for dinner, so paying for college for the two boys has consumed her."

"I understand," I said. I wondered where this thread was leading.

"She hasn't been sleeping well. Sometimes I wake up in the middle of the night and she's gone."

Iris said the second figure last night appeared to be female, so I asked the question. "Was she home last night?"

He wiped his eyes. "Not all night. Juanita said she saw the fire trucks and followed them to Lyman's house. She smelled of smoke when she came back."

"Did she see anything?" Manuel and Juanita both knew cars. She might have recognized mine as Winnie, Iris, and I left. Or she might have left before the fire trucks arrived.

Manuel stood. "She didn't say. Tater always seemed to know what to do. I thought he might give me some advice. Juanita's not acting right."

"Maybe you could talk to Pastor Brandon or your doctor," I suggested.

Manuel shook his head. "Do you know when they'll read the will? Juanita will be able to rest easy if she hears we can purchase the garage as Lyman promised. I hope he put that in his will."

"I don't know if Lyman even had a will. If anyone knows, it'll be Tater. Wait here—I'm going to get you a barbecue potato to take home." I started toward the Spudmobile then stopped. "Manuel, on the day Lyman died, who delivered the Spudmobile take-out order to the garage?"

"Not a proper delivery. Nila honked the horn and yelled for me to come get it. Pulled the boxes out of the bag and handed me the one marked with the number four. I laughed and said three was my lucky number."

"And did she give you the number three container?" I asked.

"Yes. She said they were all the same. Why do you want to know?"

"The orders were the same when they left the Spudmobile, but one ended up with crushed sleeping pills in it, powerful enough to send someone into eternal sleep."

Manuel stepped backward. "So anyone could have received the poisoned food?"

I shivered at the horrific implications of Manuel's statement. Could Donald have doctored the potatoes between here and the quilt shop? Had Nila done it on her delivery run? Or was Manuel trying to deflect attention away from himself and his beloved Juanita?

CHAPTER ELEVEN

I violated Tater's request not to see him until the next week and regretted it. I should have honored his wishes, because the visit depressed both of us. Without words, we both grieved for Lyman and the destruction of his house. And we fretted about the charges pinned on Tater. But instead of discussing what weighed on our hearts, we talked about potatoes, the weather, and the number of fish caught in the lake this past week. Anything to avoid topics that concerned us most. When I mentioned Manuel's distress about Juanita, Tater stared at me vacantly. When visiting hours ended, I felt relieved and went to Helen's house.

Even in casual clothes, she appeared tailored and a bit formal. She invited me to wait in the living room while she prepared tea and sandwiches.

"May I help?" I asked. "I don't mean to interrupt your evening."

"You're not interrupting." She placed a tray on the table in front of me and picked up her cup of steaming tea before sitting.

"Tater's not himself. In addition to the shock of Lyman's death, I think his conduct might have something to do with his disappearance. He won't tell me where he went or why," I said.

In my heart, I sensed there was something about the triangle of Helen, Lyman, and Tater that she wasn't telling me. Tater looked so down in the mouth, I believed Helen must hold the key. Since I'd moved to Birch Tree, I'd watched the two of them, and his countenance lit up every time he saw her. His face betrayed his emotions, but were his feelings reciprocated?

She placed her cup and saucer on the table and sat back in the floral-print chair. "Lyman wanted Tater to get involved in a project that involved a huge chunk of Tater's savings. I didn't approve of Lyman's badgering Tater to contribute and told him so. Well, Lyman became quite angry." She stopped talking and didn't continue.

"Did the project involve you?" I asked after a moment's pause.

"Our three lives were intertwined."

I recalled the banker mentioning a foundation where Tater deposited most of his funds. Sleuths always followed "the money trail" in investigations, so I prompted Helen. "Did it have to do with a charitable trust?"

Helen smiled enigmatically. "Being friends with a person, even more than friends, doesn't mean the two of you agree."

This questioning was going nowhere, so I changed the subject. "My goal is to move to Tater's house tonight. I'll clean and have the apartment ready for your new tenant on Monday morning. Where should I leave the key?"

"I have another. Hold on to it until Monday. Just don't invade Donald's privacy."

I gasped. "You're renting to Donald Price?"

"Yes. He has an apartment in York but wanted a base here in Birch Tree where he could observe his family's investment more closely."

"That's a shocker. He never seemed to like this small town." I added my thanks for the sandwich, and she walked me to the door.

Work helped me think, and there was a mountain of labor waiting in my apartment over the quilt shop. I needed to finish the packing, transfer my belongings to Tater's, unpack there, and then clean this apartment until it met food service inspection standards. My goal was to complete all the tasks tonight so I could observe Sunday as a day of rest. As I filled boxes, I thought about the relationships between Lyman and Manuel, Lyman and Helen, Lyman and Nila, Lyman and Tater, and Lyman and Donald. Where did Donald Price fit into the picture? Why was he at Lyman's house? Who was the woman Iris had seen right before the fire erupted? Was it a woman? Who would hate Lyman enough to kill him?

When my car was loaded, I drove to Tater's house without a single answer. I struggled to imagine anyone considering murder, much less carrying through with it. I also discounted the angle that Lyman might have taken his own life.

I lifted my voice. "'I sing because I'm happy, I sing because I'm free, for His eye is on the sparrow, and I know He watches me.'" Those words consoled me until I saw Donald Price's Jeep parked in front of Tater's house.

"Shanice, let me help you." Donald hurried to the car and waited by the trunk.

Assistance would be helpful, but I questioned Donald's sudden appearance and eagerness. I popped the trunk, pointed to the boxes, and led him to the guest room, my arms filled with hanging garments.

Donald deposited the first load and went back for more. The trunk was empty before I arranged my clothes in the closet.

"Anything more I can do?" he asked.

This man, who had behaved in such a bombastic manner last week by threatening to shut down Tater's Spudmobile, now asked if he could help. I didn't understand why he was here or willing to work, but I was too exhausted to do anything except nod.

His eyes brightened, and he seemed delighted at the prospect.

"My next task is cleaning the apartment for Helen's new tenant," I said, pretending I didn't know the person's identity.

He grinned self-consciously. "I'm the one moving in, and I've already booked a cleaning service for Monday morning. You can mark that off your list. It's late. Did you eat? That breakfast place is open twenty-four hours."

"I had a sandwich at Helen's," I said.

"Want me to break down the boxes as you unpack?" he asked.

His actions bordered on creepy. Why was he being so helpful when he seemed determined to destroy my grandfather's business?

"Donald, why are you here?" My bluntness caused him to step back.

"I—I, well, I knew you planned to move tonight, and I thought I might help. Then I planned to ask you to go to dinner with me or a concert or a play. They're doing a revival of *West Side Story* in York." He blushed as he stuttered out the invitation, looking like an awkward schoolboy.

I found both his appearance at Tater's house and his suggestion of an outing flabbergasting. His bashful demeanor caused sympathy to well up until I remembered his previous actions. I'd needed Winnie's advice to obtain my food handler's license, and I'd emptied a portion of my personal bank account paying all the city fees and permits Donald required for the Spudmobile. I also remembered the expression I'd seen on his face in an unguarded moment. Was there something more to Donald Price?

I shook my head. "Now's not a good time. Maybe in a couple of weeks, after the detective closes Lyman Ernst's case. Has the lawman mentioned you as a suspect? You did handle the daily specials for me."

"You needed a helper that day, didn't you?"

"Yes." I had often replayed the day's events in my head. Would Lyman still be alive if I'd taken the orders to the customers myself? "You didn't answer my question, Donald. Has Rilke mentioned you as a suspect?"

"Well, he told me not to leave town, and I wouldn't, since we have the big 'Welcome to Summer' promotion coming up soon."

"Right. Thanks for the help and saving me a trip back to the unit to clean." I walked him to the door. Tonight was not a good time to bring up his presence at Lyman Ernst's house the day of Lyman's death, again at Lyman's before the fire, or his Jekyll-and-Hyde behavior.

———

After I arranged my belongings in the guest room, the grandfather clock dinged eleven times, and I went to the kitchen for a snack break. Finding Tater's fridge and pantry bare, I opened the cooler with items from my apartment fridge and Lyman's cassette player.

A tingling told me this held the answers to all the questions. When I'd tried to listen to it in my apartment, the reels turned slower and slower as the batteries ran out, making Lyman's message incomprehensible, and my day had been too chaotic to steal time to purchase replacement batteries for the recorder. Tater stashed his battery supply in the pantry. If he had the right size and number to fit the cassette, I'd finally get to hear Lyman's message.

This time Lyman's voice sounded normal. "This is Lyman Ernst, and I have something to say that may shock the people of Birch Tree. If you're listening to this, I'm probably in heaven, reunited with my Savior, and free from earthly concerns. I recorded this tape on January 21, my seventy-first birthday, to serve as my last will and testament. Any listener needs to know about what's happening in Birch Tree. My goal in the next few months will be to right wrongs and see justice done. As for the distribution of my worldly goods—" Lyman chuckled. "I never accumulated a lot, but I hope those who receive them will remember me fondly."

I shut off the recorder and retrieved a legal pad from my grandfather's office so I could write down Lyman's words. The recording sounded like the man I'd known all my life—warm, friendly, caring, and funny. I'd probably start and stop the cassette multiple times, but I needed to get it right. I knew I should listen with another person, but curiosity overcame practicality.

Lyman said, "First, the Ernst Garage business, building, and furnishings should go to Manuel and Juanita Ortiz. To the best of my knowledge, there are no debts outstanding. Manuel and Juanita, you've been loyal and supportive friends who helped make the business a success. I want my estate administrator to sell the garage to you for the sum of one dollar. I read in some book that if you pay for something, it isn't a gift."

I stopped the recording and jotted the information on a pad. With that one pronouncement, the recording answered all of Manuel and Juanita's concerns. Lyman hadn't betrayed them. Instead of selling them the business for market value, he handed it to them for a single dollar. Thanks to Lyman and the Ortiz family's hard work, they could provide their boys with the college education they wanted.

When I pushed the PLAY button, Lyman's voice continued his instructions. "Second, I give my house on Lakeview Drive to Nila Tran. This is the land and structure only, no contents. Nila, you believe soldiers of my generation destroyed your home, so I give you a new home. I hope you'll learn to love it."

I pressed STOP and made notes. Nila Tran? She'd never had a kind word to say to or about Lyman, yet he gave her his house. A house that no longer existed.

A creaking sound brought a sudden shiver down my spine.

"Hello?" I called and listened with my whole being. Insects butted against the screens, leaves rustled, and an owl hooted. I didn't hear a single car on the street. Again, I called out—and prayed I wouldn't receive an answer.

You're exhausted and scaring yourself. You need sleep, I told myself. Just in case someone was watching, I ejected the cassette from the recorder and slipped it into my pocket while singing the first verse of "A Mighty Fortress Is Our God." Then I walked through the rooms and flipped the lights on and off, checking for anything out of place. Tonight I'd sleep with Lyman's last wishes between my bed's mattress and box springs.

But I didn't sleep the restful way my body needed. I slept in fits and starts. I listened to every outside and inside noise and even conjured up sounds. During the night, I padded to the kitchen for a drink of water, set the automatic start on the coffee machine, and rechecked all the window and door locks.

When the morning light filled the bedroom, I pulled the sheet over my head, craving more sleep. Tater's clock chimed eight times. Today was Sunday. Should I take the cassette tape with me or leave it here?

CHAPTER TWELVE

I poured my morning coffee and stared at the tape I'd just heard in its entirety. Lyman completed his wishes for distribution of his belongings. He'd recorded his feelings about his diagnosis of Agent Orange leukemia and coming to terms with his imminent death.

Refilling my mug, I debated with myself about trying to sneak the cassette into the jail so Tater could hear Lyman's words. Instead, I opted to call Detective Rilke at home.

"Hello?" Detective Rilke answered on the first ring.

"This is Shanice Williams. I discovered a cassette tape recorded by Lyman Ernst on January 21, his birthday. The words say he wants it to serve as his final will, and there's other important information as well."

"Where did you find it?" Rilke asked.

Rather than answer his question, I asked him one. "Could you meet me at the Birch Tree jail around one? I know it's Sunday, but it's very important."

"I'll be there." He broke the connection.

Wrapping my hands around the mug, I wondered if I'd made the right decision. I could have kept the tape a secret and investigated more on my own. Then I remembered Manuel's raw concern for his wife, the fire that destroyed Lyman's house, and my grandfather sitting in a cell, and surmised stepping out of the amateur sleuth role was the right thing to do.

———

Rilke was pacing outside the local jail when I pulled up. I'd made a quick trip back to Tater's after church to retrieve the cassette recorder. Holding a tote bag that contained the recorder and the tape, I acknowledged Rilke's invitation to enter as he held the door. I followed him to a room with a single table and some straight-backed chairs. The scene reminded me of the interrogation cubicles I'd seen on television detective shows.

Rilke moved the antiquated machine I handed him to the center of the table. "I've asked a court reporter to join us and transcribe the information."

No sooner were the words out of Rilke's mouth than an older man entered the room and set up his equipment on the table.

"Could my grandfather join us?" I asked.

Rilke shook his head. "I want to make certain the information hasn't been tampered with and is preserved. My parents had one of these, and the tapes were always breaking. Then we had to splice them together, which could cut out some sections. We'll get a transcription then ask forensics to examine the magnetic tape to make certain it is without breaks. Ready?" He glanced at the court reporter, who nodded.

Rilke, apparently eager to hear the tape, hadn't introduced the man whose fingers were poised over the keys. When the detective pushed the PLAY button, I heard Lyman, now dead, speak to the living.

"This is Lyman Ernst, and I have something to say that may shock the people of Birch Tree. If you're listening to this, I'm probably in heaven, reunited with my Savior, and free from earthly concerns. I recorded this tape on January 21, my seventy-first birthday, to serve as my last will and testament. Any listener needs to know about what's happening in Birch Tree. My goal in the next few months will be to right wrongs and see justice done. As for the distribution of my worldly goods, I never accumulated a lot, but I hope those who receive them will remember me fondly."

The transcriber recorded the bequests of the garage to Manuel and Juanita and the house to Nila Tran.

The tape continued. "Third, I give all that remains of my belongings to William Williams, known to all as Tater. By the way, Nila, Tater gets everything in the house and on the grounds of the property. Tater already has the information about my accounts and is a cosigner on my safety deposit box. He knows my wishes."

Rilke glanced at the man with the nimble fingers who indicated he had kept up with the transcription.

"Now, concerning Birch Tree, Donald Price's parents appointed the young man to oversee the food truck court. He thought the assignment was a way to remove him from their headquarter offices, and he was right. Donald discovered that his parents intended to use their company, Price Premier, to buy off the food trucks one by one. The Prices sent Donald here with the task of putting each of the businesses in a weakened condition so their firm could purchase the food trucks for pennies on the dollar. They also intended to buy Helen's quilt shop and the Creamery. Their scheme didn't work, because Donald found out what they were up to, and he asked me to help him thwart his parents' plan."

When I'd heard that part this morning, I felt sorry for Donald and the struggle he must have faced in following his own moral compass rather than the instructions of his greedy parents. Donald, Lyman, and Tater concocted the negative campaign about the Spudmobile and some other businesses to make Donald's parents think that he was following his parents' directives. But the young man prompted the individual owners to get everything in order so his parents couldn't find legal reasons for closing the food trucks. I was relieved that Lyman and Tater were never feuding. They were allies to the end. The two probably enjoyed fooling everyone with their contentious performances.

Rilke jotted down notes of his own as he listened. Then he pressed the STOP button. "I still have a murder investigation. Someone changed those spuds from luscious to lethal."

I nodded. "But why would someone want to kill Lyman? He was going to die soon anyway."

"Because of their lifelong bond, your grandfather might have helped Lyman die, which is still murder. Donald Price said he saw Tater at Ernst's house the day of Lyman's death. I see no reason to change my belief that Tater is the logical suspect."

"But I know he isn't. I have a plan that might flush out the murderer," I said.

Rilke gave me a slight nod, an invitation to explain.

"We have a big event coming up at the food court. It's called the 'Welcome to Summer' promotion. That day all the suspects will be there. I could mention that I found a cassette recording of Lyman's will and hint that Lyman suggested who might want him dead."

"That's too risky," Rilke said.

"But you could have officers watching. If the murderer tries to steal the tape, you'd have your man or your woman."

"In your scenario, you admit knowing the contents of the tape. The guilty person might decide to eliminate you as well as take the cassette tape."

I shook my head. "All the suspects are people I know, and I can't believe one of them would harm me."

"The town is filled with nice people, but Lyman Ernst is dead." Rilke sighed. "I'll think about it, Shanice."

When my parents said they'd *think about it*, I knew I'd won. I hoped Rilke was the same. "And Tater?" I asked.

"As for your grandfather, he did evade arrest. Since he's well known locally, the judge just needs assurance he'll show up for his court appearance."

"I'll make sure he does," I promised.

Rilke grabbed the keys and led me to the cells. When Tater saw us, he rose slowly from his bunk. My heart ached because he looked like he'd lost fifteen pounds and his hair seemed grayer.

"You're being released into my care. Scary idea, isn't it?" My joke failed to elicit a smile. "Don't think you'll get to sit around. You'll have to work at the Spudmobile."

He didn't answer. He shuffled behind Detective Rilke from his cell to the front desk and signed papers for the return of his personal belongings.

———

When we reached his house, I suggested he shower and change clothes while I made biscuits, fried potatoes, and scrambled eggs. He emerged wearing clean clothes, but his manner hadn't changed.

"Spent my jail time thinking about Lyman. If he's gone, guess my earthly time is almost up."

"Lyman had a terminal illness. You don't." I stopped buttering the biscuits. "You don't, do you?"

"No. Lyman badgered me to test for the leukemia that's taken so many of our comrades. I'm okay. I keep asking myself, why Lyman? Why not me?"

"I don't know. As a nurse, I saw cases where the patient should have lived and didn't, and also the reverse. It confirmed my belief that God is in charge, not us." I filled our plates and put them on the table. "Since you've been given more time, I believe God wants you to do something with your days."

Tater reached for my hands and offered thanks for the meal and for wisdom and discernment, to which I added a heartfelt "amen."

"Anything at all survive the fire at Lyman's?" Tater asked.

"No, it spread quickly. The fire department thinks it was set. I rescued the tape recorder and his tapes before the house burned."

Tater perked up. "You find any special recording?"

"I think you know."

"His will? We created our will recordings separately. I gave mine to a lawyer, but Lyman said he planned to keep his, in case he wanted to change it from time to time."

"Sheriff Rilke thinks Lyman's oral copy will hold up in court," I said.

"Did he mention the foundation?"

"The foundation that you put your life savings into? Nothing on the tape, but I want to hear about the foundation, where you went, and why you took your suit with you."

He grinned. "Wore that suit twice and hope to wear it again. I wore my fancy clothes for the announcement of the foundation to rebuild houses in Vietnam. The trust was Lyman's idea, and we contacted men from our old unit. The foundation headquarters is near Fort Dix, New Jersey, where we did basic training. The suggestion received lots of support. Second time was when I visited Helen's relatives in North Carolina." He twisted his toe like a nervous teenager. "I wanted their permission to ask Helen to marry me—but I haven't had a chance. I planned to ask her on Friday, her birthday, but went to jail instead."

———

Tater didn't like the plan I'd convinced Rilke to implement. The detective told me he would have plain-clothed officers in the crowd watching to make sure nothing happened to me. Of course, my grandfather vowed never to leave my side.

The day of the "Welcome to Summer" promotion started with light showers, but that didn't prevent a large crowd from showing up for the event. Maine vacationers and locals embraced festivals, and who could resist contending in beanbag tosses, ax throwing, and cherry-pit spitting? There were also bouncy castles, face painting, and a cherry dessert bake-off competition.

Eager patrons lined up at the Spudmobile as everyone wanted to greet Tater to welcome him back and to extend their condolences to him about the death of Lyman. I spread the word about Lyman's tape holding critical information about a killer, which proved to be good for Spudmobile business.

The spuds moved faster than a token in the children's game of hot potato until Nila Tran doubled over with cramps and claimed eating our Super Mashed Mixture had made her sick. Within minutes, Juanita Ortiz put down her fork, saying she wasn't feeling well either.

People moved away from the Spudmobile, as if being within a ten-foot radius of the food truck itself might contaminate them. Tater and I had featured the Super Mashed Mixture that day to prove that Lyman's death had nothing to do with the Spudmobile's food.

Our plan backfired.

CHAPTER THIRTEEN

After the ambulance whisked Nila away, Tater and I shut down the Spudmobile and drove to the hospital. Shortly after my grandpa and I began our vigil, Winnie and Iris arrived with blankets, bottled water, trail mix in small bags, a sudoku book, and a jigsaw puzzle.

Winnie offered me a water. "We didn't know how long people would be here. Iris and I brought blankets because I get chilled every time Pastor Brandon and I visit the sick."

"Since you two are getting married in a couple of months, you should start calling him Brandon instead of Pastor Brandon," I teased, which made her giggle.

"Have you received any word on Juanita or Nila yet?" Iris asked.

"Yes. The ER doc said they should both be fine. Rilke took their food containers for analysis, so we're waiting."

"We may as well put together a puzzle while we wait." Winnie opened the box and dumped the pieces on a round table. "Come on, keeping your hands busy will pass the time."

Winnie made certain all had a spot at the table and suggested areas each person might work on.

Helen took the chair next to mine. "I hear you have Lyman's tape."

"I do. I'll pass it over to Detective Rilke as soon as he returns from the police lab," I said.

"Did you listen to it?" Helen flipped pieces over to show the colored fronts. "Did Lyman mention me?"

"Well. . ." I paused, hoping she'd say more. "He did mention his concern about your business."

Helen's fingers went to her earrings, her nervous habit. "Lyman insisted I stop dealing with vendors I'd used for years. I refused. What did Lyman Ernst know about fabrics for quilt making?"

"He had good taste in clothes," I suggested.

Helen smiled at my joke. "He did, but I ran my own business for years, and he tried to tell me what to do and not do. I planned to open shops in Augusta and York, using my Birch Tree store as collateral. Lyman begged me not to put my shop in danger. I told him I wasn't interested in him or his business advice."

"Was that when you and Tater started dating?"

A rosy blush bathed her cheeks. "Yes. I found myself acting like a schoolgirl. I couldn't wait to see Tater each day. Imagine a woman at my age falling in love. And with someone I'd known my whole life. I believed Tater wanted to marry me."

"My grandfather seems devoted to you." I nodded to Tater pacing in front of the nurse's station.

"Lyman stood between us. Tater loved Lyman like a brother. After I started dating Tater, he told me he'd taken out a mortgage on his house and given all the money to Lyman for some project."

"Lyman was terminally ill," I said.

"I didn't know that." Helen grabbed my hand and moved a little closer.

"He mentioned wanting to protect you and your quilt shop from a takeover by outsiders."

"Protect me? Or did he want to prevent me from being successful? And Tater? Wasn't Lyman behind the rumors about the Spudmobile food?"

"Do you truly believe Lyman would harm his best friend?"

Helen put two edge pieces of the puzzle together and looked up. "He did, didn't he? I knew Tater's Spudmobile business was precarious and that my shop would have to support us if Tater and I married. That would have been fine with me. When I tried to explain my belief that Lyman was taking advantage of their friendship, your grandfather refused to listen."

"And now that Lyman's dead?" I asked.

"He shouldn't have died," Helen said.

The blunt statement caused me to suck in my breath. "You didn't put anything into the potatoes on the day Lyman died, did you?"

"Don't be ridiculous. And I didn't tamper with Juanita or Nila's food today." Helen glanced at Tater. "I love that man. I wouldn't harm his best friend or his business."

Jerry Rilke entered and waved a sheet of paper. "I have the lab results. The potatoes were harmless, and the 'sick' ladies are on their way to join us. Nila admitted pretending to be sick, and the doctor thinks Juanita's symptoms occurred because of the power of suggestion. We're going to play Lyman's tape and put this case to rest." Rilke held out his hand.

I gave him a cassette tape, and he slipped it into his pocket. No one seemed to notice that the tape recorder already had a tape in it. After Juanita and Nila arrived in the waiting room, Jerry Rilke told everyone this appeared to be Lyman Ernst's last will, and that Lyman included the people present in his bequests. Rilke pushed the button.

Lyman's voice sounded, making pronouncements that would change lives. Manuel and his sons, relieved that Juanita was fine, shared hugs and tears in amazement and gratitude at Lyman's generosity to their family.

Manuel said, "We may own the garage, but the business will continue to operate as Ernst Garage because Ernst stands for honesty and integrity. Our customers recognize that reputation, and we will follow Lyman's example and serve old friends and new clients in the same way."

When Lyman's voice mentioned Nila's inheritance, the response was different.

"What? That was my house?" Nila's reaction showed the most animation I'd ever seen her display.

"Did you torch Lyman's house?" Tater asked Nila, then turned to Rilke, who'd paused the tape. "Isn't that a crime?"

The detective nodded. "It is."

Nila appeared dazed. "Lyman Ernst gave me a house, a home, and now it's gone."

Lyman's alliance with Donald Price about tarnishing the reputation of various food trucks elicited more consternation. All eyes turned to Donald.

Donald nodded. "Lyman pretended to be at odds with Tater, put up the LETHAL SPUDS sign, and said negative things about the Spudmobile—all with Tater's consent. The three of us developed a plan, not to destroy the food park businesses, but to save them as well as Helen's quilt shop and the Creamery. On the night of the fire, I went to Lyman's place to see if I could find some proof of our agreement in his handwriting. I didn't want the townsfolk to remember Lyman in an unkind light when he was trying to save community businesses."

Winnie said, "I work in permitting at city hall, and my office has been very busy. You've been the one receiving the money, so how did you help the food truck owners?"

Winnie's strong words surprised me, but Donald appeared eager to answer.

"I knew my parents' plan was to shut down this whole operation and put in their own food stands. My goal was to make certain every local owner had done things legally and correctly so there would be no loopholes for my parents' company, Price Premier, to exploit. My actions weren't popular, but they were for the protection of Birch Tree locals. I'm a big-city boy who loves this small-town atmosphere. I hope to make Birch Tree my home."

Donald looked directly at me as he made the last statement. He obviously hadn't heard that I'd soon be leaving this small town of Birch Tree for the big city of Augusta. Our timing was off, but my heart was open. After my mother's death, my bout with depression, and my ICU nursing burnout, I found the awareness of his interest in me encouraging.

Jerry Rilke removed his finger from the STOP button. "Many of you know that I spent twenty years in military service before I became a law-enforcement officer. Soldiers share a special bond and an affinity for the places where they serve. Lyman's message on this tape moves me. I wish I'd known the man, but even without a personal acquaintance, I feel I know his character." Rilke pushed PLAY again.

As Lyman's words resonated throughout the room, I noticed Tater sat with his arm around Helen's shoulder. When the next section played for everyone to hear, Helen would realize the depth of the friendship between Tater and Lyman.

Rilke continued playing the tape, and Lyman's recitation shared his doctor's opinion that his patient had only months to live because of the leukemia caused by Agent Orange. Lyman's laughter caught on tape filled the room. He said either his heart would fail or the leukemia would get him, so he created a charitable trust that would outlive him. The room quieted as everyone listened.

"I served in Vietnam as a young man straight out of high school. Thought I was a man, but after living a few more years, I looked back and pictured that soldier, not as a man, but as a young boy. There I was in a beautiful foreign land, surrounded by people losing their homes in a horrible war. With the bulk of my money, I decided to start the Rebuild and Renew Charitable Trust. Tater joined me, taking all the equity out of his house. We contacted other members of our old unit, and word spread. I was not the only one who wanted to make a difference. On the second Saturday in June, Tater will meet with our army buddies and transfer funds to a construction company to start the rebuilding of homes in the Quang Nam province of Vietnam. The goal is to build ten houses each year."

Nila gasped. "No! I'm so sorry. I'm so sorry."

Rilke stepped forward. "Why are you sorry, Nila?"

"I put the sleeping pills into Mr. Ernst's potatoes the day he died." Nila placed her head on the table and sobbed.

Helen stared open-mouthed at Nila. "You doctored his potatoes?"

"Yes. When Price gave me the take-out orders to deliver, I decided to add a special ingredient to Lyman's order. I didn't intend to kill him. I just wanted to make him sick."

Rilke nodded and smiled at me as if I'd be happy the killer had confessed. I wasn't pleased. I'd loved Uncle Lyman, and the man I knew wouldn't want Nila to spend the rest of her days in prison.

CHAPTER FOURTEEN

After all the excitement, the return to normalcy was a blessing. Lyman's doctors testified that they had suggested their patient move to hospice care as he was in the final stages of leukemia. The sleep aid in addition to the muscle relaxants and pain medications he used could have caused him to lose consciousness and fall. While initial results pointed to the sleeping pills, the final autopsy showed the cause of death to be a bleeding in the brain. The blood thinning medications prescribed for his heart disease led to a brain hemorrhage following his fall.

The court prosecuted Nila Tran for arson and involuntary manslaughter. Nila, against the advice of her counsel, pleaded guilty. The judge sentenced the Vietnamese woman to ten years because of the petitions of her Birch Tree friends for leniency. He approved her proposal to work from prison on Lyman's trust and to offer suggestions for rebuilding a house on the Birch Tree lot as a temporary lodging for refugees.

Tater and I served a record number of customers the last week of June. Regulars flocked to the Spudmobile and brought friends, as if trying to prove their loyalty.

Walking to Tater's house after closing for the day, I brought up my departure. "Tater, I needed my time in Birch Tree to recover, but I'm going back to my true vocation."

"You like being with sick people better than serving spuds?" he asked.

"I do," I said, then turned to him. "Are you ready to say those two words?"

Tater smiled broadly, which showed the gap between his front teeth. "I'm more than ready. Pretty smart of me to ask Helen to marry me on the Fourth of July. Can you believe the city will provide fireworks for us?"

"Why not? You're a town favorite," I said.

"Can't think of a better day for a soldier to marry. Several men from our old unit are coming. I invited them when we launched Lyman's Rebuild and Renew Charitable Trust. They'll stand up with me, in place of Lyman."

"And you'll wear a suit?"

"Yep, my wedding and funeral suit. Like I said, I wore it at the launch of Lyman's trust and when I asked Helen's nephew for permission to marry her. I told him to bring all the family relatives he could round up for our wedding."

"You could have told me. I'm glad you contacted Helen's kin. She's excited about seeing her extended family again."

Tater grinned. "I like making that woman happy. Sorry I didn't start courting her years ago."

"And we shouldn't wait for a wedding or funeral to get people together. I've missed seeing my brothers and their families, even though I've only been in Birch Tree four months."

"Your stay here was not uneventful," Tater said.

"More excitement than I bargained for," I said.

The wedding day for William Williams and Helen Randall began with a light drizzle, which everyone counted as enough rain to signify good luck for the newlyweds. Donald Price drove me to the stone church where Winnie and Iris waited. We slipped into choir robes and ran over the two songs we'd sing, "Wither Thou Goest" and "Surely the Presence of the Lord Is in This Place." My eyes filled, and I sniffled during our rehearsal, so I asked for a prayer before the ceremony began. Even though any tears would be tears of joy, I didn't want my emotions to distract from the exchange of vows.

Weddings reminded me of endings and beginnings, the ending of single lives and the beginning of a unified one. This day I reflected on my endings and beginnings. I'd be ending my time in Birch Tree. My reaction to the end of Mom's life had been a self-imposed hibernation, and I'd retreated to this small town to heal. Lyman's death was the end of the life of a man I considered an uncle. But his death inspired me to live again, to search for meaning in my life, and to open my heart.

The organist began the familiar strains of the "Bridal Chorus," and we all stood to watch Helen walk down the aisle carrying a red, white, and blue floral arrangement.

Seeing the joy on the faces of Helen and my grandfather, I remembered the beautiful words from Ecclesiastes.

> *There is a time for everything,*
> *and a season for every activity under the heavens:*
> *a time to be born and a time to die,*
> *a time to plant and a time to uproot,*
> *a time to kill and a time to heal,*
> *a time to tear down and a time to build,*
> *a time to weep and a time to laugh,*
> *a time to mourn and a time to dance,*
> *a time to scatter stones and a time to gather them,*

a time to embrace and a time to refrain from embracing,
a time to search and a time to give up,
a time to keep and a time to throw away,
a time to tear and a time to mend,
a time to be silent and a time to speak,
a time to love and a time to hate,
a time for war and a time for peace.

Tater reached for Helen's hand before she reached the front, his broad grin showing the gap between his front teeth.

Would I ever see a man waiting at the altar and looking at me with the expression Tater wore whenever he saw Helen? I stole a glance at Donald and found him watching me. Considering all the "times" mentioned in the Bible passage, I wondered what kind of "time" Donald and I might share in the future.

Speculation about my future was for a different day. Today was a time to laugh, to dance, to embrace, and to celebrate love.

Linda Baten Johnson loves traveling and has visited all fifty states and many foreign countries. She also enjoys sampling regional cuisine, and finding the local food truck picnic park often provides that opportunity. She grew up in a small Texas town, where she won blue ribbons for storytelling, and she still loves telling tales. A tornado destroyed her hometown when Linda was young, and watching faith-based actions in rebuilding lives and homes after the tragedy influences her writing. Her historical fiction books for young readers, squeaky-clean romances, and cozy mysteries are available in print, e-book, and audio.

TACO TRAGEDY

TERESA IVES LILLY

CHAPTER ONE

I can't believe how many customers we've had this week," I said as I pulled the window screen of the food truck down on Saturday night. "I thought by now, since school has started again, the crowds would have thinned a bit."

I glanced at my cook, Elena Guadalupe, a woman in her midsixties, but she didn't answer. I shook my head. I'd hired Elena because she had experience at one of the Mexican restaurants in town and knew how to cook authentically, but the woman wasn't very friendly.

I wiped the counter with a wet cloth and frowned at Elena's back. There was something about her that had originally reminded me of my grandmother, and I'd hoped that Elena and I would be able to form a friendship that might help ease some of the pain I'd felt since Abuelita had grown so ill and gone to heaven. However, a friendship with Elena had not panned out.

I guess it didn't matter. She was a great cook and understood the recipes in Abuelita's cookbook better than I did. However, it irritated me that she kept asking me to share the secret recipe for my sauce for Abuelita's Holy Guacamole taco that I'd won the "Best Mexican Food in Town" award for the last four years.

I sprayed a bit of cleaner on the counter carelessly, without looking at what I was doing.

"You'll poison someone if that cleaner gets into your secret sauce," Elena said in a dull voice with a bit of a sarcastic edge. She nodded at the large stockpot sitting on the stove top. I knew Elena was offended that I wouldn't share my recipe with her, but it had been a family secret as long as I could remember. Abuelita had only shared it with me a year ago, and I'd made a solemn oath that I wouldn't ever let anyone know the secret except my own daughter, when and if I ever had one.

"Oops." I grabbed the lid and covered the pot. I wouldn't have to make a new batch for another few days if I could keep this one fresh. I carried the pot to the refrigerator and placed it inside. "I don't think any of the cleaner got into the sauce." I gave Elena a shrug.

She just stared at me with her dark eyes.

I finished cleaning the counters and hung the cloth on a hook. "I guess that's it for the night. You know the judges will be here on Thursday next week, and I hope to win the award for best Mexican food in town again this year."

Elena's shoulders were stiff, but she nodded. "*Sí*, I know you do. What time will the judges be here?"

"I'm assuming between eleven and noon. They like to show up when we're the busiest. Didn't they use to do the same at El Patrón?" I named the restaurant where Elena used to work.

She nodded again. "*Sí*, always during the hustle and bustle. Last year they came earlier than we expected, and the bean soup had not cooked long enough."

I wondered if that was why Elena had been let go from the restaurant. She'd told me once that she worked there for years and years. Until my grandmother had opened this food truck, El

Patrón, Margarita's, and the Taco Tent in town had all won the award once or twice, but never four consecutive times like the Crunchy Taco had.

It was hard to believe that the owner of El Patrón would fire Elena just because the bean soup hadn't been cooked long enough.

Well, their loss was my gain. As I said, she was a great cook.

I moved across the trailer, an envelope in my hand. "Here's your check, Elena. I've put in a little bonus since you've been working extra hours."

The woman met my eyes with a look of surprise. "*Gracias.*" She bobbed her head, took the envelope, and turned away abruptly. "I will see you tomorrow."

Elena slipped out the door of the food truck, leaving me alone, my face reflected in the small mirror I kept hanging over the sink. I had a somewhat plain look, dark hair and dark eyes, although since there were very few Hispanic women in the area, I was often referred to as "exotic." That made me laugh. *Exotic* was the last word I would have used to describe myself.

Finally, after one last glance around the interior of my food truck, I snapped off the lights, locked the door, and clambered down the outside steps. I strolled over to the lake edge and stood looking out over the water. The moon cast an iridescent glow, and I was able to see the small ripples made by a fish swimming here or there. It wasn't quite a full moon, but here in Maine it seemed as if we were close to it. As if I could just reach out and touch it.

Ever since the first time Abuelita and I set eyes on the lovely lake, I'd been in love. If I could build a house in this exact spot instead of a food truck, I would. My grandmother always told me, "Marissa, this is the most beautiful place I've ever seen. We will stay here until Jesus comes to take me home."

At the time, they were only meaningless words to me. Losing Abuelita to old age seemed many, many years away. However, losing her to a heart attack at age sixty-five was a sad reality that I'd had to endure this last year.

The last thing she'd said to me was, "Marissa, this is a good place. You and José stay here and make a good life with the food truck. When you see the moonlight on the lake at night, think of me. I will be looking down on you."

Wiping away a tear, I sniffed and tucked away the thoughts. I missed my grandmother very much, but at least I still had the lake and the food truck, and I had no intention of leaving.

As I made my way to my car, I passed by the Lucky Noodle food truck, then the Spudmobile, which was in the center of the park, and finally the Dream Donuts food truck, which was by the entrance. The lights on each food truck were turned off, and there was no one in the area. The farther from the lake I got, the less the moon illuminated the area around me. It grew darker and darker.

I pulled my sweater close. It wasn't that I was cold, although the early fall breeze was beginning to make itself known in the evenings, but there was something eerie about the food truck court when no one else was around.

Suddenly someone tall stepped out from behind a tree, blocking my way. I couldn't see the person's face. I gasped, looked up, and realized who was standing in front of me. "What are you doing here?" My voice had a startled tone.

"Can't a little brother come and walk his big sister home?" The tall, lanky youth grinned at me. José was unusually tall for a Hispanic teen, and having him to walk with gave me some comfort. "Marissa, now that it's getting darker earlier, I don't want you walking to your car alone. I'll try to be here by closing each night."

I slipped my hand into the crook of his arm, and we walked side by side. "I hate for you to have to do that, but I'm glad you're here. There's something in the air lately. I get the feeling of. . .I don't know. . .dread."

José laughed. "You're beginning to sound like Abuelita. She was always predicting bad things."

"I know, but most of the time she was wrong. I can only hope I am."

We reached my car, which was nothing to brag about, though it did get great gas mileage, and my brother's best friend, Pete, was always willing to fix it up at his auto shop if anything broke. I opened my door while José walked to the other side and got in.

When we were both inside the car, I turned on the engine.

"You know, Mari," José said, using the nickname he'd called me ever since he'd first been able to talk, "you told me all about your new relationship with God. I think you should put your trust in Him, rather than in your feelings."

I glanced at my brother. "You're right, José. I guess I was just feeling a bit nostalgic. Tonight was the type of night Abuelita would have loved. The fall breeze, the air filled with the aromas from the different food trucks, the moonlight on the lake."

José reached over, grasped my hand, and gave it a squeeze. "By keeping the Crunchy Taco going, you're honoring her memory."

I felt a tear threaten to fall, so I sniffed and began to drive, trying to shake off the melancholy. I truly hoped I was honoring her memory. I was glad that I had the food truck to keep me busy since her passing.

"Hey, wasn't there something you wanted to watch tonight?" I asked, remembering a conversation we'd had earlier.

"Yep, there's an old Sherlock Holmes movie on." He shrugged when he saw me cringe.

"Another mystery? Don't you think we've watched enough of them over the last year? And you wonder why I have bad premonitions."

"You know I've been thinking about my future, and I might just want to be a detective someday. I consider this my pretraining." He gave a quirky smirk. "I could spend my nights hanging out on the corner or drinking or smoking. . ." His tone begged me to understand him. "But, as Sherlock Holmes often said, 'It's my job to know what other people do not know.'"

I smiled. This was something new José had begun doing lately—quoting from Sherlock Holmes. I expected to hear many of the pithy sayings in the near future until he got hooked on some new detective. "You're right, and I shouldn't make fun. I'm proud of you, and if you want to be a detective someday, and you think watching old mystery movies is important, then it's important to me. So, no more talk. Let's just get home."

José settled back, a smile flitting across his face.

I was content. Since my grandmother's death, I was not only the older sister but also the mother to José, and we'd bonded more in the last few months than in all the years before. We lost our parents to influenza when I was only fourteen and José was four, and we'd been sent to live with our grandmother.

She'd moved us several times, though we lived in one town long enough for me to go to a local college. But after that we moved to the Birch Point Lake area, about thirty miles outside of York, Maine, to a town called Birch Tree. All three of us fell in love with the area, and I was glad that we'd finally settled down. At that time, I was twenty, but now I was twenty-five and José was just fifteen but looked at least eighteen, so I knew I could always feel safe with him beside me.

Grandmother had made a good life for us here, and I had no intention of changing things now. José and I were both happy in Birch Tree.

I could have asked José why he was spending his Saturday night with his sister instead of with friends, but I didn't need to. He was an introvert and had a very small group of friends. Most of them were probably at home tonight watching old movies themselves. So, for now, I was content to hang out with my brother. I was sure that one day, in the not-too-distant future, he'd be chasing a pretty girl and would be too busy for me.

We drove around the lake until we reached our small cabin. It was set back from the road, nestled in the thick forest. It was nothing special, but to us it was home. Somehow my grandmother had paid off the cabin and put it in my name before she died, but we knew we'd need to keep up with the taxes. The money we made from the Crunchy Taco was enough to take care of most things and add to our savings. We weren't getting rich, but we wouldn't lose our home as long as we continued to have good crowds at the food truck.

I pulled into the driveway and parked. José hopped out of the car and lumbered toward the front door. My heart tightened as I watched him. It was sad that such a wonderful brother had no mother, no grandmother, and no father. I was all he had, and there were many days I felt lost and alone.

Of course, since I'd heard the message preached at church about how to give my life over to Jesus, I'd felt less lonely, and I hoped that José would soon accept Jesus into his heart as well. When he did, I knew he too would feel less lonely.

CHAPTER TWO

The following Monday morning I dropped José off at school, a few minutes late, but at least he wouldn't miss his homeroom. He, however, had a scowl on his face.

"Marissa, why do I have to go to school? I'd rather work at the Crunchy Taco. You could homeschool me."

I shook my head. "As much as I'd love that, José, you know I don't have time. The customers come all day long to the food truck. Besides, you're going to be a great basketball player, and the local homeschool community doesn't offer a team for that."

I didn't really need to remind him, because we'd already hashed all this out several times. His best friend, Pete Carlin, was homeschooled. But Pete was too short for basketball. He was great on the homeschool swim team.

He sighed, grabbed his bag, and headed toward the building. I wanted José to have the same opportunities I'd had. Going to college was an exceptional experience for me. In the end, though, my heart was in cooking the traditional Mexican food my grandmother taught me to cook. Using her recipes at the Crunchy Taco was only a beginning.

She and I had hoped to save enough and open an actual restaurant by the lake. There was a small piece of land, which only one other person I knew of was interested in, that would make a perfect spot for a restaurant. Grandmother tried to buy it and made several offers, but the owner said they were too low. We had thought that in about two more years we would have enough money saved to actually make a fair offer that the owner was sure to take.

Now, without her, I hadn't been seriously considering it any longer. Still, José mentioned it quite often. As I watched him walk up the steps of the high school, I wondered if he, like me, really had his heart set on cooking, even if he did say he wanted to be a detective. If that was the case, maybe college wasn't something he needed to do.

A nearby town had a pretty good community college. Or he could go away, which would be sad for me. I just wanted him to have the opportunity if he wanted it.

Once he was inside the building, I drove to the food truck court and stationed my car in its usual place. I may have been a bit late because most of the other food truck owners were already busy opening windows, turning on stove tops, or heating oil—the activities each one needed to do to get started for the day.

The good thing was that no one but Dream Donuts started serving food early. And they weren't my truck's competition.

The Spudmobile was my biggest competitor. However, Tater Williams, who owned the converted school bus, was really nice, and he and I didn't see each other as competition. At least not that I knew of. The owners of the food truck court didn't allow direct competition, so I didn't have to worry about a Mexican food truck ever opening up here. During the summer there were more food trucks, but only a few of us were permanent fixtures.

After saying hello to some of the other owners, I made my way to the Crunchy Taco truck. I was late, but Elena was even later, which didn't surprise me. For someone who had been so adamant I hire her, she didn't take her job that seriously. I didn't mind though. Opening up the truck was one of my favorite things to do. I liked getting things set up and set out so I could reach whatever I needed for the day. If Elena got there too early, she tended to set things up her way.

After I turned on the light, I looked over my supplies. I expected a delivery later in the week with some of the supplies I was running low on, but I had enough to get me through. The only thing I needed to be careful with was what I would need for the Holy Guacamole tacos I would make on Thursday for the judges.

I currently had a batch that would last the week, but I wanted to make a new batch on Wednesday evening just for the judges.

As I set out the tomatoes and avocados for cutting, the door on the end of the food truck opened and Elena pulled herself up the steps into the truck.

I turned with a bright smile. "Good morning, Elena."

She stared at me, then gave a small nod of her head.

I wasn't even sure she spoke fluent English, because we'd had such little interaction since she started working for me. There were days I longed for a friendly smile and a bit of encouragement like Abuelita used to give. But Elena wasn't inclined to offer any such thing.

The Hispanic culture in the South was usually very friendly and family oriented, but here in Maine, those who owned or worked in a Mexican restaurant were usually third or fourth generation, and most of them had grown out of that type of community support. Only a few of the older people in the restaurant business were originally from Mexico or surrounding areas. Abuelita had been one of them.

Elena grabbed one of the full aprons, tied it on, and moved toward the surface where we made tortillas by hand. That was the most time-consuming task of our day. I didn't want to buy premade tortillas though. Nothing spoke real Mexican food like a hand-tossed flour tortilla, and I knew my regular customers wouldn't be happy if I changed that.

The day began a bit slowly. We served breakfast tacos on weekends but not during the week, so most people weren't looking for our type of cuisine until lunch. We often had a steady flow of local construction workers who would each buy about six tacos, so we knew that making enough tortillas was mandatory.

At about ten, a tall, good-looking man stepped up to the window. "Hello, miss."

I smiled. *"Hola."*

"I'd like two hundred Holy Guacamole tacos, please." He winked.

I laughed. This was a rolling joke between Rick Carlson and me. He was a local real estate agent I met when we first moved to the lake. We'd been on a few dates, although once my grandmother died, I hadn't felt up to socializing much, and Rick had been kind enough to step back a bit.

"Seriously though, I'd like three Holy Guacamole tacos."

"All right. Give me a few minutes." I turned away from the window to work on the tacos, but he called in to me.

"Marissa, I have something important to talk to you about. Can I come in?"

Usually, my answer would be no. The health inspector didn't look too kindly on having customers in the food truck, but she'd been by for inspection a few weeks earlier, and I didn't expect her again for a while.

"Sure." I nodded to the far door, and Rick's head disappeared from the window. In a few seconds, the door opened and he pulled himself up into the food truck.

I was busy creating the tacos for him, but he moved toward me and sat on the one and only stool we kept inside. There just wasn't room for more chairs, so Elena and I took turns resting on the one stool throughout the day.

"So, what's so important?" I asked in a playful tone. I didn't want him to get the impression I was irritated with him being in the food truck. I really liked Rick and wanted to continue a relationship with him.

"Well, I have some good news, but I'm not too sure how it will go over."

I stopped spreading the refried beans on the tortilla in my hand and stared at him. "Yes?"

"That spot on the lake your grandmother wanted to buy. . ."

"Yes, what about it? I thought the owner didn't want to sell." My hand stilled in anticipation.

"The owner has decided to move to Florida and finally wants to sell, but immediately."

I felt my shoulders drop. "I probably can't afford what he's asking."

Rick shook his head. "That's just it. He's not asking any more than your last offer."

My head shot up, my eyes alight. "Really?"

"Yes. However, you aren't the only one who put in an offer." Rick's voice dropped.

"Oh. Mr. Charles Burnard," I muttered.

"Yes, he put in an offer at the same time as your grandmother. Since the owner wasn't selling, the offers were rejected. But now the owner wants me to inform both of you that he's willing to sell."

I sighed. "Mr. Burnard can outbid me any day." I felt my heart crashing. It was one thing to have a dream that you never thought would come true. It was another thing to have a dream smashed.

"That's just it, Marissa." Rick's eyes met mine. "He wants you both to give him a proposal of what you want to do with the land. He isn't asking for more money, but I guess he wants to have some say in what will be built by the lake."

I dropped the taco I had just finished. "Oh, Rick. Do you think he'll sell it to me?" My heart started beating faster.

"I'm not sure what his idea about the lake is. You know Mr. Burnard wants to build a hotel there. I guess the owner has his own thoughts, but he's not sharing them with me. So, I think it's best for you to write a letter tonight, explaining exactly what you want to do with the land, and I'll present it to him in the morning. That is, if you still want the land."

I felt like jumping up and down. "Of course I still want the land. This was Abuelita's dream."

Rick reached over and touched my hand. "But what about yours? Is that your dream, Marissa?"

I could understand his concern. Not many women would want to follow their grandmother's dreams, but I did. She and I had spent hours and hours planning the restaurant.

"Yes, it's also my dream, Rick. If I can get the land, it may take a few years before I can build a building, but at least I'll know the dream is within my grasp."

Just then another customer stepped up to the window. I handed Rick his three tacos.

"I'll send you the letter tonight," I assured him.

Rick stood up, tacos in hand, and moved to the door. "I'll be praying it works out for you, Marissa."

I turned to the window and heard the door close on the far end of the food truck. Then I saw Rick, waving as he walked away.

"Can I get two chicken fajitas?" The customer at the window interrupted my thoughts.

I smiled. "Yes, do you want cheese on those?" I settled back into the work for the day, but my mind was never far from the letter I would write that evening.

———◆———

"Did you hear what Rick Carlson told me?" I asked Elena as we were doing our after-lunch cleanup.

"Sí, about you buying the land for the restaurant."

"Yes, I'm so excited. That was my grandmother's dream. Just think, we could be as big as El Patrón someday!" I turned to look at the other woman but met only a blank stare.

Goodness, Lord. I don't know why Elena always seems so cold toward me, but she continues to work here.

"Will you make a new batch of secret sauce for the judging?" She interrupted my thoughts with a question. I smiled. At least she was talking to me.

"Yes. I'll come in on Wednesday night and make my best, fresh batch. I won't serve the sauce to anyone but the judges."

Just then the door opened and José climbed into the food truck. Elena spun around and smiled at him. "*Hola, chico.*"

My mouth dropped open at her behavior. I'd noticed she always had a smile for José. I had to wonder why she liked him and not me.

"Hi, Elena. Hi, Marissa." He dropped his backpack in the corner. "What can I do?"

I turned with a hand on my hip. "What are you doing here? Why aren't you in school?"

José cocked his head. "Early release today, Mari," he explained. "Why?"

"I don't know, some kind of teacher workday." He grabbed an apron and tied it on. "Want me to work the window?"

I nodded. I felt a bit guilty that I hadn't been aware of the early release. Our grandmother would have known about it and met him at school. I walked over and gave him a hug from behind. "Sorry I didn't know."

He shrugged. "No problem." He leaned forward and started taking orders from the line that had formed. There were a lot of teenagers from the high school. Obviously other kids who'd gotten out of school early.

"How did you know we were going to need your help?" I asked, glad he was here.

"Elementary, my dear Marissa. Elementary."

CHAPTER THREE

When the alarm rang on Tuesday morning, I rolled over and slapped at it then moaned. It was going to be hard getting up because I'd stayed up late writing the letter about why I wanted the spot on the lake.

I mean, how do you write a convincing letter when you have no idea what the owner's wishes are? If he was a big businessman, more than likely he'd want to see the land turned into a hotel. If he was a conservationist, he'd rather the land stayed free of all human influence. My hope was he was somewhere in the middle and loved good Mexican food. I did highlight that my food truck had won the award for best Mexican food for several years in a row. That seemed to be my only card to play.

Then I'd spent a good hour praying over the letter, which put me in bed at midnight.

Suddenly my bedroom door was flung open. José stood there staring at me, concern on his brow. "What are you doing in bed? You sick?"

"No, just a rough night."

"Well, I gotta get to school."

I rolled over and stood up. "Okay, I'll do a rush job this morning, no shower or anything."

He shrugged. "I can walk."

I shook my head. "No, I'll drive you. Don't worry, you may have never seen it before, but I can hurry if I have to."

He laughed with a tone that indicated he didn't believe me and turned away to go get his breakfast.

I looked around my room. Normally, I'd take a leisurely shower, pick out an outfit for the day, apply a small amount of makeup, and spend a half hour reading a morning devotional. Today it was going to have to be grab a pair of jeans and T-shirt, run the brush through my hair, no makeup, and just sing praise songs on the way to work.

When I entered the kitchen in less than ten minutes, José almost dropped his spoon. His eyes opened wide in surprise. "I can't believe it," he sputtered with cereal in his mouth.

I walked by him and gave him a playful slap on the arm. "Hey, don't make a big deal of it. I'm not that bad."

He rolled his eyes.

"I guess I can get some coffee at one of the other food trucks this morning," I said, frowning at my Keurig, thinking about my own special blend with almond milk.

There was no time for coffee though. José was already out the door and waiting in the car, so I grabbed my phone, my purse, and a light jacket, and then headed out the door. Early September in Maine could mean anything as far as weather was concerned. It might be a lovely, almost springlike day, or the wind could get stronger like a fall day, or it could even snow. One never knew, so I chose the thin jacket. However, I always kept extra blankets in the car and an umbrella in case of an emergency.

The farthest I ever drove in and around the town was about ten miles. Pretty much everything I could need or want was close by or could be delivered, so I didn't worry too much about being caught in the elements.

I slid into the front seat and turned to face my brother. He had a comical grin on his face.

"You done good, Sis."

"Thanks," I said, aware of how badly I needed to wash my hair. I turned on the engine, and within seconds I had pulled onto the road and was headed toward the high school.

"José, are you going to try out for basketball?" I asked.

"Hmm, I guess so. I mean, I'd rather come work at the food truck after school." He glanced out the window.

"I know you say that, but I really want you to try out for the basketball team. You're good, and you could get a scholarship to a college. You need a chance, like I had. The food truck, or hopefully the restaurant, will be here if you decide later on that's what you want in life, the way I did."

José was silent.

"Just think about it," I murmured as I pulled into the school drop-off area. "Besides, you would need an education to be a detective."

José opened the car door and hopped out. "Bye, Sis. Have a good day." He waved and walked away.

I wished he would have been able to mingle with one of the groups of kids standing around, but then again, I knew José was a true individualist and wouldn't fit the mold of any of those groups.

I pulled the car onto the street again and began to think about the day. Suddenly I remembered the letter I'd sent to Rick last night. I hadn't gotten a response from him before I went to sleep. Now my hands itched to look at my phone, but I knew better. The police in a small town have a special sense, and I'd be sure to be pulled over if I was on my phone—especially in a school zone.

———◆———

When I reached the food park, I could almost feel a change in the atmosphere. All the owners were cleaning their trucks, both inside and out. The tables in the middle of the park, with their striped umbrellas, sparkled.

This was in anticipation of the food judges coming by on Thursday. I wasn't the only one hoping to win an award. Mine was for best Mexican food, but there were plenty of categories, so everyone worked together to get ready.

I stood outside the Crunchy Taco and stared at it with a frown. It could definitely use a good scrubbing. The truck was just a plain rectangular truck, painted bright green, yellow, orange, and red. On the top was a large fiberglass taco. I would need to get a ladder to clean that.

The menu board was in the worst condition. There were even a few items I couldn't read. Of course, most of my regular customers knew the menu. We served simple things like tostadas, burritos, quesadillas, and chimichangas. We offered authentic, fruity, bottled Mexican drinks from Jarritos.

Shrugging my shoulders at the dirt, I headed for the taco truck, determined to get a bucket of soapy water and work on the menu at least, but when I reached the steps, I noticed that the lock on the door was broken. I reached out to touch it, and the door swung open on its own.

I turned around and searched the area around the truck. What I was looking for, I didn't know. I guess part of me expected to find a group of teen boys snickering in a corner or maybe a man dressed in dark sweats and a ski cap over his head slinking away.

Nothing seemed any different. The owners of the other trucks barely noticed me, although I did get a friendly wave from one or two. It didn't seem to make any sense. Everyone in town knew that no food truck owner left any money in the truck overnight, and honestly, nothing in the truck was worth stealing. A guard patrolled the area a few times each evening, so it didn't seem possible that anyone had tried to break into my truck.

I wondered if mine was the only one that had a broken lock. I'd have to ask the other truck owners once I got things set up for the day.

I pushed open the door, stepped up, and stared into the truck. I scanned the whole area. There were no hiding places, so I was confident no one was in the truck. I slid in and began to get things ready for the day.

The first thing I did every morning was get out the supplies I needed to make my secret sauce, if we didn't already have a batch made. I looked into the big freezer and noted the one pot I'd made earlier in the week.

I was glad that was done, because I would have time to get outside and clean the truck. I'd have to ask José if he would climb up and wash the taco.

Elena was exceptionally late. A whole hour passed before she opened the door and entered.

"What happened to the lock?" she asked.

I shrugged. "I don't know. It looks like someone tried to break in, but nothing is missing."

She glanced around. "Did you call the police?"

"No, but I guess I'll think about it. Since nothing is missing, I doubt they'll do anything. I'll have to get a new lock though. I'm glad there's a hardware store right around the corner."

"I can go get a new lock while you get things ready for the day," Elena said, and then she yawned.

My mouth wanted to drop open. Elena offering to help me? Elena yawning? I couldn't fathom it. But I did need the help, so I handed her some money.

"I'd appreciate it. Just get another lock like the one I already had." She nodded and left.

I was the only one who had a key for the food truck, but I decided it might be good for José to have a copy as well, so I rushed after her and called out, "Elena, can you have an extra key made?"

She nodded vigorously.

I backed up the steps and turned around. Who would have thought sending her for a new lock could cause the woman to become so animated?

An hour later, I opened the window on the food truck. The outside menu was shiny clean, and much of the outside of the truck had been washed down. Elena had returned with the lock and two keys and put them on the counter, and then she began making tortillas.

My first customer that day leaned against the food truck and called in the window, "Do you really think this town needs another Mexican restaurant?"

I looked up when I heard that voice. I would know it anywhere. Charles Burnard. He was loud and obnoxious and could easily send my customers flying away if he were to become boisterous and rude.

I leaned out the window. "Hello, Mr. Burnard. Was there something I can get you? We have some fresh tortillas." I kept my voice low, hoping he would lower his.

He waved a hand in the air. "No thanks. I just came over to let you know I've sent my information to the seller of the lake property. I understand you did also. I wouldn't hold your breath. This town doesn't need another restaurant, especially another Mexican restaurant. What we need around here are hotels, resorts. Something to bring in visitors."

I stared at him and clenched my hands. I couldn't believe he was saying all this here at the food park. "Mr. Burnard, I'm sure you have your opinion and I have mine. However, from what I understand, it's up to the seller. I'm willing to wait for his decision. Can I get you a taco?"

"A taco? What, one of your prize-winning concoctions?" he sneered. "No thanks, I had one before, and it tasted like you'd been cooking the sauce for weeks on end. I'm pretty sure the judges won't like it this year."

I glared at him. "For your information, I'll be making a brand-new batch on Wednesday night, just for the judges. It will be fresh and wonderful." I wasn't sure why I felt I had to defend myself or my Holy Guacamole secret sauce. "So, if you aren't buying anything, would you kindly move to the side so my customers can step up?"

He turned around and glared at the three people in line behind him. "Humph. They can wait. I just wanted to warn you."

"Warn me?" My voice rose slightly, remembering the broken lock on the food truck. "What do you mean by that?"

He ran a hand through his thinning, greasy hair. "What I mean is, don't think you'll ever get that lake frontage. I will get a hotel built there, one way or another." He slapped his hand on the windowsill, upsetting the bottle of hot sauce, which rolled across the ledge and fell to the ground. He didn't pick it up. Instead, he just turned and stomped away.

The next customer stepped forward, picked up the hot sauce, placed it back on the windowsill, and ordered a quesadilla. I wasn't sure how I even got through the next hour. My mind spun, and I felt such anger at Mr. Burnard. I finally had a break from customers, so I ran to the ladies' room and, once there, took a deep breath and said a quick prayer.

Lord, the man is odious, but I can't allow his behavior to fill me with anxiety and dread. I must remember that You give me a more abundant life. I need to stay focused on Your goodness.

I rubbed my temples. This was the only way I knew to calm down. However, the man's threats kept returning to my mind, and I couldn't help but wonder if he'd already begun to put them into action by breaking into my food truck.

CHAPTER FOUR

I wiped the counter absentmindedly. For a Wednesday, it had been a good day as far as sales, but in the back of my mind two themes had been running all day. First, would the owner of the lake property choose my proposal over Mr. Burnard's? And second, what was Mr. Burnard warning me about? Was he threatening me?

If my proposal was chosen, I couldn't afford it if the man started sabotaging my business or the land around the lake.

Suddenly I straightened up. What was I doing, allowing myself to worry? I'd given this dream to God. If He wanted it to become a reality, I needed to continue to trust Him.

Just then there was a knock on the food truck door. I looked up, and Elena spun around to see who it was.

"Hello, you home?" Rick called. "Permission to enter?"

I laughed. "Permission granted." I tossed down the cloth and moved closer to the door. Elena placed the big pot in the sink.

"Your secret sauce is gone." She showed me the empty pot. "So, you are making more tonight?"

"Yes, that's my plan." I spoke a bit sharply because I'd already told her that earlier. I noticed her shoulders seemed to tighten, and her dark eyes burned into me.

Seriously, this woman needed to take a class on how to treat her boss.

Rick moved closer. "Fresh sauce?"

I pulled my attention away from Elena. "Yes, just for the judges tomorrow."

Rick feigned a sad face. "What about for me?"

"No tacos for you," I joked.

Seeming to remember the reason for his visit, Rick pulled out some papers and held them up. "I'm not sure you'll win the judging tomorrow, but I've got some great news."

I swung my head up, focusing on the papers. "What?"

"You won!"

"I won? What?"

"The seller chose your proposal. It seems he doesn't want to change the lake by bringing in more strangers."

My eyes opened wide, and I flung my arms around Rick's neck. "Oh, thank you, thank you." I started jumping up and down.

Rick wrapped his arms around me and gave an enthusiastic squeeze.

Finally, realizing what I was doing, I dropped my arms and took a step back, but I knew my eyes were still lit up—partially from the good news and partially from the warmth tingling in my body from being so close to Rick.

"What do I have to do next?" I mumbled, feeling a bit embarrassed now. He'd come here as a real estate agent, not a boyfriend.

Rick didn't even seem fazed. "Just sign the papers. We can close by the end of the month, but the seller wants the papers in his hand by tomorrow."

I blinked a few times. "Tomorrow is the judging. Will there be enough time for me—"

Rick touched my arm. "Don't worry. I know how important tomorrow is, so I'm going to pick up the papers in a half hour, then take you out to dinner. You can sign them after we eat."

A feeling of pleasure warmed me. Rick was really a great guy. "I'd like that."

"I have another meeting before that, and I'm seeing the client at El Patrón. How do you feel about eating there?"

"How unique, taking a Hispanic girl out for Mexican food. Who would have ever thought of that!" I winked at him.

He hung his head and kicked his foot. "Sorry."

"I'm only kidding." I rushed to reassure him. "I love the food at El Patrón. So, I guess you won't be picking me up, since you're meeting the client. What time shall I meet you there?"

The light of laughter in Rick's eyes seemed to come alive. "How about six? Then you can be back here by seven to make your secret sauce."

"Yes, and that will get me into bed by eleven." I laughed as Rick turned to leave. Elena blocked the way.

"Elena, didn't you use to work at El Patrón?" Rick asked.

"Sí." She answered but gave no further information.

Rick stared at her for a moment. "You know, you look a bit like Luis Lopez, the owner of El Patrón." Rick turned back to me.

Elena, in the meantime, had stepped to the side. She slipped on her Manila shawl with its long fringe. Without a word of goodbye, she headed to the door and disappeared down the stairs.

When she was gone, Rick spoke. "She's an odd one."

"You're telling me! She came by almost a year ago and told me they fired her because of a problem with the bean soup, which she assures me was not her fault. I needed someone to help, so I hired her on the spot. I hoped she and I would become friends, but she barely speaks, and, honestly, I get the feeling she doesn't like me at all."

Rick picked up my hand. "What's not to like?" He smiled.

"Um. . ." I felt a bit flustered. "I sort of wish I could fire her, but she never makes any mistakes with the food preparation. She's often late, but she's pleasant to the customers, even if she isn't nice to me."

"I guess you can't ask for more than that." Rick squeezed my hand then set it free. "Okay, I have to get going. I'll see you at six?"

I was a bit frustrated, torn between the excitement of signing the papers to purchase the lakefront property and the need for rest so I could stay up late making my secret sauce for the Holy Guacamole tacos I'd be giving the judges.

"Where you going?" José asked, walking past my room and noting my clothes. "Big date?"

I started to deny it, then realized I *was* going on a big date. "Yes, one of the biggest. I'm going to sign the papers to purchase the lake property."

José's eyes widened. "Really?"

"Yes. It seems the owner prefers restaurants over hotels." I clenched my hands and smiled. "We've finally gotten Abuelita's dream, José."

He stepped closer and gave me a hug. That in itself was nice. Lately, hugs were few and far between—typical teenage stuff.

"I wasn't sure we'd ever get the land. It'll take a few years to save enough money for the building, but if we work together. . ." My voice faded. The image of José going off to college flashed through my mind. "That is, once we've gotten you through college."

"I'm telling you, Marissa, I don't care about college. Maybe someday I'll go study to become a detective, but honestly, right now all I want is to finish school and work the food truck. If we save all the money to build the restaurant, we can decide about school later on."

I pressed a quick kiss on his cheek. "You, dear brother, are a very good person. Let's just pray about it."

He jokingly swiped the kiss away. "You know my methods, Watson," he said.

———

El Patrón is as authentic as a place can be outside of Mexico or Texas, and they served many meals I could only hope to compete against. Anytime I wanted to indulge in enchiladas verdes, El Patrón was my first choice.

Rick was waiting by the front door for me as I pulled into the parking lot. I turned off my engine and slid out of the car with a small wave.

We only had to wait a few minutes to be seated. Rick asked for a quiet corner table away from the mariachi players. Usually, I liked to hear them playing the Mexican arrangements on their bright guitars, but tonight I needed to be able to hear everything Rick had to say about the contract.

When the waitress had taken our orders, Rick opened the large manila envelope and pulled out the contract. "It's a pretty standard sale. I've written it up in the simplest way I could to assure there are no questions."

I took the contract and began reading it.

Just then, the owner of the restaurant, Luis Lopez, stopped at the table. "*Buenas noches,*" he said. His gaze seemed to settle on the contract in my hand. "Are you buying something?"

"Yes, Mr. Lopez. I'm buying the land on the lake that my grandmother always wanted."

The man frowned. "What will you do with it?"

"Build a restaurant. It was always my abuelita's plan."

"Another Mexican restaurant?" His lips pressed together in a grim line.

"Yes."

Rick laid his hand on mine and gave me a quick smile.

"Over my dead body. The last thing we need in this town is another Mexican restaurant." The man turned and stomped away.

"My, he's. . ." I couldn't think of what to say. It was obvious he was worried. Although it would give him some competition, my restaurant wouldn't be anywhere near the scale his was. Why couldn't we all just help one another?

"Don't fret, Marissa. There's nothing wrong with you opening a new restaurant. The other owners will just have to accept it." Rick's words were meant to comfort me, but it made me realize that Luis Lopez wasn't the only person who was going to be upset about a new Mexican restaurant in town.

CHAPTER FIVE

Dinner had been excellent at El Patrón; however, we didn't stay long. Although I would have liked to spend more time with him, Rick knew I was anxious to get to work on my secret sauce, so he didn't fuss when I suggested making it an early evening.

Once home, I stopped to check on José.

"I'm off to the food truck. Did you get your homework done?"

José frowned. "Yes, but I think I should come with you. You know, it was broken into the other night."

The thought had crossed my mind, but I didn't want José to be alarmed. "I'm not concerned. It was probably a lark of some sort. Kids probably. You need to get some sleep."

He rose and walked over to me and stood with his feet spread apart. "Now listen, you need to keep your cell phone on and let me know when you get there and when you're headed home."

I had to laugh inside. Sometimes I wondered who the adult was, him or me.

After promising him I'd obey his rules, I rushed out, hopped into my car, and headed for the food truck court. I didn't feel worried at all. Although it was dark out, this time of the year seemed to be when the moon was at its brightest, so things were pretty well lit up.

Before turning into the park, I remembered I was missing an ingredient I needed for the sauce, so I decided to run to the grocery store.

As I hurried down one of the aisles, I suddenly had to stop because two people blocked the lane.

"Excuse me." I had barely spoken when Brad and Kim, the owners of the Taco Tent drive-through restaurant in town, turned and glared at me.

I was a bit taken aback. The couple were young, in their late thirties, and usually were completely relaxed and genuinely nice.

"Hi, Brad. Hi, Kim," I said, trying to sound friendly.

Brad just nodded. Kim, who was usually very nice, gave a grunt of sorts. I thought her eyes brimmed with tears. They moved apart so I could pass. But as I did, Brad leaned in and whispered into my ear, "Don't think you'll ever open a restaurant on the lake."

I swung around and stared at him. "How did you hear about that?"

"Oh, word gets around. But my advice is for you to stick with your little food truck. Besides, we've decided to expand the Taco Tent. Pretty soon we'll be the largest Mexican restaurant in town. You'll just be throwing your money away. You won't be able to compete with us."

I looked at Kim, hoping to see disapproval in her eyes for what her husband was saying, but instead her head moved up and down in an agreeing nod.

I could hardly believe that these other restaurant owners would be so worried about competition. The town already supported El Patrón, the Taco Tent, Margarita's, and the Crunchy Taco. I couldn't see why my opening a place on the lake and closing the food truck would cause such a stir.

I placed my hand on my hip. "I'm sorry you feel that way, Brad. I just signed the papers for the lake property, and I'm hoping to begin building by the end of the year. I'm sure we could all help one another's businesses if we wanted to."

Kim stepped up closer after I spoke. Her words came out in a sneer. "You'll never get the place open."

At that, they both turned and walked away.

I found myself shaking in anger but tried to remember my new relationship with Jesus. So I bowed my head and lifted up a prayer for Brad and Kim, asking Him to deal with this situation. I couldn't understand their hostility. They'd never been like that before. I thought they were the most easygoing couple I'd ever met.

Two hours later, I contentedly placed the tureen filled with sauce and labeled "Judges" in the refrigerator. I was more than happy with the flavor. When I slipped out of the trailer, I double-checked the lock then headed for my car. I was tired and looking forward to my evening's rest. I made sure to text José and let him know I was headed home. We shared our respect for one another by doing this.

I didn't expect to win the competition again this year, but I had high hopes and spent a bit of time in prayer before finally drifting off to sleep.

———◆———

The next morning, I got up and got dressed. I could feel my excitement tingling in my fingers. This was the day of the judging, but I tried to remember that I had customers and their desires to consider. I dropped José off at school and arrived early at the food truck court. I wasn't the only one there early. The Spudmobile was open as well. They must be preparing for the food judging too.

When I reached my truck's door, I gasped. The lock hung open.

This time I didn't touch the door. Instead, I pulled out my phone and called the police. Tater, owner of the Spudmobile, saw me standing outside my food truck. He must have noticed my anxious face. He trotted over.

"Anything wrong, Marissa?"

I pointed at the open lock.

"Again?" His eyes opened wide. "Someone broke in twice?"

I nodded and chewed on the corner of my thumbnail. A sign I was upset. Tater waited with me for the local police to show up. The officer didn't give me much comfort. He said there didn't seem to be any way he could get fingerprints off the lock. It was a standard lock. He asked if I had extra keys, but I told him it was new and I'd only gotten two keys, one for me and one for José.

"Is there anyone you know of who would want to break into your truck? Do you keep money there?" the officer pressed.

I shook my head vehemently. "Everyone in town knows that no one leaves money in their food trucks. Have there been any strangers in town?"

The officer smiled. "Miss, we don't have time to keep up with all the strangers in town." He must have seen my frown. "But we'll do what we can. Keep our ears open, that sort of thing. Is anything missing?"

I had already entered the food truck and looked around. I even went so far as to check that no one had touched Abuelita's cookbook, but it was inside a locked cabinet, and that lock was not broken.

"Nothing that I can see. I'm just wondering what would make someone break into the truck two times. Do you think they're looking for something specific?"

The man was obviously uninterested in any further discussion. He shrugged his shoulders and walked away, assuring me he would let me know if they got any clues.

A few moments later, my phone rang. It was Elena.

"Hello?"

"I'm feeling ill. I won't be in to work today." Her voice sounded deep and far away.

I held the phone out and stared at it. The woman knew how important today was.

"I see," I said, and ended the call. Turning around and around, I wasn't sure where to begin. Of all days for Elena not to show up, this was the worst.

———

An hour later I was able to open the window on the trailer. A few early birds wandered around the center of the park by the picnic tables. Across the way I saw Brad and Kim Powers. Before running into them the other day, they had always seemed pleasant. I was a bit envious. It would be nice to work with someone I could enjoy talking to every day. The idea of José working with me flashed through my mind. We had fun working together in the summers.

Suddenly my window was filled with the sour-looking face of an older Hispanic woman, probably in her late sixties, named Maria Martinez. She was the owner of Margarita's, the other Mexican restaurant in town. I'd met her several times over the years, but like Elena, she wasn't very pleasant. I was actually surprised she was able to keep the place open. Perhaps years ago, Margarita's may have been a very good restaurant, but over the past few years the cleanliness and quality had gone down.

"Hello, Mrs. Martinez," I said.

"Just stopped by to tell you something." The woman actually smelled of some kind of alcohol. It made me wonder if that was why her restaurant had taken a turn for the worse.

Despite the smell, I leaned closer, hoping she would lower her voice. There had been a stir across the park, and I could tell the judges had arrived.

"You won't win this year!" she screamed into my face. I pulled back and covered my nose. I felt pity for her, but at the moment, I also felt anger and embarrassment.

"Might as well close up your window now and let the judges pass on by, because you are *not* going to win this year."

I wished Elena were here. Perhaps she could have spoken to Mrs. Martinez and calmed her down. I hadn't realized how this contest could affect people.

I stared over the distraught woman's head and saw that Brad and Kim were looking our way. I hoped they would step in and help me out, but I was even more shocked to see what I could only describe as a look of satisfaction cross Kim's face.

I took a breath and closed my window. Maybe Mrs. Martinez would drift away. I had to wonder why she was so adamant I wouldn't win the contest this year. Did she know something or someone? Could the judges have been bribed? No. I shook the thoughts away.

As I wandered around the food truck interior, waiting a few minutes before reopening the window, I was surprised when the door swung open and José stepped in.

"What are you doing here? Why aren't you in school?" I stood, arms akimbo.

He gave me his best puppy dog eyes. "I just had to be here for the judging." His voice trailed away into a whisper.

"What did you tell the school?" I glared at him. "Wait, did you even tell the school?"

He shook his head.

I pressed my hand against my forehead. "José! You can't just walk out of school." I grabbed my phone and began searching for the number.

José pressed his hands together. "Please, let me stay."

I spoke with the school secretary and explained what José had done. I was surprised that all she did was laugh. I assured her he would be back tomorrow and it would never happen again, then ended the call.

"Am I in trouble?" José asked, already busying himself at the preparation area.

"Not at school. They don't seem to care a bit about your behavior. She told me that your actions were nothing compared with some of the things kids your age do. But you are in trouble with me!" I slammed a towel down on the counter. "The last thing I needed today is for you to get in trouble. It's bad enough that the food truck was broken into again, Mrs. Martinez was just outside giving me some type of threat, Kim Powers was giving me some seriously bad looks, and Elena didn't come to work."

José frowned. "The truck was broken into again? Anything taken?"

I shook my head.

"Gotta be some dumb kids. Well, this is all the more reason why you need me here." He clapped his hands together. "Now, what should we do first?"

I blew out a breath and decided his true scolding would come later on, after the judging. Right now, I did need his help.

"Open the window and start taking orders. No one gets a Holy Guacamole taco except the judges, and I'll make those myself." I grabbed my hair, spun it around, and put it up on top of my head in a bun. Then I reached over and picked up a hairnet to cover it with. No sense taking a chance of any hair getting into the tacos.

José slid open the window, looked out, and gave a long whistle. "Wow. . . The place is packed. He looked down at a woman who waited in line. *"Te puedo ayudar?"* he asked with a fake Hispanic accent.

The woman's brow scrunched in curiosity. José laughed. "May I help you?" he said in his all-American voice. We both looked Hispanic, but we didn't have the accent to go along with it. We'd learned a few words and phrases from our grandmother, but that was about as far as authenticity went with us.

The woman covered her mouth and giggled. "Oh, sí." She was obviously not someone who spoke Spanish. "May I get a chicken fajita?"

"*Uno fajita de pollo*," José called out.

I shook my head. José probably spoke less Spanish than I did, but he had learned a few key phrases. He thought it made our food truck seem more authentic. I wasn't about to argue with him. The customers seemed to love it, and it made José very happy.

I moved over to the refrigerator and pulled out my pot with the secret sauce I'd made the night before. It needed to be heated up so the flavor would be at its best when served.

About an hour later, the door opened and Elena popped her head in.

I stared at her. "Hello, Elena."

She didn't speak. Instead, she stepped to the side, and Rick came up the stairs and into the food truck. Elena followed.

"Hi, Marissa," Rick said. "I just heard that your truck was broken into again."

"How did you hear that?"

"Seems to be a story that's spreading all over the park."

I clenched my teeth. That alone could ruin my chances with the judges. "Well, the lock wasn't broken, just open. Maybe there was something wrong with the lock. Maybe it didn't click closed all the way. I don't know." I put down my spoon and stared at Elena. "I thought you were sick." I looked her over. She didn't look sick.

"I'm feeling better. Did you get your sauce made?"

"Yes, I made it last night, and I've got it heating on the stove now."

She nodded. "But you aren't serving it to anyone else?"

"That's right. This batch is just for the judges. I guess when they finish, we can sell some Holy Guacamole tacos."

Elena grabbed an apron and put it on, then turned toward the cutting area, where she proceeded to cut open the avocados I had waiting there.

Rick and I stood silently, watching her. I think we were both surprised by her behavior.

Finally, he turned back and asked, "So, was anything stolen?"

I shook my head. "Nope. Again, nothing seems out of place or to be missing. A few things were moved around, but the officer didn't think he could get any fingerprints."

The crowd at the window had thinned. José turned around. "As soon as the judging is over, I'm going to start on the case."

Rick tilted his head. "The case?"

"You know. 'The Mystery of the Unbroken Lock.'"

Rick knew about José's fascination with mysteries. He laughed. "Oh yeah. Okay, Sherlock. We'll wait for your deductions."

CHAPTER SIX

M arissa, the judges are coming!" José's voice broke. He was still going through that time of life when his voice often sounded like a girl's. He blushed.

"Okay," I squealed. I turned to make one of my special tacos. My hands shook slightly. Even after four years of winning, it still made me nervous. I think it was really just the idea of competition, not necessarily the concern for winning. I mean, it wasn't like I'd be voted worst food if I didn't win. There was really nothing to worry about.

There were three judges, and each one of them covered a different type of food. Each year the judges would rotate. This year the judge who would be trying my food was probably the pickiest of them all, Mrs. Alice Caster. She was about sixty and was considered high society in our little town.

I'd seen her many times over the years, and never once had there been a hair on her head out of place. Her nails and makeup were always perfect, and I was sure she only bought dresses from designers like Christian Dior.

She lived in a huge mansion that overlooked the lake, across from the food truck court. No one else owned any of the land on that side. She owned almost all of it. It was unclear if there ever was a Mr. Caster or not. No one remembers one, and yet she called herself Mrs. Caster.

I didn't feel very enthusiastic about her judging my food. In past years, she hadn't been very kind about those she did judge.

José must have noted her moving toward our food truck while the others split off, because he turned to me with a groan. "Oh no. It's Mrs. Caster."

I nodded. "I know. I got a notice about it a week ago."

"Why didn't you tell me?"

"What for? There's nothing we can do about it. She's our judge this year."

José gave me a conspiratorial wink. "I could have bumped her off last week. Then they would have gotten a new judge."

I slapped at his arm. "That's not funny, José." Although I did think it was a bit amusing. Not that I would ever consider. . .or ever want Mrs. Caster to die. However, I did pray several times during the week that something might cause her to decide not to judge. The other two judges had been kind to me over the last few years.

"Not all prayers seem to come true," I mumbled, and finished making the taco. For a moment, I considered tasting the sauce one final time just to make sure it was perfect, but I'd done it at least ten times last night. I knew that this batch was the best I could do.

"How about making me a taco?" Rick asked. "You know I love your Holy Guacamole tacos."

"Not until after the judging!" Elena said forcefully.

I nodded and in a brash tone said, "That's right. This batch is only for the judges. After that, we'll see."

Rick held up a hand. "Okay, okay. Sorry I asked."

I tucked my head a bit. "I'm sorry. I guess I'm a bit edgy about the judging. After she leaves, you can have all the tacos you want."

Rick reached over to the pot of sauce. "Not even a taste?"

I gave him a playful slap on the fingers. "Not even a taste. Now, you need to leave before the judging begins."

Rick mock frowned but bowed out the door. "Until we meet again, I say adieu." He pretended to tip a nonexistent hat and disappeared. Those were the types of things he did that I found rather charming.

I must have been staring at the closed door, because José coughed to get my attention. "The judge is waiting!" he hissed at me through clenched teeth with a fake smile.

"Oh goodness," I nearly shouted. Pulling my attention back, I hurried over with the plate and handed it to José.

José handed it out the window.

Mrs. Caster stared at the taco and wrinkled her nose as if she smelled something foul. My spirits fell further. I wondered if she even liked Mexican food at all. How could she judge my dish if she didn't like the cuisine?

José and I squeezed together at the window and watched Mrs. Caster carry the plate toward the middle of the park. She gingerly sat down at one of the picnic tables.

Honestly, I began to wonder if she would ever take a bite of the taco, because first, she took out a wet wipe and cleaned the table. She opened a notebook, jotted something in it, then she spoke to one or two people who walked by. My hands were clenched. The taco would be cold before she took her first bite.

Elena moved around the kitchen behind us, cleaning things, but her eyes were focused on the judge. Finally, after four painfully long minutes, Mrs. Caster lifted the taco and took a bite.

I grabbed onto José's arm for emotional support. We watched as she began to chew. I think our own jaws were moving up and down.

Suddenly she turned her head and glared across the park at our food truck. The look was something I'd never seen before. My heart dropped as I realized we were not going to win the contest this year.

As I stared at her, hoping her expression would somehow miraculously change to one of pleasure, she seemed to freeze with the taco in midair, and then she dropped the taco right on her lap. Next, she stood up and grabbed her throat.

"I think she's choking," I yelled, already headed for the door with José on my heels. We threw open the truck's door and jumped out, missing the steps altogether.

I ran as quickly as I could to Mrs. Caster's side. She was no longer standing. Instead, she sat in a most unbecoming position on the ground next to the picnic bench. Her hand still grasped her neck.

As I got closer, my old CPR classes rushed through my mind. Would I be able to help a choking victim?

When I drew nearer, her head dropped.

"Mrs. Caster, are you okay?" I called out.

She didn't lift her head, so I knelt down in front of her and, with one hand under her chin, lifted her face. I was hoping she'd finally stopped choking and was recovering now, but that was not what was happening.

I sat there in front of the woman, dumbfounded. She was no longer choking, but she was also no longer breathing. From what I could tell, she was dead, and a strange bit of foam had formed on her lips.

When José reached my side, he too knelt down. "What's going on?" he asked, staring at the woman's face.

I slowly pulled my hand back, allowing her head to gently fall forward again.

"I called 911," José said. "Is she going to be okay?"

I shook my head slowly, but the words didn't seem to want to come out. "She's...she's... Mrs. Caster is...dead!" The last word came out in a huge sob, and tears began to pour down my face. Not that I liked the woman much, but I'd never seen anyone so soon after they'd died. It was awful. I knew I should shield José from the sight, but I felt as if I could barely move. I felt lethargic and unable to get up.

"Are you sure? Shouldn't we do CPR or something?" José lifted Mrs. Caster's head again, looked at her blank eyes, then slowly let it rest forward. Her body began to fall sideways. José helped until the body lay on its side. Then he stood up and stepped back.

The Holy Guacamole taco lay on the ground. My first instinct was to pick it up and toss it, but when I reached out for it, José stopped me.

"Don't, Sis."

I looked up at him curiously.

"Sorry to say, but...the police are gonna want to see the taco." His expression, which earlier had been so excited, now was downcast. A look of shock had settled into his eyes.

"But why?" I asked. "It's obvious she choked on something. Does it matter what?"

José nodded. "Yes. It's evidence."

"That's ridiculous. No one is going to care exactly what she choked on," I said. But knowing José's preference for mystery and detective shows, I agreed to go along with his suggestion. He did know more about this type of thing.

In the distance, I could hear the sound of sirens headed toward the park. The town had very little crime, so anything that caused a stir would be enough to get the entire police, fire, and medical force to show up. I knew it wouldn't be long before there was a whole gathering of police officers, firefighters, and EMTs.

I hadn't even thought about the other people in the park, but when I lifted my head, the two other judges, along with Maria

Martinez, Brad, Kim, and some of the other food truck owners, were gathered nearby. From what I could see, there was plenty of whispering and pointing going on.

This is definitely not going to be good for business, I surmised. Gossip in a town this size could spread like wildfire, and if it wasn't stopped it could destroy a person's reputation or their business within days. My knees ached from the position I was in, but I thought that it would offend the crowd if I simply stood up and stepped back.

José was standing though. I think he was setting up a perimeter in his mind. One or two people tried to move toward us, but he held up a hand and stopped them.

My teeth chattered even though it wasn't cold out, and I could feel my body shaking. I assumed those were signs of shock. It was the first time I'd actually seen someone die.

When the EMTs appeared, I finally stood and stepped away. Even though I had expected the firefighters and police to show up, when they all appeared, it felt overwhelming. I was already pressing back tears. I really did feel awful about the judge dying.

An officer opened a small notebook and began asking me questions.

"Did you know the deceased? What was she doing here? What was she eating? Did anyone else eat the same thing?"

At that question, I stopped him. "Well, what does that matter? She choked on the food. I couldn't get to her fast enough to give her the Heimlich maneuver."

The man blinked. "Choked?"

A bad premonition swept over me.

"Yes, choked."

The officer moved away for a few minutes. He spoke to the EMT, then returned to my side.

"I'm sorry, but the deceased didn't choke."

It was my turn to blink. "Of course she did." I stared at him. "Oh, then she had a heart attack?"

The man shook his head. "We don't know for sure yet, but the EMT believes she was poisoned."

My hands began to tremble. "Poisoned? But how? Did she eat something before she got here? Maybe she stopped for coffee?"

The officer had slipped on some latex gloves and opened a plastic evidence bag. I felt the blood rush out of my face as he bent over and placed the Holy Guacamole taco into the bag. A lump formed in my throat, and I couldn't speak.

The officer handed the bag to another officer, then turned back to me again. "Who exactly made this taco?"

I felt my knees beginning to grow weak, so I backed up to a bench by one of the picnic tables and sat down. Everything began to spin.

"Marissa, what's wrong?" José asked.

All I could do was shake my head. I felt my eyes beginning to roll back, and a wave of giddiness came over me. José must have realized what was happening, because he grabbed my head and pressed it between my knees.

"Take deep breaths, Marissa." It sounded as if José's voice came from far off. A few seconds later, everything went black.

CHAPTER SEVEN

W hen I opened my eyes, two EMTs stood over me. I tried to sit up, but they pressed me back down. "Not so fast," one of them said as he removed a blood pressure cuff from my arm.

"I'm fine." I sat up slowly. I was perspiring, which was probably an aftereffect of fainting.

José was sitting on the ground beside me. His face showed raw emotion—fear and sympathy all in one.

I reached out.

"I'm okay, little brother." I spoke gently. I could see he was trying to keep tears back.

Suddenly I remembered the reason I fainted. The judge had died of poison, and it seemed like the officer was indicating it was my taco that killed her.

I turned to face José. "Did anyone else eat any of those tacos?"

"Nope. Remember, you insisted they were only for the judge."

My eyes flashed over to the Crunchy Taco. There was a short line of customers. I guess the police hadn't gotten around to closing us up yet.

I scrambled to my feet. "We've got to make sure Elena doesn't give anyone a Holy Guacamole taco."

I could tell by their reaction that the EMTs thought I should sit back down, but José and I both took off running toward the food truck, yelling out incoherent things. I reached the truck first and pounded up the steps.

"Elena, don't serve the secret sauce!"

She turned around and glared at me.

I scanned the room for the pot of sauce. It was nowhere.

"Elena, where is it?" I was still shouting. I pulled open the refrigerator door, hoping to find the sauce, but it wasn't there either.

"I got rid of it. You said it was only for the judges, so since you already served the judge, I dumped it in the garbage and washed the pot." She pointed at the big pot on the drying stand.

José pressed past me. "Elena, don't you know what's going on outside?"

The woman's brows pulled together in a question.

"The judge died after eating the Holy Guacamole taco," José said.

I gulped down a bit of bile. Those words just didn't seem real.

"Died?" Elena actually screamed.

"Yes."

Elena turned to me, her face filled with anger. "You have to close the food truck right now." She reached over and pulled down the window and the shade. "No one will ever buy another taco from you." She moved across the trailer, picked up her purse, and walked to the door. "I quit!" She stomped down the steps and disappeared.

I looked at José. "Do you think she's right? Will this ruin our business?" The image of the restaurant on the lake slowly faded away.

"No way. So far it hasn't been proven that the judge died from the taco, and if for any reason it is the case, then it has to be that someone slipped poison into the sauce."

My heart fluttered with a little hope. "The trailer was broken into."

"That's right. We need to talk to the police again." José began to look around.

"What are you searching for?" I asked him.

"The garbage. If the sauce was poisoned, the police will think it's strange that you got rid of the evidence."

Again, I realized he was right. The garbage can had a new bag in it, which meant Elena had taken the old one, filled with the secret sauce, out to the dumpster. As I headed to the door, I lifted up a prayer.

Lord, help me. I don't know why this has happened, but You know I didn't poison anyone.

When I reached the dumpster, I scanned the bags on the top. I could see the one from my trailer toward the back. Elena must have flung it hard. I walked to the end of the dumpster and began to climb up the side. When I reached the top, I leaned over as far as I could.

"Excuse me, Miss Valdez, what exactly are you doing?" I looked down at the officer, my eyes opened wide, my mouth opening and closing as I tried to explain. But before I could say anything, I felt my body tilting dangerously sideways, and suddenly I fell right into the dumpster.

———◆———

Two hours later, I stepped out of the shower. The officer had collected the garbage bag filled with my secret sauce. He'd interviewed me and questioned me for over an hour. Two other officers had searched the food truck. José told me that they needed a search warrant, but I didn't care about that. I was more afraid of appearing guilty by not allowing them to search the trailer.

I wasn't sure what poison the judge had died from, but I was hopeful they wouldn't find it in the trailer. Then and only then would I be able to insist that whoever broke in the night before must have tainted the sauce.

With a towel on my head, I dropped onto the couch and took a deep breath. A part of me wanted to break down crying, but I felt almost frozen. It was as if I had no emotion at all.

José came in and sat beside me. I leaned my head on his shoulder, and we just sat there quietly for about an hour.

Finally, I stood up. "We need to get some sleep."

He stood and stretched. "Marissa, what are we going to do?" I could hear the worry in his voice. He'd been so strong the whole day, I'd almost forgotten he was my little brother.

I gave him a hug. "Don't worry. It's all going to be all right. Remember, we have God on our side."

He gave a small smile.

"Let's agree to just keep praying and let God work this out."

The next morning, my phone rang at seven o'clock. I eyed it with dread, and as I suspected, it was an officer from the police department asking me to come to the station. I didn't ask any questions but immediately got up to get ready to go.

José was dressed for school and eating a bowl of cereal. I debated on telling him about needing to go to the station, but if for any reason I was detained there, he would need to know, so I told him.

He dropped his spoon. "What?"

"Well, not that I'm worried, but they probably have more information about the judge's death."

José's eyes met mine. "What if. . .if they arrest you?"

A huge knot twisted even tighter in my stomach. "Nonsense. Of course I won't get arrested. I didn't poison anyone."

José tried to talk me into letting him come to the police station with me, and although I actually could have used his support, I knew he needed to be at school. Finally, he agreed to let me take him to school, but I don't think he believed the facade I put on. He knew I was a nervous wreck.

"I'll have my phone turned on all day, school rules or not. Text me, call me, as soon as you know anything." I could see the worry lines on his forehead.

"I will."

After dropping José off, I headed toward the police station. I wasn't in a huge hurry, although I didn't want to show up very late. On my way, I passed by El Patrón. I could see the usual morning crowd through the window, which didn't bother me. There were always those who preferred the Crunchy Taco. However, I was more than surprised to see Elena through the window. She was waiting on one of the tables.

All I could imagine was that she really had decided not to work for me anymore and had gone and asked for her old job back. She was an enigma to me. I drove on, shaking my head. What did it matter? She never seemed happy working for me, and from what I'd just seen, the smile on her face indicated she was very pleased to be working at El Patrón again.

When I reached the police station, I parked, making sure I was in a legal spot and there wasn't a parking meter nearby that I should pay. The last thing I needed was to get a parking ticket.

Satisfied, I headed into the building and asked to speak to the officer in charge of the Crunchy Taco case. Those words sent a shiver down my spine. I didn't want the Crunchy Taco to be involved in this at all. I pressed my hand to my forehead, thinking about how bad this whole thing was going to be for business. I even wondered if it might somehow affect the sale of the land on the lake.

The officer who interviewed me the day before came to the front and met me. I noted his name on his desk as he steered me to it and asked me to sit down. I sat, placed my hands in my lap, and looked up at him. "Now, what can I do for you, Officer Brown?"

The man sat across from me, moved a few papers on his desk around, and then looked straight at me. "Miss Valdez, can you explain to me how Mrs. Caster could possibly have been poisoned by your secret sauce on the taco you gave her?"

All hope swept out of my chest. The woman had died because of something I cooked. I felt awful, but I knew this was no time to acknowledge that. I needed to give the officer some idea of who might have wanted to make it look like I killed the judge.

"Well, sir. I know I didn't poison the sauce. Someone broke into the food truck the night before, and they must have put the poison in it."

The man leaned forward. "Oh, really? And do you have any thoughts on who might have done such a thing?" His voice dripped with sarcasm.

Five faces came to mind. Charles Burnard, who wanted the lake land for a hotel, Luis Lopez and Kim and Brad Powers, who didn't want any more competition in town, and Maria Martinez, who had been insistent that I wouldn't win the food contest this year. I could only imagine her reason would be pure jealousy over the fact that the Crunchy Taco had won the contest so many times.

CHAPTER EIGHT

I was a bit surprised I hadn't been arrested, and as I walked out of the police station, I lifted my face to the sunshine and smiled. It was as if I'd been in prison and had been set free. Of course, I'd been warned to stay in town and not to discuss the case with anyone. I was also given the bad news that my food truck needed to be closed down until the case was solved. The police had already wrapped it in yellow caution tape.

That was going to be hard. What if it took several months to solve? How would I make money? It wasn't like many people in town would hire me with the suspicion of murder over my head. And what about the land by the lake? Would that deal go through? How would the seller feel about selling to someone accused of murder?

When I reached home, I texted José a simple message that everything was all right. I knew we'd have to discuss the immediate future later, but for the rest of the day I wanted him not to worry.

I sat on the couch, my open Bible in my lap. I glanced at it and was surprised to find a verse that was perfect for my situation in Joshua chapter one verse nine. I read it out loud.

"'Have I not commanded you? Be strong and courageous. Do not be afraid; do not be discouraged, for the LORD your God will be with you wherever you go.'"

That was exactly what I needed. I mustn't be afraid or discouraged by all that had happened. I needed to be strong and courageous, for José, for myself, and for God. I slipped onto my knees—not something I did often, but I felt I really needed to show God how much I honored Him.

I spent a long time in prayer, thanking Him for all he'd done for José and me over the years and asking Him to help clear me and the Crunchy Taco of suspicion. I knew that even if all these things were cleared up, the business might still suffer from long-reaching repercussions, so I needed God to fix it all.

———◆———

When I picked José up from school, he got in the car and turned to face me.

"Well?"

"Well, all is well for now." I tried to joke it off, but José could see right through the farce.

"Tell me!"

I sighed. "I wasn't arrested, but the police have shut down our food truck until the case is solved."

José knew exactly what that would mean to us. I saw him silently gulp.

"I'll get a job, Sis."

"It may come to that if the case doesn't get solved soon, but for now, I think we're all right."

José pressed his head back against the seat. I could tell he was thinking. I drove along in silence.

Suddenly he sat up. "I have it! You and I will solve the case. We both know you didn't poison the sauce, so we have to assume someone else did. So, either someone hated the judge or someone hates you."

I squeezed the steering wheel harder, trying to imagine how many people in town hated Mrs. Caster. She did tend to be quite a snob, and although I didn't think anyone hated me, there were the five who definitely didn't want me to win the contest this year.

I shared my thoughts with José. "If we concentrate on those five, maybe the police will look into anyone who hated Mrs. Caster."

José nodded and pulled out the small notepad he always carried with him. "Let's start making notes about each of the suspects right now."

I couldn't help but feel that this was all just a game to José, but at the same time, I had no other ideas about what else to do, so the rest of the way home we discussed each of the five, although we considered Kim and Brad as one suspect. It wasn't likely one of them would have done something without the other. They were always together.

"So, let me get this straight," said José. "Our suspects are Charles Burnard, Luis Lopez, Maria Martinez, and Kim and Brad Powers?"

"Yep. They're the only ones I know of who seem to be upset at me and the Crunchy Taco recently. If we'd won the award for best Mexican food another year, I think all of them except Mr. Burnard might have flipped their lids."

José stared at me in surprise. "Excuse me, but one of them obviously flipped their lid before you won the award. One of them snuck into the food truck and put poison in your sauce, knowing it would kill someone."

I think having José actually spell it out like that really hit home. Tears began seeping out of my eyes. "Oh, José. I can't believe that our sauce was used. . .was used to murder someone."

He reached over and patted my arm. "Don't let it upset you."

"I can't help it, and you know that even if we can solve this case, we'll never be able to serve another Holy Guacamole taco in our lives. Abuelita would be heartbroken. It was her secret recipe." I sniffed loudly.

José located an old wadded-up McDonald's napkin I had in my cup holder and handed it to me. I took it and dabbed my eyes then wiped my nose with it.

"Sis, we'll just rename the taco. We won't have to worry once we solve this thing. Now, why don't we start with Luis Lopez at El Patrón? Maybe if we can talk to some of his waiters, we can get an idea of how he really feels about you."

Since I had no other idea, I agreed and steered the car in that direction. It was going to be a bit weird to go into El Patrón again so soon, but there was no other choice.

———◆———

There weren't many customers at El Patrón, and we obeyed the SEAT YOURSELF sign. Both José and I scanned the restaurant, for what, I didn't know.

After a few minutes, the door to the kitchen opened and a woman stepped from the back. I couldn't help but gasp. It was Elena.

She didn't look at us until she reached the table. Then I saw her shoulders tighten, and she spoke slowly. "What can I get for you?"

I tried to break the ice with a smile. "Hello, Elena. You're working here again?"

She nodded but didn't speak, and I wasn't sure what to say. José, on the other hand, was a bit overly eager and blurted out, "Elena, do you think Mr. Lopez might have poisoned that sauce? We know he isn't happy about us opening a restaurant on the lake."

I watched in fascination as a look of scorn filled her face and her hands clenched. "Luis would never have done that. How dare you accuse him. He works hard to make this restaurant the best and—" She stopped speaking almost as quickly as she'd begun then just stared at us. I was a bit surprised by her words. I mean, the man had fired her because of a bowl of beans. Why was she now defending him so adamantly?

A minute later, the kitchen door opened again and a young man came out. When Elena saw him, she turned and walked away from the table without taking our order. The young man must have noticed, because he came over and asked us if we knew what we wanted.

I wondered if we should ask him some questions, but I was still reeling from Elena's reaction. I had been under the impression that she'd been fired by Luis Lopez before coming to work for me, so I was a bit surprised at her reaction to our question.

José realized that he knew our waiter from school, so when he returned with our plate of quesadillas, José introduced the subject. "Hey, Marcus, I didn't recognize you at first."

The young man smiled.

"How long you been working here?" José asked.

"A few months." He set the plates on the table. "It's a good job."

José nodded. "Yeah, I help my sister at the Crunchy Taco food truck. I like that."

Marcus' eyes opened wide. "You mean where the murder happened?"

I cringed at the words, but José just kept talking. "Yep, and the police are trying to pin it on my sister, but I know she didn't do it. We think there's someone in town who hates her or doesn't want her to open a new restaurant."

Marcus froze. He turned his head slightly toward the kitchen. "Hmm, I know what you mean. Mr. Lopez complained to his mother about it the other day. I overheard him say that if you opened a new Mexican restaurant by the lake, it would ruin his business. His mother told him he shouldn't worry about anything.

She said there was no way the Crunchy Taco would win the contest this year."

José leaned closer. "Marcus, do you think there's any way that Mr. Lopez would have. . .you know. . .put that poison in my sister's secret sauce?"

Marcus shook his head. "No way. He's a good guy. His bark is way worse than his bite."

José sat back with a laugh. "Yeah, that's what I figured."

Marcus gave a little shrug and walked away.

I leaned over and asked, "Why did you say that? You didn't really figure that Mr. Lopez didn't do it."

"I know, but I could see Marcus was getting protective, and I don't want him telling his boss that we're out here asking questions."

I nodded. "I see. That was the right thing to do. What do you think about what Marcus said?"

"I believe him. It didn't seem like he was covering up for the man, and I think employees sometimes know their boss better than anyone else."

"Well, Marcus doesn't think Mr. Lopez did it, and from what Marcus said, Mr. Lopez's mother didn't think he did it, so maybe we should move on to our next suspect."

"Most mothers would do anything to protect their kids, even someone as old as Mr. Lopez, so we can't count what Marcus said about her anyway, especially if we don't interview her. But I agree we've gotten about all the information we're going to get here, so let's finish these quesadillas and move on." José took a bite.

I wasn't sure I could even eat, but the food was enticing, so I began. I thought for a minute. To José, Luis Lopez must seem very old, but in reality he was probably in his late forties. I imagined his mother was pretty old though.

After a few minutes, José spoke again. "Sis, we can't just go in the front door of all the Mexican restaurants in town and ask if they know who poisoned your sauce. I think we need to be a little sneakier than that. I'm thinking we could slip in the back door, find a place to hide, and see what we can overhear."

"Hmm, sounds sketchy, but I think you're right about the front door. Maybe we can try it at Margarita's next. If we find it works, we can return to El Patrón later."

José gave a huge grin. "The game's afoot," he whispered, and stood up. I wondered if allowing him to help me on the case was a good thing after all. I mean, did he really know the difference between fact and fiction?

CHAPTER NINE

I t was almost eight thirty when we finally pulled up to Margarita's. I had insisted we go home, freshen up, and discuss our strategy. I even spent a good amount of time trying to convince José that there had to be a flaw in his plan, but as younger brothers often do, he just grew grouchy and told me I never go along with anything he wants.

So, without any further argument, I drove us slowly to the back entrance of the restaurant. I really wasn't sure where we would hide once inside, and I sort of hoped there wouldn't be a good spot. That way José would give up his crazy idea.

I parked on the street that ran behind the restaurant. Maria Martinez's van was parked right behind the building. She didn't drive anymore, but her son used the van. He brought her to work each day and picked her up in the evenings. We got out of the car and silently made our way to the back door. The restaurant was going to close in a half hour or so. I wasn't even sure what we could overhear in that little bit of time.

As we got closer but were still behind the van, José held out a hand to stop me from taking another step toward the building.

"Shhh, someone is out here."

I glanced around him, and sure enough, Maria's son, Mario, was sitting on the back stoop. For a moment, I thought we'd gotten there too late, but then he stood up and went inside. From the look on his face, I could tell he was unhappy about something. I suspected it was hard to work for a mother who drank too much, too often. Mario was about thirty-five, but life had already taken its toll on him. He looked about forty-five.

José and I slipped quietly to the back door. The main door was open, but the thin screen door was closed, and from inside, we could hear an altercation between mother and son. I heard Mario's deep voice. "Just tell me what you did." From where we stood, we could see Mario's back. He faced his mother in the dining area of the restaurant. His words caused my heart to start pounding. Was she about to admit to him that she'd poisoned my sauce?

José grasped the handle on the door and turned it slowly. To me the creaking door sounded like a loud baby crying. I expected to see one of them turn around, but they were deep in conversation.

José stepped in first. We were in the kitchen, and from what I could see, there was nowhere we could hide. José hurried to the left, out of their line of vision. I followed. There was a pantry of sorts at the far end of the room, which we slipped into. I moved toward the back, and José stood by the front, holding the door partially open so we could hear their conversation.

"Really Mario, it wasn't anything," Maria said. I could picture her, facing him with her hand on her hip.

"But Mom, the police are involved now."

My heart skipped a beat. Surely we hadn't really stepped into a conversation that would solve our mystery this easily? I pressed closer to José so we could both hear everything. I noted that José had his phone out and had pressed record.

"I don't care, Mario. I had to get rid of the pest. She was making my life miserable."

José turned to look at my reaction. I believe my mouth was gaping open. If these weren't the words of a murderer, I didn't know what was. However, when Maria spoke again, my shoulders dropped.

"Mario, it was only a dog, and it's not like I killed her. I simply took her to your uncle's farm."

José turned to me again, and we both mouthed, *A dog?*

"Yes, but Mom, it wasn't your dog to give away. The neighbors have had that dog for three years."

I almost burst out laughing when the reality of the conversation hit me. Obviously, Maria Martinez didn't like her next-door neighbor's dog and had kidnapped it and taken it to somebody's farm.

"Face it, Mario. That dog is better off on the farm. All it did here was bark and bark and bark. It was lonely and spent all day chained up."

"I know it, and I can't say the dog didn't deserve a better life, but really, Mom, I'm not sure. If anyone finds out, you could be arrested."

I heard an indignant snicker. "Who will ever find out?"

I guess Mario must have finally given up, because the room grew quiet. We stood still a few minutes more, but suddenly it got very dark.

"Oh no!" José whispered.

"What?" I almost shouted, my nerves were so wound up.

"They just turned off all the lights and went out the back door. It looks like they decided to close up early for the night."

My eyes were wide. "What does that mean for us?"

José shook his head and shrugged. "We might be locked in."

I sank to the floor. I was shaking. This was going to be a very bad situation. First, I was accused of murder, and now I would be caught trespassing.

"I doubt they have a good alarm system. We can probably move around the restaurant easily enough. But when we open the door, the alarm will go off. We need to be ready to move fast and get out before anyone hears the alarm and comes to investigate."

I wasn't surprised that José already had the whole thing figured out. Of course we needed to be worried about who was going to see us pulling away in our car.

"What about our fingerprints?" I whispered, not sure why I bothered, since no one else was in the shop.

José pulled his shirt out and began wiping anything we'd touched. "I'll make sure to wipe the door handles as well." He gave a little wink, trying to lighten the tension.

Somewhere inside myself, I heard the Holy Spirit speaking. Maybe telling me I'd gotten myself into this mess by doing something illegal in the first place. I realized I shouldn't have only tried to talk José out of it. I should have prayed about it.

I reached out and took José's hand. "Listen, little brother. I've been going along with this whole crazy plan because I'm afraid of losing our business. But you know it was wrong for us to sneak in here, and trying to 'get away' isn't any better."

I pulled out my phone and called Maria Martinez.

———◆———

It took a while to explain to Maria that José and I were locked inside her restaurant, because she kept asking what we were doing there, but I avoided the question.

"I don't want to open the door and set off the alarm, Maria. Can you and Mario come back to the restaurant and let us out? I can explain it all to you then."

José and I moved into the dining area and sat down at a table. This was by far the craziest thing we'd ever done. I even began to wonder if I could end up in jail and José in a juvenile center if Maria pressed charges.

I shook my head to rid it of those thoughts. Surely that couldn't be what God wanted for my life. Although He obviously didn't want me breaking and entering either.

We didn't have long to wait before Maria burst through the back door, followed by Mario. She rushed up to the table and glared at me. I stood up to meet the situation head-on.

"What do you think you're doing? Why are you in my restaurant? Are you planning to poison my food and kill off someone else?"

Her words struck me, but her last statement brought out the fight in me. I lifted my head.

"Hey, I'm sorry that we were snooping around and got locked in your place, but I never poisoned anyone. In fact, that's why we were hiding here. We were wondering if we might hear you or Mario admit to putting the poison in my secret sauce."

Mario plopped into a chair across from José. They gave each other a nod. I think they both knew better than to get involved in this conversation.

"Why would I put poison in your sauce? I hardly knew the judge." Maria's voice rose.

"But you were so certain I wouldn't win this year. How could you have known that unless you did something to make sure?"

Mario cleared his throat, and Maria turned to him and shook her head.

"Mom, you'd better just own up to it. I don't want the police to start suspecting you of murder."

My eyes met hers, daring her to tell me any more lies.

Finally, her gaze dropped to the floor. "I sent the judge a letter, promising her free meals for a whole year if she didn't choose the Crunchy Taco this time."

I sat back down, feeling flabbergasted. "You're kidding! This is just a silly little local competition."

She crossed her arms over her chest and blew her breath out of her nose. "Maybe to you, but you have no idea how much my business has gone downhill since you started winning that contest every year."

I wanted to speak but really didn't know what to say.

"Mom, I've told you over and over, the restaurant's business is going downhill because you're drinking so much." Mario looked up at me apologetically. "I'm not sure why things have gotten so bad for her, but I think it's time she retires."

I thought Maria might get angry at these words, but instead I noticed she seemed to relax.

"I agree. I'm getting too old for this. You can run the place without me, can't you Mario?" Her voice softened.

He stood up, walked over to her, and put an arm around her. "Sure, Mom." Mario glanced over at me.

I stood up. "Um, I hate to ask, but do you plan to call the police about us being here?"

Mario stared into my eyes. "You say you were both in the pantry and overheard everything Mom and I talked about before we left the shop?"

I nodded slowly, remembering the conversation about the dog.

Mario cocked his head and grinned. "I guess it will be better all around if we just pretend this never happened." His eyes actually pleaded with me for understanding. I wasn't sure if covering up the facts that Maria had kidnapped her neighbor's dog and that she'd tried to bribe a judge was a great idea, but I didn't want the police involved either.

"I think that's the best thing for all of us." I walked over and gave Maria a hug. "I hope you enjoy retirement, Maria."

She turned tear-filled eyes to me and gave a small smile.

It was obvious we'd gotten all the information here that we could, so José and I left the restaurant, hurried to the car, and quickly drove home.

On the way, José sat back with a huge grin on his face.

"What could you possibly have to smile about?" I asked.

"I'm just thinking how funny that whole event is going to sound when I write it out in my detective journal."

A flutter of worry passed through me. "I hope you plan to change the names of the characters."

José nodded. "Indubitably."

CHAPTER TEN

José and I had a late-night dinner and rehashed the evening's events.

"I could do that every night." José laughed.

I assured him it would never happen again.

"Well, Marissa, you have to admit we accomplished something. We at least know it wasn't Maria Martinez who poisoned the secret sauce."

I nodded but realized that her whole story about bribing the judge could have been made up. However, I tended to believe it. Besides, she lived with her son, and unless he was in on it too, she wouldn't have been able to get to the food truck without a driver. And by his reaction to her stealing the next-door neighbor's dog, Mario didn't seem like the type to want to poison someone just to win a contest.

"It's funny, the secrets you find out about people when you're a detective," José said.

I didn't smile. I thought it was rather sad to know so much about Maria Martinez. She was an unhappy woman who drank

TACO TRAGEDY

too much and was a dog thief and a cheat. "I think I liked it better when I didn't know so much about her."

I wasn't sure what her future would look like, but I knew I'd be praying for the woman from now on.

"So, who's next?" José asked, clapping his hands together.

I looked at him quizzically.

"You know, who's our next suspect?"

I leaned back and groaned. "You've got to be kidding. After today's fiasco?"

"Well, we won't be hiding in any pantries anymore, but we still have Luis Lopez, Brad and Kim, and Charles Burnard to consider."

"I thought we decided it wasn't Luis Lopez?"

José shook his head. "We aren't positive one way or the other. All we have is the word of his employee."

"We probably should interview his mother. Maybe she can give him an alibi."

José nodded. "But not yet. We don't want to make Luis suspicious by showing up at his restaurant again so soon. Do you know where his mother lives?"

"No, as a matter of fact, I've never seen his mother. At least, I don't think I have." I tried to recall the times I'd eaten at El Patrón, but the image of an older woman I didn't know did not come to the surface.

I got up and walked toward the front window and pulled the curtain to the side. The sky was lit with stars. Here in Birch Tree, Maine, the stars seemed so close. Especially over the lake. One of my favorite things to do in the evenings was sit out on the small dock on the lake and watch for shooting stars. But until this mystery was solved, I didn't have time for stargazing.

I turned around. "I guess we can try to interview Brad and Kim tomorrow."

José's eyes lit up. "That's a plan. We need to find out where all these suspects were on the evening before the judging. One of them was breaking into the food truck. And poisoning your secret sauce."

I tried to picture each suspect. It was almost impossible to see Maria Martinez doing it. Kim and Brad might do it together, and Luis Lopez seemed more the type to shoot someone if he wanted to do away with them.

"I wonder about Mr. Burnard. Would he really murder someone to get the land on the lake?" José asked.

I thought Mr. Burnard would easily hire a hit man if he wanted someone out of the way, but would a hit man use poison? That seemed more like something a woman would use. But who was I to say how a murderer chose their murder weapon?

"We can at least try and find out if he was home the other night."

I agreed, and we headed off to our rooms for the evening. It had been a long day, and I was ready to get some sleep.

Mr. Burnard worked out of a small office in town, which he rented by the month. He didn't actually live in the area. He only rented, and if he didn't find a place to open a hotel soon, I began to doubt he would settle in the area. He, like many others, had come to town to try and establish a new business, but most had failed to convince the mayor and town board to agree to let them build. Birch Tree wasn't a town that was interested in much growth, and I was glad. I hoped it always kept its charm. My opening a small restaurant on the lake wouldn't hurt the town a bit. However, a big hotel, bringing in hundreds of visitors, could change things drastically.

So, José and I found ourselves walking into the small rented office at exactly nine on Monday morning. We were both still overly nervous after the events at Maria's restaurant, but we didn't want to lose momentum. Of course, I had declared we were not to put ourselves in any more dangerous or compromising situations. José had just given a wink and a nod. I'm not sure what that meant, but I had to take it as an agreement.

I opened the door, and we entered the office. It was hot and stuffy and small. I wasn't impressed at all. The man usually dressed in expensive suits, but he obviously didn't care about his work environment.

A rather worn-out woman, who appeared familiar, looked up from behind the desk. "Can I help you?"

I stared at her for a few moments then remembered she'd visited the Crunchy Taco quite often. "Hi, yes. We would like to speak with Mr. Burnard."

She stared back, and I saw recognition dawn on her face. "Oh, you're the owner of the Crunchy Taco?"

I nodded.

"Your flautas are the best anywhere. I was upset when I found out you'd been closed down." Her eyes met mine, searching. "You didn't. . . I mean, did that judge really die eating your food?"

I felt the urge to laugh. "I didn't kill the judge, but yes, she died eating one of my Holy Guacamole tacos. However, someone broke into the food trailer the night before and slipped some poison into the sauce."

The woman's eyes opened even wider. "Really?"

"Yes. Now, is Mr. Burnard in?" I asked in a sweet voice.

"No, he's gone to a developer's convention in Florida. Was there something you needed to ask him?" Her smile flattened to a grim line. "Oh my. You didn't come here to ask him if he was the one to poison your sauce, did you?"

I just kept a steady gaze on her.

She turned a desk calendar around and pointed at the day before the judge had died. In bold red letters was written Boss to convention for the week.

"I drove him to the airport myself," she said.

José leaned forward. "Why should we believe you? You could be covering up for him."

The woman pulled back. "Why would I do that?"

José drummed his fingers on her desk. "You could be in love with him. Afraid to lose your job. . . Oh, any number of reasons."

The woman turned the calendar around and stood up. She pointed at José. "Now, look here. I am a happily married woman, and this is only a temporary job. I barely know Mr. Burnard, and I don't care for him a bit. He's a nasty piece of work, but it's my job for now. So you can just get out of here, and don't let me find out you've been spreading wild gossip about me or my feelings about my boss."

While she was speaking, I realized that the police had probably already checked into Mr. Burnard's trip. They would know if he had really been gone that day. From what I could tell, this irate woman was telling the absolute truth.

José and I backed out of the office, smiling and thanking the woman. She seemed a bit calmer as I closed the door. We ran down the street once we were out of the building. Finally, we stopped by a city bench, sat down, and began laughing.

"She was something else," José squeaked out between fits of mirth.

"Yes, but we have to admit, unless she's a really great actress and covering up for him, Mr. Burnard was probably not in town the day of the judging, or the night before, so he'll have to be moved to the very bottom of our list of suspects."

We sat side by side for a while. Then I stood up. "Come on, little bro. I kept you out of school for this, and you skipped school the other day. We don't want to get in trouble about that."

José stood and stretched. "Okay, but promise not to do any more snooping around until I can be there."

I crossed my heart. "Promise."

I was true to my word; however, I did jot down the names of all our suspects and start some notes beside each. From what we knew, Mr. Burnard could not have poisoned the sauce. I was also unable to believe Luis Lopez had done it, although he still remained a viable suspect. Maria Martinez was also not a real suspect in my opinion any longer.

Next to Kim and Brad's name, I put a big question mark. They sure were upset about the idea of me opening a new restaurant. However, their attitude was more in the line of arrogance. I truly believed they simply wanted to own the biggest Mexican restaurant in town.

I supposed I should stop by and assure them I was planning for my restaurant to be a very small, intimate venue with just a few tables overlooking the lake. In fact, the more I thought about it, the more that idea grew on me. This town didn't really have any fancy places to eat. Perhaps if we offered a very select menu, with dim lights and just the right ambience, we could pull it off. I could continue to run the Crunchy Taco as well. It was something to think about.

I decided to go to the food truck court and wander around. Just because I couldn't open my truck didn't mean I wanted to be away from it. So I took the car and headed for the lake. Once parked, I began to walk toward the Crunchy Taco. I stopped at the Dream Donuts truck and grabbed coffee and a plain, glazed donut.

I took small nibbles of the sweet treat as I made my way through the park, waving to the other owners. Most of them seemed friendly in return. They'd all known me for a while, and I didn't think any of them believed I was capable of murder.

I walked to the small dock and leaned over the edge, taking in deep breaths of the crisp lake air. This was truly a place of peace for me. However, I wasn't completely alone. To my surprise,

Kim and Brad stood on the end of the pier. Kim's shoulders were slumped over and shaking.

From what I could tell, she was crying.

Not wanting to interrupt, I began to walk away, but some twigs beneath my feet made a loud crunching noise. Brad's head shot up, and he turned.

"What are you snooping around for?" he shouted angrily at me.

I was taken aback by his apparent irritation. "Um, sorry. I wasn't sneaking around. I was just getting some fresh air. I didn't mean to disturb you. Is Kim okay?"

Brad's shoulders relaxed. He shook his head and beckoned me to come closer. I imagined he needed some female support.

I moved closer and placed a hand on Kim's back. "Kim, I'm not sure what's wrong, but I'm here if you need someone to talk to," I whispered.

She took a few gulps of air, and her shaking shoulders calmed a bit. She looked up at me.

"Oh, Marissa. I owe you an apology."

I was stunned. "Me? What for?"

"The way Brad and I spoke to you recently was just awful, but we are so upset."

"I know, but I can promise that my new restaurant isn't going to be bigger than yours. I'm planning a very small—"

She shook her head, cutting me off. "That's not important anymore. We aren't really upset about you opening a restaurant."

"You're not?"

She shook her head. "We're upset because I was pregnant, only six weeks along, and I lost the baby a few days ago. I'm sorry for yelling at you at the grocery store. It's been an emotional time." Her tears began to flow again.

I hugged her and choked back my own tears. "I'm really sorry, Kim."

"We haven't been able to open the Taco Tent since finding out. We spent the whole night before the judging in bed weeping. We came to the food trucks that day to tell Mrs. Caster that we weren't entering the contest this year."

While she spoke, I silently asked God to comfort her and Brad. Finally, she stopped crying and wiped her eyes. Brad stood a few steps away with his back toward us. I knew he'd been crying too.

"Thanks, Marissa. I hope you can forgive us," Kim said.

I gave her another big squeeze. "There's nothing to forgive, Kim. I've never gone through what you're going through, but I can understand it would make you very emotional. I'll be praying for you both to heal."

Kim turned to Brad and took his hand, and they walked back toward the food trucks. I felt a deep sorrow and knew I'd be praying for them every day.

At that point, it was time to pick José up, so I jogged to the car and headed toward the school.

I wasn't sure how much about Kim and Brad I would share with José, but I knew one thing. They surely weren't in my food truck poisoning the secret sauce the night before the judging.

CHAPTER ELEVEN

José was saddened to hear what I shared with him about Kim and Brad, and he also agreed that they weren't suspects any longer. We were both stumped. So far, not one of our suspects had panned out. Unless some totally unknown killer was running around town, it made no sense that none of them had done it.

José and I looked over my list and my notes, discussing each suspect again and again. One small note I'd written next to Luis Lopez's name was *Mother sure we wouldn't win the contest.*

"I wonder why his mother seemed so sure?" I cocked my head.

José shrugged.

Just then my phone rang. It was Rick.

"Hello," I answered.

"Hi there. Wondering if you'd like to go out to eat with me?"

José leaned forward. He'd heard Rick's request. "What about me too?" he called out.

Rick laughed. "Sure. Any place special you both want to go?"

I covered the mouthpiece and frowned at José. "You can't just invite yourself along like that."

He smiled cheekily. "I know, but he said I could go. Anyway, we need to go back to El Patrón and find out about Luis Lopez's mother."

I nodded. That made sense.

"Um, Rick, could we go to El Patrón?"

The phone got quiet. Then he said, "Again?"

"Yeah, well, I really love the food there and—"

"Does this have anything to do with your brother and his Sherlock Holmes obsession?"

I cringed a bit inside.

"Yes, I guess it does. We're both interested in finding out who Luis Lopez's mother is. She may know something about who poisoned my secret sauce."

Rick groaned. "Please don't tell me you and your brother are playing detectives. That could get you into serious trouble."

"Well, we are, sort of. And we did sort of land in some trouble. But it's okay now. I'll tell you about it at dinner."

"Okay," he grumbled. "I'll pick you up in a half hour."

I smiled at José and gave him a thumbs-up. "Thanks, Rick. We'll be ready."

When I ended the call, José gave me an impish smile. "Sorry, Sis. But we need to figure this thing out as soon as possible. If our food truck stays closed, we can't afford to buy the lake property."

"I know. I'll forgive you this time, but once this case is solved, no more inviting yourself on my dates."

José held up three fingers in the Boy Scout promise. "I promise."

———◆———

Rick held the door open, and I stepped into the traditional Mexican restaurant. A mariachi band was playing in the corner. Sometimes I wondered how a small town in Maine could have ended up with so many Mexican cuisine places. Although we each had our own special fare. I had to keep that in mind if I ever got to open on the lake; I would need to offer dishes that were completely different from the other Mexican restaurants in town.

We stood by the door, waiting to be seated. I glanced around. The waiter we spoke to the other day was there, and I noticed Luis heading into the kitchen. The door swung open, and Elena stepped out with a tray. She carried it to a table and handed out the plates, a smile on her face.

I shook my head. I would never understand why she was never able to give me a smile. What was it about me that made her frown so much?

Finally, another waitress approached, grabbed some menus, and told us to follow her. She led us to a table in the far corner away from the mariachi players and closer to the kitchen.

When we were seated, Marcus stopped at the table.

"Hi, are you ready to order?" he asked.

We all gave our orders.

A few minutes later, Elena stopped at our table, her lips pressed together in their usual grim line.

"Why are you here again?" she said.

I sat back, and my mouth dropped open.

Rick spoke up. "We just came for dinner, Elena. We love the food here."

She gave him an incredulous stare then walked away.

José leaned over. "Wow, I don't know what her problem is. It's not like we ever treated her badly, but she acts like we're the scum of the earth."

I patted his hand. "Let's try to enjoy the evening. Maybe we can ask Marcus about Luis' mother."

José nodded.

We all nibbled on chips and salsa until Marcus showed up at the table with a tray full of food. He wasn't smiling.

"What did you all say to Elena? She refuses to serve you." He handed Rick his plate. "All I'm supposed to do is take the orders." He slammed the next plate down in front of me. "I've got too much to do."

I looked up at him. "We were wondering the same thing. I hired Elena when she got fired from here, and although we never became friends, she seems pretty upset that we're here."

Marcus tilted his head. "Got fired? I don't—"

Just then, Luis called across the room for Marcus, so he didn't get to finish his sentence. I wondered what it was he was going to say. Why had he looked so confused when I mentioned Elena being fired?

After Rick led a quick prayer, we began to eat, and I scanned the restaurant. On one wall I noticed the plaques that El Patrón had won over the years. Several were for the best Mexican food in town. I recognized them because I had four of my own. There were also some photos in frames. I couldn't make them out very well, except I did recognize Luis and Elena in several of them.

Rick noticed my interest and glanced that way. "Did you see the new plaque? I can't believe the judges gave out a prize after that judge died."

I turned once more to the wall. Sure enough, there was a new plaque for "Best Mexican Food" hanging on the wall. I couldn't believe my eyes. I dropped my fork and stood to my feet.

"I've got to see this." I headed toward the wall.

Marcus actually bumped into me on my way. "Oh, sorry."

"El Patrón won the contest?" I asked.

Marcus shrugged. "Yeah, I guess they decided to give it out even after what happened to the other judge. I didn't think they were going to do it, but Luis' mother called them up and insisted on it."

I shook my head in utter surprise.

"She knew we would win. She said something about the Taco Tent not being open, and everyone knows that Margarita's wasn't going to win. Then the judge died eating your food, so we were sure to win."

Marcus walked away, and I stood in front of the wall, staring at the award. Then I began to peruse the photos. There were many scenes from inside and outside of El Patrón. There were several photos of Luis and Elena holding the winning plaques. I wondered why Elena was in so many of the photos. Why would a waitress be holding a plaque? I couldn't find one photo of anyone I would even have imagined to be Luis' mother.

There was a recent photo beside the new plaque. Once again, it was Luis and Elena. Below the photo was a small index card on which was written, *"Mamá y yo ganamos de nuevo."*

I waved for Marcus. He came over.

"Yes?"

"Marcus, what does this say? I can read some Spanish, but does this say what I think it says?"

Marcus squinted at the small card. "It says, 'Mom and I win again.'"

"Mom?" I gulped.

"Yes."

"Elena is Luis' mother? She seems too young to have a son as old as Luis."

"Yes, she had him when she was very young."

"But her last name is Guadalupe, and his is Lopez."

Marcus nodded. "She got married again after having Luis."

I felt my body start to tremble

"Then Elena is Luis' mother, and she told Luis not to worry about winning the contest this year?"

Marcus nodded again. "Listen, I need to get back to work." He walked away.

I turned toward our table, but across the room, my eyes met Elena's.

She must have recognized the look in my eyes, because hers narrowed to angry slits. She waved for me to come over.

I didn't even think twice, which I should have, but at the time all I could think of was confronting her. There was no doubt in my mind that Elena was the one who poisoned my secret sauce, and I wanted to know why.

———◆———

I hurried across the restaurant, not sure if Rick or José had seen me. Elena had moved into the back room. I pushed open the doors and entered the kitchen. Luis was cooking, and several waiters and waitresses ran around getting trays ready.

I turned to the right and saw Elena again. She gestured for me to follow, so I did. I should have known better, but at the moment I couldn't think straight, so I simply walked across the kitchen and followed Elena into the hallway. Luis' back was to us, and the waiters and waitresses were too busy to notice.

I followed Elena down the hallway, where she stopped beside a large silver door and turned to face me. Her eyes were barely slits, and her lips pressed hard together.

"What are you doing here?"

I almost laughed. "I was trying to figure out who poisoned that judge, and now I know it was you." I glared at her.

She bit her bottom lip.

"Why, Elena? I hired you. I was nice to you. Why would you do this to me? Or did you have something against the judge?"

She shook her head. "I had nothing against the judge."

"Then why did you poison her?"

"I didn't mean to. I just meant to make her sick. I thought if she got sick from your food, she wouldn't choose your food truck to win again. You've won the last four years in a row, and it's not fair."

"But to put poison in the sauce? You had to know it would kill her!"

She continued to shake her head back and forth. "No, no, I didn't know. I was desperate. I promised Luis we would win this year. I tried and tried to get you to tell me your recipe for the secret sauce. Luis and I could have made it and added a few extras to make it even better, but you kept it hidden."

"I assume you're the one who broke into my food truck both times?"

"Sí. The first time, I wanted to search for your recipe. I knew it was not in your grandmother's cookbook, but I searched every nook and cranny."

"I don't keep the recipe there. I have it memorized."

"I know that now."

"You must have gotten a third key made for the lock, and that's why it wasn't broken."

She nodded.

"So, you just came over, let yourself in, and put poison in my sauce?"

Her shoulders slumped, but her head moved up and down. I could hardly believe I was looking at a murderer.

"I wasn't going to come to work that day so no one would suspect me, but then I decided I could throw away the sauce and no one would even know for sure if it was the sauce or not. That's why I came to work after all."

She obviously didn't know to what extent police officers would go to find clues.

"Elena, I'm sure the police will understand it was an accident. I'm sure they'll—" I reached out as if to comfort her, but she pulled away from me.

"Police? No police! Luis will be so mad."

I was taken aback at her tone of voice and could hear panic taking over. I'd been so busy trying to figure out what Elena had done, I hadn't noticed the surroundings I was in. Too late, I realized I was standing right beside the freezer door.

She must have noted the same thing, because suddenly she grabbed my arm and, with her other hand, ripped open the door and pushed me in. I tripped, and while I tried to stand up, she closed the door and locked it behind me.

My mind went blank for a few moments. The small room was dark. There was a glass window which I began beating on, but Elena had her back turned to me. I imagined she was keeping an eye out so no one would notice me in the freezer. I wondered if anyone could hear me through the thick glass.

I started to panic. Was I going to die in the freezer? Surely that wasn't God's plan for me.

I began praying. *Lord, please help me out of this situation. I know I tend to jump into things without thinking, but I know that You, Lord Jesus, can help me.*

Just then, and to my relief, my phone rang. I'd forgotten it was in my pocket. I grabbed it and answered.

"Help, help me, I'm locked in the freezer!" I screamed into the phone, but when I put it to my ear, there was only silence.

I stared at the phone in horror. Did I have any reception? I dialed José, but the phone didn't ring. My eyes were completely blurred with tears. I didn't want to die. I tried the phone again. My fingers were already getting cold.

Before I could press 911, the freezer door was yanked open. Rick stood there, and over his shoulder I saw José holding on to Elena. I fell out of the freezer and into Rick's arms.

"Marissa, what's going on?" He started rubbing my arms and hands. I didn't think I was even slightly frozen yet, but I felt comforted by his actions.

Elena tried to squirm away from José, but he kept a tight hold on her. She murmured threats in Spanish over and over again.

Just then, Luis appeared.

"What's going on? What are you doing to my mother?" He came closer, but Rick turned around and put a hand out to stop him.

"Luis, I hate to tell you this, but your mother is the one who poisoned the judge the other day."

The man's eyes opened wide, and he faced Elena. "Mama, what have you done?" His voice was loud and demanding.

"I was trying to help you, son." She sank back at the look on his face.

Luis looked at me. I pointed at Elena. "She tried to kill me. She locked me in the freezer." My teeth chattered, not so much from cold as from fear.

Rick had pulled out his phone and had dialed 911. We heard him ask for the police, but all I could see was the defeated look on Luis' face.

"Oh, Mama, why?"

I couldn't help but feel bad for him. Even if his mother was the one who poisoned the judge, El Patrón would get a pretty bad reputation because of it.

Luis turned away, his shoulders slumped.

Rick walked me out to the table, and I sat down. My legs trembled, but I felt better. José led Elena out and pressed her into the chair beside me. She didn't look at me. She looked like a crushed rag doll sitting in the chair.

I turned to her. "Elena, I want you to know I forgive you for everything. I believe you didn't mean to kill that judge, but I'm pretty sure you did mean to kill me just now."

She glanced up. "I wouldn't have let you die. I was just. . .just. . . Oh, I don't know." She dropped her head onto her arms, sobbing.

I couldn't blame her. She'd ruined her own life and her son's career.

———◆———

The police arrived a few minutes later. It didn't take long to explain everything to them. One officer gently placed a hand under Elena's arm and guided her out to the police car. He didn't even put handcuffs on her, because she was obviously not going to give anyone any more trouble.

Luis called out for Marcus to lock up the restaurant, and he followed the officer and Elena out the door. It was going to be a long night for him. Would Elena actually go to jail, or was there some kind of institution she could be placed in that would actually help her?

Finally, Rick helped me up, and we headed out to his car. If the police wanted a statement from me, it would have to wait until the next day. All I wanted to do was soak in a hot bath and get some sleep.

CHAPTER TWELVE

The next morning my phone rang, and I could see it was the police station. With a huge sigh, I rolled over and answered. Sure enough, they wanted me to come and give my statement as soon as possible.

I walked past José's room. He was still asleep. I wondered if we would ever get back on a regular schedule. I stepped into his room and gave him a soft shake. His eyes popped open.

"What's up?"

"Nothing, but I need to go make my statement. They'll probably want yours too, so get up and get ready."

Without hesitating, José slid off the bed and headed for the bathroom. It was just like him to have no trouble getting up to go to the police station, but school was a whole other thing.

———

We arrived at the station within the hour. We did make a stop to pick up some coffee, so we walked into the station, cups in hand, ready to set the account straight.

"Morning, Marissa." Rick already sat there. I assumed he'd been called early as well.

"Have you heard anything about Elena?" I whispered as I sat on the bench beside him. José strolled across the hall and sat on a chair.

"Yes, they told me that once Luis pressed her, she admitted to everything. No one thinks she wanted to kill the judge, so that may help her case unless you give them evidence to prove otherwise." He glanced at me with a serious question in his eyes.

I shook my head. "No, that's what I think. But she could have killed several people that day if I'd tasted the sauce again or given you or José some. Plus, she did lock me in the freezer. Her jealousy took her down a very dark road."

"She needs help, that's for sure."

The officer took each of us into his office to take our statements, one at a time. I was last. I guessed by that point the officer had heard the story so many times that he'd run out of questions. I simply told him what I knew, from beginning to end. A stenographer typed out my statement. I read it and signed it.

When I stood up to leave, I asked if I could have access to my food truck again. The officer frowned, reread my statement, and nodded.

Relief washed over me. Once the news hit town, suspicion on the Crunchy Taco would end and business would pick up again. It wouldn't be long before José and I could begin to work on the plans for the new restaurant on the lake, but I needed to know for sure what José wanted to do for the future.

"How about I take you out for dinner tonight?" Rick's voice interrupted my thoughts. "No Mexican food though." He smiled, and I agreed wholeheartedly.

———◆———

Later that evening, I stood by the small pier, overlooking the lake. I'd gotten into the Crunchy Taco and done a top-to-bottom cleaning. I threw away the pot that had held the tainted sauce.

Now, as I stared at the sky, the stars twinkling, I felt a true contentment. God had seen me through this hard time. I had learned so much through it as well. I felt closer to Kim and Brad, and I felt sorry for Luis Lopez and Maria Martinez. From what I was told at the police station, Mr. Burnard had found another town to build his hotel, so I had nothing else to worry about from him.

José had helped to clean the food truck and had tossed out the trash bags. Then he joined me on the pier.

"Well, now that you've been through a real mystery, what's the verdict? Do you want to go on to school to be a detective?"

"No, I don't want to be a detective anymore."

"Oh really? What brought you to that conclusion?"

He shrugged. "To quote Sherlock Holmes, 'When you have eliminated the impossible, whatever remains, however improbable, must be the truth.' I've eliminated the desire to be a detective and realized that what I really love, as improbable as it seems, is running the Crunchy Taco. And I have a lot of ideas for the new restaurant. So, the truth is, I think I'll take some business classes at the community college that'll help us run a great restaurant."

I turned and gave him a big hug. That meant the world to me. "Thanks José. You're the best partner anyone could ever ask for."

Like a typical teenager, José allowed me to hug him for only a few moments, then walked away. I was pleased with the decision he made, knowing that he and I together would be able to open the restaurant and fulfill our grandmother's dream.

In the distance, I saw Rick. He gave a short wave, beckoning me to join him. He'd been there for me so often, and now that the future plans with José were set, I looked forward to concentrating on giving a relationship with Rick a chance to grow.

I glanced up once more.

Thank You, Lord, for helping to solve this murder and setting me on a new, exciting path.

I headed toward Rick and smiled when I noticed him hang an arm over José's shoulder. Although my Abuelita was gone, I had a very special family right here in Birch Tree.

Teresa Ives Lilly has been writing for over forty years. She has written and published more than thirty books and novellas with Lovely Christian Romance and four collections with Barbour Books. She wrote over one-hundred unit studies which are used in private and public schools. Her articles have appeared in a variety of magazines, including *Turtle*, *Vette*, *Corvette Fever*, and more. Her novel *Orphan Train Bride* was a number one bestseller on Amazon and several others have been in top ten. She gives God all the glory for allowing her dream of being a published writer to come true.

YOU MIGHT ALSO ENJOY...
MISSING PIECES

What could go wrong when jigsaw puzzle enthusiasts get together?

How about four murders and a couple of thefts? Can clues be pieced together to solve these puzzling crimes?

Elvis Has Left the Building by Cynthia Hickey

Cee Cee is hosting a jigsaw puzzle party in Apple Blossom, Arkansas, and everyone is expected to bring a brand-new 500-piece jigsaw puzzle to work on that depicts something from the 1950s. With a vintage car show, vendors, live music, and a dance, the night promises to be a great one—until the Elvis impersonator is murdered and a priceless puzzle is missing.

The Puzzle King by Linda Baten Johnson

Jane enters a jigsaw puzzle competition at the Fargo, North Dakota, fairgrounds. When a fellow competitor is poisoned, all suspects are confined at the hotel during the investigation, and Jane is determined to use her puzzle-solving skills to root out the killer.

A Puzzling Weekend by Teresa Ives Lilly

Tabitha's first event at her new bed and breakfast in Pumpkin City, Pennsylvania, is a jigsaw puzzle mystery weekend. All is going well until the hired cook is found stabbed to death. As the prime suspect, Tabitha works with the handsome investigator—and two wily beagle dogs—to clear her name.

Mystery at the Jigsaw Swap by Janice Thompson

Mariah hopes to sell her vast puzzle collection at a jigsaw puzzle swap in Camden, Maine, at the historic opera house. But her most valuable puzzle ends up missing when another vendor is stabbed to death.

Enjoy four short cozy mysteries—all involving jigsaw puzzles!

Paperback / 978–1–63609–289–8

YOU MIGHT ALSO ENJOY...
GONE TO THE DOGS
Series of Cozy Mysteries

The town of Brenham, Texas, has gone to the dogs! The employees of Lone Star Veterinary Clinic link arms with animal rescue organization Second Chance Ranch to care for the area's sweetest canines. Along the way, there are mysteries aplenty in this series of six books by authors Janice Thompson and Kathleen Y'Barbo-Turner.

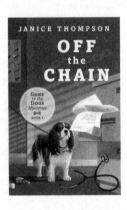

Book 1 Off the Chain by Janice Thompson
Marigold Evans' first attempt at rescuing an abandoned pooch lands her in the underground sewer lines of Houston's Buffalo Bayou. . .and almost in jail, until Parker Jenson comes to her defense. Then a bad day only gets worse as the Lone Star Vet Clinic, where they both work, is vandalized and the list of suspects starts to climb. With the help of her fellow employees, Marigold sets out to simultaneously solve the crime, rehab the rescued dog, and help more dogs in crisis. But why would anyone continue to work against all their good efforts?
Paperback / 978–1–63609–313–0

Book 2: *Dog Days of Summer* by Kathleen Y'Barbo, 978–1–63609–394–9
Book 3: *Barking up the Wrong Tree* by Janice Thompson, 978–1–63609–451–9
Book 4: *The Bark of Zorro* by Kathleen Y'Barbo, 978–1–63609–517–2
Book 5: *Every Dog Has His Day* by Janice Thompson, 978–1–63609–587–5
Book 6: *New Leash on Life* by Kathleen Y'Barbo, 978–1–63609–662–9